Disney and the Wonder Within

BOOK TWO:
THE WATCHMAKER'S GIFT

Charles E. Zitta

Theme Park Press
The Happiest Books on Earth
www.ThemeParkPress.com

Editor: Bob McLain
Layout: Artisanal Text
Cover Illustration: Jamie Hood

ISBN 978-1-68390-245-4
Printed in the United States of America

Theme Park Press | www.ThemeParkPress.com
Address queries to bob@themeparkpress.com

THE
WATCHMAKER'S
GIFT

Chapter One

It was 1959. Sleeping Beauty was showing in theaters across the country. In one such theatre; near Anaheim, California, sat an artist, slouched low in his seat near the very back, as not to be seen—a shadow amongst others. Maddened. Furious. Enraged. The jealous artist sat, staring at the big screen before him with fists clenched, teeth grinding and legs twisted up like a pretzel—critiquing each and every creative element, in each and every scene. The more the audience applauded the movie, the more furious he became. *I was the chosen one. Full-length animated movies were my idea. I was the one who should have succeeded. This should have been me, not him. No, no, no. Not him,* he thought to himself.

This was not just any artist, not by any means. This was a man who had once worked side by side with a young artist named Walt Disney. This was an artist who had worked just as hard and just as long as Walt. A young, confident man who had grown as a budding artist alongside Walt. Had had meaningful and creative conversations with Walt. He'd brainstormed with Walt about the future of art, animation, it's impact on society and the power of imagination. He had worked with Walt at the Disney Animation Studios as a lead character animator. And at one point, had even been considered for the position of creative director over all Disney films. But the position was eliminated. Walt thought it best to spread the creative responsibility amongst many; as in *the nine old men,* in order to develop the best product possible. But this decision did not sit well with the talented artist who's name never made it onto a Disney movie credits list. He felt slighted. Passed over. Humiliated. And now, here he sat, alone, a failure, a nobody—his mind filled with hateful, vengeful and evil thoughts as he watched a movie that could *very easily* have been his creation.

Then, *she* appeared; green skinned, piercing eyes, cloaked in black with staff in hand and armed with a personality which commanded attention. The dark fairy. Maleficent. She fit his mood—strong, dark, intimidating. She was a true leader of undesirables. She made sense. This was to be his motivation. All the years of anger, all the years of jealousy—the built up hatred inside him finally had a purpose, a goal—a dark and devious goal. Take Disney's very own villainous creation, or better yet, creations, and use them to bring Walt's creative empire to its knees.

Marching down the rainy sidewalks of Burbank—head down and continuously mumbling mad gibberish to himself, the shell of a man made his way back to an old dilapidated hotel complex with a red neon no vacancy sign that read: NO V AN. He barged through the front door, striding into the lobby in wet shoes that squished with every step. He turned right, then made his way to the elevator doors, completely ignoring the front desk staff in the process, as he left a trail of water behind.

"Quite the odd fella, don't you think Elsie?" one of the desk clerks said to the other.

"Oh yes. That man hasn't spoken a word to me since I started working here. And that was over a month ago," she replied.

"Yeah, well I've been here almost two years and the only time I ever recall him speaking to *anyone*, including me, was the day he checked in. And even then, he didn't make eye contact with me. He's a real piece of work, that's for sure. I mean, what kind of person wants to make an old rundown hotel like this their permanent residence anyway?"

"I agree, Ed. I agree," the woman said, while staring over the rim of the reading glasses resting upon her nose, continuing to study the eccentric artist in drenched clothes who stood by the elevator doors.

Feeling unwanted eyes upon his back, he eagerly tapped the up button with his boney right hand index finger. Slowly, the arrow above the door started to move counter clockwise towards the first floor. The rickety old elevator clanked and thunked its way down to its caller, louder and louder, until it came to rest with a sudden THUNK. The doors opened and he stepped inside. With fifteen buttons to choose from, the brooding artist hit number nine, then nine again, and one more time. If this were a properly functioning elevator, the button would illuminate, but not in this case. Money for repairs did not exist in hotels such as this. Soap, shampoo and even towels were considered luxury items. The doors awkwardly closed and the elevator ascended, floor two, three, four...and finally, nine. The doors clanked open, exposing a dimly lit hallway. Only two lights out of eight were working, one of which, flickered on and off. The floor was covered with a thin coat of what used to be blue carpeting; it was flanked by water-stained walls—covered with sixty year old floral-patterned wallpaper that once may have been white, but now was dirty yellow with streaks of brown and peeling everywhere. The first door to the left, facing the elevator, was his destination. Apartment nine thirteen. With a shaky wet hand he reached deep into the front right pocket of his rain drenched trousers, the water from his long dark bangs dripped down his forehead, over his crooked nose, across his lips, and off the end of his chin, before finally hitting the junky old carpeting which sat between his oversaturated shoes and the door to his room. Pulling out a single key, his shaky hand repeatedly aimed for the key hole—once, twice, a third time—a difficult thing to do for anyone in such dark accommodations. Finally, the key and lock became one, his hand turned, the lock clicked and he bumped open the old battered door with his right forearm. Anxiously rushing inside, he slammed and locked the door behind him, taking off his coat and casting it to the floor. He immediately headed for the drawing table in the back corner of the room near the window and turned on the dusty old table lamp. Instantly flooded with a fluorescent yellow-cast light, the table revealed layers of sketches, notes and diagrams—and more sketches notes and diagrams, piled high in an unorganized fashion. Alongside the table was a trash receptacle, overflowing onto the floor with countless crumbled balls of paper containing hopes, dreams and ideas—all of which, had been crushed by the realities of the harsh world. But that was all in the past now. *No more,* he thought to himself, *no more.* The drenched artist mounted his stool, and in one full swoop, pushed all the spent piles of paper covering the table to the floor. Grabbing a pencil and a clean sheet of paper, he began to plot his scheme.

"Name, hmmm," he mumbled to himself while scratching his head. *Evil. Evil is to be key,* he thought. *Villains against Walt? No. United Villains of Evil? No. The Evil Doers? Nope, not scary enough.* For nearly two hours, the crazed artist obsessed over the perfect name for his diabolical organization—writing and scratching out names, again and again. It had to carry purpose. It had to be dark. It had to strike fear in the hearts of ALL Disney lovers who heard it. Something memorable, something simple...something, undoubtedly sinister.

He stared out the window at the rain; messaging his temples, thinking...thinking. The soft glow of the lonely street light on the corner whispered for his attention. And then, it went dark. *Wait, that's it.* He had it. *Yes! It's perfect. Frightfully perfect. It shall be called, The Dark Order.*

Deep into the night, the dejected artist scribbled down his thoughts, filling sheet upon sheet of paper, until all the thoughts in his head had been emptied out. His plan of attack; to build a secret army, a dark collective group that will possess the ability to destroy, crush, and abolish all the joy, all the happiness, all the goodwill Walt and his company had worked so hard to build and spread throughout the world. Indeed, this was to be the beginning of the end for all things Disney!

Chapter Two

As the years slowly passed, The Dark Order continued to increase in size, silently growing more powerful with each passing day. Days turned to weeks; which turned to months, years, and decades. The unknown artist who had founded the Dark Order continued to secretly and tirelessly build his army. He visited the most horrid places around the country; and even the world. From the deepest, darkest holes imaginable; like run down pubs and trash covered alleys, to condemned old buildings and rat infested sewer lines, there was no place too dark, too dirty or too dangerous to find new prospects for his army of undesirables.

But the evil artist knew that recruiting more and more members, that numbers, were not enough. These soldiers, his dark soldiers; needed to be taught the ways of the villain. They needed to be taught the art of deception—trained to lie, cheat, steal, con, and sabotage. To do anything in their power that would bring Disney's reputation and the quality of their creative community to its knees, and inevitable demise.

However, to the dismay of the dark artist, Disney had already put into place something rather brilliant to prevent such evil threats from penetrating their positively charged, *creative world.* When Disney animation was making a name for itself, and Disneyland was on the verge of opening, a select group of imagineers secretly developed a magical world, a world created by their dreams and ideas. They called it, the World of Natural Dream Enhanced Realities, or WONDER, where both reality and dream-like fantasy coexist. Its purpose, to preserve everything positive Disney instills upon the world.

It was only then, after the imagineers had created WONDER, that the evil intentions of the maniacally twisted artist and his Dark Order were exposed. In response, the select group of imagineers wasted no time in calling together all their Disney brethren to dream up, design and build in safeguards to protect WONDER from any unfriendly threats. Five of those safeguards included the Kingdom Crystals.

This clever move by the imagineers generated an insurmountable barrier for the Dark Order, pushing the crazed artist and his evil organization back into the shadows of society. It was there they laid dormant for many years; scheming, planning, waiting for the day when the Dark Order would once again reach full strength, and destroy all that Walt and his team of loyal imagineers and animators had worked so hard to build.

But the seamless years of waiting proved to be too much for the artist to bear. His mind had grown overly impatient, his body, older, weaker, and more frail. Those who knew him well insisted he step down as leader of the Dark Order. But to their dismay, he refused— still driven by the personal hatred for Disney that lay deep within his heart, until eventually, it cost him his life. The artist who had once shown so much promise, talent and creativity was left with nothing more than lost hope, anger in his heart, and a concept sketch he had once drawn for Walt's first full length animated Film, *Snow White and the Seven Dwarfs*. He was laid to rest shortly after on a cold and rainy Halloween afternoon—the sketch, nestled between his arms. Some say he was buried in a secret tomb his followers carved out in an underground cave on the west coast. Others say his ashes lay near, or under, the Haunted Mansion at Disneyland. To this day, nobody really knows. Two months later, after his passing; the Dark Order disbanded.

Nearly thirty years had passed. It was the end of the Disney Decade; an incredible era in the history of Disney animation and the parks. The masters of family entertainment and theme park magic were sitting on top of the world. Everyone and their families were talking about the latest Disney movies, *The Little Mermaid, Beauty and the Beast, The Lion King, Aladdin* and so on. If it wasn't a Disney movie they were talking about, moms, dads and grandparents were planning their next big vacation to one of the Disney theme parks—to give their families the experience of a lifetime. Whether you were a child, or child at heart, the nineties were indeed the perfect time to be alive. And with the millennium just around the corner, the anticipation of what Disney might do next was overwhelming—but in a good way, as far as fans were concerned.

However, to one very young lady, the Disney Decade had been nothing more than an unpleasant reminder of all the suffering, all the disappointment, and all the frustration her great-uncle had gone through in his creative, yet unfulfilled life. Which, according to her mother, was largely due because of one man—who most considered to be a great individual, a creative genius and a true family man. But who, in her mother's tainted opinion, was nothing more than a ruthless thief who stole ideas from helpless creative talent, such as her great-uncle. A man named Walt Disney.

She was just an innocent little girl living in Florida with her mother when the Disney Decade had begun. While most girls her age were dreaming about being a Disney princess, Lila could only remember the agonizing stories about her once great-uncle from

California. Stories her mother had shared with her throughout her childhood, over and over again—pushing out any thoughts of princes, princesses and happily ever afters that may have existed in a mind so young, so fragile, and so impressionable.

The twisted stories weighed heavy on the young girl's thoughts. As she entered her teen years, she was pulled even deeper into a world most chose to avoid. School became an awkward daily nuisance, and by the time Lila was a junior in high school she had disowned her friends, sat in the back of the classrooms, and hardly said a word to anyone—except to criticize or complain about someone or something. She began to avoid color in her clothing choices; blacks and grays were the norm. Only on a very good day, which was a rarity, would she throw a subtle hint of purple into her outfit. Her skin, though not pale, was lighter than most girls her age, who enjoyed going to the Florida beaches and pool parties to look at boys. Nobody cared, or even tried, to befriend the strange girl who had a dislike for others.

By the end of her junior year of high school, she had truly become the school's most popular outcast—a title nobody really wanted to claim. This made her an easy target for cruel jokes, rumors, lies and even a nickname—given to her of course, by the most popular girl-click of the class. She was known amongst her peers as, "Looney Lila". But the name never really did concern her. To a girl who had much more significant things to think about, a silly little nickname was nothing but a foolish distraction—mere child's play for someone who's thoughts ran much broader, much deeper, and much darker than pretty much anyone else in the entire school.

During the summer, between her junior and senior year, it was rumored Looney Lila had traveled abroad. Where she went, nobody ever really knew. The only whiff of rumor to be had, was that her mother had sent Lila away to learn the ways of the Dark Order. Hoping one day, Lila could *finish* what her twisted mess of an uncle had started, many years before her daughter was even born.

It was 1999, Lila's senior year had finally arrived. The northern fall air blew across the school yard, rustling the trees, which swayed to and fro—marking the end of summer and the beginning of a new school year. All the popular kids and their friends were gathered in the front window-lined hall of the school—the traditional meeting place for the popular students before the bell rang to begin the day. There were conversations about summer break, who went where, which blockbuster movies people saw, or who kissed who. There was even talk about class schedules, who was in who's class, or what lunch period people were in. Overall, everyone was happy to be back—to be amongst friends they hadn't seen in months. Even Principal Allen was perusing the halls, asking kids how their summers had went, and if they had had a good time.

One of the main entryway doors clicked open, and a sudden wave of silence swept through the hallway as Lila entered the building. Even Principal Allen was slack jawed. Like a graceful swan parting the calm pond waters, she made her way through the crowded hallway of kids, who were gathered in clusters like lily pads. All, unable to get a single word out—or for that matter, even a blink. The girl who had once hidden behind a loner personality, drab clothing, and a lack luster hair style, with crooked bangs and sunglasses, was now commanding full attention of those around her without saying a single word. A dazzling purple outfit, with black belt and boots, complimented her long black hair, ruby red lips and green, catlike eyes—which pierced the heart of every teenage boy, as she passed them by like afterthoughts.

The girls stared jealously at their supposed boyfriends, who's heads turned and followed the unexpected surprise dressed in purple. It was as if they had never seen her before. And to be fare, they really hadn't—at least not like this, and all the females new it. They also new—as the ring leader of the popular girls whispered, "This changes everything," to the others, that Lila had undergone a life changing experience over summer break. She could no longer be addressed as "Looney Lila". From now on, she would just be called, Lila.

While the circle of popular girls all respectfully nodded to confirm their approval of Lila's miraculous transformation, she thought to herself, *if they only knew the true story behind what they see.*

On the surface, Lila had indeed undergone incredible changes. Changes that could fool even the sharpest of minds. But hidden deep within her jaded heart, she was still the same dark-minded teenage girl who despised everyone.

As the first day of school progressed, the dark-spirited teenager wasted no time in plotting her revenge against those who had repeatedly ridiculed her throughout the past decade of school. She started with number one atop her list of those she despised the most. The most popular girl in school; blond hair, tan skinned, blue-eyed Vicky Anne Brighten. A true real life Barbie, as far as Lila was concerned. The two girls shared first hour English together. Vicky grabbed a seat right next to Lila, eagerly wanting to strike up a conversation.

"Uh. Hi there. You're like, Lila, right?" Vicky asked in her best fake valley girl accent, half heartedly attempting to befriend the swanlike girl she had shamed into submission over the past ten years—mainly due because of the way she had looked. "My name is Vicky, and I guess you could say I kind of, like, run things around here, as far as the popular girls go. So, if you need anything. Like, anything at all. Don't hesitate to ask. Especially when it comes to boys. I think we're going to be, like, really good friends. I mean, I *so* have a special feeling about you."

Lila turned and stared emotionlessly with her marble green eyes at Vicky, giving her a lukewarm smile—not wanting to appear overly anxious to hear what Vicky had to say.

"We're having a movie night this Friday at my house if you're interested?" Vicky said.

"Really, me? Why, I don't know what to say," Lila replied.

"Oh, it's pretty simple. You say yes of course. It's going to be *so* much fun. You'll get to know all the other girls, eat bad food, and watch some really good movies."

"Well, that does sound like a lot of fun. Sure. I'll come. I mean, if you really want me to?"

"Don't be silly, of course we want you to come. I mean, like, I wouldn't be asking if we didn't want you to hang out with us. I can't wait to tell the other girls. They'll be so excited. We're going to have such a great time, and that's like, just the beginning. This is going to be the greatest year *ever*. I promise," Vicky said, as she gave Lila a great big smile, before turning to face Mrs. Woddle, the English teacher at the front of the classroom.

Lila flashed a fake smile back to the golden girl, then turned to face the teacher as well—looking sternly out the corner of her eyes at Vicky and thinking, *yes, maybe Miss bright and shiny is on to something. Perhaps it will be the greatest year ever.*

The first two months of the school year had been a blur of girl get-togethers, football games, dances, movie nights, day trips to Disney World, shopping sprees, and a little homework in between all the social activities. The days had grown shorter, the nights cooler, and the theme parks, spookier. And one of their biggest nights of the year was only a day away. An after hours trip to *Mickey's Not So Scary Halloween Party.*

To get ready for their big night, Vicky and her girlfriends—including Lila, decided it would be really cool to watch a few of Disney's key villains in action before the big party. So the night before they went, the girls all gathered at Vicky's house for movies, popcorn balls, caramel apples, pumpkin pie, and many other traditional Halloween favorites. Only the *best* villain movies were chosen to honor such a spooky occasion. Included in the lineup were; *The Little Mermaid, Snow White and the Seven Dwarfs,* and *Sleeping Beauty.* All of which featured iconic Disney villains such as Ursula the sea witch, the Evil Queen, and Maleficent. More importantly, all the starring villains in each movie chosen were female. Perfect for such an occasion as this.

"OK ladies," Vicky said, "now that we're all here, I say we, like, put in a movie and enjoy some of the tasty treats over there on the table."

"Yeah, I mean, like, your mom must have worked so hard to prepare all this stuff for us," one of the girls replied.

"Totally. This is going to be so awesome. Like, way better than any Halloween, like, ever before in the history of Halloween," another girl added.

Lila sat quietly. Patiently waiting for the movie to start.

"What do you think Lila?" Vicky asked—which caught the newcomer off guard.

"Oh, sure. Yeah. Like, totally. This is going to be the most awesome Halloween ever. For sure," Lila replied in her fake happy voice. All the other girls bought into it and responded with a barrage of "woo-hoos."

Vicky had selected *Sleeping Beauty* to begin their Halloween movie marathon. The girls admired and cheered on the dark fairy as she dominated every scene of the movie she was in. It was at that moment, later in the movie, during the final battle scene between Maleficent and Prince Phillip, that an evil idea struck Lila's thoughts like a thunderous bolt of lightning. The *words* Maleficent recited as she cast a spell across the land to prevent Prince Phillip from reaching King Stefan's castle struck a chord in Lila's heart:

> "A forest of thorns shall be his tomb. Borne through the skies on a fog of doom! Now go with the curse, and serve me well! 'Round Stefan's castle, CAST MY SPELL!"

Those words, she thought to herself. *So wicked, so powerful, so perfect for the purpose I seek to carry out.* Lila continued on in her own head, while the other girls spat out mindless babble about their upcoming night of events at *Mickey's Not So Scary Halloween Party.*

"A forest of thorns." Yes, that's it. My great-uncle's legacy of the Dark Order shall once again rise up from its past to take on new life, and it will have a new name. A name that will strike fear in the hearts of ALL who believe in Disney's goodwill, pixie dust, and happily ever afters. It shall be known as...the Forest of Thorns Order. Having reached a deep, dark conclusion within her mind, Lila calmly sat back on the sofa and enjoyed the rest of the movies Vicky had selected for them to watch.

While the other girls continued with their half witted discussions about what they were going to wear, if they should dress in costume, or whatever; the girl who had once been an outcast among the group began secretly planning her own agenda for the Halloween party. A plan much different than the other girls could ever imagine.

"Hey, what do you think we should do?" one of the other girls asked Lila. Who at the moment, appeared to be happily staring off in thought. "Should we like, dress in costumes or not? And what are we going to do? Like, there's so many options during Mickey's Not So Scary Halloween Party."

"I think we should let Vicky decide for us. After all, she is the leader," Lila calmly replied.

"Oh Lila, sometimes you have such brilliant ideas," the red headed girl named Trixie said, as Lila rolled her eyes in response. "That's perfect. So does everyone else agree that we should let Vicky decide?"

The other girls raised their hands to vote yes for Vicky.

"Great, it's settled then. Vicky our night of spooky fun and tasty treats is in your hands. So, fearless leader. What is our plan?"

Your "plan" will be to flee for your pathetic little lives in terror and turmoil, all wrapped inside a shell of fear, Lila thought to herself as she giggled inside while staring at Vicky.

"Like, we could crash the Kingdom at four," Vicky said, "cause I heard from this podcast guy that like, they will let you into the park at four if you have a ticket for Mickey's Not So Scary Halloween Party. And then we could like, hit the rides and grab a snack or two before the party actually begins."

"That sounds totally awesome, Vicky", Katie, another blond haired, blue eyed Barbie girl type, replied.

Trixie chimed in as well. "Yeah, that's like, the best plan *ever.*"

Vicky continued on, "Then, when the Halloween party officially begins at seven, we can like, check out some of the cool shows, see the parade, do a little trick or treating, watch the fireworks, and like, ride more rides until the park closes."

"And what about the costume thing? Like, are we doing it or not?" Bunny, a long haired brunette with big brown eyes and a model-like figure, asked.

"That's the best part of all," Vicky replied. "I've been thinking about it as we were watching the movies tonight. Since it's like, Halloween—and the villains get to steal the show this time of year, we could all dress up as our favorite, like, bad girls of Disney."

The girls all looked at each other, then back at Vicky, and in one unanimous vote, agreed that this was the greatest idea ever. Even Lila was happy with Vicky's decision, as she put on a big smile, a deceitful smile, a smile for something much darker than what Vicky had in mind.

"So now that everyone agrees, that like, Disney female villains will be the theme for our costumes, we need to decide who's going to be who," Vicky proclaimed. "And since Katie and I have been friends the longest, I'm going to let her have the first pick. That is, after me of course. And then we'll go Bunny, Trixie, and our newest friend, Lila will have the final pick. Oh, and everyone has to pick a different villain. No, like, copy catting or anything."

As it turned out, all the girls had a preference for a different female villain, so the selection process went smoothly. Vicky chose Maleficent, Katie picked Ursula, Bunny went with her favorite, Cruella Deville, Trixie selected Madame Mim, and Lila was genu-inely excited to have the Evil Queen as her villain—with whom she shared a personal bond. The Queen was one of several characters her great-uncle had secretly admired during the development of *Snow*

White and the Seven Dwarfs. This was a personal *connection* she did not share with the other girls. It was a secret she kept deep down inside—buried in a dark place within her thoughts. Within her heart. Only her mother was aware of the true powers her daughter now possessed—powers she had been trained to use by one of the last remaining members of the Dark Order during last summer's vacation. Indeed, Lila was ready, and well-trained, should the occasion arise, to showcase her wickedly-dark powers. An occasion such as Mickey's Not So Scary Halloween Party—now only a day away.

It was mid afternoon, Halloween day—the Florida sun, still warm and full of radiant light, highlighted the palm trees flanking the road where Lila resided. The house in which she lived was quite small, with only two bedrooms and one bath. But it was plenty large enough for her and her mother. Lila's bedroom, unusually decorated, was void of color. Her walls were mostly empty, except for one small eight by ten photo in a black frame, which dangled awkwardly on a crooked nail. It was a photo of her mother as a young girl being held by her great-uncle in front of the Disney Studios in California. It was the only photo she had of him—her only memory of the man who's legacy she wished to carry on.

Lila was sitting on her bed, already dressed as the Evil Queen—going over in her mind how the night was to play out, as she stared at the photo of her mother and great-uncle on the wall.

"Hello Lila," her mother said calmly, as she walked into the bedroom. "Thinking about your *special* night?"

"Yes, mother," Lila said in an eerily calm tone.

"I'm sure you've been trained well for what needs to be done this evening."

"I have no doubt that my powers will be quite sufficient."

"Nor do I dear." Her mother giggled quietly under her breath, as she turned to look at the photo on the wall. "Nor do I."

The fifteen minute ride over to the Magic Kingdom from where Lila lived was nothing short of annoying to a young lady who had serious thoughts running through her mind. Since she lived the furthest from the other four girls, and was the newest member of the group, she was the last to be picked up. Vicky's parents were quite well off and had offered to rent the girls a limo service to and from the park. So by the time they pulled up into Lila's driveway, the vehicle was filled with the sound of non-stop teenage girls chattering like chickens in a hen house. To the point that Lila had to cover her ears when she opened the passenger side rear door to get in.

"Well come on Lila, like, jump in," Vicky said. "It's time to get this villain party started. Woo-hoo!" The other girls followed suite, with a barrage of "woo-hoos" and "yeahs".

Before stepping into the limo, Lila turned and looked back at her mother, who was standing in the window, gazing out. She nodded to her mother, who nodded back. After climbing into the limo, Lila managed to tolerate the other girls who were chattering about whatever popped into their empty heads for the entire ride over to the park. It was as if they all had had nothing to eat for the entire day except caffeine and sugar. When they reached the park, Lila eagerly opened the door of the limo and quickly exited—trying to clear her mind and re-focus on what was really important. But of course, the other girls jumped out quickly as well— all were excited for their big night out at Mickey's Not So Scary Halloween Party.

"Okay girls, this is it," Vicky said, "put on your best villain attitudes and lets go have a ball."

"Yeah, like a monster ball or something," Trixie replied.

All the girls laughed, though one of course, was fake.

The energetic girls turned and headed for the front gate, all striding and playing up their roles as villainous characters. As they entered through the check points and showed their party passes, cast members happily played along with the girls and their wicked attitudes. They were truly enjoying every minute of the situation and the attention they were getting. Bursting onto Main Street in villainous style, the girls began discussing where they should head first.

"So, we've got like, three hours before the party officially begins," Bunny said. "Where do we start?"

"Well I say we head to the Haunted Mansion, so we can like, set the mood for the night. What do you girls think?"

Perfect, Lila thought to herself.

"That's a fab idea, Katie," Vicky replied, "and then maybe a little Pirates of the Caribbean?"

"Yeah, like, and then we can get a dole whip or something," Trixie chimed in.

"Ha-ha-ha. And now you know why we're all friends," Vicky said. "It's like, we're all on the same wavelength."

"You are so totally right, Vicky," Bunny said. "It's like, you read my mind. You are *so* awesome girlfriend."

The girls broke out in laughter after hearing Bunny's reply— agreeing that what she had said was true.

While Lila pretended to like the other girl's jokes, using a fake laugh, the true motivation for her laughter—which only she knew, came from knowing that everything was falling into place for her big *Halloween surprise* later that evening.

Seven o' clock creeped in, as the hot, sticky air began to cool. The park lights were fully illuminated in hues of green, purple, blue and orange. Haunting tunes merrily danced through the fog-filled air, setting the mood for a frightfully jolly night of spooktacular fun for guests of all ages.

Vicky and her villainous girlfriends were enjoying their early evening, which was filled with attractions, snacks, laughs, and even a few unexpected screams. But for one of the girls, it would be much more than that.

Before riding the Haunted Mansion, Lila had managed to set up a secret meeting with an old friend of her great-uncles. That meeting was to take place in a hidden room of Gracey Manor, where they would plan out the most diabolical of endings for that night.

When it came time for Lila and the other girls to ride the Haunted Mansion attraction, the clever young witch told the others she would ride in her own Doom Buggy, and that this would allow them to pair up and leave room for a hitchhiking ghost at the end of the ride. The other four girls—thoughtless as they were, all jumped at Lila's suggestion, proclaiming it a "brilliant idea".

When it came time to enter the buggies, Lila cleverly lagged behind—letting the other girls board first, making it difficult to see what she was doing in the buggy behind them.

When her turn came to board a Doom Buggy, the wickedly clever teenager faked as if she weren't feeling well. Naturally, a cast member directed her towards the nearest exit door. But as she was walking away, Lila veered right instead of left; back towards the stretching room—then right again, passing up the stretching room doors, as she made her way down a secret, dimly lit corridor which was mostly used by cast members to move around behind the scenes of the Mansion. It was there, in the hallway, that she grabbed her cape with one hand and pulled it over and across her head and body, while spinning in a circle. As she completed her turn, the cape disappeared, and her head rose up from behind her arm. She had transformed from the Evil Queen into a cast member with blond hair, blue eyes, and shiny white teeth. No cast member working the attraction that evening would know her true identity.

Continuing down the dark corridor, the crafty teenager witch recited the words, "illuminate the way," while holding her right hand in a half cupped position. Instantly, light shot out from the palm of her hand—making it easy to see six feet in any direction from where she stood. Quickly, Lila worked her way down the crooked corridor—the haunting sounds of the attraction echoed in the background. She went left six paces, then right four—left eight more paces, then right seven. The young witch scoured the hallway walls for signs of a doorway, yet still she had no luck. As she rounded the next corner, two cast members (both college age) came from the opposite direction, nearly colliding with Lila. Thinking quickly, she extinguished her hand.

"Whoah! That was close. It's really tight quarters back here isn't it? My name is John, by the way," the young man said, as he extended his hand out to shake.

"Hi, I'm Kathy," Lila replied—playing off the name on her tag.

"Hi there, I'm Shelley. So good to meet you," the young lady said. "Welcome to the house of happy haunts."

"Nice to meet you too, Shelley," Lila said, while shaking her hand.

"So where did your flashlight go?" John asked.

"Flashlight?" The young witch replied in a dumbfounded manner.

"Yeah, it looked like you were carrying a flashlight just before we bumped into you," Shelley said curiously.

"Oh, right, my flashlight. It's very small. I just put it in my pocket," Lila replied.

"Right. In you pocket," Shelley replied sarcastically, while John continued to look intently at the young witches pocket—still not convinced Lila had a flashlight.

Seeing that John and Shelley were not going to let the flashlight thing go, the quick-minded witch said, "Here, I'll show you". While reciting the words, "memories removed," she pulled her hand from her pocket, a flash of green light shot out from her palm and struck the two cast members in their heads simultaneously. Seconds later, neither could remember what had just happened, nor were they aware of Lila's presence.

"I think we need to hurry and get over to the load area, Shelley. It's almost time for a shift change, and I bet Joe is getting hungry."

"Yeah, that's a good idea, John," Shelley replied, with a blank expression on her face.

The two cast members quickly darted off—opposite of where Lila was headed, and faded into the darkness of the dimly lit hallway.

Again, the young witch recited, "Illuminate the way," as her half-cupped hand lit up like a flashlight. Just beyond the next corner—behind the clock room, a seam was revealed. Its definition was so fine, that seeing it in such dim lighting was nearly impossible. Lila gave a subtle smirk and whispered softly to herself, "This has to be it." Facing the secret doorway, she positioned both hands—with palms facing each other, and in one quick motion, opened her hands like a butterfly spreading its wings, thrusting them forward towards the wall she said, "REVEAL".

The hidden seams in the wall suddenly began to give way to piercing rays of blue light that were pushing through from the other side. Lila quickly pulled her hands away from the wall—the hidden doorway swung open. Carefully, she bent over and stepped through the opening. The door slammed closed behind her. Standing before her, only five feet away, was a steep wooden stairway that led upwards. It was flanked with hand carved railings textured with raven feathers. The haunting sounds of the Mansion that had been present just a moment ago, could no longer be heard. *Where am I*, she thought to herself while gazing up the stairway—wondering what may lay ahead. As she began her ascent up the dusty, untraveled steps, paintings once hidden on the dimly lit walls came into view, each resembling fictional family members or previous occupants including pets, of the Mansion. Continuing up the stairway, the eyes in each painting slowly followed her.

At the top was a small room, no more than the size of a child's bedroom. The floor was covered with intricately detailed, burgundy carpeting. The walls were lined with fully-stocked book shelves—covered in decades of dust. In the center of the room, opposite the staircase, was a small circular table—barely four feet in diameter. Above it hung a miniature chandelier, highlighted by the flames of five wax candles. In the back right corner of the room was a bronze pedestal. And atop it sat a large black crow with blood red eyes—which followed every movement Lila made. As she approached the table, the bird cawed, as if telling her to be seated. She obliged, and sat down. The bird turned slightly to its right—now facing the back wall, and cawed three more times. A hidden doorway, making up the center shelving unit, slowly began to creek open, exposing an eerie, narrow hallway covered with spider webs. Some fifty feet away, an animated mass of grey, smokey haze was quietly and effortlessly making it's way closer towards the table where Lila sat. Trails of smokey-green vapors followed its path, as it floated through the air. The grey mass grew larger and brighter as it approached. Gradually, a face, arms, body, legs and feet began to materialize from within it's core, until it became clearly evident what Lila was looking at, the spirit form of a woman, suspended in air—her silvery blue hair, floating around her pale face as if gravity did not exist. Slowly, she descended to the floor, walked over, and sat down at the small circular table. "Good evening child. I've been...expecting you. Please, sit down," her voice echoed graciously.

Lila hesitated—giving the mysterious woman a look of distrust.

"What's the matter, dear, don't you recognize me? It is I, the *real* Madame of the house."

"Madame Leota?"

"No child, I am the shadow spirit, Madame Sera. True ruler of this humble abode. But please, call me Madame S. Sera is so old fashioned, and I really cannot stand being referred to as old fashioned like my aunt. You know, the one who works the seance room downstairs and out west at Disneyland."

"Madame Leota? She's your aunt? Interesting," Lila said.

"Yes, I guess you could say we're related. Except for the fact that she was created and duplicated by Imagineers, while I was conjured up by a darker force. A past admirer of your great-uncle, I believe."

"So the imagineers know nothing about you?"

"Precisely young lady," Sera replied—which allows me to roam freely within the manor and do as I wish, when I wish, and to whom I wish. And *all* without the imagineers even knowing," she said, followed by an eerie bit of laughter. "Regardless, that's the least of my worries, darling. I understand you are here to carry out your great-uncle's wishes?"

"That's right. How did you know?"

"He stopped by for a visit not too long ago, we're good friends you know. He told me you would be coming by. You would be surprised how many roaming spirits frequent our establishment. It's a shame we have to turn most of them away. There's just simply not enough room here. Too much spiritual activity going on, if you know what I mean. Anyway, here *you* are. So, how may I be of service?"

"Oh, we have *many* things to talk about," Lila responded, while showing Sera her villainous grin—her blue eyes giving way to their true color, green, as they sparkled with evil intentions. "And, did I hear you mention that you can *only* roam freely 'within' the manner?"

"Yes, unfortunately that is correct, dear," the Madame of the house replied. "Because of how I was created, my presence can only exist within the walls of Gracey Manor.

"Well, Madame S, I may have a solution to your problem."

While exiting the Haunted Mansion, the girls were all curious as to where Lila had gone?

"Have any of you guys seen Lila?" Vicky asked.

"I thought she was like, right behind us or something," Bunny replied.

"Yeah, I swear, she like jumped in the Doom Buggy right behind us, Vicky," Katie added.

"Well we can't just leave her behind. That would be so rude," Vicky said.

"I agree, Vicky. That *would* be rude," Lila replied in a chilling manner—gaining everyone's undivided attention, as she came walking around the corner of the exit area—dressed once again in her Evil Queen costume.

Vicky laughed half heartedly, as did the other girls—who were all caught off guard, even somewhat shocked, by Lila's sudden reappearance. "Hey. Uh, hey Lila. Like, what happened to you? I mean, I thought you were right behind us?" Vicky asked.

Lila had already woven a story in her wicked little mind to cover her tardiness. "Oh. Well, one of the paintings on the wall near the loading area caught my attention, and I wanted to get a closer look before boarding a doom buggy. So by then, like the next wave of stretching room guests had flooded the area, which put me even *further* behind. Next thing you know, there were like, fifty or sixty people ahead of me! Oh, it was horrible", she said in an overstated manner.

"Oh Lila, how terrible. You poor *thing*," Bunny replied sarcastically. Lila had fooled them all, which really, was an easy thing to do for such a smart young witch like herself.

The other girls enjoyed a big chuckle over Lila's overdramatized story, then immediately moved to the next conversation.

"So girls, what do we do now?" Trixie asked.

"Vicky?" Katie asked, queueing their leader to reply.

"Oh. Yeah. Right. Well, I'm kind of feeling a little *playful* tonight. So what do you *say* we head over to Fantasyland and take a little flight on the Peter Pan ride? And then maybe Dumbo and Small World?"

"You rock, Vicky," Bunny responded.

"It's like, you could read my mind or something," Trixie threw in.

"For sure," Katie added.

"Definitely," Lila contributed—just to keep the other girls believing she was one of them. "Of course, being the Evil Queen and all, I wouldn't mind taking a spin on Snow White's Scary Adventures," the young witch said with a raised brow.

All the girls broke into a hysterical laughing fit over Lila's facial gesture. She had *definitely* won them over.

"Okay-okay-okay. Ladies, it looks like Fantasyland wins," Vicky replied, as they all mutually agreed and darted towards Peter Pan's Flight.

As the girls made their way through the portal from Liberty Square to Fantasyland, Katie made a comment which caught Lila's attention. "So, did it seem like the Haunted Mansion ride took forever to you guys?"

"I felt the same way, Katie," Vicky replied. It was like, the longest ride *ever.*"

"Yeah, it felt like we were in that buggy for like, one or two centuries," Bunny added.

"That attraction is quite involved, I must say," Lila injected— trying to make light of a topic she knew much more about than the others. As it turns out, when she had met with Madame Sera, the shadow spirit had placed the entire attraction under a time-and-motion spell. This made time move much slower for anyone who was in the Haunted Mansion queue or on the attraction. That is, except for Lila and herself—who, durning the duration of the spell, were able to conjure up a most devious plan to be launched later that Halloween night.

Midnight was quietly approaching, the moon, unusually large and orange in hue, glowed ominously in the southern sky—highlighting Main Street and the rooftop of the Walt Disney World Railroad Station. Mickey's Not So Scary Halloween Party was in its final hour of tricks, treats and ghastly family fun, as creepy colors danced across Cinderella's Castle to the beat of the spooky park music.

Lila and her unsuspecting friends had just finished trick or treating and were strolling past Rocket Tower Plaza—all with fully loaded bags of tasty Halloween goodies they had received along the way.

"What are you girls up for next?" Vicky asked.

"How about a little spin on Buzz," Trixie shouted out.

"Or the tea cups," Bunny added.

"And of course, we have to make sure we're in the last group they let through the Haunted Mansion tonight. I mean, it *is* Halloween after all. Am I right, ladies?" Lila cleverly slipped in.

"Oh, like yeah. Without a doubt. That *has* to be our last ride of the night," Katie replied. "Right, Vicky?"

"Absolutely," she said. Vicky looked at her watch, noting the time—three after eleven. "Looks like we have just enough time to hit Buzz and the tea cups before visiting the Mansion for one last ride. So let's like, get moving girls—before the clock strikes midnight."

Nobody else had to say a word. Like greyhounds darting out of the starting gate, the girls took off walking at a brisk pace towards Buzz Lightyear's Space Ranger Spin and never looked back.

Lila could not be any happier. As she kept pace with the other girls, a devilish smirk came across her face—hidden from the others, who were too busy huffing it to notice. Her plan was working. Less than one hour from now, her great-uncle's wishes would be set in motion.

The peek hour of Halloween was upon them—eleven fifty six. Only four minutes remained until midnight. The girls had timed the end of their evening perfectly. They slowly walked through the empty Haunted Mansion queue as a female cast member, dressed in creepy fashion, chained off the entrance to the attraction behind them. They would be the last guests to experience the Mansion that evening.

The girls briefly paused at the entryway doors, as a pale-faced figure with sunken cheeks and ill-shadowed eyes appeared from the darkness within. His sinister smile led the way, welcoming the five young ladies into the mansion for a visit. No words were spoken, as the cryptic butler quietly guided them under the cobweb-ridden chandelier, and towards the stretching room, to begin their haunting experience. But unlike their earlier visit to the Mansion that day, the girls were the only occupants in the stretching room besides the butler. The emptiness surrounding them only drew *more* attention to the chilling sounds echoing throughout Gracey Manor—increasing the scare factor exponentially, and adding yet another level of ghoulish delight to an experience already considered spooky enough for the average guest. The five young ladies looked at each other, then up at the iconic paintings, as the door closed behind them—and on queue, the ghost host started in with his welcome speech.

"Welcome, foolish mortals. To the haunted mansion. I am your host. Your, ghost host."

As he continued on, the room slowly began to stretch—all eyes were wide open and filled with spine tingling excitement, as the girls watched the paintings around the room grow taller, revealing their dark secrets. Then, everything went black! There was a flash of lightning, a crack of thunder, and a blood curdling scream—as a corpse, dangling from the ceiling above, was highlighted by another sudden flash of light. The room went dark again...but instead of the stretching room doors opening up to the hallway, which led to the doom buggies, everything remained dark. And stranger still, the room felt as though it were actually *descending!* Which, as any serious Walt Disney World fan knew, was not possible in this version of the Haunted Mansion. Five, then six seconds passed, and still the floor continued to descend into the unknown darkness below. The frightened girls held on tightly to each other's hands, not knowing what to expect next—each, in a silent state of horrified panic. Finally, the silence was broken.

"Like, what is going on? This is *not* normal," Vicky whispered to the other girls.

"Yeah, I mean, if Disney is trying to freak us out, they're doing a *really* good job," Bunny nervously replied.

"Maybe like, it's a secret entrance into the utilidor tunnels?" Trixie said. The other girls all whispered hopeful replies, wishing Trixie's proposal was actually true.

Lila played along, pretending to be scared as well, though inside, she was thoroughly amused by the other girls reactions to everything going on around them.

There was a deep sudden THUNK, which shook the room. The floor had finally come to rest. Candle-like fixtures resting in the hands of Gargoyles above simultaneously lit up, as a hidden doorway just behind where Lila was standing, slowly opened. Beyond the opening sat a large expansive room, fairly circular in shape. Its jagged walls were cave-like, the floor, made of black polished marble. Engraved in the floor, at the center of the room, was a large ten foot, ornately decorated crest. In the center of the crest were the letters MS. And around the circle's outer perimeter, facing inward, sat five sturdy, tall-back chairs. They were made of intricately carved, black stained oak—with the seats and backs covered in diamond-patterned, dark purple, velvet padding.

The girls remained motionless, too petrified to move, as they cautiously looked over every square inch of the unexpected room that sat before them.

"Well Vicky, what do you think?" Lila asked, in an attempt to get the girls moving. "It looks like this is our only way out. And I don't see anything very threatening. Do you?"

"I think she's actually right, Vicky," Bunny replied while peering out the doorway into the large, mysterious room.

"Well..." Vicky hesitated.

"After all, it is Disney, Vicky," Lila added. "I'm sure this is probably just some kind of special Halloween stunt they pull every year to *up* the experience for select guests. Don't you think?"

"I guess you're right, Lila," Vicky replied in a relieved tone. "It's like, Disney World—the most magical place on earth. I'm sure it's just part of the show. Okay, c'mon girls. Lets go check out those awesomely cool chairs the imagineers left behind for us to sit in."

"Yeah, like the one on the left has my name written all over it," Katie confidently replied.

"I call the one closest to us," Trixie hollered.

Like a game of musical chairs, each girl anxiously claimed their spot until all five were taken. As they sat and admired the chairs they were sitting in, a great debate rose up from within the group of self-centered teenage girls. Whose chair was the best of the five, and why? Spiraling out of control, the discussion reached a state of verbal chaos, with red faces, loud screeching voices and wild hair flips. In fact, it had gotten so far out of wack, they had completely forgotten about their immediate surroundings.

Except for Lila, that is.

"Wait. Did you feel that?" Katie said. "Whoop! There it is again. It feels like—"

"Like the floor is moving," Vicky confirmed.

"Yeah. And we're headed towards the ceiling," Bunny added.

Everyone looked up at the ceiling, which was slowly opening to make way for the circular section of the floor the girls were sitting on. Beyond the crack of the opening ceiling, bright rays of moonlight pushed their way through—highlighting the crest in the center of the rising floor. As the opening grew larger and the floor rose higher, it became apparent to the slack-jawed girls that they were headed outdoors. The floor locked into place, sealing off the opening through which it had just passed.

Not knowing how to react, the girls sat silently in their large black chairs; looking around in utter disbelief.

The large Halloween moon sat high in the midnight sky, flooding the area with its bright orange hue. Long, dark shadows cast from willow trees, prickly thorn bushes, and a large stone wall topped with pointed iron rods, surrounded most of the area where the girls sat.

"Where are we?" Bunny asked. "I don't recognize this part of the park."

"I'd say it's pretty obvious", Vicky said, pointing behind Bunny.

Overlooking the moonlit courtyard, in ominous fashion, sat a familiar structure to all who visited the Magic Kingdom. Though none had ever seen it from a vantage point quite like this.

Bunny turned and was immediately taken by surprise, as the words "I don't get it" flowed from her lips. Before her stood what was only too obvious. It was the back of the Haunted Mansion.

"Yeah, like why would Disney put us in the back yard of the Mansion?" Trixie said.

"I didn't know the Haunted Mansion even had a back yard," Bunny added.

"Like, yeah, I don't really think it does," Trixie said, and that is what's creeping me out."

"And what's going on with that crest?" Vicky asked.

The engraved crest centered between the chairs began to glow orange, as if it were energized by the moon's rays. Brighter and brighter and brighter—until six small meteor-like bursts of light shot out from the crest and began rapidly traveling in small, random motions above it. They continued to move faster and faster—creating trails of yellow-orange sparks, which formed a large globe-like mass of intense orange light in the center of all the activity.

"Oh, I think I know", Lila said in a diabolical tone.

"What? How would you know?" Vicky snapped at Lila. The bright glow of the light mass highlighted her face in the darkness like a large bonfire, as she gave Lila a perplexed look.

"Wait. Who's touching my arm?" Bunny screeched out.

"And my leg," Katie followed.

The tall chairs had suddenly sprung to life! Their intricately carved details broke free from the rigid structures that lye beneath—moving in vine-like fashion, they quickly restrained the arms and legs of the four frightened girls.

"Why, why is this happing?" Vicky cried out. Too scared to say anything else.

The other girls shrieked out for the very same reason.

"And how come *she's* not tied to her chair?" Katie yelled out, while directing her attention to a smiling Lila.

"Yeah, how come you're still free, Lila?" Trixie asked.

Lila looked at Trixie with a sly grin, her green cat-like eyes began to glisten—startling the other four girls. "You'll see," she said with suppressed laughter. Slowly standing up from her chair and turning her attention towards the ominous moon, the green eyed girl raised her arms towards the dark sky and spun around—as her silky-black cape covered, then revealed, who she really was. A young and powerful witch! Lila had waited years for this night to finally arrive. The night when all her great-uncle's darkest desires would become reality.

Her long, black hair was now streaked with violet hues, as it fluttered in the wind. Her perfectly toned skin contrasted beautifully with her burgundy lips and piercing green eyes. An intricately textured purple bodysuit with flowing black cape and knee high boots added to her stunning, yet very intimidating, appearance. Quickly, she scanned the circle with her evil eyes, looking at each of the four girls, before gazing upon the large black staff she now possessed in her left hand. Atop the staff, held in place by a vultures claw, sat a crystal-like sphere—five inches in diameter and transparent green in color. Its appearance, one could say, closely resembled the staff of her great-uncle's inspiration, Maleficent.

The confident young witch waved her right hand in a circular motion over the top of her staff, which ignited into a green fireball—illuminating her evil, yet very beautiful, facial features. Gripping the staff with both hands, she thrust the blazing head towards the bright orange globe above the crest. A bolt of green lightning shot from the staff, striking the core of the radiant, orange mass centered between the chairs—which immediately burst into thousands of tiny blue and white light particles and transitioned into a giant tornado-like funnel around the area in which the girls sat. As the particles continued to rapidly orbit the area, the wind grew stronger and stronger—the hair of each girl was flying around so uncontrollably, they could hardly see what was happening.

Unaffected by the wind, Lila spread out her arms and raised her hands above her head; commanding the funnel to rise towards the eerie, moon-lit sky. Higher and higher it went, until it was at least thirty feet above the ground—all along, picking up speed. Again, the young witch took her staff with both hands, only this time she thrust it towards the funnel. A continuous stream of green lightning shot from her staff and into the center of the whirling mass of wind and light—transforming it into giant, free-flowing shapes of blue, green and white light—which moved in and around each other. As four petrified girls looked up to observe the unexplainable events taking place right before their very eyes, Lila raised her hands above her head yet again, as she called out to the moon above, "Halloween moon of spirits dark, let her roam throughout the park!"

"Her?" Vicky questioned. "What does she mean by 'her'? I hope she doesn't mean one of us."

"I...don't...think...so," Bunny replied. "Look", she said while nodding towards the floating shapes above them.

As the colorful shapes continued to move in and around each other, a pale white face began to take shape, and then a neck. Gradually, facial features, silvery-blue hair, slender arms, and a long, tattered grey dress—that effortlessly flowed through the air, became more pronounced. The smokey blue and green shapes formed an eerie aura-like border around the floating figure, then faded into the surrounding midnight sky.

"Who is that?" Katie asked.

"You don't know me?" the floating figure replied with a grin.

"No, we don't," Vicky replied.

"Let me give you a clue," the lady spirit answered back. "A 'head start' in the right direction, you could say. You can usually find my aunt floating about the seance room, if you know what I mean."

"The lady in the crystal ball?" Bunny asked. "How can she be your aunt?"

"Yeah," Trixie added. "Isn't Madame Leota just a ride prop?"

"Don't be silly, Trixie. She's more than just a ride prop," Vicky replied.

"Silence!" Lila shouted. "It's time you learn to *respect* those around you."

"Thank you my dear. Please ladies, call me Madame S."

"So, Madame S, are you really, like, related to Madame Leota?" Bunny asked.

"Yes, I guess you could say that, in a roundabout way. But enough about me," Madame S replied. "Tonight your friend, Lila, has freed me from the boundaries of the mansion walls. In return, I have agreed to help carry out her great-uncle's wishes."

"Wishes?" Vicky repeated.

"Oh, Lila didn't tell you?" The floating spirit said as she glanced over at the young witch with a grin.

"Tell us what?" Katie asked. "We didn't even know she had a great-uncle."

"Ah, splendid," Madame S responded. "So this whole thing is like one big *surprise* to the four of you? Wonderful," she said with a sinister laugh.

"Surprise? Like, what does that mean?" Vicky said with the look of terror written across her face. "Lila, what have you done?"

"Well, considering I had such simple minds to work with, it was really rather easy," Lila replied, signaling to Madame Sera to begin the ceremony.

"What? What are you doing, Lila?" Bunny asked.

"Preparing for big changes," the young witch answered back.

"Changes for what?" Katie asked.

"All of this," Lila calmly replied, as she raised her arms—looking in all directions.

"Huh?" All four girls responded simultaneously. Flabbergasted by Lila's response.

"I know, it's too much for your feeble little minds to comprehend," Lila said, "but in time you will understand." The young witch walked over and calmly sat in the fifth chair, poised and ready for what was about to happen. Then she signaled to Madame Sera to begin.

The intimidating female spirit closed her eyes and slipped into deep concentration, while four frightened girls hung on her every word.

Still restrained by the chairs, they could do nothing but watch and wonder. Would they make it through this horrible nightmare?

"Chairs of black, it is blood you need. Prick a finger to do the deed."

Instantaneously all the girls screeched out, startled by the sudden prick of their right index finger. The five chairs had each drawn a single drop of blood.

The shadow spirit continued her seance: "Moon of orange, which shines so bright. Call out the spirits this hallows eve night." The wind began to swirl around the area as villainous streaks of light came flying in from all corners of the Walt Disney World property. Each was led by an obscure facial image of a spooky ghost, ghoul or skeleton, and each, shot into the crest—giving it a life-force of its own.

Lila, still poised in her chair, sat confidently with her chin up and eyes closed. She felt the energy building around her, and the wind blowing through her hair.

Madame Sera's dark, piercing eyes opened and gazed down at the energized crest, as she finished her calling. "Powers of shadow and evil that scares, rise from thy crest to all nested chairs. Inject them with darkness, Thorns they'll become. So darkness may rule, all good that's been done!" The energy of the wind was instantly sucked into the crest—the air went silent and still. In one giant burst, violent streams of orange and yellow light shot out from the crest's center and into the five chairs—jolting and sending them into uncontrollable variations of transformation!

All five girls fell to the ground as their seats suddenly vanished and were replaced by tall, dark figures standing behind them. Each wore a hooded, long black cloak which covered their bony frames. Their skin was pale blue and wrinkled. Behind dry chapped lips were sets of uncared for teeth, past which, the most foul of breath flowed. Their large eyes appeared lifeless and black as night. Their hair, white as the polar caps, was lined with streaks of bright blue.

Lila rose to her feet and walked to the center of the crest, slowly turning three hundred and sixty degrees, admiring what she and Madame Sera had just accomplished.

The other four girls had been knocked unconscious by the light streams that had passed through their bodies and into the chairs— erasing all memories they had just witnessed. They would have no recollection of how their Mickey's Not So Scary Halloween Party ended that evening.

Madame Sera's spell had worked to perfection. Standing before her and the young witch, Lila, was their future—their legacy to be.

"Welcome," Lila said, as she walked around the crest, "my new conjurers of villainy and chaos. We have brought you here, this Halloween eve, to lead a new Order. One that will carry on the legacy my great-uncle so unwillingly left behind. Each of you possesses the power of dark magic. The ability to call on characters and creatures in shadow, manipulate environments in *and* around WONDER, or whatever else your ruthless minds can think up within Disney's precious little World of Natural Dream Enhanced Realities. Your only goal, crush the Disney spirit. Put an end to *all* happily ever afters. Build your armies, teach your leaders the ways of villainy—how to deceive, lie, cheat, steal, con and sabotage. Anything, that would lead to Disney's inevitable demise and give birth to the *new* kingdom. A *dark* kingdom, where new villains will rule and evil shall triumph over good." Lila raised her arms, staff in hand, and looked to the moon. Her voice echoed these words: "I declare the five who stand before me, *supreme rulers* of the new Order. To honor the villain my great-uncle most admired, the *new* name of this Order shall reflect Maleficent's inspiring words: 'A forest of thorns shall be his tomb. Borne through the skies on a fog of doom! Now go with the curse, and serve me well! Round Stefan's castle, CAST MY SPELL!' And that name shall be... the Forest of Thorns Order. Each of you, my Dark Thorn leaders, shall rule over a segment of the Order. Elontra, my dear, you will control the Magic Kingdom. Senkrad, Epcot shall be yours. Oltar, Hollywood Studios is now yours to command. Kunn, the Animal Kingdom shall fall under your ruling. And Tanion, you are to be Roamer for *all* of Disney World. As Dark Thorn leaders, you will answer to one, and only one, person... me. Is that understood?"

The five Dark Thorns kneeled, bowed their heads, and answered in unison, "yes your majesty".

"Very well then," Lila said. There is work to be done. Seek out your lairs, build your armies, nest, conjure, and plan the fate of all you rule—in darkness and WONDER alike. Now, off you go!" The young witch slammed the base of her staff into the crest—instantly launching the five Dark Thorn leaders, like a series of sizzling-green fireworks, into the night sky towards their new respective territories.

The shadow spirit hovered close to Lila, who was still standing on the large crest tablet. "I should get back inside the mansion, my dear. I can sense my presence is needed."

"Perhaps you're right," Lila replied. "But remember, you are free to roam the Kingdom as you please, now. The walls of Gracey Manor no longer define you."

With a devilish smirk, Madame Sera said, "If you ever require my services again, just call on the spirits. I will hear you."

Lila and Madame Sera gave each other a look of appreciation, as the tablet on which they stood slowly descended back underground. The grass-covered panels moved back into place—leaving only the foggy, hidden courtyard behind Gracey Manor to be highlighted by the Halloween moon.

Chapter Three

Sometime in recent past.

It was a blustery Sunday evening in snowy February. Typical winter weather for Michigan. Charlie, his parents, and brother had just finished with dinner and were gathered in the family room for what had become known as "Disney movie night" in their household. And tonight's selection was no exception. It was Charlie's turn to choose, and his choice was a family favorite—as were most Disney movies in the Zastawits household, *Alice in Wonderland*.

The fireplace was cracking and popping, as it filled the room with an amber-like glow and steady, flowing heat—making the entire family comfy and warm, while they all nestled under blankets—ready to enjoy the movie.

Their father inserted the disc, the castle appeared, and the Disney movie theme song began to play. Showtime had arrived.

The entire family was enjoying the movie—sharing wholesome conversation, as the white rabbit came scampering across the screen. "Oh my fur and whiskers! I'm late, I'm late, I'm late!," the white rabbit said.

Mrs. Z, as she was known throughout the community, burst into laughter. "Oh, how I adore that silly bunny."

"You say that every time we watch this," Mr. Z replied.

Charlie and his brother looked at their parents, then each other, as they rolled their eyes.

The family cats, Cocoa and Skats came scampering into the family room to see what all the giggling was about. Skats, the grey cat with a lean build and floppy belly, favored Charlie. While Cocoa, the black cat with a portly build and short legs, belonged to Michael. Both quickly claimed their napping spots next to the kids, while curling up to enjoy the humble comforts of a well heated room.

Charlie was gently stroking Skats, who purred in appreciation while kneading the blanket upon which he laid. It was the perfect end to another weekend. Until that is, something rather odd happened—something, only Charlie could see. The white rabbit suddenly stopped in his tracks, turned, and looked straight at Charlie as if he were in the same room.

"Oh, hello there," the rabbit said with a startled reaction. "I was told you'd be here tonight, hiding in the bushes. It's okay, you can come out. I have a little secret a friend of yours wanted me to share with you."

Charlie quickly looked around the room to see if anyone else had noticed what was going on. "Are, are you talking to me?" the startled boy asked.

"Why of course. Your name is Charlie, is it not?"

"Uh. Yeah?" Charlie replied.

"Well then, there's something I need to tell you—I haven't much time to waste," the rabbit said, while looking at his oversized watch. "Your friend down in Florida wants you to watch the Disney vacation planner disc he sent to your house a few months ago. He said there's something REALLY important you need to see on it before you come down to visit in June."

"Huh? How would you know that?" Charlie asked.

"Heh, heh. Cause he told me, he did. And now I'm telling you."

"But why? And how?"

"Never mind that, young man. Just make sure you watch the disc. I have to be on my way now. No time to waste."

"But?"

"No time for buts. No time at all."

"Okay?" Charlie doubtfully replied.

The rabbit quickly spun around, as if he'd heard a noise. "Oh! I gotta go," he said, disappearing from the screen. Then suddenly, he popped back into view. "I almost forgot. Make *sure* you watch it alone. Got it? OK then, I'm off."

As quickly as their discussion had begun, it was over. Everything in the room returned to normal, including the movie.

Charlie looked around the room, and just like his experience on the Small World attraction the year before, no one had seen or heard a thing but him.

"Charlie, would you like some popcorn?" his mother asked. "Charlie, can you hear me? Charlie? Charlie, you need to wake up. Hey, Charlie!"

What? What's happening? Charlie thought to himself as he opened his eyes and looked around his bedroom—his mother's voice blaring through the hallway and into his room. He sat up, scratching his head, wondering, *was it all just a dream? Did I actually have a discussion with the white rabbit from Alice and Wonderland?* Charlie raised the blinds on his window, allowing the early morning sun to burst into the room. The birds were singing, the neighbors were setting out their yard waste bin full of grass clippings—it was another beautiful late spring morning, which confirmed what Charlie had thought to be true. He had indeed had another unusual dream. A dream infused with a message from his good friend, Frank Wellington, by way of micro dream particles and the Magic Dream Expander. *But I didn't eat any "special chocolates" last night?* Charlie thought, as he got out of bed and headed for the bathroom to clean up.

"Hurry up Charlie, breakfast is almost ready," his mom called out.

Unfazed by his mother's voice, he continued to review in his mind all he had eaten the day before—trying to figure out what could have possibly contained the micro dream particles. But as hard as he thought, nothing came to mind. Even after cleaning up and eating breakfast, Charlie still could not pinpoint a moment from the day before when he may have consumed something outside of his daily diet. Frustrated for lack of an answer, he decided it was best to move on—to focus more on what the white rabbit had told him, which was to watch the vacation planner disc and make sure he was alone when doing so. *Easy enough*, Charlie thought, as he sat in the passenger seat of his dad's minivan.

Mr. Z was taking Charlie and his younger brother, Michael, to begin one of their last full weeks of school before summer vacation. The daily drop-off routine now required two stops. First, the middle school, to drop off Charlie. Then Washington Elementary, to drop off Michael.

"Hey Dad, don't you have some errands to run after you pick us up from school today?" Charlie asked.

"Yes. Yes I do. Thanks for the reminder, Son."

"Do you think you could drop us off before you go? I have a bunch of homework to do."

"Actually, I have to take your brother to find a pair of new shoes for our trip to Disney World in a few weeks. But yeah, I can drop you off if you have school work to get done."

"Great. Thanks Dad," Charlie replied. In his head he was thinking, *perfect, I can watch the vacation disc and no one will ever know.* He smiled while looking out the passenger seat window—the morning sun, comforting his face.

At last, school was out and Charlie's father had dropped him off at home. It was the ideal time to watch the Disney vacation planner disc. Alone, without anyone else around to interrupt. He popped in the DVD, which started off with a friendly barrage of testimonials, informative updates and entertaining details regarding the Walt Disney World parks, hotels, restaurants and more—all of which, excited Charlie for their upcoming trip. But just as the video was transitioning from water parks to Disney Springs, the recording was interrupted by a very unusual message. One clearly not intended for the everyday viewer.

The screen jumped to Frank Wellington's small studio apartment, just above the Plaza Ice Cream Parlor in WONDER. And in the background, was his abnormally large cat, Midnight, rolling about on the oriental carpet without a care in the world.

Startled by the noise of something falling in the background, Midnight sprung to his feet and addressed the person shooting the video.

"I say, man, can't you see that I was trying to relax," the well spoken cat said. "Well go on then, get on with it. Don't let *me* interrupt your precious message. What? I'm sure he'll see it. You sent him a message in his dream the other night, did you not? Well, you have *nothing* to worry about," Midnight said, rolling his sparkling green eyes at the one working the video camera. "Right, right, right. I understand. But you're wasting time. You need to get on with it so I can be fed for lunch."

Frank's face popped into view, up close and large—very large, from the right side of the camera lens, with wide open, bug-like eyes. "Oh, hi Charlie. It's your friend Frank. I hope you uh, had a great school year? The other Patrons and I are very much looking forward to seeing you again," he said, smiling. "Now then, let me get you up to speed on what you and your brother have to look forward to when you arrive in a few weeks. As you know, there are five Kingdom Crystals, one of which, we found last year. Thanks in part to the Ears of Virtue, and more notably, the courageous efforts of you and Michael. For that, we are truly grateful. This year, your trip down will have a similar goal in mind. To find the second of five Crystals—though how you achieve this, will most likely involve a set of *very* different experiences. Perhaps even more challenging, and dangerous, then last year's. And of course, as you also know, there are five Objects of Magic—each of which, has its own special set of powers. More importantly, each magical piece has the ability to guide the one who controls it, to one of the Kingdom Crystals. And *that* of course, would be you Charlie, the chosen outsider of the Patrons. Which, brings me to my next point. And this is *very* important. We have already removed the Object of Magic from safe keeping to be used in your search for the second Kingdom Crystal. And you should know, as I did not tell you before, each Object of Magic is bonded to one *specific* Kingdom Crystal by the powers of Disney imagination. And more importantly—"

White noise covered the screen. Frank had been cut off.

Then he returned. But this time, under much distress and in a place Charlie did not recognize. It was very small and cramped—crowded with books, hats, jackets and things. The lighting was dim. From what little Charlie could see, it appeared Frank was in a closet, and very out of sorts. *Perhaps he was hiding from someone evil? Like the Dark Thorns?* Charlie pondered in his mind.

In a very quiet and cautious manner Frank looked into the camera as best he could for such a cramped area, and with a nervous voice said, "Charlie, something *terrible* and unexplainable has happened. The watch, which I'll explain further once you arrive, was struck by lightning tonight while the *Alice and Wonderland* rabbit was transporting it to Uptown Jewelers by way of the Disney Festival of Fantasy Parade. Where, if all had gone according to plan, was to have been held until your arrival. We were *certain* the parade would be the perfect cover for the Object of Magic transfer, but it appears we were wrong. One of the Patrons claimed the green lighting strike came from somewhere over by Big Thunder Mountain Railroad and *not* the sky—which tells us it was not a natural occurrence, but rather some form of black magic. Perhaps by a Dark Thorn, or possibly even a shadow villain who had been called out of WONDER and into reality by either a Dark Thorn or their superior. I'll explain shadow villains later. Regardless, they knew the white rabbit was carrying the watch. They knew about our plan to transfer it to the jewelers. And they knew we were using the parade to do so. Some way, some how, they knew. Fortunately for us, our furry rabbit friend was still able to get the watch to the jewelers, where it is being carefully guarded by the strongest magic we can provide at this time. Just minutes ago, I was informed the magic watch is too damaged to function correctly."

The eccentric Patron paused and looked away—his facial expressions told Charlie that his friend may have just heard an unexpected noise, possibly from someone who was opposed to Frank contacting an outsider, which in this case, was Charlie.

The worried Patron returned his attention to the camera—pulling his hat further down over his forehead. "Where was I? Oh yes. As I was saying, this lightning strike, wherever it came from, damaged the watch so badly, that it is now unable to function properly—putting us in a *very* difficult situation. Without the magical powers of the watch, finding the second Kingdom Crystal will be unachievable. However, there is one tiny glimmer of hope, which will greatly depend on you and your brother. It is a favor I hate to ask, but have no alternative. And that is; take the watch, transport into deep WONDER, and *find* the watchmaker. I cannot tell you who he is at this time, but if anyone has the ability to fix the watch, it will be him. He, is the only chance we have at getting the watch repaired. It is imperative that you and your brother find him—with our assistance of course."

Frank paused a second, then came in closer towards the camera—speaking in a tone even softer than before. "Knowing that what happened here tonight was most likely an act of dark magic, this journey we're asking you and Michael to take with us...well, we may be facing forces more powerful, more treacherous, and much more evil than anything we have ever experienced before. Once you arrive on Walt Disney World property, you and your brother will have to be *extra* careful who you talk to. DO NOT speak to anyone about what I told you today. Trust no one, even the friendliest of cast members or characters may be your enemy dressed in disguise. We will contact you the day of your arrival. How, I'm not certain yet. And be *sure* to bring Merlin's magic looking glass with you. You will need to use it when"—Frank paused again. A pair of glistening green eyes appeared from the darkness beyond the camera's light. It was Midnight.

"Frank, we need to go," the cat said.

Upset from the news, Frank rolled his eyes towards Midnight, then back to the camera. "I'll explain the rest later, Charlie. Remember, trust no one."

There was a blip of video noise—the regular vacation planner material resumed.

Worried that he may have missed something, Charlie scrambled in a frantic attempt to try and jump back to the same spot on the DVD where the secret message was located. However, this time when he watched it, only the regular Disney vacation material played. Frank's message had somehow magically been erased, as if it had never existed on the disc.

Chapter Four

The past two weeks of school had been filled with many fun projects and activities for the kids, though Charlie had hardly noticed. It was the end of the school year—which to most students, was a very exciting time of year, if not *the* most exciting time of year. But for Charlie, his mind had been so consumed with thoughts of what lied ahead in Disney World, that those two weeks seemed more like two days.

Classes dismissed for the year as kids scurried for the buses or their parent's cars. The halls looked like a chaotic ant farm. Kids wove in and out of each other, trying to avoid any catastrophic collisions, as they lugged around a years worth of projects, all crammed into their backpacks or tucked under their arms. Teachers conducted hallway traffic as best they could, though the only kids following their direction were a handful of sixth graders. The rest of the middle school students completely ignored the teachers—being they were too cool for such childlike direction. On the east side of the school was the teacher's parking lot and pickup area for kids getting a ride home from their parents. It was here, that Charlie stood, leaning against the building; waiting for his father to arrive.

"Charlie Z," someone called out.

He turned and spotted a familiar face. It was his best friend, Johnny Bibbs, loosely dressed in a faded teeshirt, baggy shorts and flip flops.

"So buddy, all set for your big trip?" Johnny asked, while leaning into his friend.

"No. Not at all. In fact, I had completely forgotten about it until just now when you asked me."

Johnny laughed out loud at Charlie's response. He knew his friend was a Disney fanatic, and that there was no way he would *ever* forget about a trip to Disney World.

"What?" Charlie replied with a straight face. "I've been busy with school work.

"Yeah, whatever," Johnny spat back. "You think I'm going to fall for that load of garbage? Maybe someone else, but not me, friend."

Charlie continued to stare at his friend with a straight face—which gave way to laughter. "Ha ha ha! Of course I'm ready Einstein, was there ever a doubt? C'mon."

Johnny laughed as well. "Geez Charlie, you almost had me on *that* one. Not. So, I suppose you've been packed for a week?"

"More like two," Charlie replied.

"Two weeks? Obsess much, pal?"

"Hardly. I *was* ready to pack a month ago, but my mom said it was too early."

"Well yeah, I'd say she was right on that one," Johnny added. "Anyway, you'll call me when you get back, right? I'm sure you'll have plenty to tell me about your trip. And, maybe something to show me? Like a little something-something?" Johnny hinted.

"Oh. What is that? A something-something?" Charlie said jokingly.

"You know, a little token of appreciation for your best buddy, perhaps?"

"My best buddy? Let me think for a minute...I don't really *have* a best friend. At least I can't think of one at the moment," Charlie said, looking towards the sky—pretending to be in deep thought.

"Aw c'mon dude. Right, like I'm not your best friend in the *whole* world. I mean, do I have to remind you about what you brought me back last year? The Mickey ears?"

"That's right, I did bring you back something, didn't I?"

"Well, to me they were much more than just *something*, Charlie. Why, you even had them personalized with my name stitched on the back. Only a best friend would think of something like that."

Charlie looked out of the corner of his eye at his friend and gave him a smirk. "True."

"Okay then, at least we've established the fact that I *am* your best friend."

"Of course you are, Johnny. I couldn't think of a better person."

"So that's a yes then?"

"A yes for what, again?" Charlie was stringing his friend along.

"A yes, as in you'll bring me something back, ya knuckle-head."

"I'll try and remember," Charlie replied with a giggle—though deep down inside he knew he would never forget to bring something back for his best friend, Johnny, who's family could not afford such a trip, and thus, had to live vicariously through his best friend's experiences.

"Thanks buddy."

Mr. Z pulled up in the pickup line and Charlie got into the car. As they were pulling away, he rolled down the window and yelled out to his friend, "I'll call you next week when I get back!"

"Okay, I'll see ya soon!" Johnny smiled as he watched the Zastawits van pull out of the school parking lot.

Michael was filled with giddy anticipation, while his brother's stomach was turning like a cement mixer. Charlie, now twelve, and Michael ten, were in a restless state of pre-Disney thought—each for different reasons.

The Zastawits house was buzzing like a beehive as their mother, upstairs in the bedrooms, was double checking the boys luggage for the trip—making sure each boy had everything packed they were told to bring.

Downstairs, their father was going over tomorrow morning's itinerary for their flight, transportation to the resort from the airport, and activities planned for their first day at the most magical place on earth. It was a masterful plan as usual. Mr. Z was a fanatic when it came to planning out the daily family itineraries for Disney World. Not a second would be waisted, nor an attraction missed. And every meal of the day would be accounted for. Their father knew well that trying to do it all was not within the realm of possibility, so he always asked the boys, and mother too, which attractions, shows, and other activities they most wished to see. From there, he scheduled out the details of each day, including meals, then added in a little fun time for unplanned activities or magical distractions that may arise.

The early evening passed quickly, Mr. Z had just wrapped up his masterful plan for their vacation and was walking into the kitchen, where the rest of the family had gathered. Stomachs were growling and talk of food was the conversation at hand.

"Okay, okay everyone, I've got everything figured out. So, who's up for food?" Mr. Z asked. It was clearly a question he already knew the answer to.

Instantaneously, the boys and their mother shouted, "Me!"

"Great," Mr. Z replied. "So of course, the next question is, what does everyone feel like eating?"

"Didn't we have burgers from Roxy's last year?" their mother asked.

"Oh, I believe you are right," he replied.

"Yeah, Roxy's Dad," Michael added.

"Good with you, Charlie?"

"Sure Dad, burgers work for me."

"Alright then, tell me what you guys want and I'll take care of it." Everyone spat out their requests as Mr. Z quickly jotted them down on a sticky note. Seconds later, he was out the door and off to Roxy's. Disney adrenaline fueled his body as he took off in the family van down Cleveland Avenue to fetch dinner.

Somewhere underground, hidden from all wandering eyes, in a secret room of the Magic Kingdom's Pirates of the Caribbean attraction, Captain Plank and Dark Thorn Elontra were having a meeting. A crazy rumor had gotten out and was spreading like wild fire amongst the lower tier Thorns. A rumor that one of the Objects of Magic has been destroyed by a bolt of lightning—ending the Patron's rule over all things Disney. And that a creature of great evil, more powerful than all the Dark Thorns combined, had delivered the fatal blow.

"So Plank," Elontra said, while staring into the Captain's soul with her deep, dark eyes from across the table. "I understand that you and the rest of the foolish Thorns have spread a rumor that the Patron's are finished?"

"Yes. Yes, oh great one," Plank stuttered in response—unable to get past the intimidating appearance of Elontra's pale blue skin, white, blue-streaked hair, and deep black eyes. All of which, were encompassed by a black cloak that created a reaper-like silhouette, cast by the amber glow of the torches on the wall behind her.

"Well, let me ask you a question, Captain," she said in a raspy voice—the bony fingers of her right hand tapping on the small wooden table top.

"Uh, yes? What do ya wants to ask me? Uh, master of darkness," Plank nervously replied while starring at her tapping fingers—his eyes, too scared to look directly into hers.

"A simple question," she replied. "One a small child could *easily* answer, I would imagine."

"Sure. What, what is it?"

"If the Partron's are no longer in control, how come we're still hiding down here in this retched room while they are roaming free in the Kingdom above?"

"I. I don't know? Because we ain't in control?"

Elontra tilted her head upward and let out a horrifying laugh. "Ha-ha-ha-ha-ha-ha! Because we aren't in control," she said while staring at the damp stone ceiling above. "And if *we* aren't in control, who is?"

Plank swallowed deeply, then answered. "The–the Patrons?"

"The Patrons!" Elontra shouted, as she slammed her boney fist on the table. Her soulless eyes, now staring directly into the Captain's. "So *why* would you, and all your babbling fools for friends, ever think for one second that we were in control?"

"I don't kno-know your excellency."

"Ah, very well—I figured as much. Obviously the Patrons still control things. And because they are still in control, we still have much to do."

"Right. Right your dark excellency. But what about the one who cast the bolt of lightning which destroyed the Object of Magic? I, I mean, we heard it was someone with *great* powers—enormous powers. Even more powerful than yours." Plank turned to shield himself, waiting for Elontra to strike him down with a dreadful spell for saying such a thing.

Elontra stared at her Captain—void of all expression, her arms crossed.

"I don't mean any disrespect your excellency, but, but we heard—"

"Shut up, you buffoon, and listen." She slammed both her fists on the table, then pointed at Plank with her long, crooked index finger. "*That,* is not important at this time, in fact, it is the most ridiculous thing I have EVER heard. What *is* important, as far as you are concerned, is this. We received word today from one of our elite spies that the Patron's chosen outsider will be returning to Walt Disney World any day now. What they have planned, we do not know. I'm leaving it up to you, Plank, to find out. We need you to gather your crew, track down any vital information you can within the Magic Kingdom, then report back to me. The Shadow Queen has laid this upon me and I *will not* fail her. Which means, *you* can not fail. Understand me?"

"Yes, I'll get right on it. Consider it done, dark leader," Plank said, nervously jumping up from his chair.

"Very well then. Go fetch your soldiers, spies, or whoever and get me some answers."

"Aye-aye your highness. I mean, I'll get on it straight away. You can count on me."

"Oh... and Captain."

"Yes, your excellency?"

"Try to be smarter next time. You wouldn't like me when I'm... angry."

"Of course your excellency," Plank replied with a fearful heart.

Dark Thorn Elontra stood up, then quickly lifted her arms upwards. Blue flames shot up from the floor, engulfing her completely. Seconds later, she was gone. The only thing remaining were scorch marks where she had stood.

Dinner had been filled with conversation about the next day's trip to the one place on earth the whole family enjoyed, Disney World. Everything that could be packed was. All required documentation was sitting on the kitchen counter next to the luggage, and the kids were in bed trying to overcome the unbearable urge to stay awake. Their parents were triple checking everything one last time before they themselves retired for the short evening ahead. Departure time was four thirty a.m. This assured they would be in the parks by no later than noon the next day.

Charlie laid in bed, his eyes wide open—nervously thinking about tomorrow and the dangers he and his brother may face. He could faintly hear his parents talking, as they walked up the stairs towards their bedroom.

"You have the money for snacks tomorrow morning and the parking fee at the airport, right?" his father asked.

"Yes, Ed. I've got plenty to go around."

"Okay, good. Once we get on property we won't have to worry about any other expenses. We're all covered."

"So where are we staying again, dear?"

"Beach Club Resort."

"Oh, that's right. I think you told me last week. And which park will we be at tomorrow?"

"The Magic Kingdom. *And*, we have a dinner reservation for seven o'clock at The Plaza Restaurant."

"That sounds perfect, Ed. The boys are going to have such a great time. I'm so worked up right now, I don't know if I'll be able to sleep tonight. I sure hope the boys sleep better than I plan to. They really need to get a good nights rest before all the fun begins."

When Charlie heard his mother's words, he rolled onto his side to exhale, then mumbled to himself, "I don't think I'll be sleeping much at all on this trip." His eyes remained open, while his mind kept looping thoughts about the spoken words of his friend, Frank Wellington.

The hallway light went dark, as did the soft glow from their parents bedroom. Morning was just a few short dreams away.

There was a spark of light. A swirl of color. And then...the white rabbit. Running through the colorful, and very lush, woods of Wonderland. A quick turn around a giant oak tree and BAM, he collided with Charlie—who was standing smack dab in the center of the pathway upon which the rabbit was traveling.

Both fell hard to the ground. And each was equally confused about what had just happened.

"I say lad, you caught me quite off guard. The last thing I expected was for someone to be standing, well, where you just were."

Charlie shook, then rubbed his head—still trying to figure out where he was at.

"What's the matter boy, lost for words?"

"I'm just trying to figure out where I am. And how I got here?"

"Well clearly you're not here," the rabbit said.

"What? Not here? What's that supposed to mean? I don't understand," Charlie replied with a look of confusion painted across his face. "And where'd my pajamas go? This isn't what I wore to bed."

"Settle down there laddie, settle down. No need to get yourself all worked up over a little dream interaction."

"Dream interaction?" Charlie said.

"That's right, dream interaction. Frank sent me into your dream to provide all the valuable information you'll need to know prior to your arrival at the Magic Kingdom tomorrow."

"He did? Like what kind of information?"

"Oh, you know, the four w's kind of stuff?"

"The four w's?"

"Yes. Who, what when and where. Surely you're familiar with that sort of thing? I mean, you *are* the chosen outsider."

Charlie thought for a second, then it occurred to him that Frank actually never did tell him *who* he and Michael were to meet, *where* they were to meet, nor *when* the meeting was to take place. All he really knew at the moment was the *what*. Which was the watch. And that the Patrons were to contact him once he arrived at the Magic Kingdom. "Uh, I guess you are right Mr. Rabbit, Frank didn't really get a chance to tell me much in the video I watched a few weeks ago. All I know is, there's a magic watch and someone is supposed to contact me when we arrive at the Magic Kingdom."

"Quite right, good fellow. That's *exactly* what Frank told me. Now then, would you like to hear more?" Quickly answering his own question, the white rabbit replied. "Of course you would. You'd be silly not to, right-right. Very well then, let's tackle the four w's one at a time, shall we?"

"Sure," Charlie replied—barely able to get a word in on the quick-tongued rabbit.

"First off, *who* are you meeting with? Well, for starters, you will be looking for someone you are already familiar with. A chap by the name of Ben, I believe?" The rabbit pulled a note pad out of his jacket pocket to double check. "Ah yes, that *is* correct, Ben."

"Oh, Ben. Ben Glimmer. The little red headed fellow? Yes, I know Ben," Charlie said, with a chuckle of relief.

"Excellent chap, that's swell. Now, for the *what*. You are already aware that the Object of Magic to be used in your search for the second Kingdom Crystal is a watch, is that correct?"

"Yes. A watch. Right," Charlie replied. "I already said that."

"Good-good," the rabbit said with a smile, as he nudged his glasses back up his nose. "Next we have the *when* and the *where*. You are to look for Ben at the *very end* of the Buzz Lightyear's Space Ranger Spin attraction. Plan on entering the ride between two forty five and two forty eight. Fastpasses for you and your family have already been secretly added to your magic bands. So you should have little difficulty boarding a ride vehicle during the appropriate time. Are we clear?"

"Uh, yeah, I guess so."

"You guess so?" The rabbit mocked.

"Oh. I mean, yes sir. I mean, Mr. Rabbit. Sir," Charlie answered back.

"Hmm? Let me hear you repeat what I just told you, *just* to make sure," the rabbit insisted.

"OK. I—I mean, Michael and I are to meet Ben at the very end of the Buzz ride. We are to get on the ride between two forty five and two forty eight using the Fastpasses already on our magic bands. Oh, and we will be discussing information regarding the magic watch," Charlie said, nearly out of breath after such a long spout of words.

"Splendid, young fellow. That was spot on. Well, it's time for me to carry onward." The rabbit turned and was just starting on his way, when he stopped and turned for one last word of advice. Pointing at

Charlie with a squinted eye, he added, "Now don't forget young man, you must be on that ride between two forty five and two forty eight. Two forty five and two forty...it's four thirty, Charlie."

"Charlie? Wake up. It's almost four thirty. We gotta go. Dad's already loaded the van. C'mon Charlie", Michael said, as he literally pulled his brother out of bed and onto the floor. "Hurry up. Get dressed and brush your teeth, Charlie. Mom just said we're leaving in ten minutes!"

Morning had come. It was dark, it was early. Way early. Charlie's mind was still in a heavy dream-like fog. But it did not matter, he knew today was no ordinary day. It was a special day—a magical day. It was the first day of their Disney World vacation.

The families morning travels had passed quickly, Charlie and his brother were sitting in the hotel lobby of the Beach Club Resort waiting for their parents to check them in.

Prior to arriving at their resort, Charlie had secretly told Michael what their plans were for the day using text messages—explaining all the important details Frank and the white rabbit had brought to his attention over the past few weeks. At first, Michael thought his brother had made up the stories about the secret DVD message and the white rabbit dream. But eventually it sunk in—especially after he thought back to what had happened on their previous visit to Disney World.

"Okay boys, we are all set. Is there anything you want to leave here at bag check before we head to the Magic Kingdom?" Mr. Z asked. "Our room isn't ready yet, but we can leave our carry on luggage here and they will take it up to the room with the rest of our luggage once it is ready."

Charlie saw this as an opportunity to pull the magic looking glass out of his backpack and hide it in his pocket for later. "Yeah, Dad, I need to leave my backpack, if that's OK?"

"Me too, Dad," Michael added.

"Of course guys. Just give them to me and I'll check them in."

Charlie quickly unzipped the pocket where he had stored Merlin's magic looking glass, pulled it out, and began to stuff it in the right front pocket of his shorts, when his mom noticed what he was doing.

"Charlie, isn't that the toy you bought last year when we were here?"

Caught off guard, he quickly thought up a story. "Uh, I had so much fun last year, that I brought it back for good luck."

"Oh, I like that Charlie. A 'Disney World good luck charm'. That is such a *neat* idea. Don't you think so, Ed?"

"Yeah, really cool, Charlie. So, you guys got everything you need?" Their father was so preoccupied on getting to the Magic Kingdom that the magic looking glass was hardly a blip on his radar. A big relief for Charlie.

"All set," their mother replied.

"Okay Zastawits family, let's go find a ride to the park. There's a sign over there pointing to the bus pickup area."

They all headed out the front door of the lobby, veering left down the pathway, with their father enthusiastically leading the way. It was going to be a fun-filled day at the Magic Kingdom.

The remainder of the morning passed quickly for the Zastawits family, as did lunch at Cosmic Ray's Starlight Café, thanks to a wonderful midday performance by Sonny Eclipse and some tasty burgers.

Before Charlie realized, it was two thirty five. They had just finished riding the Tomorrowland Transit Authority and Walt Disney's Carousel of Progress, only ten minutes remained until he and his family were to enter the Buzz attraction so the boys could meet up with their red headed friend, Ben Glimmer. It was still too early to hit the attraction, so Charlie stalled for time.

"Hey Dad," don't we have Fastpasses for something?" Charlie asked. A question he already knew the answer to.

"Let me check the app here. Yes, we have two forty five Fastpasses for Buzz. So in about five minutes we'll head over there."

Charlie looked to his brother and grinned, to assure him that everything was running just as Frank had planned.

Five minutes of people watching passed like one, and it was time to go ride Buzz. The Fastpass line was barely occupied, allowing them to reach the boarding area of the attraction in no time at all. As they waited to board, Michael stood and admired the large Buzz Lightyear figure, one of his all-time favorite characters.

"Okay, watch your step please," the cast member said, waving Charlie and his family to enter the boarding area walkway.

"Is it alright if Michael and I ride together, Mom?"

"Sure Charlie", she replied. "We'll be right behind you."

Charlie and his brother jumped into a ride vehicle—a cast member locked them in and they were off. Being the older of the two, Charlie immediately claimed control of the vehicle, which Michael did not mind since he saw it as an opportunity to zap more stuff with his cool laser pistol. The boys had a blast shooting, spinning and shooting some more. And while Michael focused primarily on targets, Charlie concentrated on steering, in an attempt to spot Ben. The deeper into the attraction they went, the quicker he spun around—desperately trying to find their little red headed friend. But before he succeeded, the ride had come to its final stage. The vehicle spun forward and locked into place, no longer allowing Charlie to steer.

"Did we miss him?" He quietly asked his brother.

"Miss who?" Michael replied.

"Ben, you idiot."

"Ben?" Michael asked—still not catching on.

"Yes, Ben. The little guy with red hair. He helped us get the Kingdom Crystal last year? You know. Ben."

"Ohhhh, that Ben. Right."

"Yeah, that Ben."

"I didn't see him anywhere on the ride."

"Are you positive?" Charlie asked.

"Yes, Charlie, I'm positive."

As they exited the ride vehicle, fear swept through Charlie's body like a wave of nervous energy. *Had he somehow missed Ben?* He thought to himself. The sounds around him became muffled. His vision blurred as his eyes began to well up with tears. Tears he could not let his parents see. Suppressing his emotions, Charlie walked up to the monitors to help his brother look for their photo. He felt a hand on his shoulder. Thinking it was his father, Charlie quickly wiped the water from the corner of his eyes and turned to look up. Only he didn't have to look as high as he had anticipated. It was a shorter man, a jolly man, a man with red hair. It was their friend, Ben Glimmer.

The wee man held a finger to his lips, signaling the boys to be quiet. "Hey lads, good to see ya. I'm only here to tell you one thing. Keep your eyes on monitor number three."

"But Ben, I don't..."

"Shhh, lad. No time to talk details. Just watch the monitor," Ben said, as he turned the boys heads towards the third screen. OK, I gotta get going now. Good luck."

Charlie turned around to speak, but it was too late. Ben had left and his parents were rapidly approaching. "You distract Mom and Dad while I watch the monitor, Michael. Got it?"

"Ten-four, big brother," Micheal replied. He jumped into character immediately. "Hey Dad, did you guys find your picture yet? I think I see it over here." Michael pointed in the opposite direction from where monitor three was located.

His parents bit, following the clever ten year old, and leaving Charlie to focus on the third monitor.

As he stared intently at the screen, waiting for something to happen, he noticed the monitor was rapidly alternating between a picture of them and a black screen with words. The harder he stared, the clearer the message became, until it was so clear that the photo was almost non-existent. It read:

It's time to visit the hatter and take a spin.

The screen went blank—then a photo of the next group appeared. The message had disappeared. But not before Charlie had committed it to memory and typed it into his phone. All of this had happened in a matter of mere seconds.

His brother, ready to move on, gave Charlie a look of desperation. He had run out of ideas to keep their parents distracted.

Charlie read his brother's eyes and came to his rescue. "Hey Dad, I think we should move on to Fantasyland. I heard they've made some changes since last year."

"You know, I heard that too, Charlie," his mom added. "Besides Ed, we still have a lot to see, eat and do before the day is over."

"I think you guys are on to something," Mr. Z replied enthusiastically. "Looks like we're headed to Fantasyland."

As they approached the Mad Tea Party, Charlie spotted the Mad Hatter, just left of the queue line entryway, triggering the message he had just received on the Buzz attraction. Tugging his brother's shirt, he pulled Michael close enough to whisper. "This is it."

"This is what?" his brother barked back.

"Shhhh. The Mad Hatter. We need to speak to him before we get in line for the ride." Charlie thought quickly. "Hey Mom, Michael and I want to get our photo taken with the Mad Hatter, is that Okay?"

"Sure dear. You boys go right ahead. I'll take a photo or two as well."

Charlie and his brother walked up to the Hatter, who strangely enough, already knew their names. "Oh, hi boys, you must be Charlie and Michael. I've heard *all* about you, I have."

The noise from the crowds and attraction music masked their conversation. Their mother could not hear a word they were saying.

"How did you know our names?" Michael asked.

"A cat told me," the Hatter replied.

"A cat?" Michael snipped back.

"Yes, I believe you know him? He's kind of big, fluffy, and he loves to talk a lot."

"Oh, you mean Midnight?" Charlie asked.

"Yes, that's his name. Midnight."

"It's Frank's cat, Michael. We met him towards the end of our trip last year in Frank's apartment, remember?"

"Oh yeah, right," his brother replied.

"Anyway, speaking of Frank, you two ready to take a spin on the cups?"

"Sure, that's why we're here," Charlie replied. "But let me ask my parents if it's okay, first."

"Go right ahead, young man."

"Hey Mom", Charlie called out. "Is it okay if we ride the teacups with the Mad Hatter?"

"Sure honey, you go right ahead." She was not worried in the least, since her boys were with an "official" Disney character.

The Hatter smiled and waved, then bowed to their mother to show his respect.

In return, their mother did a curtsey and smiled back at the Hatter. "Have fun boys."

"Very well then, a rhyme I have for you," the Hatter giggled out.

A rhyme?" Michael questioned.

"Shh, Michael, shut your trap and listen," Charlie snipped.

The Hatter nodded to Charlie, thanking him for his help, then he spoke in rhyme.

"Ride with me and you shall see this ride is quite the treat. I'll spin you left, then spin you right, be sure to stay in your seat. A great un-birthday journey we'll take, to a place unknown to most. Where you shall meet above Main Street, a friend, a Patron, your host."

Charlie and his brother looked at each other with smiles on their faces, impressed by the Hatter's rhyme.

"Come-come gentleman, it's time to climb aboard."

"What about our parents?" Michael asked.

"Not to worry young fellow. The tea cups will occupy their time during your absence."

"And how are they going to do that?" Charlie asked."

"Easy. I've set their cup for what we like to call an 'animated spin'. Once they get going fast enough, the cup will take over—sending them into a spin so fast in the opposite direction of time, that *time* will literally stand still, as long as the teacup continues at a certain rate of rotation. Once you return, the cup will slow down, returning your parents to the present moment. Trust me, they won't miss you at all—in fact, they'll never know you were gone."

Charlie and Michael looked at their parents, who were seated in a blue teacup on the other side of the attraction, and waved with their best fake smiles. Charlie turned and looked at the Mad Hatter. "Are you *sure* they won't know what happened?"

"One hundred and twelve percent," the Hatter replied, with a crazed expression of happiness on his face.

As the tea party floor began to move, the boys instinctively reached for the wheel with both hands to spin their cup.

"No-no-no," the Hatter said, while he gently placed the tip of his index finger on the wheel. "One finger is *all* you'll need."

The boys followed the Hatter's lead—each placing a finger on the wheel. Their teacup began to spin, faster, and faster, and faster. The people in the other cups surrounding them turned to blurry swirls of color and sparkly gold dust. The surrounding sounds blended together into one harmonious jingle. The boys looked at the Hatter, who was sitting erect with his index finger still on the wheel and eyes closed, as if he were in a meditative state.

The ceiling above became an inverted whirlpool of orange, yellow and red, as it began to pull their spinning teacup upwards. The cup was spinning, the ceiling was spinning, *everything* was spinning! Charlie and his brother lost all sense of orientation as they were pulled into the eye of the ceiling—screaming, hollering and waving their hands in the air. It was indeed a *mad* tea party!

The spinning cup blast through the ceiling like a shooting star, leaving behind a trail of magical dust—only to come to an abrupt stop seconds later. With their heads still spinning, the boys tried to gather their bearings. It appeared they were no longer on the attraction, but rather, in the hub of the park. All the guests passing by were perfectly dressed, perfectly groomed, perky and happy. That's when it dawned on Charlie, they were in WONDER. He turned to the Hatter and said, "So, my guess is, our *host* is Frank Wellington?"

"Ahh, you *are* a very observant young man, just as Midnight had told me." The Hatter pointed with his gloved hand to the window above the Plaza Ice Cream Parlor with a whimsical smirk on his face.

Charlie looked, then grinned. "Of course, it's Frank's apartment."

"Well, go on," the Hatter said. "Take your brother and go see your old friend. He's been expecting you."

Charlie and Michael took off running for Frank's apartment—crossing the hub lawn, before running into the ice cream parlor where they searched for a stairway. The kind cast member working behind the counter looked at the boys and said as she pointed, "It's right back there gentleman."

"Thanks", Charlie replied, as he pondered how she knew what they were looking for. But then again, this was WONDER. They scurried up the narrow stairway, which opened up to a hallway of doors. One to the left and three to the right. It was clear to see which one to choose. The first of three doors on the right with the brass sign that simply read, FRANK.

Charlie knocked on the vintage-styled wooden door and stepped back. There were clicks, clacks and a clunk—then the handle turned and the door opened up to a grinning man with wavy grey hair, bushy eyebrows, clear rimmed glasses and colorful clothes. "Hello Boys, so good to see you again. Won't you come in. I have plenty to share with you."

The boys ran up and wrapped their arms around Frank, squeezing tightly.

"Now-now, no need to get all sentimental when there's work to be done. We can save that for later," Frank said, patting the boys on their backs.

"But Frank, I thought you were in trouble?" Charlie said, as he pulled away to look up at his friend.

"Why would you think such a thing?" the Patron replied, closing the door behind them. "Please, have a seat. Would you or your brother like something to drink?"

"I'm thirsty," Michael shouted.

"It was probably the video, Frank."

The boys turned to see who had spoken. It was Midnight—Frank's oversized, and very sarcastic cat, who had just crawled out from underneath the bed and was stretching.

"Hi ya Midnight," Michael said.

"Hello to you too, young man," the cat replied with a yawn.

"Yes, it was the video," Charlie replied. "The way it ended, I thought you were in danger."

"Oh, right. I can see why you might think that," Frank replied. "I did look a little nervous in the video, didn't I. The truth is, we weren't in any danger at that time, but that's not to say danger wasn't lurking near by. You see, ever since the lightning strike a few weeks back, things have been sort of shaky around here."

"What lightning?" Michael asked, as he sat down at the small wooden table near the kitchen area.

"Your brother didn't tell you?"

"Ohhhh. *That* lightning strike, now I remember," Michel replied.

Charlie stopped petting Midnight, then walked over and sat next to his brother at the table, preparing himself for what the wise old Patron had to say.

"So, he did tell you. Good," Frank said. "As I've already explained, the watch was struck by a green bolt of lightning while being transported by the white rabbit during the Disney Festival of Fantasy Parade. And because of this, the magical watch will not function properly—making it impossible for us to track down the second Kingdom Crystal. We need the two of you, Charlie and Michael, to pick up the watch later tonight at Uptown Jewelers on Main Street."

"So someone will be there to give it to us?" Charlie asked.

"Well, something like that. You see, if somebody working there knew where it was, that would make them an easy target for the Thorns—who would work over the cast member until they found out where the watch was hidden. And we can not take a chance like that. Not in the least bit. That's where Merlin's magic looking glass comes into the picture. It will help you find the hidden Object of Magic." Frank leaned down towards the boys, stressing the importance of what he was about to say. "This evening, shortly after your dinner, go to the jeweler's shop on Main Street, but don't go inside. Take out the magic looking glass and look closely at the shop sign out front. From there, you'll know what to do."

"Oh really," Michael said. "And how's that going to happen. Is the sign going to tell us what to do?"

Charlie gave his brother a smack on the arm.

"Ow! That hurt," Michael shouted.

The wise Patron calmly held a finger to Charlie, encouraging him to be calm. "I thought you might ask that, Michael."

"And how come we have to let a stupid sign tell us where the watch is? Why can't *you* just tell us now and we can go get it?"

Frank remained calm, as if the young boy's words were a mere pebble of sand between his toes. "The whereabouts of the watch is protected by magic in order to keep it out of Thorn hands. Only the chosen outsider possesses the power to seek it out. And that, young man, would be your brother and the magic looking glass he's carrying in his pocket."

Charlie looked at Frank and humbly smiled in appreciation.

"OK then," Michael replied. The expression on his face turned from anger to curiosity. "But how did you know when we were going to eat dinner? I mean, doesn't the person we're meeting at the jewelry shop need to know what time we'll be arriving?"

"They already do."

"But how?" Michael asked.

"Let's just say I know people who know people," Frank replied with a grin, which then turned serious. "Now remember, this lighting strike—we don't believe it was a natural occurrence, but rather some form of black magic created by either a Dark Thorn, or possibly even a shadow villain."

"Yeah, I remember you saying that in the video. What is a shadow villain?" Charlie asked.

"Just like we use WONDER to grow and preserve all the *good spirited things* from Disney, the Dark Thorns and their Superior, whom is yet to be unveiled, use black magic to grow and preserve all the *evil* which lurks in the shadows of WONDER—where they can reimagine villains in any form they choose, and from the looks of things, may now be able to bring them into reality.

"I don't like the sound of that," Michael hesitantly replied.

"As you shouldn't," Frank answered back. "If the Dark Thorns have in fact started to summon shadow villains into reality, then our task of seeking out the five Kingdom Crystals will have become exponentially more difficult, and worse yet, more dangerous than we could have ever imagined."

"That sounds like one giant nightmare", Charlie replied. "So Frank, why is the word 'shadow' used to describe these villains?"

"Well, Charlie. Everything created by Disney is technically a concept until it is brought to finalization and released to the general public. There are endless concepts and dreams created durning the development of Disney movies, park attractions, resorts and more, which never reach the public audience. Through many years of hard work, the Partons have figured out how to secretly preserve many of these concepts in WONDER, where they are magically used to protect the five Kingdom Crystals and all other things sacred to Disney. Unfortunately though, many concepts also include villainous works of imagination. And over time, they have been taken by force and reimagined by FOTO in the 'shadows' of WONDER. It's been an ever increasing problem for the Patrons to say the least.

Sorry, I guess I forgot to mention that part when you were here last year?"

"Oh great, so now we have Thorns *and* villains to worry about?" Michael replied sarcastically.

"Shush, Michael," Charlie snipped. "So Frank, everything that exists in WONDER is created from concepts and dreams—good or evil, and NOT from what we see in reality, such as Disney movies, and everything in the parks?"

"Precisely, Charlie. And, they can also be combined, added to or reimagined without any limitations—like the WONDER version of Hollywood studios you and your brother experienced last year. Which was a combination of everything that has ever existed in Hollywood studios, but in a conceptual state. You could say, WONDER is a giant melting pot of all concepts ever created by Disney imagineers and animators. Some are good, while others are, well, evil."

"But why would they ever create anything evil for Disney?" Charlie asked.

"You have to have balance, Charlie. Just imagine what it would be like if heroes had nothing or no-one to overcome, to defeat, to rise above and conquer. Without evil, good would struggle to define itself—to exist."

"So there's a very good chance we may have to battle these shadow villains during our search for the second Kingdom Crystal?"

"Precisely, young man. Which is why I initially hesitated to ask the two of you to come back and help us", Frank reverted back to a positive note. "Uh, where was I? Oh, right. Yes." He cleared his throat. "Uh-hmm-hmm-hmm-hmm. However, we *do* have the watch in our possession and we know who can fix it. Which are *both* good things—very good things. Yes, very good, very good indeed. So the only question that still remains is, are you and your brother willing to help the Patrons, Charlie?" Frank asked with a glimmer of hope in his eyes.

Charlie and Michael looked at each other, then turned to their friend. "We're here aren't we, Charlie said."

The old man smiled. "Oh good, so glad to hear it. Welcome back, boys."

Charlie and his brother stood up from the table and gave Frank a group hug to show their support.

"Very well then, I believe that's all I need to tell you for now. Any questions before I send you back to your parents?"

"No, I don't think so. It seems pretty simple", Charlie replied. "Eat dinner, go to the jewelry store, read the sign, and get the watch."

"Perfect," the old man replied.

"Oh, I do have one question," Charlie added. "What do we do after we get the watch?"

"Ah yes, good question. Chances are, I will be there when you pick it up to explain what is to be done next, OK?"

"Got it," Charlie replied.

"But remember Charlie, and you too Michael, between now and then, trust no one except those you know well enough to ask a personal question that only they would know the answer to. Understand?"

The boys nodded to confirm.

"Alright then, you've both done this before. Each of you place a hand on the lamp and I'll see you soon," Frank noted. Charlie and his brother touched the lamp and vanished.

Charlie and Michael appeared back in the cups with the Mad Hatter as the ride slowed and came to an end. They exited right behind their parents, who were unaware of what had just happened.

"So, anyone up for a snack?" their dad asked. "They have lemonade slushes at The Friar's Nook."

Everyone unanimously agreed that a nice cold slushy would hit the spot on a hot Florida day, such as the one they were experiencing. Within a few short minutes they had gathered around a small shade-covered table and were enjoying their ice cold lemonade slushes. It was an ideal time to plan out the remainder of their day.

"It's four o'clock," their father said. "We have three hours until dinner time. So where would everyone like to go next?"

"Well, we're in Fantasyland, Ed, there's plenty to do right here," their mother replied.

"Yeah Dad, Charlie added. "We have Dumbo, Small World, Seven Dwarfs Mine Train, Peter Pan's Flight... like Mom said, plenty to do."

"I guess the two of you are right," Mr. Z said while laughing.

"Where are we eating tonight, Dad?" Charlie asked.

"We are eating at the Plaza Restaurant. Should be a nice casual dinner. I didn't want to overdo it on our first night. Besides, they have real tasty deserts from what I read."

"Awesome," Charlie replied.

"Hey Ed, what do you say we do a little Main Street browsing after dinner? I bet the boys wouldn't mind a break from the ride lines. Especially if they found something cool in one of the shops to buy."

Charlie chimed in, knowing the jewelry shop was located on Main Street. "Yeah Dad, I like Mom's idea," he said while kicking his brother in the ankle to agree.

"Yeah Dad, I want to go shopping too," Michael awkwardly added.

"You see honey, the boys like my idea. Besides, I think Charlie mentioned something earlier about looking at watches. Right, Charlie?"

"Watches?" Mr. Z questioned. "Since when do you like watches, Charlie?"

"I don't know," Charlie replied while shrugging his shoulders.

"Oh, leave him alone, Ed. After all, he is a middle schooler now. I'm sure lots of the kids in middle school wear watches, don't they, Charlie?"

"Yeah, they actually do," he replied.

"There, you see, Ed. Our little boy is becoming a young man."

"I guess you're right honey," her husband giggled, while observing the crowd.

Charlie smiled, knowing inside he had won. The evening was now set up perfectly for what he and his brother needed to accomplish. They would be able to pick up the magic watch shortly after dinner. It was going to be a great night in the Kingdom...or so he thought.

Just two tables over from where the Zastawits family were enjoying their lemonade slushes sat three spies with ears wide open. They were disguised as everyday, happy guests, thanks to the belt buckle cloaking devices all the Thorn spies wore. Their boss was Captain Plank, the scraggly looking leader of the low life Thorns in the Magic Kingdom.

"Did you hear that matey's?" One of the spies growled. "Sounds like the Patron's little friend likes watches."

"Quite a coincidence, I'd say Robert," replied Joe, the second of three spies.

Martin, the third spy in the group, joined the conversation. "Yeah, and he wants to take a look at 'em later on after dinner. Ha! But we knows what the little fella is really look'n for, and it ain't no regular watch," he said with a snarl.

"Ok boys, I say we gets back and tells the Cap'n the good news," Robert said.

"Right you are Robert. The Cap'n will wanna be making plans for this evening once he hears the news," Martin added.

Robert signaled with his index finger for the other two spies to lean in closer so he could whisper. "When that little booger and his brother show up tonight they'll be in for a big surprise, I tell ya. A very *BIG* surprise." The half-wit spies enjoyed a good laugh around the table over Robert's statement, who then continued, "Okay, gents, let's go tell the Cap'n the good news."

The three Thorns stood up from the table and walked to a nearby dream dot that was typically hidden from everyday guests. They set coordinates on their wrist band devices for Plank's liar and vanished.

Chapter Five

Evening settled upon the Magic Kingdom with a soft orange glow. The Zastawits family had just finished up with desert at the Plaza Restaurant. All bellies were full, though evil was lurking near by.

Captain Reginald Plank, Segment One commander of the Thorns, was sitting at a table on the far end of the restaurant with his two most trusted spies. His forearms rested upon the table, as he stared with his one good eye—concealed by mirrored sunglasses, at the chosen outsider. All three men were cleverly disguised as common park guests thanks to the signature Thorn belt buckle masking device they all wore, though most of the time the buckles were concealed by untucked shirts. The only noticeable detail that truly separated Thorns from common guests were the wrist bands they wore. Unlike a colorful Magic band, their bands were made of brushed metal and featured a thick round face with blue LED coordinates—used to jump from one dream dot to another within WONDER, and around its outer ridge—more commonly known as the Disney World properties.

"You mates have the crew in place?" Plank asked his spies in a soft, gravely voice—his one good eye still focused on the outsider.

"You bet ya Cap'n," Jolly, the spy with the Donald Duck teeshirt, replied.

"Yeah Cap'n, we gots three of our best mates all set and ready inside the shop, just wait'n for the little fella and his brother ta show up," the other spy added.

"Very good," Plank replied. "Once those two medaling kids get their stink'n little hands on the watch, you tell our boys to grab 'em. Understood?"

"Yes Cap'n, understood. We'll take care of them little brats for ya.

"And the watch too?, you blither'n idiots," Plank snarled back, as he kept his eye on Charlie.

"Oh, yeah-yeah, yes sir. And the watch as well. We'll be make'n double sure we gets that too, Cap'n. Don't you be worrying about that," Jolly replied.

"I'll stop worrying when the watch is sitting in me hands mateys, you get what I'm saying to ya?" Plank said, his hands opened up in a ready-to-receive position on top of the table.

"We hears ya loud and good Cap'n," Jolly answered back.

"Yeah, loud *and* good", the other spy, Smith, added.

"Now that's what I likes to hear mates. Cause if ya don't come through for your cap'n, well, then I might have ta have ya walks the plank and keep me twin tiger sharks company. They're *always* ready to eat, ya know." The captain grumbled, then broke into a fit of sarcastic laughter.

Mr. and Mrs. Z had gone inside Uptown Jewelers to browse, while the boys still remained outside on Main Street near the corner entrance. Charlie had told his mother he wanted to take a few photos of Main Street before going into the jewelers, which bought him and his brother an extra bit of time outside—just long enough to pull out Merlin's magic looking glass and search for what he'd come for. The secret message concealed within the letters of the Uptown Jewelers sign. He held the magic looking glass up towards the sign, then pushed the button on the handle. The glass began to spin—faster and faster, it's frame glowed brilliant green as the spinning glass Charlie was looking through turned the letters on the sign into blurred streaks of white, aqua and golden light. Quickly, Charlie scanned the letters on the sign for hidden words. Just as the first word "Up" appeared, he felt a tap on the shoulder! Frantically, he turned around—almost dropping the magic looking glass, which immediately snapped to a halt and dimmed.

"Excuse me young man, can you tell me where I could get one of those light toys for my daughter?" a well rounded lady dressed in Disney apparel, complete with Minnie ears, asked.

Charlie momentarily found it hard to focus on her question, as he was distracted by the buttery popcorn dropping down from the corner of her mouth and onto her shirt. "Oh, this old thing?" he replied with a nervous chuckle.

"Yes," the woman replied as she continued to cram handful after handful of popcorn into her mouth. "Where did you get that little spin thingy that lights up," she said, pointing towards the magic looking glass with her buttery index finger.

"Yeah-ah, were'd you get that? I *want* one," the lady's eight year daughter screamed, as she peeked out from behind her mother's leg. She was a spitting image of her mother, only smaller, with the same pushy personality.

Charlie found it hard to be rude to others, even if they deserved it. Though his brother did not.

Michael spat out a blunt reply, which upset the lady so badly, she could not even find words to respond. With a beet red face covered in popcorn butter, she grabbed her daughter's hand and stomped off towards the castle—leaving a trail of popcorn, which spilled from the bucket attached to the side of her backpack.

"Thanks," Charlie said, with a smirk on his face.

"Glad I could help. Now would you please hurry up and finish what you were doing," Michael replied, as he motioned towards the jewelry store sign.

"Oh, yeah. Right." Charlie looked around to make sure no other snoopy guests were passing by, then he reactivated the magic looking glass and quickly began to scan the sign. Just like before, the first word "Up" appeared in bright gold letters. Then the next word, and the next, until the message had been completed and the magic looking glass shut down. Remembering what Frank had told him the year before, Charlie pressed the button on the looking glass handle to play back the message he had just discovered. He quietly read it to his brother, who typed it into his phone. "OK, Michael, read it back to me."

Michael read the message: "*Up above the show floor you'll find, a lady in white, nice and kind. A timepiece she'll reveal, from a bright shiny box. Take it you shall, to a maker of clocks.*"

"Good," Charlie said. He stuck the magic looking glass back into his pocket.

"So we're supposed to go inside the jewelry store, and head upstairs?" Michael asked.

"Yep."

"But I didn't think there was an upstairs?" Michael said.

"Oh, don't worry about that right now, Michael. We need to go find Mom and Dad before they get suspicious."

"This is your Captain speak'n, any sign of that watch yet?" Plank spat into his transmitter.

"Nothing yet Cap'n. The kids just entered the store."

"Well, keep a good eye on 'em mateys. Once they grab the watch, you grab them, got it?"

"Aye-aye Cap'n. We're standing by in the store, ready to engage," one of the crew members whispered into his transmitter. "Ope, wait a tick. They just walked in. Me eyes is on 'em, Cap'n."

"Good. Don't let 'em out your sight," Plank replied.

"Aye-aye Cap'n. Wait. Hold on."

"What? What is it?" Plank impatiently asked.

"Well Cap'n, a cast member just led those two little buggers past the watch counter, towards the back of the store, and right into the employee's private quarters."

"Why, why would they do that?" Plank spat out. "There's nothin' in the back of that bloody store."

"What should we do, Cap'n?"

"You follow them, you baboon! Grab the other two men and go find those boys. THAT'S AN ORDER!!!"

"Yes. Yes, right away Cap'n. We're on it."

The crew member on the transmitter frantically signaled to the other two, as they rushed towards the back of the store. But when they reached the private doorway, they were headed off by a large, very well fit, cast member who's name tag read, Timothy.

"I'm sorry gentleman, cast members only beyond this point," Timothy said with a smile.

"But we just saw two little fellas run in there. Are you tellin' me they work in this store?" one of Plank's crew members rudely asked.

"I didn't see anything," Timothy politely replied.

"Well, ya must be blind as a bat matey, cause *we* just did."

"Why don't you three run along and enjoy the park," Timothy said, smiling and politely gesturing towards the store entryway.

"I'm afraid we're not going anywhere's without them two boys," the lead crew member said with a snarl.

Timothy shook his head, giving the three crew misfits a look of disappointment. Then he signaled for four other cast members to join him. "Now, you fellas can leave quietly and enjoy the rest of your day, or I can call in security and we can deal with this matter *another way*. So what's it going to be gentlemen?"

Outnumbered five to three, with security standing nearby, Plank's crew members begrudgingly obliged. They turned and stormed out of the jewelers—where they were immediately greeted by more of Plank's men.

The crew members were guided around the corner on the right, then down East Center Street—where Plank was furiously pacing in circles.

"So boys, *where* is it?" Captain Plank asked.

"Uh. Sorry Cap'n, but we ain't got it", Glubber, one of three crew members, nervously said.

"That's right, we was ambushed by Disney's stink'n cast members," another crew member, added.

"Ohhhh, is that right?" Plank responded—his face turning red as his sunglasses steamed up. "Well, well. I assumed you at least had the watch since you didn't have those two little buggers with ya. So, you're tell'n me you came back empty handed?" the captain asked, as he leaned in closer towards his three failed crew members.

"Gulp, yea, yeah Cap'n, that-that's what we be saying," Glubber replied, as sweat ran down his forehead.

Plank turned away from all three momentarily, scratching his head, then slowly turned back to face his men. His sunglasses were now in his left hand—exposing the unsightly area where his left eye once existed, thanks to the sword fighting skills of a lost boy from Peter Pan's Flight. "Now, I know you boys didn't mean to disappoint your old Captain, did ya?"

All three shook their heads no, then one of them said. "No, no we didn't, Cap'n. Honestly, we didn't," Jimmy replied.

Plank pushed in close—so close that the three men could count the hairs on his nose. "Oh, I believe ya Jimmy, I do. You two as well,

Glubber and William," the captain said, as he pointed at each of their faces—his finger nearly touching their skin. "And that's why I'm give'n ya until midnight to GET ME THAT BLOODY WATCH!"

"Yes. Yes sir," Jimmy stuttered out.

"I want you three to wait here, no matter how long it takes, and you follow those two boys until you gets a chance to grab 'em. And if they don't have the watch, you bring them back to me and *I'll* find a way get it out of 'em. Is that clear?" Plank said.

"Crystal clear, Cap'n," Glubber replied.

Plank put his sunglasses back on, turned his back to the three crew members and began to walk away, as he calmly said, "And if you fail me again...you'll be finding yourself behind a set of bars without a key."

As Charlie and his brother were escorted by the cast member into the employee's quarters of Uptown Jewelers, a white door with a highly detailed brass handle magically materialized in the wall just to their right. An ornately-etched brass sign on the door read, COME IN.

Following the sign's queue, and a little encouragement from Timothy, Charlie opened the door, revealing a virtual set of silvery-white stairs. The boys followed the stairway up to a second floor that did not exist. As the boys reached the top of the stairway, they heard a soft voice call their names from the far side of the room.

There, across a room of white, stood a frail, little woman. She was at least ninety years young. Dressed in white, her appearance resembled someone from the late nineteenth century. Her silvery grey hair was neatly wrapped in a bun atop her head. Light silver-rimmed glasses rested upon her nose, while a decorative eyeglass chain hung from its sides. Behind the glasses her crystal blue eyes sparkled with sincerity, as her kind smile effortlessly welcomed the boys.

"Come in, boys. No need to be shy, I won't bite," she said in a soft tone. She was standing behind a brilliantly lit crystal showcase, filled with unimaginable antique jewelry.

The boys walked up to the showcase where two white stools awaited their company. "Please, have a seat", the lady said, as she turned her fragile hands palm up, welcoming Charlie and Michael to sit. "So, Charlie...and Michael," addressing each boy respectively, "you've come to collect something, *unique*? An Object of Magic, perhaps?" she asked, while gently polishing the showcase top with an old weathered dust rag.

"Hey, how did you know our names?" Michael blurted out in a rude manner. As was usually the case.

"Michael, you don't have to say it like that," Charlie said, attempting to tame his brother's behavior. "I'm sorry. You see, sometimes my brother doesn't know his place—as in when to speak, and when not to." He gave his younger brother a scolding look.

The kind lady giggled softly then said, "Oh that's quite alright young man, I've dealt with every type of personality through the years, and if there's one thing I've learned from past experience, it's that people are entitled to their own personalities. That's just the way we are. Different. Each and every one of us."

Charlie looked into her blue eyes and smiled. "So, may I ask your name?"

"It's Ruth, dear. And thank you for asking. Now, where was I? Oh yes. So, as I was asking earlier, you've come for the Object of Magic, correct?"

"Yes, that's right. We're here to collect a watch," Charlie said. "But I'm not quite sure what it looks like?"

The old lady giggled again. "Just a minute, sweetie", she said, while turning and picking a watch box decorated in silver and gold floral patterns off the shelf behind her. She sat the box on the countertop, then peeked up over the rim of her glasses at the boys. "I always enjoy this part." Gently she opened it up to take a look. A soft, warm glow radiated outward from the box and highlighted her face, as she marveled at what lay within. Slowly she turned the open box to face the boys. Nestled within its purple velvet lining was a watch like none the boys had ever seen before. It was a Mickey Mouse skeleton watch—which meant all the workable gears were visible. It was mostly made of colorfully painted wood, except for the face glass. The watch was badly damaged with scorch marks from the lightning strike, making it illegible. Mickey's gloved hands and arms were splintered, partially in tact, and unable to function properly. Wooden gears and springs protruded out the sides. The thick band was also made of wood, with intricately carved details—and painted in a variety of playful colors as well. It too had suffered from the lighting strike and was in poor condition. The details on the band resembled some form of ornate symbology.

"I can see why Frank wanted us to pick up the watch," Charlie said. "I mean, it's definitely broken."

"Yes," the lady said. "The watch has indeed suffered a terrible experience. And that is why we need the assistance of you and your brother—to help us right the wrong which has been cast upon such a beautiful Object of Magic."

"What are all those pictures on the wrist band?" Michael spat out. Again, with no respect for the kind old lady.

The sound of someone clearing their throat rumbled from behind them. "Those carvings, Michael, tell the story of the five Kingdom Crystals and how they came to be," a man's voice said with authority.

Charlie and Michael, surprised by the voice, turned to quickly discover the source. "Frank," Charlie said with a smile.

"Hello boys," Frank replied, while resting his hands on the boy's shoulders. "I see you've met Ruth, one of our most *valued* members.

She is the one we refer to within the Patron circle as, *The Keeper of the Watch*. Why, if it weren't for Ruth, FOTO most likely would have found, and stolen, the Watch of WONDER many decades ago."

"Ohhhh, it was really nothing at all."

"Well you know what they say young lady, 'with age comes wisdom and beauty,' and that certainly holds true with you, my dear," Frank said, as he gently cupped the elderly ladies hand with his own atop the counter.

Her cheeks began to slightly blush as she looked upon Frank with her gentle blue eyes. "You are too kind, Frank...thank you."

Frank closed his eyes and nodded to Ruth, to show his respect.

Michael, being only ten, and lacking appreciation for such things, rudely interrupted the moment. "So, what's the big deal about this watch again?"

"Michael, shut it," his brother snipped. "Sorry ma'am. If you could please tell us more, we would really appreciate it. I mean, our father collects Mickey watches, and I have NEVER seen one like this before."

Ruth broke eye contact with Frank, stepped back, and focused on the boys. "Indeed boys, this Mickey watch is, without question, different. Unlike any watch you have ever, or will ever, see again. Forwards, backwards, sideways and magic," she said while making corresponding hand motions with each word.

"What? I don't get it?" Michael replied."

Charlie gave his brother another dirty look, then returned his attention to Ruth. "Sorry about that, please go on."

The kind woman continued. "This watch, the Watch of WONDER, is not really a timepiece at all, but rather, allows one to travel to *conceptual realities* that Disney has dreamt up, or will dream up— which are all connected in WONDER. More importantly, it will lead the chosen outsider, that being you Charlie, to the second Kingdom Crystal by utilizing these magical places."

"So it's like a time travel device?" Charlie asked.

"Sort of, my dear. Unlike normal time travel, which jumps to places or events based on reality, the Watch of WONDER is used to travel amongst all conceptual *realities* created by Disney imagineers and animators. These include park, resort, ship, movie, and other concepts, combined with all dreams that never even reached the concept stage. And, as you know, they are ALL bottled up in WONDER."

"Fascinating, isn't it boys," Frank added.

"So it's kind of like the Ears of Virtue we used last year to jump around within WONDER?" Charlie asked.

"Yes," Ruth replied. "But different as well. First, you can have the Watch magically send you anywhere within WONDER by simply asking it to go to a specific Disney-related place in time, even those around the Magic Rim—making it easier to control when and where you transport to. For example, if you and Michael wanted to explore a simulated Pirates of the Caribbean attraction from the fall of 2002, or a conceptual rendering of Captain Hook's ship from the 1953 animated movie, all you would have to do is ask the watch to take you there, and it would."

"So it works for both, Disney park and movie concepts?" Charlie asked.

"That, and any other ideas ever dreamt up by Disney's imagineers and animators."

"Neat," Michael replied.

"And I should add," Frank said, there *are* two limitations the Objects of Magic bare. They *cannot* access any of the finalized scenes or characters used during production of a Disney movie. Nor will you find the actual parks, resorts, ships, etc., we have in reality, stored within WONDER, using the Objects of Magic. Only conceptual realities, which includes all ideas dreamt up by Disney Imagineers and artists, can be found in WONDER. Sorry Ruth, I didn't mean to interrupt. Please continue."

The boys each nodded, to confirm their understanding, though Frank knew all to well the boys would have questions later regarding these details.

"Also," Ruth added, the Watch can be used as a dream dot locator. Making it easier to navigate your way around WONDER."

"But how can we use it if it's broken?" Charlie asked.

Ruth looked to Frank for an answer. "That's why I'm here boys," Frank replied. "Now that you have the watch, we need to get you safely to the watchmaker so he can fix it. And THAT is going to take a good plan, a little bit of magic, and flawless execution, to keep it away from those pesky Thorn's. But I think we've given you *more* than enough information for now. I want the two of you to go back and enjoy the rest of tonight vacationing with your parents. I'll contact you tomorrow once I've figured things out. Until then, enjoy yourselves, go spend some quality time in the parks with your parents, and just try to let what we told you today sink in slowly and naturally. I know it's a lot to take in all at once, but don't worry, we are here to help. Understood?"

"Sure," Charlie replied, "but how will we know when you're trying to contact us?"

"I'll make certain you know," Frank said with a humble smile. "Now, you need to go, before Captain Plank's men figure out where you went."

"How are you going to get out of here, Frank?" Charlie asked.

The wise old Patron lifted the light charm necklace from under his shirt and winked. He touched the charm with his right index finger and was gone.

Charlie shook his head in amazement and laughed. Then said, "It was nice to meet you Ruth."

"You as well, Charlie. And you too, Michael," Ruth said, attempting to warm the boy's heart. "You best be on your way now, boys. Just take the stairs to get back down to the store. I'm sure your parents are still wandering around there somewhere."

"Thank you," Charlie replied. He signaled to his brother, who was impatiently pacing around the room, waiting to head back down stairs.

"You should hide the watch in your pocket, just in case someone is looking for it once you get down there."

"Right. I mean, yes ma'am", Charlie replied. He placed the watch in his pocket.

The boys headed down the virtual staircase, which vanished behind them as they descended. When they reached the door at the bottom of the stairs, they opened it and walked back into the cast member room. The door slammed behind them—magical dust shot out from its seams in all directions, as it vanished, leaving behind nothing but a solid wall.

Chapter Six

Darkness was ninety minutes away and the watch was safe and secure in Charlie's pocket, as the boys and their parents headed through Adventureland. Little did they know, they were being followed by three of Captain Plank's men—Jimmy, Glubber and William, who were waiting for the right moment to move in and grab the watch.

"What do ya say we stop and snag a Dole Whip while we waits for the boy to get off the Jungle Cruise ride," Jimmy said.

"Good thinking, mate," William replied.

"Yeah, I could use a good coolin' off," Glubber added.

"Yeah, a good coolin' off indeed," Jimmy said, as they all laughed.

Charlie's father eagerly led the way, trying to squeeze in as many attractions as possible before the fireworks show began. "OK, we've done the tree house and Jungle Cruise, so what's next?"

"I suggest we head to Pirates of the Caribbean and work our way back towards the hub for the fireworks," their mother said.

"Brilliant idea, honey."

"Look at you, Mom," Charlie added with a smile, "that's a great idea."

"Hey Cap'n, we haven't had a chance to grab the little rascals yet, but they just left the Jungle Cruise and looks like they're headed for our neck of the woods, Jimmy said into his phone."

"That's good enough for me," Plank replied. "I'll inform Dark Thorn Elontra, so she can set a Dream Dot trap for our two little friends. And I'll make sure we have one of our boys disguised as a cast member put them in their own boat, cause we don't want the parents complicating the situation, if ya know what I mean."

"Aye-aye, Cap'n, we've got 'em now."

The Zastawits family arrived at the Pirates of the Caribbean queue.

"This looks like as good a place to start as any," their father said.

"And look, no lines," Michael added.

Charlie and his family made their way through the unoccupied queue, passed the skeleton's chess match, and came to a stop with only ten riders ahead of them in line. Because it wasn't crowded, the cast member, one of Plank's men in disguise, suggested the boys hop in one boat and the parents in another.

Their parents climbed into the lead boat and departed, looking back to wave, while the boys quickly climbed into the next vessel—each claiming their own row of seats.

The air was filled with that familiar musty water smell, as their boat slowly banked right, past the waterfalls, and through the damp, water-like fog, reflecting a projection of Black Beard. Their ride vessel continued right, passing skull rock, and shipwrecked skeletons, who's boat had been shattered to pieces and laid scattered throughout the sandy shore. Sounds of the sea winds grew stronger and stronger, as a woman softly sang a salty pirate song that echoed throughout the cavern. To their right, another skeleton, sporting a bandana, captained the wheel of the shattered ship, as the stormy sea skies rushed by in the background. The wind continued to strengthen. Just ahead, their parents boat vanished into darkness—shooting down the waterfall. Screams echoed through the cave-like setting—then everything changed.

The skeleton at the wheel of the shattered ship suddenly took on a life of its own. Stepping away from the wheel, it began to walk in an awkwardly-disjointed fashion along the shore, following the boy's boat as far as the jagged terrain would allow. Placing one boney foot on a large raised stone, it leaned forward and pointed towards the hidden fall where their parents had just dropped.

"Grab hold and prepare yourselves mateys, there be no pretending here tonight. You have somethin' we needs, and we intend to take it."

Placing both hands on his hips, the skeleton laughed and stared at the terror-struck boys, who had no route of escape.

The skeleton's laughter continued to follow them into the darkness, as they braced themselves for the dark unknown.

Sounds of crashing water rose up from the darkness far below. The boat began its rapid descent—four, five, possibly ten times deeper then would normally be expected for the attraction. As the plummeting boat continued to pick up speed, Charlie and Michael held on white-knuckle tight to the railings in front of their seats—screaming uncontrollably, as their vessel continued to dive.

There was a gigantic SPLASH, throwing a large wave of water up and over the front of the boat, which soaked the boys from head to toe. As they looked around, the unimaginable danger of their surroundings made it clear that reality had been left far behind.

The boys had been pulled into a part of WONDER dreamt up by an unknown evil, which lay deep in the shadows of creativity.

Their small vessel was flanked on both sides by more than a dozen pirate-infested ghost ships, all docked and floating just above the water's surface. Charlie and Michael spun around in all directions, taking in the spooky sea-side town overrun by nonliving things, as their boat slowly moved along. Everywhere they looked; left, right, forwards, backwards, upwards and down, the boys could see nothing but ghostly pirates, skeletons that were once pirates, and dangerous luminescent sea creatures. There were sharks, eels, squids and unimaginable things that lit up the clear water in a vast array of colors with their glowing bodies, which at times, highlighted the treasure-covered bottom of the haunted cove. Obviously, it was treasure to be seen but *never* touched. To the right was a swash buckling battle between two ships for possession of the treasures the other had. The pirates battled to fend off a surge of corrupt skeletons who attacked their ship like a swarm of ants. While on the other vessel, the skeletons struggled to fend off a swarm of ruthless pirate ghosts attacking from the air. Neither appeared to have an advantage over the other. And though the pirates were transparent, had the ability to go through physical objects, and could fly, they also possessed the physical qualities of real matter when desired. This made the pirates very difficult to deal with, no matter how skilled or powerful their opponents were. To the boy's left were three more ships—all fighting together against a giant octopus that had grabbed hold of the middle ship, causing it to upend and start sinking into the water, while at the same time, flailing its free tentacles, in an attempt to grab hold of the other two ships or anyone occupying their masts or decks. In the dark, starlit sky above, skeleton seagulls swarmed the docks, waiting for, and diving at, every opportunity to snatch up whatever tender morsels they could snag from the local fisheries, eateries and other food related establishments—while at the same time, being chased off by the flying ghost dogs who belonged to each facility.

As the boy's vessel crept further into the cove, and inevitable trouble, it became more and more apparent that they were quickly becoming the center of attention. Heads began to turn and take notice that the outsider carrying the watch was amongst them, and ripe for the taking.

"I don't like the looks of this, Charlie. It's like someone took the Pirates ride, gave it a Haunted Mansion twist, then threw in even more spooky stuff," Michael said.

But what the young boy forgot to mention, was that everything they were experiencing was much greater in scale and much more real than the pirate attraction in the park.

"There's a group of pirates and skeletons looking at us over there by the tavern," Charlie said.

Michael started to turn his head.

"Don't look, Michael, just keep staring straight ahead. Maybe they won't notice we're here."

"Ha! I think it's a little too late for that."

Just as Michael finished speaking, the entire cove fell silent. All except for the rum runner, who's horse and wagon were being ransacked by a rowdy group of thirsty pirates. There weren't too many things that took priority over a good bottle of rum, let alone a whole wagon filled with cases of rum, as far as the pirates were concerned.

"We need to keep moving forward," Charlie said quietly to his brother.

"Forward towards what?" Michael replied. "There's nothing ahead of us but more trouble."

And perhaps the younger brother was right. Just ahead, where the cove narrowed down to a crystal clear river, was an old wooden bridge that crossed over the waterway. On that bridge were at least sixty skeletons, all with swords and pistols out, waiting for the right opportunity to attack the boy's boat.

"Michael, are you ready for this?"

"Ready for what?"

"You know wha—watch out, Michael! Skeletons! Right behind you!"

No sooner had Charlie gotten his words out, when three skeletons, all with swords ready, jumped onto their boat and started climbing over the empty rows of seats towards the boys.

Michael turned to check the boney attacker's positions—the lead skeleton was already upon him.

"Ay there matey," he grabbed Michael around his upper torso— spun him around, and held a sword to the young boys throat.

Michael remained perfectly still, there was nothing he could do.

The lead skeleton stared Charlie down, his hollow eye sockets glowed amber.

"If you want yer brother here to live, you'd best be handing over that watch matey."

Two more skeletons, both flanking Michael, stared Charlie down as they pulled their pistols and aimed directly at the outsider.

"Sorry Michael," Charlie said in a defeated tone. He slowly reached into his pocket to pull out the Watch of WONDER

CLANK, CLANK, CLINK, THUNK!

"Not so fast there ya greedy bunch of boney what nots!" a pirate captain hollered from a nearby riverside dock. "We'll be take'n the outsider, and that watch, if ya don't mind. Heave-ho ya landlubbers!"

On their captain's command, a group of pirates tugged on the ropes attached to the four grappling hooks they had tossed onto the small boat. Their first tug jerked the boat radically to the right, throwing the boys and three skeletons off balance.

Two of the skeletons stumbled to the left side of the boat and fell into the water, while the one holding Michael managed to hang onto the boy's shirt, but had fallen between the seat and floor, struggling to get back up.

"Heave-ho!" The ghost pirates gave a second tug, which threw Charlie backwards into his seat, but gave Michael the momentum to shrug off the skeleton holding his shirt. The younger brother leaped over two rows of seats, quickly joining Charlie—who stood up and grabbed onto the railing in front of him as the pirates gave a third tug.

"Now... what... Charlie?" Michael asked in between breaths.

"First we take this boney guy out," his brother replied, while dodging a strike from the skeleton's sword. The sword blade cut deep into one of the seats. Too deep for the skeleton to pull free. Thinking quickly, Charlie yanked a leg bone right off the skeleton and struck him solidly in the skull—which flew into the water and was crushed instantly by the jaws of a circling, luminescent shark.

"Good contact," Charlie," Michael said.

"Michael, behind you!"

Just as Charlie hollered, the two skeletons in the water had managed to work their way back to the boat, and were attempting to climb back on.

Michael jumped to the side, clearing the way for Charlie, who swung and connected with one of skeletons heads just as they were climbing aboard. The skeleton's head bounced around in the boat with chattering jaws—hopping from one section to another, until Michael finally grabbed hold of it and threw it far into the water.

"Heave-ho!" The pirates tugged again, just as Charlie was trying to swing at the other skeleton attempting to climb aboard. He lost his balance and fell hard to his right—losing control of the leg bone, which fell and was lost to the water.

There was another SPLASH!

"Michael!"

"Charlie! Charlie! Help me! There are sharks everywhere!"

"Swim, Michael!" Charlie said, while continuing to battle the skeleton attempting to board. "Grab hold of his bones, Michael, then pull yourself up."

Filled with frightful adrenaline, the young brother swam up, grabbed hold of the back of the skeleton's rib cage and pulled himself up out of the water, over the shoulders, and eventually, over the head of the skeleton. Then he grabbed his brother's hand, who pulled him aboard. As he fell forward into the boat, he gave the skeleton a hard kick square in the face, knocking the sack of bones into the water, where he was overtaken by tentacles of an unfriendly squid-like creature and pulled out of sight.

"Heave-ho!" The pirate captain yelled. "We've almost got 'em mateys."

"Quick, Michael, uh..." Charlie went speechless. Before he could say another word, he realized that their boat had been docked.

A small group of pirates and their captain looked down upon them from above, eager to take what the young outsider had in his possession.

"Hi there, fellas, me name's Captain Goolie. What do ya say you get out of that boat and give us that watch," the captain said, looking down from the dock into the boy's boat. His appearance was exactly as you'd expect from a pirate captain; he wore a three point, feathered hat, with a captain's jacket and large sword on his left hip. His pointed beard and curled mustache surrounded a crooked smile filled with crusty teeth. And beneath his hat grew long wavy hair. But unlike living pirate captains, he was transparent with a blueish-green hue, and his legs faded into thin air—as he hovered slightly above the surface of the dock alongside his crew members.

"You heard the Cap'n," one of the crew members spat out, pointing his pistol at the boys. "Get out of that boat and give us the watch."

"Yeah, you heard 'em, give us that watch ya smelly little bugger," another crew member with a tattooed face added.

"Why should we give it to you," Charlie snipped back while remaining seated in the boat. "The watch belongs to the Patrons, not some filthy pirate like you."

"What? Why you little stinking rascal. Get out of that boat so I can cut your—"

"Now-now," Goolie said to his crew. "We don't need to go scaring the young lads. We're just asking for a little cooperation. So, what do you say boys? If you hand over the watch without a struggle, I'm sure we could work out a deal with Elontra to go easy on ya."

Elontra was the Dark Thorn in charge of Segment One—the Magic Kingdom, and like all other Dark Thorns, she was very ruthless and unforgiving when it came to mistakes being made by her soldiers. Which included anyone, and anything, under her command in the Magic Kingdom. So the captain was hard pressed to make sure the outsider surrendered the watch before going any further.

But what he didn't know, was that Charlie had just caught sight of the skeletons from the wooden bridge, who at that very moment, were aggressively making their way straight towards the dock where Charlie, Michael and the pirates were. The young, but clever, outsider was stalling for time—his brother caught on to his strategy.

"Watch? What makes you think we have a watch?" Michael said. "Do you see a watch anywhere? I don't."

"Shut it you little landlubber," the captain shouted back, "or we'll be making sure you and your big brother never get out of here. Well, at least not alive, anyway."

The crew burst into laughter, but suddenly were blind sided by the skeletons, who engaged the pirates in a fierce battle. Members of the skeleton crew quickly swarmed the group of pirates on the dock, who took off flying in all directions and positioned themselves for an aerial counter attack. The swashbuckling sound of steel on steel filled the air, as the two adversaries battled for control of the dock, and ultimately, control of the watch. Pistol shots fired out from all directions, filling the air with a haze of gun smoke and hot lead—knocking many of the skeletons to pieces, who immediately reassembled themselves—shooting and slashing pirates to the ground—who quickly rose up and to fight again after a momentary lapse of afterlife. The jaws of the skeleton crew clicked and clunked loudly, as they hollered out orders. The pirates shouted out an endless barrage of counter attacks, as the heated battle for control of the dock continued.

"It's time we stop playing around, mateys, and show these worthless bags of bones why they ought not be messin' with the likes of us," the captain said to his crew.

On his command, all the ghostly pirates took to the air, flying high in to the dark star-lit sky. Paired in groups of three and four, they began to dive-bomb the skeletons—either knocking them into the water, or picking them up and dropping them into the surrounding trees, or on top of nearby buildings. Several were dropped onto a flagpole, resembling a shish kabob.

While it appeared to be a victory for the pirates, it actually was quite the opposite. Having been distracted by the surprise attack of the skeletons, Goolie and his crew had completely lost track of their original intention, to take the watch from the outsider and present it to their dark leader, Elontra.

"Hey captain, I'm not sure, but it don't look like them two boys are in the boat no more. As a matter of fact, I don't even see the boat."

"What? Of course the boat is there, you buffoon. Fly in and take a closer look."

Following the captain's orders, his first mate flew back to look by the dock once more, and sure enough, his first observation had been true. Both the boat and boys were missing. Amongst all the chaos between the pirates and skeletons, Charlie and Michael had managed to free the boat from the dock and quietly slip away unnoticed. "Uh, Cap'n...I don't know what else to say, but it looks like those two young landlubbers snuck away in the boat while we was fight'n off the boneheads."

"Holy mermaids of the sea," the captain replied, "gather the crew, and the row boats. Those two yellow-bellied youngsters can't be too far down the river. And when we catch 'em, the first thing we're gonna do is get that watch.

"I'm tellin' ya Frank, I know what I heard in the Dole Whip line, and those three guys were definitely Thorn spies. They must have known the boys picked up the watch at Uptown Jewelers. Charlie and Michael are in for a dangerous night, and I really think they're gonna need our help," Ben said.

"Hmmm, so you think we need to send someone to shadow their activities for the rest of the evening?" Frank asked, while searching his apartment for something.

"Yes. Yes I do. In fact, I think I know the perfect one for the job. Someone who works best at night."

"Someone who sleeps best at night?" Frank questioned. "Then how would they stay awake to follow the boys tonight?"

"No-no-no. Not someone who 'sleeps best.' I said someone who 'works best'."

"Works better," Frank said, half listening, as he continued searching his apartment for something he obviously could not find.

"Oh my goodness. Have you *even* heard a word I said? And what on earth are you looking for?"

"My lucky tie," Frank replied.

"Luck tie?"

"Yeah-yeah. Do you see it laying around here anywhere?"

"Uhhhhh, no. Nope. No, I don't see any tie around here," Ben replied as he scanned the apartment with his eyes. "So what do you need a tie for, Frank? I don't believe I've ever seen you wear one before."

"I have a meeting with the Patron Council tonight and I need my lucky tie."

"Must be an important meeting, eh?"

"Anytime the heads of the council call a meeting, it's important, Ben, and when we meet, I have to wear my tie. It helps clear my mind."

"Hah! There it is."

"Where?"

"Right over there," Ben said while pointing, "on the chair. Is it that funky colored thing sticking out from underneath the cushion?"

"Yeah, that's it. Boy, that's quite an eye you have there, Benny. Thank you. Now I'll be able to think straight tonight when I go to that meeting."

"Well, while you're on the subject of 'thinking', what do you *think* about what I said a few minutes ago?"

"And what was that again?" Frank asked.

"You know, to get someone who *works best at night* to watch over the boys this evening. Someone who has excellent night vision."

"Ahhhh, yes-yes-yes. Now I remember. I was thinking the exact same thing. I agree one hundred and three percent. He would be the perfect fit for an assignment such as this, wouldn't he."

"And I'm sure it would help us all rest much easier tonight," Ben added.

"Right you are. I'll put him on the job right away, as soon as we're finished here."

"Put your backs into it mateys," the captain said to his row men, who paddled tirelessly down the calm, clear river, for fear of what Elontra may do to them if they failed. Faster and faster the ores of the three row boats cut through the water, as the captain barked out the pace of the strokes. They passed one opportunity after another for looting and plundering. There was The Sleepy Ghost Grill and Tavern, The Angry Crow's Nest Bar, Skeleton Bones Hotel, Blackbeard's BBQ Shack, and a host of many other riverside establishments ripe for the taking. But the captain had only one thing burning in his mind, to capture the outsider and get the Watch of WONDER.

"Keep rowing mateys, those two little buggers can't be more than a few strokes away."

Meanwhile, Captain Goolie's first mate, Mr. Farkle, was leading an aerial search party high above the river and palm trees, as he and a dozen ghostly pirates combed the area in search of the two young lads who had cleverly escaped their capture.

Just as they approached a moonlit bend in the river, a small boat appeared on the water's horizon. *It had to be them*, the first mate thought to himself. "Yo-ho, Cap'n," he shouted from above. "Small boat just ahead near Blue Beards Bend."

"Yes-yes-yes, Mr. Farkle, but is it them?" The captain hollered back.

"Hard to tell, Cap'n. We'll have to move in for a closer look."

"Push ahead and report back immediately," Goolie ordered.

"Aye-aye, Cap'n. You heard 'em boys, attack speed."

The flying pirates shot ahead, leaving only blurred streaks of blue and green behind.

"C'mon, Michael, we have to keep moving," Charlie said between deep breaths. "I think I can actually hear them now, which means they're getting closer. We have to go faster."

"But I'm tired, Charlie," Michael whimpered.

"Not now, Michael. *Not* now."

A sudden BOOM accompanied by a giant burst of bright light, exploded in the air above—and through it, a majestic, silvery-white owl came shooting into the night sky, followed by a sparkling trail of glittering dust. Immediately, the mighty owl began scanning the island below with his large yellow eyes—shielded by a pair of black rimmed glasses. Seeing great distances at night was no issue for this courageous creature, as he was Alexios, mighty owl of the Patrons, and loyal defender of the Kingdom Crystals. But tonight, his task was one of smaller scale. To keep the outsider, and his younger sibling, out of harms way. *A simple task for someone such as I,* he thought to himself, as he soared through the night skies.

"What do ya mean they're not in the boat!" Captain Goolie replied to his first mate, after receiving the disappointing news that the boy's boat was empty. "Paddle faster mates, I needs to see this for me self," the captain hollered in frustration. A few short minutes later, Goolie and the other two boats rowed ashore next to the empty vessel. The captain now believed he had no chance to retrieve the watch, yet still, he continued to rant and rave. "How can this be? Those two little rats were in the boat right before the bloody skeletons showed up. And if they had tried to escape, one of us would have *surely* seen 'em. We was right there on the dock for Pete's sake."

"We were a little distracted, captain," one of the crew members said. All the other pirates turned and looked at him as if he had just made a big mistake.

"What? What did ya say?"

"I, I said, we was a little distracted, Cap'n," the crew member repeated and smiled— hoping the captain would make lite of his comment and pardon the interruption.

Captain Goolie turned beet-red with anger, as smoke poured out of his ghostly figure. "Ohhhh! Take him back to the ship and lock him up. There'll be no rum for you this evening. And if you say anything else, it'll be two nights with no rum. I might even make ya marry the brewmaster's daughter." It was common knowledge amongst all the pirates that the brewmaster's daughter was the most unfriendly lady ghost in all of Pirates Cove, and to marry her would surely be the harshest of all punishments known to man—dead or alive.

"Hey. Did you see that?" Mr. Farkle said, pointing towards the sky.

"Yeah, I saw it too, it looked like a great big explosion in the sky," another crew member added.

"I didn't see it, but I heard the explosion," another pirate said.

"Alright, alright. That's enough ya anchor heads," the captain replied in annoyed fashion. "There *are* other pirates on this island ya know—and I'm sure, other battles as well. Wouldn't ya agree?"

"Oh, right captain. Other battles—I'm sure that's all it was, a little friendly fire, an explodin' ship or something like that, heh-heh," Mr. Farkle replied.

"Now then, you two fly Mr. Know-it-all back to the ship and lock him up below," Captain Goolie said, while pointing to two of his crew. "And the rest of you split up into two groups. Half will come with me on this side of the river, the other half will fly to the other side with Mr. Farkle and start searching there. We'll find those boys and the watch before sunrise, or my name isn't Captain Goolie."

An easy achievement, being it was eternally night time in Pirates Cove. Though none of the crew had the courage to say it.

Just beyond the shadows, not far from the boat, Charlie and Michael were crouched down—having just listened to the pirates discuss their plan to capture the outsider.

"OK, Michael, it looks like they're all gone. Let's make a run for the boat and get out of here before they come back. On the count of three, ready. One—two—."

"Hold on—hold on, young squires. No need to rush into a bad decision."

"What? Who?" Charlie and Michael replied, as they searched for the source of the voice that had just interrupted their conversation.

While staring into the heavy foliage covered by darkness and shadow, Charlie said, "Reveal yourself."

"Is it too much to ask that you try and look a little harder?" the mysterious voice asked.

"If we try any harder, our eyes are going to pop out," Michael replied.

"I assure you, no such thing will happen. For goodness sake— here, I'll make it easier for you." Amongst the vast blanket of wooded darkness two large, yellow spheres appeared and gazed upon their youthful disciples.

"Alexios?" Charlie responded, "it's been so long, I—"

"Forgot the sound of my voice?" the owl said.

"Yes, exactly. But now that I know who it is, it's clearly obvious."

"Why yes, Charlie, the mind works in mysterious ways," Alexios said with a chuckle.

"Now that you've got that figured out, can we get in the boat and go," Michael blurted out impatiently.

"Absolutely the wrong thing to do," Alexios sternly replied. "Your pursuers will be expecting it. In fact, I'm sure they left somebody behind, who's lurking in the shadows, to watch and make sure you *don't* return to the boat."

"Wait, I hear something," Charlie said, pausing the discussion with a raised index finger.

Rising up from their silent surroundings, came the clinking and clunking of bones—which grew louder and louder.

"Quick, back into the bushes," Alexios whispered.

Not thirty seconds later, a crew of skeletons came rushing buy— three of which, stopped abruptly to scan the boat before continuing on along the shoreline.

After all had cleared, the owl continued. "OK, if you want to get back to your parents with the watch safely in hand, here's what we're going to do..."

Captain Goolie and his raucous crew of pirates had combed both sides of the entire river up to Deadman's Drop, a perilous waterfall which dropped hundreds of feet straight down upon a cluster of jagged rocks.

"Surely they haven't gone beyond this point, Cap'n," Mr. Farkle said, as they all observed the drop.

"It appears you are right, Mr. Farkle," the captain replied. "OK, mateys, time to double baaaaa—attack! Grab your steel and have at it lads."

Goolie and his crew were under attack from the skeletons, who were also tracking the watch, and thought the pirates had it.

"We don't got it you bone heads," the captain yelled out.

But the captain's words had no effect. The skeletons continued to battle under the belief that the watch would be revealed. Swords clanked and shots were fired as Goolie and his crew were pushed back to the river bank by the surge of greedy skeletons.

"Alrighty men, it's time we show these boneheads who's in charge. Everyone to the air."

On command, the pirate crew took off into the sky—gathering a good fifty feet above the sea of swarming skeletons, now rendered harmless.

"Call your dogs and have em flush out the woods," the captain shouted to his men.

"Aye-aye, Cap'n. Right away."

Half the crew took off out of sight, leaving behind blurred trails of smokey, blue light, as the the captain and remaining ghosts hovered above the skeletons below, who continued to stir out of frustration—unable to reach the flying pirates.

Suddenly, a faint noise rose up in the distance—growing louder and louder.

The skeletons all stopped and turned towards the sound.

Highlighted by the moonlight, a stampede of ghost dogs came streaking across the sky, flying over the skeletons, and deep into the woods. Barking madly, they maneuvered in and out of the trees and foliage. Seconds later, a wave of partially decayed bats came shooting out of the woods—and right behind them, the ghost dogs, who were guiding the swarm toward the gathering of skeletons along the river's shore. Like a screeching tidal wave, the bats hit the skeleton crew with a mighty force—knocking them backwards and into the water.

Laughter rained down from the sky above at the misfortune of the skeletons, as the ghostly pirates bid the bats farewell and began to celebrate their victory.

Below, the skeletons struggled to regain their composure as they swam back to the river's edge and crawled ashore.

Suddenly, a quick reminder of their purpose floated by—stopping both pirates and skeletons alike in their tracks. It was the boat Charlie and Michael had brought into their world. Though now it was empty—quietly making its way downstream.

"Now boys!" Alexios shouted. He took off from the low-lying bushes, high up into the air. The mighty owl performed a variety of random loops to distract the pirates and skeletons—enabling Charlie and his brother to sneak off to the boat and make a clean getaway downstream.

But it only lasted a minute. The captain quickly caught on to the wise owls trickery.

"What kind of fool do you take me for ya silly owl," Goolie said. "Forget the bird mateys. Go after that boat. We need the watch!"

"You heard 'em, get that boat. We needs that watch."

Goolies crew mounted a charge towards the young boys. Through the air, over land and water, they swirled, ran and flew directly towards the boat, swords and pistols waiving in the air, as they shouted and screamed out piratical threats.

Not to be left out of the mix, the skeletons, who had made it to the opposite shore of the river, began their relentless pursuit for the boat as well, while those still in the water quickly snapped together like a set of Tinker Toys—forming a large paddle boat made of bones. Upon its completion, the remaining skeletons climbed up the sides and onto the upper and lower decks—packing the boat full. The rowdy skeletons, who were also waving swords and pistols, anxiously hung over their boat's railings, as they battled for a clear view of the outsider's boat, just ahead.

Alexios swooped down from the sky and onto the boat to give his young apprentices a shot of encouragement. "Well young squires, it appears we've gotten ourselves into quite a mess."

"Really, ya think?" Micheal said with a dose of sarcasm.

"I hate to say it, but I kind of agree with him at the moment," Charlie added.

"Yes. Yes, I can see that," the owl replied. "But now is not the time for opinions."

"It's not the time for philosophies either," Michael snapped back.

"Right. So I think it's wise to listen if you and your brother want to survive this dreaded mess," the owl said, giving the boys a stern look over the rim of his glasses.

Neither said a word.

"Now then, I need the two of you to keep the boat on course and moving forward, no matter what happens. You must reach Dead Man's Drop. Is that understood?"

"Yes, but then what?" Charlie asked with a horrified expression. "Do you mean we're supposed to take this boat *over* the waterfall and get smashed to bits on the rocks below?"

"Never mind the rocks for now," just focus on what you've been told and trust me. If you can do that, the rest will take care of itself."

"Trust you?" Michael said with a snicker.

"Well, you could always come up with your own plan."

"No-no-no, we'll do exactly as you say, won't we Michael?" Charlie demanded of his brother.

"Of course," Michael replied against his will.

"Thank goodness we've got that settled," the owl said.

"And why's that, Michael snipped back.

"Cause, here they come!" The mighty owl took off into the sky like a shooting star, attempting to draw the flying pirates away from the boat. On cue, they immediately changed course in pursuit of the elusive owl. Flying in crazy pretzel-like patterns, Alexios twisted, turned and confused the low-level thinkers. On his last turn, he flew near the boat, practically paused in midair, and said in slow motion, "Keeeeeeep mooooooving fooooooorwaaaaaard." Then, POW—he exploded back to full speed, leaving his ghostly pursuers just out of reach, as he soared skyward.

No longer had the boys taken their eyes off the brave owl, when a wave of pirates came flying in low towards their boat, their swords and pistols raised high. "We've almost got 'em boys," one of the crew members called out, as the rowdy pirate crew closed in on the slow moving boat,

Charlie and Michael began to fret, feeling helpless and vulnerable for the taking. They were convinced no good could come from what was about to take place. With only twenty-five feet before the pirates reached their boat, the boys closed their eyes, covered up, and prepared for the worst. Twenty feet, fifteen, ten—

Suddenly, the charging pirates were pulled backwards by a large and powerful vacuum-like wind.

The boys each opened an eye, then the other—squinting to see beyond the struggling ghosts, who were trying as best they could to resist the hurricane force winds pulling them backwards. To Charlie and Michael's amazement, they saw a white, supersonic blur flying in a circle perpendicular to the top of the water's surface—creating the powerful wind tunnel, which sucked up the pirate ghosts and shot them out the far side of the tunnel in all directions as disfigured spirits. Eliminating any immediate threat to the boys.

CLANK, CLINK, CLUNK, CLANK. "What in the—" Michael said as the boys spun around to face the other side of the river.

"We're hooked, Michael," Charlie said.

The skeletons on the far side of the river had managed to grab hold of the boy's boat using grappling hooks attached to ropes. They were now holding the small boat against the will of the river's current. What Charlie and Michael failed to realize was that this allowed the skeleton's paddle boat to catch up to their boat.

Within seconds, the boney paddle boat carrying hundreds of skeletons was upon them. Four crew members from the lower deck crouched low, then jumped onto the boy's boat, as they pulled their swords. All sported bandanas of various colors wrapped around their skulls, weathered shirts, shredded pants, and a gold tooth or two. One had a peg leg, another an eye patch.

But as intimidating as they were, Michael refused to let it hinder his actions. Without delay, he charged the peg legged skeleton—kicking the wooden peg clean off and into the river. This threw its rightful owner off balance and allowed Charlie to easily push the wobbling skeleton into the water. "One down, three to go," he said.

Thinking quickly, the older brother reached out with his right hand, grabbed hold of the Femur bone from one of the remaining three skeletons, and tugged with all his might—pulling it clean off. With great ferocity, Charlie took a mighty swing—smashing his aggressor into countless pieces, which flew into the water.

Inspired by Charlie's actions, Michael dodged an oncoming sword, and charged his attacker—making a clean wrap around the skeleton's legs, he lifted up and dropped the helpless sack of bones into the water. "Wow, they're really lite," Michael said with enthusiasm.

"Yeah," CRACK, Charlie connected with the fourth skeleton—"I can tell. One swing and they fall to pieces."

"Ha-ha. That's a good one—"

Before Michael could finish his sentence, six more skeletons jumped aboard, and again the brotherly duo—now brimming with confidence, made quick work of the aggressors. Three times, four times, then five—the boney attackers boarded and were quickly defeated by the boys. As a sixth group readied to board the small boat, Charlie said to his brother, "We need to figure something out. At this pace I don't think we're going to last for too much longer."

"Cut the ropes," a voice called from above. It was Alexios— still flying in crazy patterns, as the ghostly pirates continued their pursuit.

"Right," Michael said. "Charlie, when they jump on board, smack one of the skeletons in their sword arm."

"Good idea, Michael." As the first skeleton jumped aboard, Charlie swung and made solid contact with his forearm—knocking it clean off, which allowed the sword to drop free. Michael seized the sharp weapon, and with four quick strikes, cut their boat free—sending them towards Dead Man's Drop.

As they pulled away, the skeleton boat tried to keep up. Several skeletons attempted to dive onto the smaller boat, missing and splashing into the water. The gap between the boats grew larger, as the sound of crushing water against the jagged rocks of Dead Man's Drop grew closer.

"We're almost there, Michael."

"Almost where, Charlie?" We don't even know what we're supposed to be looking for, or doing, once we get to the waterfall. How can you be so calm right now."

"Simple. We have to trust the words of the owl," Charlie replied.

"Really, that's it?"

"Yes, Michael. That's it."

"What about the skeletons, the pirates, and whatever else we've seen in this crazy place?"

"Trust the owls words and keep moving forward, that's it, Michael. Period"

"Well I think that's the craziest thing I've ever heard."

"Sometimes you have to put your faith in others, Michael."

"Whatever," Michael said sarcastically. Though inside, he knew his brother was right.

As their boat approached the falls, steadily gathering speed, even Charlie began to doubt the words of Alexios. *Does he really want us to stay in the boat?*, he thought to himself. Unexpectedly, and in dramatic fashion, the answer revealed itself.

Above a moonlit hillside just off in the distance, a small fleet of flying pirate ships with cannons blazing appeared in the sky. They were chasing the mighty, white owl, who landed next to Charlie and said, "Hurry boys, they're coming."

"Who is 'they'," Michael questioned.

"All of them. I tried to keep them distracted as best I could, but once they got word that you still had the watch and were attempting to escape back to the real world, they quickly lost interest in me and gathered all the ghosts of Pirates Cove to come after you."

"So now what?" Charlie asked.

"Get to the waterfall, no matter what," the owl said. "And hold on tight."

"You mean you want us to go *over* the waterfall with the boat?" Michael said. "Are you crazy!"

"Yes, I guess I am," Alexios replied. "I'll try and draw their fire as best I can, while the two of you make way for the waterfall."

"But—"

"No time for questions, Charlie. Just stay on course." The owl took to the air towards the fleet of flying pirate ships—dodging cannon and gun fire along the way. As he grew smaller in the distance, he hollered, "Trust meeeeee."

BOOM-BOOM-BOOM, POW, POW-POW-POW, SPLASH, SPLASH-SPLASH. The boys tiny boat was in range of both cannon and gun fire from the ships above. The canons and pistols continued to fire from the flying vessels, as the watch-hungry pirates closed in on the boys. Some of the pirate crew left their ships and soared high into the sky, while others jumped overboard and began flying low, just above, and below, the water's surface. All were headed directly towards Charlie and Michael with one thing in mind, to get the watch at all costs.

"Hello there mateys, care if I join ya," an overweight pirate with a striped shirt said, as he popped up through the bottom of the boat between the boys.

Another came down from the sky, landing right behind Michael. He put a pistol to the boy's head.

And then a third popped up through the bottom of the boat, right behind Charlie.

"How about ya give us that there watch in your pocket," the pirate behind Charlie said in a soft gravely voice.

"Watch? What watch?" Charlie said.

"Don't be playing those games with me boy. I know it's in your pocket."

"And how would you know that, if you can't see it?"

"Cause me little friend here told me."

To Charlie's surprise, he turned and saw a mouse with a tattered head band and a tiny patch over one eye, perched atop the pirate's shoulder. Excited to see such a thing, the young boy kept calm and played along—knowing the waterfall grew nearer with each passing second. "Since when can mice talk?"

"Yeah, he can't talk," Michael added, pointing at the mouse.

"Well this one here can, right fella?"

"You're bloody right, mate," the mouse replied in an unusually low-pitched voice for such a tiny creature.

"Alright, so he can talk, but that doesn't mean anything," Charlie replied. "He still hasn't seen the watch."

"Why of course I have," the mouse confidently replied.

"Oh yeah, I never felt you in my pocket, Charlie said.

"I'd reckon you'd have a hard time feeling something as little as him snooping 'round your pockets, boy," the lead pirate with the mouse said.

"Alright then," Charlie said to the mouse, "what does the watch look like?"

"Hold on there, little guy," the pirate said while petting the mouse. "We ain't got time for all this nonsense, boy. Now hand over the watch or my friend over their is gonna pull the trigger on that pistol he's holding to your brother's—"

SWOOOOOSH!

Before the pirate had time to finish his words, the mighty owl swept in and snatched the mouse off his shoulder—carrying the helpless rodent high into the sky.

"Bring him back you filthy owl!" the pirate yelled to Alexios, who was now several hundred feet away.

"Not until the three of you leave my friend's boat," the owl yelled back.

"We're not going nowheres until we get that watch," the pirate replied.

"Well, then I guess you wont be getting your little friend back," the owl proclaimed.

"Ohhhhhhhhh! Shoot that bloody owl while I grab the watch!" the angry pirate said to his mates.

The other two pirates opened fire on the flying owl above, as the third pirate lunged for Charlie's pants,—tugging on the pocket which held the watch.

"No!" Charlie yelled, "get your stinking hands off it."

"Let him go or you'll never see your mouse friend again," Alexios said. He zoomed down and knocked the pirate's hat crooked—obstructing his vision and setting off a chain reaction. Out of frustration and a lack of vision, the pirate behind Charlie tried to stand up and lost his balance. As he did, he accidentally shot the pirate behind Michael—who, as he was falling out of the boat, shot the pirate in the middle of the boat. He too, fell overboard.

Before the three ghostly pirates could recover and climb back aboard, the boat reached the rough waters of Dead Man's Drop and began rocking from side to side—making it difficult for the boys to maintain a grip on the seat railings.

With only fifty feet to go, Alexios flew in and hovered erratically next to Charlie, continuing to flap his wings. "There's one last thing I need to tell you. Well, two actually."

"What's that,?" Charlie said.

"Tonight, after you get back to your parents, make sure to watch the left side of the castle during the fireworks show using the magic looking glass."

"OK, and what's the other thing?" Charlie yelled, as the noise of the waterfall intensified.

"Hold on tight," the owl yelled back.

"What?" Charlie yelled.

"Hold on tight," Alexios repeated even louder. "That means you too young squire," he yelled at Michael. The mighty owl took off over the mist of the waterfall, as he yelled, "I'll see you again my friends!"

The boys replied in unison, "OK Alexioooooooooooooooooooooooo!"

Their boat took a header over the falls, diving towards the jagged rocks below. It began to pick up speed, traveling faster and faster, their surroundings grew darker by the second. Everything went pitch black. The wind increased in intensity, as the crashing sounds of water on rock grew louder. The speed at which they were falling was almost unbearable. The boys held onto the railings with all their might.

THUNK-KAPLOOOSHHH!

The boat made contact with calm water and leveled out into a peaceful floating pace, as Barbosa's ship slowly came into view on the left. They were back on the Pirates of the Caribbean attraction. Their parents, in the boat just ahead.

The boys were exhausted from battling ghostly pirates and skeletons, and their bellies were full from a hearty dinner at Liberty Tree Tavern—making it difficult to fend off the sleepiness that had taken over their worn out bodies. As the sun sank low in the sky, everyone in the Magic Kingdom began to gather around the hub and Main Street in preparation for the Wishes fireworks show, including Charlie and his family.

"Dad, it looks like there's a good spot over there by Sleepy Hollow Treats. Not too many people," Charlie said, trying to establish a good vantage point on the left side of the castle as Alexios had advised.

"That looks perfect. It'll keep us away from the crowds. OK with you, dear?"

"Sure, fine with me," his wife replied.

Just a short while later the skies had darkened and the fireworks were in full bloom, lighting up the sky in spectacular fashion. Three members of the Zastawits family stood and admired the show, while the fourth, unbeknownst to the the others, was watching through a looking glass. A magic looking glass.

Charlie carefully positioned the magical device so he could clearly see the left side of the castle, while not being noticed by his parents. Pushing the button, the glass began to spin rapidly, as it lit up green. A full minute passed without a trace, and then, illuminated words—cast down from the fireworks above, began to appear on the west wall of the castle. One word followed another, disappearing as the next appeared—each in position as if you were reading a book. When the looking glass had completed the message, Charlie quietly snuck it back into his pocket.

Shortly after the fireworks show, everyone agreed a relaxing ride on the Tomorrowland Transit Authority would be a perfect way to end the night. Charlie requested he and Michael ride in a separate car on the TTA so everyone could spread out. His parents happily agreed. This allowed Charlie to replay the message captured with the magic looking glass and type it into his phone. It read; 9:45 *Breakfast. Epcot. Sunshine Seasons. Emergency meeting. Frank.*

Chapter Seven

Charlie woke the next morning—day two of their vacation, with an exuberant amount of adrenaline flowing through his body—fueled by thoughts of what Frank would have to say in just a few short hours. Only on rare occasions did he wake before his brother. An emergency breakfast meeting with Frank was such an occasion. No matter what their friend had to tell them, Charlie needed to know as soon as possible. He needed to move forward—to face and conquer any fears, doubts, hesitations or potential dangers that may lay ahead for him and his younger brother.

"Michael, rise and shine. We gotta get going. Dad's already out taking a walk and Mom's in the shower. Epcot opens at nine—which is only about an hour away."

"I'm awake," Michael grumbled from underneath his blanket—still tired from the day before.

"Then why don't you get up?" Charlie replied. "I'm already clean, so that means you're next once Mom gets out of the shower."

"It's not that big of deal. I'll still be ready before Mom."

"You could at least get your clothes out."

"I already know what I'm going to wear."

"Really? I don't see anything."

"Don't worry about it, Charlie." That was the last thing Michael said before going into silent mode. Something he did quite often when he didn't want to be bothered. Especially by his pesky brother.

Charlie had seen it many times before and knew better than to push the issue. So instead, he accepted it and quietly went out on the balcony to enjoy the sunrise, as he waited for his mother to come out of the bathroom. If anyone could get his brother moving without a fight, she could. Her secret weapon, baby talk. Michael had very little, if any, tolerance for such child-like nonsense—which she knew, and used to her full advantage.

Just like clockwork, and as Charlie had patiently anticipated, his mother came out of the bathroom and immediately began to baby-talk her youngest to the fullest degree—her long, wet hair dangling down just enough to tickle Michael's exposed cheek.

Unable to take it anymore, he jumped out of bed, grabbed his clothes from the dresser, and stumbled to the shower to clean up. Charlie continued to take in the morning from the balcony. He quietly celebrated another small victory over his brother.

Their meeting with Frank was only minutes away, as Charlie and his family approached the meal checkout line at Sunshine Seasons in the Land pavilion of Epcot. Looking around, he tried hard to spot his eccentric, Patron friend amongst the crowded dining area, as his parents paid for their meals. Though such a task—even for the sharpest of eyes, was quite the challenging.

"Excuse me." Charlie heard a voice from the right as they were wandering to find a table. "I'm finished eating if you and your family would like this table." It was an older man wearing a Yankees baseball cap, orange bird t-shirt with red suspenders, khaki pants and dark blue Converse All-Star tennis shoes.

"Are you sure?" Mr. Zastawits replied, "we don't mean to rush you."

"Absolutely, I was just getting ready to leave anyway, I have a FastPass to use for Spaceship Earth in just a few minutes. Here, have a seat," the man said, as he got up and motioned with his arms for Mr. and Mrs. Z to sit down. "Right on time, Charlie," Frank quietly mumbled, before turning his attention back to the parents. "Hey, have you seen the latest necklaces they're selling over in the Mouse Gear store? They're really kind of neat," he said, pulling out the light charm necklace out from underneath his orange bird t-shirt to wave in front of their parents. Instantly they fell into a memory knot, a powerful, yet harmless memory-blocking spell the Patrons of WONDER used quite often on park guests to protect their secrecy of operations.

"So now what?" Charlie asked.

"We sit down so I can tell you what I learned yesterday at the Patron Council meeting."

"Really? And our mom and dad won't remember a thing?" Michael asked.

"Not a thing," Frank said, motioning the boys to sit.

Their parents proceeded to eat and talk as if they were alone.

"Now, where do I begin. Oh yes, the watch, as you know, does not work because it was struck by lightning. After yesterday's meeting with the Council, I can confirm, unfortunately, that the source of the lightning did indeed come from the black magic of a shadow villain pulled out of WONDER by the Dark Thorn's mysterious Queen."

"So who is this Queen of the Dark Thorns?" Charlie asked.

"We don't really know yet, but we have a small task force specifically assigned to find out."

"You mentioned shadow villains the other day, and told us they are basically reimagined by Dark Thorns and this 'mysterious leader' of theirs in the shadows of WONDER. But what exactly are these shadows?" Charlie asked.

The shadows of WONDER are like small, concentrated spots of evil, created and hidden by the Dark Thorns throughout WONDER. Since the Dark Thorns and their superior cannot create new realms within WONDER, nor permanently alter any of their existing characteristics—such as the themed lands or the attractions, they have created hidden shadows throughout WONDER to plant and grow their evil ideas, including shadow villains. And it is for *this* very reason they wish to gain control of the Objects of Magic we possess and find the five Kingdom Crystals. This would allow them to access a key element, which, when paired with the Magic Dream Expander I told you about last year, can penetrate the Dream Core of WONDER. Ultimately, they wish to control all of WONDER—a nightmare of a thought at the very least, as you already know quite well from your past experiences. Including the one you just had yesterday.

"Talk about a bad dream, I can't imagine what it would be like to deal with that every day,"Charlie said.

"Wonderful," Michael added.

"But Frank, last year the Dark Thorn leader of the Animal Kingdom was able to control the *entire* park when we were searching for the Vision Stones to help rescue you. So why would they need to go through *all* the trouble you just mentioned, if they can already control entire realms, parks or whatever of WONDER?" Charlie asked.

"You're correct Charlie, Dark Thorn Kunn *did* control the entire park. But, that type of dark magic only lasts for a short period of time, it is not a *permanent* spell. If you had gone back and visited that particular realm of WONDER the next day, you would have found that everything had returned back to its normal state."

"Hmm, interesting," Charlie replied while scratching his head.

"So, I have a question. Why didn't we run into any of these shadow villains last year?" Michael asked.

"Good question, Michael. The Patrons and I can only assume it was because the Dark Thorns and their superior did not see the two of you as a big enough threat to warrant the use of shadow villains. But I assure you, that has now changed. Worse yet, as I already mentioned, the lightning that struck the watch came from a shadow villain called out of WONDER by the Dark Thorn's Shadow Queen. Which means the dark forces have found a way to bring them into our world, where they can actually interact with physical reality. Something we didn't think they were capable of doing until now. In fact, it's quite concerning, being we, as in the Patrons, are still unable to do such a thing."

"The Patrons can't bring animated characters into reality?"

"Precisely, Charlie. It's a technology we still have not perfected. And since the Thorn Order has, that makes them even more dangerous than we expected."

"Terrific, looks like this is going to be one big jolly *hoot* of a vacation," Michael replied.

"Unfortunately, you're probably right, Michael," Frank replied with a sigh.

"Well, at least we were lucky enough not to come across any shadow villains yesterday on the Pirates attraction," Charlie said, attempting to change the mood.

"Yeah, our hands were full enough as it was, with all those pirate ghosts and crazy skeletons," Michael added.

"That's right, thank you for reminding me, Michael. Why don't the two of you tell me more about your run-in with the pirates and skeletons yesterday. That's a story I'd really like to hear."

"Oh, Frank, it was the strangest thing," Charlie said. "We went on the Pirates of the Caribbean with our parents. They rode in one boat and Michael and I took another. Everything seemed normal until we got to the skeleton captain just before the waterfall, and that's where things got weird."

"Yeah, the skeleton guy started to follow us, and the next thing you know, we went shooting down a giant water fall that seemed to last forever," Michael added.

"And when we finally hit bottom," Charlie said, "we were in this creepy cove. I think I heard one of the ghost pirates call it 'Pirates Cove', or something like that? But anyway, it was one of the creepiest looking islands I've ever seen."

"There were flying ghost ships filled with pirates, other ships filled with skeletons, and crazy looking glow-in-the-dark sharks, squids, eels and other weird sea creatures," Michael said.

"Yeah, and flying ghost dogs, skeleton seagulls, partially-decayed bats, and even a boat made out of skeletons," Charlie added. "Luckily, Alexios showed up to help us get out of there before they could take the watch from us."

"Well you can thank your old friend, Ben, for that," Frank said with a smile. "He's the one who told me to send Alexios to help you."

"I'll have to remember to thank him," Charlie replied.

"I'm sure you will," Charlie. Anyway, you said 'they' were trying to get the watch from you?"

"Yes, three of the pirates hijacked our boat and were trying to take the watch out of my pocket, but Alexios swooped down from the sky and set off a chain reaction that knocked all three out of our boat just before we plummeted down a waterfall, and back to reality."

"Ah, good 'ol Alexios. He sure knows how to get things done," Frank said with a chuckle. So, from what you're telling me, it sounds like the Thorn Order knows we've given you the Watch of WONDER. But I'm *quite* sure they have no idea what we plan to do next."

"I sure hope you're right," Michael said.

"Well, whether I'm right or wrong, we still need to be ready for them, no matter if we're in WONDER or on the Magic Rim."

"What's the Magic Rim?" Charlie asked.

"Oh, I'm sorry, I thought I had told you. Evidently I haven't. The Magic Rim is the outer ridge of WONDER, where inanimate objects in the real world can temporarily come to life—such as the sun on the Small World attraction, the tree at the Shoot'n Arcade and the tiger and snakes on the Jungle Cruise attraction you encountered last year—by way of magical powers. But of course, those powers can come from forces of good, or forces of evil."

"Now I see," Charlie replied. "So really, no matter where we are, there's a chance the Dark Thorns could throw something wicked our way."

"Exactly, Charlie," Frank replied. "So please, make sure to always, and I DO MEAN ALWAYS, be aware of your surroundings, who's around you, etc., when you are here at Walt Disney World. Especially now that they know you are a formidable threat. The Dark Thorns do not like to be outdone."

"Well they better get used to it, cause me and my kid brother here aren't going to be scared off *that* easily. Right, Michael?"

"Speak for yourself," Michael replied, stone faced.

"Really?" Charlie challenged his brother.

"You know I'm here for ya," Michael said, cracking a smile.

Charlie and Frank laughed heartily at Michael's comment.

"Now that's what I like to hear. I knew the Patrons made the right choice when we picked you as our outsider, Charlie. And Michael here is the icing on the cake." Frank said, while patting the boy on the shoulder. "Oh, speaking of cake, does anybody want a piece?"

The boys jumped at the opportunity without hesitation.

Frank returned with two scrumptious slices of chocolate cake for the boys and a tasty slice of carrot cake for himself. He closed their conversation with a few more words of wisdom, while they all enjoyed desert. "First, as I mentioned earlier, we've confirmed that a shadow villain was the source of the lightning strike that damaged the watch. Why the Thorn Order would want to destroy it is beyond our knowledge at this time. They need it as much as we do to obtain a key element required to penetrate the Dream Core, by way of the Magic Dream Expander."

"That's unsettling," Charlie replied.

"Yes, it is Charlie, and quite concerning for the Patrons as well. Secondly, speaking of the Magic Dream Expander, in recent months, several Dark Thorns have attempted to locate the whereabouts of this device by way of casting truth spells upon some of our best Patrons. Fortunately for us, none of those affected by the spells knew where it was hidden. Regardless, this tells us the Dark Thorns and their superior are now aware of its capabilities and that they need it to penetrate the Dream Core."

"So it sounds like they have two things they are chasing after at one time now? Objects of Magic and the Magic Dream Expander?"

"Exactly, Charlie. Which means they have more than likely doubled up on their forces—so you will be twice as likely to face a dangerous situation when you're out there searching for the watchmaker to get the watch fixed. I thought it only fair to tell you this upfront, though some of the Patron Council disagreed with my views, thinking it may scare you off."

"We're here to help, Frank," Charlie said with commitment in his eyes.

"I know you are, young man. And you as well, Michael," Frank said with a kind smile. "Which brings me to one more thing." The old man leaned in close to the boys and whispered, as not to let any unfriendly ears around them hear what he was about to say. "Tonight at 8:15, meet me by the Neptune fountain in the Italy Pavilion. From there, we will begin our search for the watchmaker. Until then, be safe my young friends." Frank leaned back and began to talk in a normal tone—playing the role of a solo tourist. "Well, it was nice to meet all of you. Thank you so much for letting me share time with you and your wonderful family." As he stood up, he turned and faced their parents, snapped his fingers three times, then said quietly to the boys as he leaned in. "They'll be back to normal in a jiffy." Frank tipped his cap, winked, then turned and walked towards the escalators.

"It was nice meeting you too, Mr. Smith," Charlie said as his friend walked away.

"So who's up for Soarin'?" Their father asked, having just snapped out of his memory knot.

"We have FastPasses, right Ed?" Their mother replied with a smile.

"It's the only way the this family does attractions," he said jokingly.

"I'm ready for a little Soarin'," Michael replied. He turned and looked at his brother with a smirk—making fun of the fact their parents had no idea what had just taken place.

Charlie smiled back at this brother and gave him a little shoulder bump. "Yeah, me too, I'm up for it," he replied, while finishing off the delicious chocolate cake Frank had bought for him.

Chapter Eight

Charlie and his family had just come off Test Track, his mother's hair—frazzled from humidity and wind, looked like a nest of mess. It was their third attraction in a row. If there was one thing riding attractions did, it was eat up time. Noon was rapidly approaching.

Having had a late breakfast at Sunshine Seasons, both parents were still plenty full. But growing boys with hollow legs never stay full for long.

"Mom, can we eat lunch? I"m starving," Michael said in his best whiney voice.

"Really? We just ate breakfast a couple hours ago."

"But all those rides are making me hungry."

Thinking quickly, as all good mothers do, she scanned the area and came up with a solution to make them both happy. "Listen, it's hot, you're hungry, and I'm, well, in need of a makeover. How about the three of you go over to Test Track Cool Wash and grab a few frozen raspberry lemonade slushies and a bag or two of chips? That should tide you over for a little while. Besides, it'll give me a chance to freshen up a bit."

"A nice cold raspberry slushy would sure help take some stickiness out of this humidity, don't you think, boys?"

"Yeah Dad, slushies," Michael replied.

"What about you, Charlie? You need something cold to drink? You are starting to look a little pink in the cheeks," his mother added.

"Yeah, a slushy would hit the spot, Charlie replied."

"OK, honey, you go freshen up and we'll meet you inside the Mouse Gear store. C'mon boys, let's go, so we can get out of this heat."

Charlie and Michael enjoyed a cool break inside the Mouse Gear store while slurping on their ice cold beverages. Their mother, who had just returned from freshening up, was busy gift hunting for their nieces and nephews. There were, cups, pins, stickers and keychains—princess clothes, pirate clothes, candy and toys. Everywhere you turned, something playful and fun was strategically placed to catch the eye of those passing by. In fact, much of it did for Mrs. Z. With her husband aimlessly following along, she picked up and awed at one thing after another.

"I can't believe how well Dad is dealing with Mom's shopping addiction," Michael said jokingly.

"It's OK, I think he actually enjoys looking with her. It makes her happy, and I think that's what he cares about most," Charlie replied. "I'm actually more worried about those guys over there by the candy wall that keep staring at us."

"Over where?" Michael replied, turning to see for himself.

"Don't turn around, just keep looking straight ahead. Besides, one of them is a short fat guy with a sunburned head and flip flops. And it looks like"—Charlie squinted as he looked closer, "like he's grabbing candy right out of the dispensers with his hands and eating it. How disgusting is that?"

"Well I guess I'm not getting any candy," Michael replied.

"How are my boys?" their mother asked. "You see anything you like?"

Michael was about to speak, but his brother headed him off.

"No, I think we're good Mom." Then he turned and whispered to his brother. "We need to keep an eye on these guys, Michael. We can't be shopping right, now." Then he turned back towards his parents. "Do you think we have time to go on one more ride before lunch?"

"Sure, Charlie. We can eat lunch whenever and wherever we want," his father replied. "Did you have something in mind?"

"How about Frozen?"

"That would be fun, but we don't have FastPasses for it, and I bet the wait time for the regular line is pretty long. But, let me check the Disney app on my phone."

While his father checked the app for wait times, Charlie peeked over to see if the fat guy and his two suspicious friends were still by the candy. Surprisingly enough, they were gone—which put his mind at ease.

"It looks like there's a ninety minute wait for Frozen, so maybe we shoot for that attraction later this evening? Unless you guys want to wait? But then we won't be eating lunch for at least a couple hours," Mr. Z said.

"So which rides have short wait times?" their mother asked.

"Journey into Imagination with Figment has a ten minute wait, Spaceship Earth is fifteen minutes, and O Canada is only five minutes."

"That sounds good," Charlie said.

"Which one, Charlie?"

"O Canada. One of my teachers at school said that I should go see it. She said it was really cool,."

"That *does* sound good," his mother added. "That gets us out into World Showcase. Then after the show, we'll have plenty of choices for lunch."

"I like the way your mind works," her husband replied.

"So we'd better get moving, Mrs. Z said. "It'll take us five minutes just to walk over there, and we don't want to miss the beginning."

As they exited O Canada, Charlie noticed something quite alarming. The candy man and his two shady friends from the Mouse Gear shop were about thirty feet behind them. And worse yet, they quickly looked away when Charlie made eye contact. Charlie's heart dropped to his stomach. "Michael, we're being followed," he mumbled to his brother. "The short round guy in the flower shirt, and his two buddies, are right behind us. We gotta make sure we stay out in the open with Mom and Dad so they can't touch us."

Michael took a quick peak as they wound their way out of the Canada Pavilion and headed towards the United Kingdom. "Looks like your'e right," he confirmed.

"Did you say something honey?" their mom asked Michael.

"What? Oh, I'm just talking to Charlie," he replied.

The boys tried to keep a far enough distance from their parents to talk freely about the situation, but at the same time, close enough so the candy man and his two shady companions could not grab them.

"Don't let those little rascals get away, understand boys," Captain Fibs said, flip-flopping along with sweat pouring over his puffy, red face, down the trunk of his neck, and onto his double-X luau shirt— which was two sizes too large.

"We won't let 'em out of our sight," Grim replied.

"That's right, there's nowhere for them to hide now," Duke added, as the three Thorns kept pace with Charlie and his family.

"Good, cause if the two of you fail me, I'll have to—"

Fibs struggled to catch his breath as they briskly marched along.

"Have to what?" Duke asked.

Captain Fibs stopped in his tracks—panting and sweating like he had just run a marathon. "Just...make...sure...we don't lose that... boy. We need the watch."

"Righty-O, Captain," Grim replied.

"Now...we need to... keep after 'em," Fibs said, still trying to catch his breath. His over-fed body leaned heavily on a trash can in the shade, as he struggled to point towards the Zastawits family with his free hand.

"C'mon Duke, let's go get us a watch."

"Now you're talk'n mate," Duke replied. "You just rest here a minute, Captain, while we go fetch us a watch."

Charlie and his family had stopped at the Yorkshire County Fish Shop to grab a tasty bite of fish 'n chips, and shady relief from the heat, along World Showcase Lagoon. While most of the family had enjoyed their meals, Charlie did not.

Savoring his last hearty chip smothered in catsup, he caught a glimpse of the candyman's two henchmen go storming by. He knew they were looking for him. He knew what they were after. He knew... they would never quit. Slowly, the food in his mouth became tasteless—as it no longer mattered. The only thing that was important now, was their safety and keeping away from their unfriendly pursuers.

As Mr. Z discarded the remains of the meal into a trash receptacle, the boys and their mother got up and slowly meandered towards the United Kingdom shops to officially begin their World Showcase shop hop.

Charlie had other things on his mind. "Michael, keep an eye out. They're still looking for us, I just saw them a minute ago," he whispered. Cautiously, he and his brother scanned the area while crossing the promenade—tying not to look directly at anyone in their immediate surroundings. Their mother was five steps ahead, their father, seven behind. First up on the right were the Crown and Crest and Toy Soldier shops.

While their parents were talking, laughing and making jokes with the cast members in the shops, the boys were experiencing something quite different. All they could think about was what lied around the next corner. Where was the candyman and his two goons? What were they going to do if they caught them? And what would happen to their parents?

The family wandered to the other side of the road to check out the Tea Caddy, where, for a brief moment, they found a tiny bit of joy. It was an assortment of deliciously scrumptious cookies and candy—which their mother gladly purchased for everyone to split up and enjoy as a belated lunch desert.

As Charlie and his brother were savoring melted chocolate in their mouths, rounding the outside corner of The Queen's Table shop, trouble found them.

There stood Fibs, blocking their way, as Duke and Grim came walking up from behind.

Their parents had been distracted by something in the shop and were nowhere to be seen.

The captain, in all his splendor of disgustingness, spat out, "Grab 'em, gents, while I fish out the watch."

"It's doesn't belong to you," Charlie said.

"Well kid, that ain't for you to say, now is it," Fibs replied, as sweat rolled down his face. "We've been following you for half the day, waiting for an opportunity to get that watch. And it looks to me like all that hard work is about to pay off."

Duke and Grim grabbed each boy by their arms, while Fibs moved in for the watch.

"No, stay away from him. You're not getting it," Michael yelled, as he struggled to break free of Duke's grasp. He watched as the captain closed in on his brother.

"Captain, what, what is that?"

"Huh, what are you talking about Duke?" Fibs replied—unaware of what was happening behind him.

"The, the hedges, they're movin', Captain," Grim said.

"Come off it boys, I think this heat has melted your brains—what little there is to melt, that is."

"No, really, Captain. The hedges behind ya are movin' and growin', me and Grimsly aren't pulling your leg. You see it too, right, Grimsly?"

"You bet I—ow! Why you little—"

Through all the distractions of conversation, Michael managed to kick Duke square in the shin, causing him to let go of his arms. He took off running towards the hedge maze.

"Go get him, you fool!" Fibs shouted.

Duke took off after the speedy little runner, which distracted Grim just enough, enabling Charlie to break free and take off towards the other end of the hedge maze.

"Oh! What's wrong with you numbskulls! Don't let them get away, I need that watch!" Fibs shouted in frustration. "Duke, forget the little one. Go help Grim catch the outsider. He's the one we need."

"Right, Captain," Duke replied. "Uh, and why do we need him again?"

"Because he's the one carrying the watch you bloomin' fool."

"Oh, that's right," Duke replied. He changed course and headed towards Charlie. Attempting to cut him off before he reached the hedge maze, which had now grown to over ten feet tall—totally concealing the band pavilion, which sat in its center.

"Hurry, he's almost in the maze," Fibs yelled.

As the hedges continued to grow upward, now nearly fifteen feet in height, a magic gust of wind stirred up and knocked the two men chasing Charlie off their feet—allowing him to make it into the maze. *Why am I going in here, I don't even know if this was created for our escape or not?* Charlie thought to himself. Whether it was a trap or an escape route, Charlie came to the quick conclusion that it had to be better than the alternative.

Within a matter of seconds, he and his brother disappeared into the maze—both from opposite ends.

"No-no-NO!" Fibs screamed out, his face now red as a tomato. "Get up, up-up-up, you stinkin' fools! I need that watch. Go in there and find him. Find him or else." Even though the captain's words sounded like a threat to Duke and Grim, it was really Fibs worrying about his own consequences if they failed to bring back the watch. Consequences he most certainly wished to avoid.

Earlier on he had made a promise to his leader, Dark Thorn Senkrad, to bring back the Watch of WONDER by the end of the day. Which Senkrad replied, "With that promise comes two consequences. The first being, if you and your men succeeded, you will be greatly rewarded beyond your wildest imaginations. If however, you fail, you and your men will be wrapped in shackles and thrown into my dungeon of doom, for two *full* weeks, with one piece of bread and a single glass of water to live off each day."

The captain had no problem being shackled up in a dungeon for two weeks—he'd done it before. But being forced to live off one piece of bread per day, one single piece, would be more than he could tolerate. Especially for a man who enjoyed eating as much as he did.

The maze was tall and vast, much more so than it appeared from its exterior. The four foot wide pathways, flanked by fifteen feet high walls of shrubbery, seemed to go on forever.

Charlie called out to his brother, "Micheal, Michael, where are you?" but there was no response.

Not more than a few steps behind, the voices of Duke and Grim bickering could be heard.

Charlie increased his pace to assure they would not catch him. Left, right, straight twenty feet, then two rights—the young boy kept moving forward, trying not to look back. For five long minutes, he silently continued on—not wanting to give away his location to Fib's two flunkies. Just as he made another right turn into a long straightaway, he noticed that the left side of the hedge began to move.

From within its walls, a human form slowly emerged, stepping out of the hedge. It was a female figure of a full grown woman. Her hair was long, yet twirled up into a unique shape atop her head. Her facial features resembled those of a princess— very well defined and beautiful, while her body was draped in an elegant dress, with long, flowing sleeves, that effortlessly moved through the air as if gravity did not exist. All was made of foliage from the hedge.

"I've been expecting you, Charlie," the hedge maiden said. "I'm here to show you the way out."

"And who exactly are you?" Charlie asked.

"I am Lady Hedgemaze. Please, follow me. I will lead you to safety."

"But my brother is in here as well. I need to find him before I leave."

"I have already visited your brother and have started him on his way. You will meet him at the crossroads, where you both shall be shown a secret way out."

"How do I know I can trust you?"

"I was summoned by the magic of your Patron friend, Frank. He must have sensed you and your brother were in trouble and needed assistance. I am here to help as a loyal servant of the Patrons."

Having earned Charlie's trust, the two set off through the maze to find Michael. Lady Hedgemaze flowed in and out of the maze walls in a ubiquitous manner, pointing the way for Charlie to go. And every so often she would disappear to help Michael, then reappear, seconds later, to keep Charlie on the right path. This continued on for several minutes, until finally they met, face-to-face.

"Michael."

"Charlie."

Then suddenly, rising up over the walls, the unpleasant voices of their pursuers came into range. "They're getting close, Michael. We need to keep moving."

"We can't go back the way I came," Michael said. The candyman is probably waiting for us.

"Hmm, perhaps, you're right, Michael. Lady Hedgemaze," Charlie said, "do you know a way out? A way that's safe?"

"Your path to safety lies right behind you," she said while pointing.

The boys turned and looked. A section of the wall began to shift right—and behind the gap it exposed, more hedge walls shifted and turned, creating an alternate pathway that did not exist until that very moment. Charlie and Michael looked at each other with astonishment.

"Here lies your path to safety."

"Thank you, uh, Ma'am, I mean, Lady Hedgemaze," Charlie said respectfully.

"You are very welcome. Now move along before the others arrive."

"Thank you again," Charlie said. He and his brother headed down the secret pathway towards a safer place.

"Yes, thank you," Michael added as he trailed behind his brother— looking back at the hedge maiden. She closed her hands together and disappeared behind the hedge wall as it slid back into place.

Magically, when Charlie and Michael walked out of the maze they were near the front of the France pavilion, where another hedge maze existed. To their left, stood their mother and father, taking photos of fanciful flower arrangements.

The afternoon has slipped by. Filled with shows, shops and snacks in several of the countries. The Zastawits family had thoroughly enjoyed their time together touring World Showcase. From the Tangier Traders in Morocco, to the Mitsukoshi Department store in Japan, and the Stein Haus in Germany—there was something for everyone in the family to add to their list of possible souvenirs. Between the shops, everyone enjoyed a multitude of delicious snacks including fresh caramel corn in Germany, cool and refreshing kakigori (shaved ice) in Japan, and tasty gelato sandwiches from Italy, to help take the edge off Florida's summer heat.

Charlie and his family managed to make it all the way to Norway, before realizing it was almost time to head back to Italy for dinner.

At that moment, inside The Puffin's Roost in Norway, Charlie and Michael were addressed by someone rather unusual. A giant troll.

The room where the troll stood was unoccupied except for the boys and a single cast member—who acted as if she knew what was to happen next.

Their parents were in the room next door looking at clothing. Close enough to see their sons, but far enough to not hear their conversations. Nor could they see the troll's movements, which were cloaked by magic.

"Hello there, boys, I have a quick couple of words for ya."

Charlie and Michael looked at each other, then all around to see if anyone was watching.

"No need to worry about that little ones, only you and the kind lady over there can see me for who I am," the troll said, pointing to the cast member—who was straightening up merchandise and keeping an eye out for unwelcome guests.

"And who exactly are you?" Charlie asked.

"Just a messenger for your old friend Frank."

"So you have something to tell us?" Charlie said.

"Indeed I do," the happy troll replied.

"Well go ahead and spit it out," Michael said impatiently."

"Michael, hush," Charlie said. "Go ahead Mr. Troll."

"Uh-hmm-hmmm-hmm. Sir Charlie and Sir Michael, it is with GREAT privilege that I remind you Mr. Wellington has requested your presence after dinner by the Neptune fountain at precisely 8:15," the giant troll said with a mischievous grin.

"Is there anything else, Mr. Troll?" Charlie asked.

"No sir, that is all."

"Please, you can call me Charlie."

"OK, Sir Charlie."

"Just Charlie is fine."

"OK, just Charlie."

Charlie giggled. "No, what I meant was, you can call me, Charlie, without 'Sir' in front of it."

"OK, Charlie."

"And what is your name, Mr. Troll?"

"I never really thought about a name, but my friends call me, Mort."

"Well, nice to meet you, Mort," Charlie said, as he shook the troll's giant hand. "And this is my brother, Michael."

"Hello, Michael."

"Hey ya, Mort," Michael said in an uninterested manner.

"Oh, don't worry about him, he was born cranky," Charlie said, to lighten the moment.

The troll and cast member laughed at Charlie's comment.

"Thanks for nothing, Charlie," Michael replied.

"See, what did I tell you, Charlie said, with a funny facial gesture—triggering more laughs from Mort and the cast member.

"OK boys, looks like Mort's time is up," Brit, the cast member said.

"Ope, heh-heh, guess I gotta go fellas," the troll said. "It was nice chat'n with ya."

"You too, Mort," Charlie replied. "Maybe we'll get a chance to talk again some day."

"I'd like that, the troll replied with a giant grin. He returned back to his normal pose and froze in place.

"Thank you too, Brit," Charlie said, reading the cast member's name tag.

"You're welcome, I hope we get to see you again some day," she replied with a smile.

"Me too," the boy said.

"Yes sir. I know sir. I, I remember what I promised," Captain Fibs said to Dark Thorn Senkrad, as they stood high above the Bijutsu-kan Gallery, near the back of the Japan Pavilion.

Senkrad stood tall, cloaked in a black robe. He was looking through a small window, staring out into World Showcase, as an unnerved Fibs pleaded his case.

"But sir, they were rescued by Patron magic. The hedge maze, it, it came alive and provided an escape for those two little brats."

Captain, are you telling me *you* and your two pudding-for-brains spies—what were their names again, Dink and Groogle?, are incapable of dealing with a little measly spell from some old washed up Imagineer?"

"There names are Duke and Grim, sir. And no, the hedge incident was just a minor setback. I've got my boys out tracking down those two little worms right now as we speak. In fact, I expect a call any time now saying they found 'em."

Senkrad turned and gazed upon Fibs with his dark, soulless eyes. "I do hope so for your sake."

The captain swallowed hard, almost chocking on air. "Yes, I do as well, sir."

"Then go, bring me the watch. And the boy if you must. Either way, I need the watch by midnight, and not a second later."

"Yes, dark leader," Fibs replied obediently—which was very unusual behavior for the captain. But Senkrad, like all other Dark Thorns, had an intimidating presence.

"I know they are still in the park. I can *feel* the magic of the watch," Senkrad said, turning back towards the window—he looked out into World Showcase. "The evening is upon us Captain, I suggest you go now. Midnight will be here before you know it."

"Yes, yes sir," Fibs replied. He slowly backed away towards the staircase.

Senkrad stood in silence, continuing to stare out the window, as if Fibs were not even there.

The intimidated captain took it as a sign to leave. He excited the room, headed down the stairs, through the Bijutsu-kan Gallery, and back into World Showcase—alone, and desperate to find the watch.

Dinner at Via Napoli Ristorante e Pizzeria was a big hit for the Zastawits family.

As the waiter took orders for desert, Charlie texted his brother: *Reminder: Frank, Neptune fountain, 8:15.*

Michael texted back: *Over and out.*

Moments later, the waiter returned with four scrumptious Zeppole di Caterinas, which consisted of ricotta cheese fritters covered with whipped cream and tasty chocolate sauce. A perfect way to end a great meal before heading out to find the watchmaker. At least that's what Charlie was thinking.

A large group of fifty or more guests were gathered near the Neptune fountain. All were colorfully dressed in Venetian-styled outfits with wildly decorated masks they randomly held up to their faces as the mood struck them. They were dancing, talking and laughing in celebration, while enjoying music piped in from all around the Italy Pavilion.

Charlie's parents were amused by the enthusiasm and positive energy the Venetian group was spreading throughout the area, and stopped to watch the celebration.

The boy looked at his phone, it was 8:13; only two minutes before their meeting with Frank. Quickly, he thought of a reason to walk up to the fountain. "Hey Mom, Dad, is it alright if we go over by the fountain, so I can take a picture?" Charlie asked politely.

"Of course, I was actually thinking of doing the same thing myself," his father replied.

As they moved closer towards the fountain, Charlie scanned the area, trying to spot anyone that may look, or that was acting, a little different compared to the rest of the group. The only possibility appeared to be two men sitting on a bench next to the stone wall, who were having a private conversation. *Had Frank forgotten about their meeting?* Charlie thought to himself, then he texted his brother: *see anything?*

Michael walked over to his brother. "I wasn't really looking."

"What? I told you back at the restaurant we were meeting Frank at 8:15," Charlie replied.

"Yeah, but I figured you already knew exactly where he would be, so we wouldn't have to look."

"Well, he said to meet him by the Neptune fountain at 8:15. It's actually 8:18 now, so he *should* be here. Since you haven't even *tried* to look, why don't you take a peek around and tell me if you see anything."

"OK, fine," Michael said reluctantly. Turning slowly, the younger brother searched the area, analyzing each person that came into view. Then he spotted a possibility. "What about the guys on the bench, Charlie?

"Hmmm, you might be onto something, Michael."

"So what do we do now?"

"I guess we go over and see if one of them is Frank?"

The boys slowly approached the two men, not knowing if what they were doing was right or not. As they edged closer, Charlie mumbled to Michae, "If we're wrong, then what? Will we get in trouble?"

"I don't know, it's your idea," Michael replied quietly.

They reached the two men on the bench, who turned to look at the boys. Both with masks held to their faces—concealing their identities.

"Excuse me, I know this may seem kind of weird, but, we are supposed to meet somebody by this fountain and we thought you might be who we're looking for?" Charlie said with a confused look on his face.

The two men broke into laughter as they dropped their masks—speaking rapidly in Italian. Neither was obviously Frank. Back and forth they bantered with each other in their native tongue, while the boys just stood and stared, not knowing what to do or say next.

"Why don't the two of you come dance with us," a voice called out from behind the boys—who immediately turned to see who it was. "Come, join the fun." It was a thin man sporting a long white wig of curly hair. He appeared to be a little older, but very spry and full of happiness. His outfit, including his shoes, was mostly purple with shiny silver and white accents. The mask which hid his face was white with floral swirls—also purple and silver. And though they could not see his face, his eyes and voice seemed very inviting in a non-threatening way.

"And how do we know we can trust you?" Charlie asked. "We were told by a very wise friend of ours to trust no one."

"Ah, it sounds like you have a very caring friend. If he were here now, I'm sure he would approve."

"And why is that?" Michael questioned.

Suddenly, another man, a shorter, more portly man, jumped out right in front of the boys—making them flinch. "Because, he *is* your friend."

"What?" Charlie said—finding it hard to follow the short man's words.

"Because, he *is* your friend lads. Take a closer look," the jolly little man said with a giggle and a twirl.

"Hey, I know that laugh," Michael said, smiling.

"Yeah, me too," Charlie added. "Is that you, Ben?"

"As sure as a pickled pickle," Ben replied, as he removed his gold mask and continued to dance around the boys in his outfit of white and green with a 3-point hat.

"Do you trust me now?" The man in purple asked, as he lowered his mask, then flung it high into the air, which burst into silvery-gold dust.

"Oh, hello, Frank," Charlie said.

"Now come along boys and dance with us, we have to keep moving to avoid any complications," the wise Patron advised.

Charlie and Michael each took a hand of Ben's, who led them towards Frank and into the fray of celebration. Around and around they went, dancing and humming to the music surrounding them. Blurred streaks of color and light passed by their eyes, as they continued to dance, while Frank explained how their parents had been brought into the Venetian party using the magic of a memory knot. He assured them they would be happily occupied until the boys returned.

"So now what?" Michael asked.

"We're about to transport into WONDER," Ben replied with a big smile."You're gonna really love this one, boys. See the dolphin on the right side of Neptune? We're gonna fly into his mouth."

"His mouth?" Charlie said, as they continued to spin faster and faster. "My head wouldn't even fit into that dolphin's mouth."

"Not to worry boys, Frankie here is going to fix that," Ben replied.

"Huh?" Michael replied with a confused look.

"Hold on boys, it's time to go," Frank said. The light charm around his neck rose up and floated weightlessly in the air—glowing brilliantly.

Round and round they went, each boy holding a hand of a Parton to form a complete circle. They continued to spin, faster and faster, until everything around them was one continuous blur with no definable shapes.

"Aghhhh, spinning fast!" Michael hollered.

"OK, when I say GO, Charlie, you let go of our hands," Frank shouted.

"What? Really?"

"Yes, Charlie, really." Are you ready?"

"Ha-ha, sure."

"GO!"

Putting all his trust into Frank's words, Charlie released his grip and was launched towards the dolphin's mouth from fifty feet away. Half way there, Neptune came to life and blew a series of magical notes on his conch shell, which made Charlie feel as though he was shrinking. The closer he flew towards the dolphin, the smaller he became, until finally he was no more than four inches tall—allowing him to easily fit through the dolphin's open mouth. A split second later, he came to an abrupt halt in Franks apartment—again, full size, where he was quickly joined by Michael, Ben, and finally, Frank.

Fibs, Duke and Grim had just come out of Tutto Gusto Wine Cellar.

"That's right dark leader," Fibs said into his wristband device. "We were just walkin' out of wine cellar, and there they were—all of 'em, being sucked right into the mouth of Neptune's dolphin."

"Ahhh, well done. You've redeemed yourself, Captain," Dark Thorn Senkrad replied. "You know where they have gone, don't you?"

"I would imagine to find the watchmaker, sir?"

"Precisely. I want you to follow them into WONDER, just to make sure our assumption is correct. Then report back to me once you have confirmation that it is true."

"Yes sir, right away, Senkrad. But uh, how are we supposed to know where they transported to?"

"No need to worry about such details, Fibs. I have already activated a dream dot and set its coordinates for the watchmaker's realm in Deep WONDER. Just walk over to the fountain and you will instantly be transported."

"Thank you, sir, thank you."

"Once there, locate them and find out their intentions. But do it *without* giving yourselves away. We don't want to alarm them just yet. It may be wiser for us to let them first find the watchmaker and allow him to fix the watch, before we TAKE it away," Senkrad advised with an evil laugh.

"Yes, Senkrad, we understand," the captain replied with a nervous chuckle. He disconnected his wristband device. "C'mon boys, we're going fishing."

"Huh? What?" Grim said with a perplexed look on his face.

"We're going after the Patrons and those kids."

"You mean we're gonna get sucked up by that dolphin? Ain't that gonna hurt?" Duke asked.

"Oh, for goodness sake man, it's a dream dot. You ain't gonna feel a thing. Now come on, we've got work to do. Or would you rather tell Senkrad you don't want to do it?"

"No-no-no-no. We'll do it, Captain," Grim replied.

"Very well then, time's a wastin'. Let's get a move on," Fibs hollered while leading his men to the fountain. Seconds later, they exited reality through the dolphin's mouth, while the large group of Venetian partiers continued on with their celebration.

"Hey there, Midnight," Charlie said to Frank's large, black cat with electric green eyes, "it's good to see you."

"So good to see you again as well, Charlie," Midnight replied. "I hear we'll be traveling together?"

"Traveling together?" Charlie questioned.

"Yes, to find the watchmaker."

"You mean you're coming with us?"

"Most certainly."

"Hey, Michael, did you hear that," Charlie shouted to his brother, who was admiring all the artwork on Frank's desk.

Excited to hear the news, Michael turned and quickly replied, "No way, you're coming with us?"

"Yes sir. Fortunately it looks like you'll be stuck with me during your journey to find the watchmaker," Midnight replied.

Frank broke away from the conversation he was having with Ben on the other side of the apartment and walked over to the boys. "That's right, Midnight is going to assist the two of you and Ben with your journey."

"Wait, what about you, Frank?" Charlie asked. "Aren't you coming with us?"

"Unfortunately no. I have to attend a meeting with the Parton Council later today regarding whoever, or whatever, may have tried to destroy the watch."

"But Frank—"

"No buts, Charlie, this is serious. We need to get to the bottom of it. Shadow villains are nothing to sneeze at."

"But—"

"It's for your own safety," Frank replied with a concerned look. "And the safety of all others who are involved as well—including Michael *and* your parents."

"Our parents?" Charlie questioned.

"Now that the Thorns are aware who your parents are, there is always a chance they may try to use them as leverage against you. In other words, hold them hostage to get what they want—such as the watch."

Charlie's demeanor became very placid. "I understand now."

"But no need to worry," Frank replied in an upbeat manner, "with Ben and Midnight at your side, I'm VERY confident you will succeed in finding the watchmaker."

"Absolutely, why Midnight and I are two of the best trackers in all of WONDER."

"I'd have to agree," Frank added. "With these two on your team, finding Raphael should be like a walk in the park."

"Raphael? Who is Raphael?" Michael asked.

"He is the watchmaker," Frank replied.

"I see," the boy replied.

"Very cool," Charlie added.

"OK, fellas, are we ready?" Frank asked, as he gave everyone in the room a look for confirmation.

"I was created ready," Midnight said in a jokingly smug tone.

"Ha! Indeed you were," Frank replied—being he was the one who dreamt up the cat to keep himself company in his apartment.

Everyone enjoyed a laugh, then put a hand or paw on Frank's magic lamp.

Then Frank recited the words, "Light so bright and grand, take us to the watchmaker's land."

The light from the charm around his neck grew large and bright, encompassing the circle of friends. Spark trails raced around its parameter, faster and faster, until its core burst into a brilliant array of light. SHWOOP, they were gone.

The animated countryside was filled with rolling hills, covered with trees and lush grass—all set before enormous snow-capped mountains. Everything, highlighted by a brilliant blue sky with only a whiff of cloud. The birds chirped in unison with the clear stream, which rushed over countless century old stones as it traveled down the mountainside and through the flower covered valley below.

Charlie, Michael, Ben, Midnight and Frank were now, animated as well—resembling their real selves, but in a stylized, cartoon-like way.

"Welcome back to Deep WONDER," Frank said. "Your search for the watchmaker begins here. There is a trail leading through the woods just over that hill," he said while pointing. "It will get you headed in the right direction."

"Huh? Oh, I'm sorry Frank, it's just I'm always amazed at what we look like when we turn into animated figures. I mean, look at my hands—my fingers are so plump and fat compared to normal. What were you saying, again?"

Frank let out a chuckle. "That's quite alright, Charlie. I was just saying, there's a trail leading through the woods just over that hill." He pointed again. "That will get you headed in the right direction."

"OK, that's all we need to know? You're sure?"

"Pretty much, well, yes," Frank replied. "Just follow the trail and trust your instincts, which from what I can gather, are very good."

"Really, that's it?" Michael snipped. "Two kids, a little round guy and a fluffy cat are supposed to wander their way through a strange land and find somebody they've never even met before?"

"Whoa-whoa-whoa, lad," Ben said. "There's no way I'm round. I'm more like, oval shaped."

"Oh you silly little man," Midnight replied. "Michael, I think what Ben was going to eventually say is, you are in *very* good hands, or paws, and have absolutely nothing to worry about."

"Well, alright. I guess?" Michael said with little confidence.

"It's all about trust, Michael," Charlie said.

"Precisely," Frank added, with a humble smile. "It's time for me to go. Take care of the boys, will ya, fellas."

"Indeed we will," Ben replied.

"You can *count* on us," Midnight added.

Frank nodded, and touched the light charm. "I'll see you real soon." There was a flash of light and he was gone.

Little did they know, that just over the hillside, beyond the edge of the woods, danger was lurking.

Chapter Nine

Far beyond the reaches of light, a meeting of evil intentions was taking place. It was hidden in a dark place—a shadow, which to the knowledge of the Patrons, did not exist, and was sure to remain a secret from all believers of good intentions. Populated by a densely wooded forest made of twisted trees with partially rotten trunks, moss-covered rocks and leaf-covered terrain, it was a dark and foreboding place— lying somewhere in WONDER between the simulated realms of the Magic Kingdom and Epcot. It was here, in a secret cave buried deep under an enormous old oak tree, that the Dark Thorns arrived one-by-one, so they could devise a plan for taking the magic watch.

First to arrive, via a giant purple ball of flames, was Dark Thorn Oltar, ruler of Hollywood Studios.

Next was Dark Thorn Kunn, mighty master of Animal Kingdom, who burst onto the scene through a bolt of lightning.

Immediately following Kunn, Dark Thorn Tanion, overseer of Disney Springs, arrived as a stormy-blue cloud of smoke which swirled in, then all at once, broke up—revealing its creator.

Next to arrive was the evil leader of Epcot, Senkrad, who flew in as a vulture, then transformed into his his recognizable self.

Last to arrive, but most certainly not the least powerful of the Dark Thorns, was Elontra, supreme ruler of the Magic Kingdom. Twisting like a mini tornado, she came storming into the cave before coming to an abrupt, and thunderous halt.

All five leaders of darkness took their respective seats in chairs made of twisted wood, forming a circle in a cathedral-like area of the cave.

Being the only female in the room, and the natural center of attention with her long, flowing white hair, Elontra took control of the meeting. She grabbed everyone's attention with her wickedly charismatic personality. "Of course, we all know why we are here. It appears, our little guest with the watch has transported into the watchmaker's realm. Is this true, Senkrad?"

"Very much so. In fact, my captain and two of his best spies have followed them in. I am expecting an update at any time. But if someone deems it necessary to check on them, let's just say, it would not offend me."

"I would be more than glad to do so, replied Dark Thorn Tanion."

"Be my guest," Senkrad said.

"Very well, let us take a peek, shall we," Dark Tanion replied. He stood up from his chair, turned to the green flame torch on the wall, and pulled from it a stream of flames that spiraled into the center where the Dark Thorns were seated. As the stream of flames gathered in the circle and continued to swirl, they formed an egg-like shape which crystalized and revealed images of what appeared to be Charlie, Michael, Ben and Midnight, walking over a grass-covered hill towards the woods.

"There's our little friends," Elontra said with an evil smile.

"It looks like they are headed into the woods," Oltar added. "Tanion, you know this realm well, yes?"

"But of course," he replied.

"So answer this question. Where might they be headed?"

"There is a path through the woods which splits into three. One leads to a lake, one to a small village, and one to the mountains beyond."

"So there are three possibilities. Two of which, most likely, would lead to the watchmaker," Elontra replied.

"Only one if we head them off before they get to the split in the path," Kunn added. "I could summon up a congress of baboonagins to attack from the trees above, and have the outsider and his friends brought back to us for interrogation?"

"But the Object of Magic would not yet be repaired," Senkrad replied. "I have already come to the conclusion that it would be most wise if we let them find the watchmaker first, so he can fix the watch BEFORE we take it from them."

"Senkrad makes a good point," Elontra said.

"But if we attack before they reach the divide in the woods, why can we not just fix the watch ourselves with dark magic?" Kunn replied.

"The Watch of WONDER is protected by its own magic. Only the watchmaker has the ability to right its undoing," Senkrad said.

"Yes, I see where that may be true. But if a shadow villain was able to strike it down with lightning, should they not be able to reverse the damage as well?" Kunn asked.

"From what the Shadow Queen has told me, the answer is no," Elontra said. "The power to destroy it and the power to fix it are two different forms of magic. Neither of which, can be possessed by the same being, whether they are from reality, or a creation of WONDER. Therefore, it will be in our best interest to heed Senkrad's words, and allow them to get the watch fixed *before* we take it away."

"And what do we do until that time arrives?" Oltar asked.

"We devise a plan to take the watch," Senkrad replied.

"Yeeeees, I see one beginning to form. A plan involving a few of our favorite, *creations*?" Elontra added.

"We can use them to collect the watch," Kunn said with a devilish grin.

"A most delightful plan," Tanion added.

"And I'm sure they will have fun in doing so," Oltar said.

"Then it is settled," Senkrad said. "We will call on the shadow villains most familiar with this realm."

"Perfect," Elontra said with a cackle.

Fibs, now fully animated, along with Duke and Grim, looked quite different from how they appeared in reality. The captain was still short and round, though now he appeared twice as wide, including his head, with legs as thick as an elephant, arms not much smaller, and enormously large feet—all bearing down on a pair of double-wide flip flops. His partially bald head was still sun burnt, though his sunglasses were extraordinarily large and sat cockeyed upon the bridge of his sweaty nose.

Duke and Grim no longer fit into the clean-cut Disney crowd. In the animated world their clothes were torn, dirty and weathered, their hair uncombed, and their partially toothed grins—framed by unshaven faces.

Fibs and his men had arrived slightly ahead of the Patrons—who had stopped by Frank's apartment to pick up Midnight before starting their journey. The three-Thorns had been waiting patiently, just beyond the old wood's edge, for the Patrons to arrive. And now it was time to carry out their duties.

"That's right Senkrad," Captain Fibs said into his Thorn wristband.

Not only were the wristbands used for transportation, but also as transmitters for speaking to Dark Thorns. Cell phones and other real world devices were of no use in WONDER.

"The boy and his Patron pals are well on their way to where the pathway splits in the woods," Fibs added.

"You are doing a fine job, Captain," Senkrad replied.

"Thank you sir, I mean, supreme leader. So what do you want us to do when they get to the split in the pathway?"

"Just keep following them as we discussed before. Remember, all you need to do for now is keep an eye on them until they find the watchmaker and get the watch fixed. After that, I will provide more information. Understood, Fibs?"

"Yes sir."

"Good. Until then, just keep track of where they go. And if possible, find out what their intentions are once they get the watch fixed. But, let me be perfectly clear. And this is *extremely* important. DO NOT give yourselves away. When it's time for us to move in and take the watch, it needs to come as a total surprise. Otherwise we may lose our best opportunity to gain control of the magic watch. Is that clear"

"Perfectly, Senkrad," Fibs replied—while nervously looking at his men.

"Very well, back at it then." The Dark Thorn leader disconnected.

"I guess that's it for now boys," Fibs said, as he closed the top of his wrist band device. "We just need to lay low and keep an eye on 'em until the watch is fixed."

"Aye-aye, Captain. That we can do, right Grimsly?"

"Right you are, Duke."

"Oh, and one more thing, fellas. If we get a chance to listen in on their conversations, we need to find out what plans the Patrons might have in store once the watch is fixed."

"That sounds easy enough," Duke replied with a chuckle.

"But, here's the kicker boys, we can't let them know we're doing it. Otherwise, the Dark Thorns ain't gonna be too happy with us."

"Now that might be a little more challenging," Grim said.

"Right," Duke added. "But I'd say we're up for it, don't you agree, Captain?"

Fibs lowered his head, peering over his sun glasses at Duke and Grim. "You best hope we are boys, for our sake."

The five Dark Thorns had summoned three diabolical shadow villains from deep within the darkest depths of the watchmaker's realm. All of which, possessed skills for the task at hand, and had worked within this realm before. A place inspired by the conceptual artwork for the animated movie, Pinocchio. A realm, which through the years, had taken on many changes.

First to arrive was the incredibly sneaky, silver fox—a real silver-tongued swindler, who was very sharp in the mind and could talk anyone into anything with his hypnotic eyes and conniving ways. One dared not look at, or listen to, him if he engaged you in conversation. His hairy physique of silvery grey, was dressed in a shabby, dark brown beggar's suite, and his eyes of yellow could pierce one's soul—making him ten times harder to say no to and much more dangerous than any normal swindler. And though he could walk on all fours, he preferred to only use his hind legs—claiming his left front paw was lame.

Second to show was the coachman, Mr. Jollysnaps. As he landed his flying, mule-drawn coach of gold, which was covered with emeralds, rubies and diamonds, it was clearly obvious he was quite different from any coachman that had ever been seen before. A tall, well-dressed, stick-like fellow with long, blond hair and a big white grin, the commander of the flying mules was known for much more than just his transportation services to the FOTO army in WONDER. Upon his head sat a tall, gold top hat with a white feather. And held in his right hand was a golden rod with a magical whip attached at its end that could extend outward—snapping its victims, which released a burst of silver and gold sparks. Unfortunately, the victims were usually the winged mules, who when struck, would fly faster at the command of the evil, jolly man with the bright, shiny whip. As wheel man and maker of money, he provided expedited services which not only turned naughty boys into working mules for cash, but girls as well. At the end of the third pathway, just beyond the woods, was a lake. And on the far side of the lake sat Mr. Jollysnap's island, known to those in WONDER as Mischief Island, where his mine of golden statues was hidden away. It is believed all his statues were at one time naughty children who had instantly been turned to gold by a single crack of his magical whip if they had not changed into working mules after spending time on the island. Either way, Mr. Jollysnaps was sure to profit.

Flamario was last to arrive. Originally known throughout WONDER as the Fire Breather, his sketch lines were similar in style to those used for the character Stramboli in Pinocchio, only Flamario was a much larger, and mightier, man. The ground and trees shook, knocking birds, squirrels and raccoons from their living quarters, and flushing rabbits, deer, and other woodland creatures out of their hiding places, as he stomped through the woods to meet up with his villainous counterparts. It was clear to see how the very presences of this colossal man brought fear to all those who looked upon him. He was easily twice the size of any normal man. Standing nearly twelve feet tall, with shoulders as broad as a car, arms like totem pulls, hands the size of beachballs, and legs the size of tree trunks, Flamario was a force almost unmatched in size and ferocity. He was an easy choice for the Shadow Queen, a natural fit for the FOTO army, and a one-man wrecking crew for Dark Thorn tasks such as this. The frazzled black hair upon his head was curly and wild. His long pointed beard reached well past his knees and acted as a focal point for the true power this beast of a villain possessed. One never before realized throughout the history of shadow villains, until that is, this large mountain of a man was reimagined by the Shadow Queen and given the power to breath fire like a dragon. A talent the leader of FOTO saw fit for a man who originally went by the name of Fire Breather. All that was needed was the source of a flame, such as a torch, a fireplace or a campfire, and his enemies stood little chance to survive. Flamario's only limitation, he could not transport into reality.

Standing in a clearing of the woods stood five ghost-like images of Dark Thorn leaders: Elontra, Senkrad, Oltar, Tanion and Kunn. Ready to address the three shadow villains.

"Welcome faithful friends," Senkrad said. "By orders of the Shadow Queen, we have called upon the three of you for a single purpose. To seek out, and TAKE, the Watch of WONDER."

"This is what you are to look for," Elontra said, as a fiery sphere of blue rose up from her boney, cupped hands, revealing a holographic image of the watch. "At this very moment it is on route through the woods to be delivered by a young boy, his brother and friends to the watchmaker."

"All we have to do is find the boy, take the watch, and deliver it to you?" the silver fox asked. "Doesn't seem like much of a challenge."

"I don't mean any disrespect, but are you sure you need our help for such a simple task?" Mr. Jollysnaps added.

"DO NOT underestimate the task we have set before you," Oltar replied. "This is who you are to find." He expanded his hands to form a miniature cloud which displayed a live image of Charlie, Michael, Ben and Midnight walking through a field.

Flamario bent down and squinted, as he stroked his beard—sizing up his enemies in the magic cloud. "Why, I could take this watch you speak of, crush the puny little boy, and throw all his friends up into the trees with one hand tied behind my back," he said with a big thunderous voice, followed by laughter.

"If it were merely that simple do you really think we would ask for help? Hmm?" Senkrad said in a sarcastic tone.

"Well, I suppose not," Jollysnaps replied.

"Then where does the challenge lie?" the silver fox asked. "Obviously there is more to it than meets the eye."

"To begin with, you cannot take the watch until *after* the watchmaker has fixed it, and explained to the boy how to use it," Elontra said.

"And why is that?" asked the fox.

"Because it is broken and needs to be fixed before it is of any use to us," Elontra replied.

"Isn't there anyone you know who we can pay to fix it? Say, someone we can pay in gold?" Mr. Jollysnaps asked.

"Nice try, but no," Elontra replied. "Only the watchmaker has the ability to return the Watch of WONDER to its original state—before it was struck by lightning."

"What? Was someone wearing the watch out in a thunderstorm?" the fox asked.

"You will learn more about that at a later time," Senkrad said with a stern look—ending the topic of discussion immediately. Even the shadow villains, as powerful as they were, dared not tangle with a Dark Thorn, let alone, all five at one time.

"But for now," Elontra said, "all you need to do is follow them to the watchmaker's dwelling."

"And once you are there, wait for the watch to be fixed, and for the watchman to explain how it works," Kunn added.

"And once's that is done?" Mr. Jollysnaps asked.

"TAKE IT," Elontra replied with a devilish grin.

"We look forward to seeing you soon," Oltar said, "you may go now."

"Contact us once have the watch," Senkrad added.

The holographic image of the Dark Thorns vanished, leaving the three villains alone to stare at each other.

Back in the cave where the Dark Thorns had gathered, one last detail was being discussed before they disbanded.

"Do you think we should have told them about Captain Fibs and his flunky crew?" Oltar asked.

"No," Elontra replied. If anything, it will give them time to *share* a special bonding moment together."

The five Dark Thorns enjoyed a private moment of diabolical laughter, which echoed through the dimly lit cave, buried deep in a shadow of WONDER.

Chapter Ten

Dreams are like subconscious acts of creativity and emotion, occurring while we're sleeping. Where ideas, or concepts, are more akin to intentional thoughts of the conscious mind. When the two are combined together, they can produce extraordinary things. Which was exactly what the Imagineers had in mind when they created WONDER—the World of Natural Dream Enhanced Realities. Realities shaped by dreams and ideas. A world where real people could experience and explore boundless imagination created by Imagineers and animators of past and present day. Where all the good Disney instills upon the world could be protected from darkness, and preserved forever within its magical realms.

In one such realm, Charlie, Michael and their loyal Patron friends, Ben and Midnight, had just begun an incredible journey.

Though they had visited Deep WONDER before, this was the first time Charlie and Michael had entered a fully developed realm. There were forests, rolling meadows, villages, snow-capped mountains, streams, lakes and animals. A place where no boundaries or end existed. And all of it was animated.

As the four brave explorers made their way over and through the grassy, rolling hills, the boys noticed many unusual, and quite extraordinary, things. The first of which, was a grey field mouse that crossed their path. His body was small and plump, with a long, skinny tail that trailed behind and curled somewhat when he paused to stand on his large hind feet. His enormously large blue eyes looked like two giant saucers of kindness, as they took in the four strangers. Indeed, this was no ordinary mouse.

"Oh, hello there," the mouse said with an English accent.

"Uh, hello," Ben replied with a smile.

"Going somewhere, are we?" The mouse asked politely.

"Yes, indeed we are. We're uh, on our way to find the watchmaker," Ben answered.

"Really, the watchmaker, eh? I can't say I've ever met him."

"He's a plump old fella with grey hair, crooked glasses and a big nose who likes to make watches, toys and things out of wood," Midnight added, attempting to jog the mouses memory.

The mouse squinted and scratched his head, trying to remember. "No, nope. Sorry, can't say that I ever recall meeting a fella like that."

"That's OK," Charlie replied. "So, do you have a name?"

"They call me—"

"SREEEEECH, SCREEEEECH!"

"What was that?" Michael said with a startled voice.

"It's a hawk and he's looking for an afternoon snack," the mouse replied. He quickly ducked into the shadow of Charlie's legs to hide from the threat above.

"Don't worry little fella, I won't let him get you," Charlie said. He looked up at the hawk, then down at the frightened little mouse—who was now doubly scared, seeing a cat was in his presence as well.

"What, what about him," the mouse said, pointing at Midnight with his shaky little paw.

"Oh him," Ben said, "he only eats prepared food, like spaghetti, tacos and macaroni and cheese. You don't have to worry about him."

Midnight shook his head and rolled his eyes.

"Looks like the hawk is gone," Michael said. "You can stop hiding now, little guy."

"Oh, thank you young man." The mouse slowly came out from underneath Charlie's shadow, continuing to look towards the sky.

"I don't believe we've introduced ourselves yet. My name is Ben, Ben Glimmer" the happy Irishman said. He extended a pinky finger to shake the mouses tiny little paw.

"Around here they call me Provo, cause, well, you know, I like cheese. Especially provolone cheese."

"It's nice to meet you, Provo," My name is Charlie, and this is my kid brother, Michael."

"Hello," Michael said with nod.

"Nice to meet you, boys," Provo replied.

"So glad to meet you Provo, I am Midnight—and yes, as Ben here already said, if there were ever a cat you could trust, it most certainly would be me."

"Well, heh-heh, that's good to know," the mouse nervously replied. "It's uh, nice meeting you as well."

"Oh, why don't you just tell him how you *really* feel," a young feminine voice called out from just beyond the tall grass.

"Who's there?" Ben asked, trying to identify the source of the voice. But all he could see was an old, grass-covered log, and a tiny gathering of yellow flowers.

"Why don't you leave me alone," Provo replied. "You are always trying to tell everyone what to do."

"At least people know where I stand when I speak to them," the voice snipped back.

"Yeah, well I'm not the one who's too afraid to show their face to strangers," the mouse said with a frustrated expression.

"Oh, alright. Have it your way," the mysterious voice rambled on in mumbling fashion. "You're always making me have to get up and move, after I just settled in to a nice, comfy spot and all."

Unexpectedly, and to the amazement of all four travelers, the log in the grass moved on its own—rocking back and forth as two appendages grew out from its mid section to form arms with three-fingered hands. Then two longer appendages grew out from its bottom end to form legs and feet. As the log rolled over and sat up, a youthful face was revealed, with two horizontal slits for eyes, robust cheeks, one oddly shaped hole for a mouth, and a knot for a nose, that twitched back and forth to shake off a spot of moss. A long shaggy lump of grass swayed back and forth atop the logs head as it shook itself off to remove all loose dirt and debris.

"What in the world is that?" Michael spat out.

"That? I am much more than a THAT," the log replied, glaring at Michael."

"Now-now, take it easy, he doesn't know any better," the mouse said, attempting to minimize the friction between the young boy and the log.

"Is it possible you have never seen a magic log before?" she asked Michael in a firm tone.

"Well, noo...not exactly," he replied.

"But we did see an entire tree come to life in the Frontierland Shootin' Arcade last year. That was pretty neat," Charlie said, trying to make light of the situation.

"It just so happens that this *beautiful, little* log was cut from the same enchanted forest as Pinocchio by an old carpenter named Mr. Raspberry. "But unfortunately, she was never transformed by a master craftsman into a whimsical marionette, like Pinocchio when he was just a raw piece of wood. Instead, she remained an ordinary log. However, Sassyfran was *never* just and ordinary piece of wood. After patiently waiting for over ten long years at the bottom of Mr. Raspberry's log pile, she finally decided to get up and walk as far away as her legs could carry her. Eventually, her tired body fell to the ground in the rolling meadow of grass you see before you, where she has remained until this very day."

"So your name is Sassyfran?" Charlie asked.

"Oh, come now, Provo, I am *sure* they don't want to hear my life's story," she replied with a kind smile. "Yes, I am Sassyfran, the wood maiden. But you can just call me Sassyfran, like everyone else around here. So what, may I ask, are the four of you doing here?"

"We're here to find the watchmaker," Ben replied.

"The watchmaker is a very nice man. Usually keeps to himself, merrily working away in his shop."

"So you know him? Do you know where he lives?" Charlie asked.

"Not exactly," Sassyfran replied, but I can get you headed in the right direction.

"You never told ME you met the watchmaker before," Provo interrupted.

"Would you be so kind as to tell us what direction that is?" Midnight asked.

"You never asked," she snipped back at the mouse. Then she calmly addressed Midnight's question. "Of course I will. You follow this path through the woods until you come to a divide, then you—"

Provo interrupted again. "It may be easier for you to just show them, then tell them. Don't you agree?"

"Yes, I think you may be right," Sassyfran replied, looking towards the woods.

"Fine with us," Ben replied. "I mean, we could use all the help we can get. Don't you agree, Midnight?"

"The more minds the better, as far as I'm concerned," the black cat confirmed with a large feline grin.

"So they're coming with us?" Charlie asked.

"And the mouse too?" Michael added.

"Why yes, lad," Ben said. "Oh, I'm sorry. I didn't mean to assume."

"Not to worry. It would be our pleasure to take you to the watch-maker," Sassyfran said.

"Brilliant. Very well then, if you wouldn't mind, miss wood maiden," Ben said, motioning for her to lead the way.

"All right then, c'mon Provo, climb aboard."

The small grey mouse with large blue eyes climbed to the top of Sassyfran's grass-covered head, and nested—happy to have been invited.

"All set and ready," the mouse confirmed.

"Very well, let us be on our way. Follow me gentleman," the wood maiden shouted out.

With Sassyfran confidently leading the way, the small band of explorers marched off towards, and into, the woods, singing out in wondrous harmony to a made up song with the most playful words imaginable.

An hour or two had passed, though it was really difficult to keep track of time in WONDER. Charlie and company were now well into their journey, deep within the forest. The trees and all the surrounding foliage was lush and green. It's inhabitants, such as rabbits, squirrels, deer, turtles and blue birds frolicked and played, as they followed along from a safe distance. A winding stream intersected the path they had chosen, and at each point, a small stone bridge allowed them to safely cross over and observe schools of brightly colored fish and playful frogs. The water ran over smooth, weathered stones, and around winding banks. Highlighted by rays of sunshine peaking through the trees, ripples in the water danced rhythmically to the flow of the stream.

It was a serene environment, relaxing Charlie's mind to a point where he almost forgot why they were there.

They continued to move along. The sunshine that had shown brightly through the trees for most of the day, was now lower, creating a soft, warm glow. At that moment, Charlie and the others reached a fork in the path. There were three choices. The path to the left led towards the mountains. The one to the right, towards a lake. And the path in the center, led towards a small village. All were clearly marked by elaborate, wood-carved signs.

"So are we heading to the village?" Michael asked confidently. He thought for sure he knew the answer to his own question. In fact, he was absolutely positive that Raphael the watchmaker, lived in a workshop located in a tiny village.

"Under normal circumstances you would be correct," Sassyfran replied.

"Remember, Michael, the craftsman we are looking for is quite different from any you may be familiar with in reality," Ben said.

"*Including* where he lives," Midnight added.

"Your friends are right, Michael, we are actually headed towards the mountains. The watchmaker moved out of his village workshop long ago to keep any potential evil away from his friends," Sassyfran said.

"I, I don't understand, why would anyone evil be interested in a woodworker who makes cuckoo clocks, nutcrackers and other harmless things?" Charlie asked.

"Because dear, he's the *watchmaker*. The one who created the watch you carry in your pocket," Sassyfran replied.

"Which also means he is the only one who can fix it," Ben added.

Midnight continued the conversation. "As a result, he was marked as a threat to *all* members of FOTO, including the Dark Thorns and their Shadow Queen."

"When Raphael caught word of this, he chose to move away from his beloved village and the people who lived there, to a place beyond the mountains. There, no one he cared for would ever be put in harm's way," Sassyfran said, with sadness in her wooden heart.

"Oh, come now, he's not THAT bad off, is he?" a small, yet deep voice said.

"Who's there?" Charlie asked, not knowing where to look.

"Up here, on top of the sign."

Charlie looked upward towards the road sign for the lake.

"Not that sign," the mysterious voice said, "the village sign, over here."

As the young boy gazed upward a small creature came into view. It was a little, planetary purple frog with large, lime-green eyes and lime-green finger tips and toes. He stood upright and carried himself like a human—walking on his hind legs only. He was wearing a tiny leather pilot's cap and goggles, with a yellow scarf wrapped around his neck. And growing out of his back was a set of dragonfly wings.

"Is that you that's doing all the talking?" Charlie asked.

"Indeed it is," the frog replied.

The young boy rubbed his forehead and thought for a second.

Everyone else except Michael stood in amusement. They had met the tiny amphibious creature before, and knew his overly confident personality well.

"I suppose you're going to tell us how to find the watchmaker, little frog?" Charlie asked.

"I guess you could say that."

"So what brings you here today, Featherwink?" Ben asked.

"Funny, I was just about to ask you the same thing."

"You don't say," Ben replied. "Well, we're on our way to see Raphael."

"And why would you need to do that?" the frog asked.

"We have a watch that needs fixing."

"A watch, you say?" The frog squinted and gave Ben a curious look. "You wouldn't be talking about the Watch of WONDER would ya?"

"Maybe."

"Rumor has it there are two young boys, paired up with a couple of Patrons, who are searching for the watchmaker."

"Oh really now," Ben replied—acting as if he didn't know.

"I also heard there might be a bit of trouble following close behind."

"Trouble you say? What kind of trouble?"

"The kind that might get you and your friends into all sorts of bad situations."

"Is that right?" Ben replied—refusing to give up any information to the frog.

"Shhhh, watch this Ben," Midnight whispered. "Gentleman, please, there is no need to fight. "Yes, it is true, our young friend here, Charlie, is carrying the Watch of WONDER. So, speak your mind, Featherwink, and we'll be on our way to find Raphael."

"Heed my warning, Mr. Cat, there is trouble brewing, and it's headed right for you. Big trouble—the kind that you never come back from. If I were you, I would think twice about continuing your search," the frog said in a serious tone.

"If you know such things, why don't you come with us?" Sassyfran asked.

"Why yes. If you know where the trouble is, maybe *you* can come along to help us avoid it. Then we can find the watchmaker even faster," the mouse added.

"That's a brilliant idea," Charlie added.

"Well, if you knuckle brains aren't going to take my advice and turn back, then I'm afraid I'll just have to come along to *try* and keep you out of trouble," Featherwink said begrudgingly.

"See, I told you it would work," Midnight mumbled to Ben.

"What, what you mean by *work*? You guys are trying to twist around everything I'm saying," the frog said.

"Really, it was nothing," Midnight replied with a giggle.

"Yeah, it was nothing at all Featherwink," Ben replied, giggling too.

"And what's so funny? I don't see anything *funny* going on here."

"No, you're right Featherwink, nothing funny going on here," Ben replied, rolling his eyes.

"Fine," the frog snipped. "You, the young man with the watch. Come over here and crouch down so I can hop onto your shoulder."

Charlie walked up to the frog, who's eyes were still red from frustration. "I know your name, but you still do not know mine. I think it best we formally introduce ourselves to one another before you jump aboard," the boy suggested.

"Right, good point young man. They call me Featherwink." The frog stood up, looked the young boy in the eye, and extended his webbed hand out to shake.

"Hello, Featherwink, I'm Charlie." The boy crouched down and extended a finger to shake the frog's hand. "There, that's better."

The frog hopped aboard and made himself comfortable on the boy's shoulder.

"So which direction are we headed again, Miss Sassyfran?" Charlie asked.

"Miss Sassyfran?" The frog interrupted, feeling offended. "I'm the one who is leading the way here. You DO want to avoid the trouble I was telling you about, don't you?"

"Charlie looked at Sassyfran with a smirk and replied, "Right, I'm so sorry, Featherwink. How silly of me to forget. Which way do we need to go, uh, Mr. Frog?" the young boy asked. Though he already knew the answer.

"Towards the mountains," Featherwink replied.

Even though Featherwink had been upset, his words carried with them a truthful wisdom. Lurking close behind was trouble of the worst kind.

Captain Fibs, Grim and Duke, were coming up on the fork in the pathway, where just minutes ago, Charlie, Michael and their friends had run into Featherwink.

"Look Captain, fresh tracks," Duke said, pointing towards the fork in the path.

"I'd say our friends are headed towards the mountains, eh boys," Fibs replied.

"I can almost smell 'em," Grim added, tilting his head back to sniff the air.

"Good, that means they're close," Fibs said. "Remember boys, we stay out of sight until the watch gets fixed."

"Right, Captain," Grim replied.

The three men continued on down the pathway.

High above the forest of the watchmaker's realm, traveling through the sky like Santa in his reindeer powered sleigh, were the three shadow villains in a sparkling gold coach pulled by flying mules. Mr. Jollysnaps sat above, guiding his drove of mules, while Flamario and the fox sat facing each other in the comforts of the coach below. They were discussing their plan to capture the watch when the moment presented itself.

"I say you sneak in, grab the watch, then jump into the coach while I burn down the watchmaker's workshop," Flamario said in a loud, confident tone. "That will teach him to stay away from dangerous things like an Object of Magic. And the little boys would be so scared, they will run off to their mommy and never want to help the Patrons again."

The silver fox rolled his yellow eyes. He saw Flamario's proposal as amateurish and immature. "My dear friend, and a very large friend you are indeed, to acquire something as valuable as an Object of Magic requires much more planning and sophistication. Not to mention, a strategy which will allow us to extract more than just a *physical object*."

Flamario's face turned red at the response of the silver-tongued fox. He was already frustrated from how cramped he felt in the coach, on account of his enormous size. And being insulted by a tiny little fox did nothing but worsen his emotional state. "If you are *so smart* little fox, what would you do to make a perfect plan, such as mine, better?"

"My dear friend, if you think this heist is *only* about the watch, then you are sadly mistaken," the fox replied.

Jolly began listening from above.

"Go on, explain this philosophy of yours little fox," Flamario replied.

"You see, the Dark Thorns want the watch, which for obvious reasons, we all understand. But if you were to step back and take a careful look at the overall scheme of things, the Watch of WONDER is just a small piece of the puzzle, that will lead to bigger and better things. And in order for the Dark Thorns to execute the Shadow Queen's wishes, they will not only need the Objects of Magic, but knowledge as well."

"What do you mean by this knowledge? Flamario asked."

"He means that having the watch, in and of itself, is not enough for the Dark Thorns to accomplish what they have set out to do," the coachman said from above. "They will need to know how to use it, when to use it, and where to use it as well."

"Precisely," the fox added. "And that is why we need to let the watchmaker tell the boy how to use it, before we take it."

"I don't recall those words. And why is this 'how, when and where' so important you speak of?" Flamario demanded in a loud, thunderous tone. Clearly, he was outmatched by the fox and coachman when it came to brain power.

"You see, my big friend, I heard through the grapevine that there is *much* more to the Watch of WONDER than what the Dark Thorns have told us. You might say," the fox added, "telling time is *not* what the watch does at all."

"Really?" Flamario said, as he began to calm down and listen.

"You are quite right, Mr. Fox," Jolly added, "I heard a few things myself. It is so much more than a watch."

"Yes, and therefore," the fox continued, "learning how to use the watch to its fullest potential could take weeks, months—even years."

"Well, the little boy only has eight days to figure it out," the ginormous man replied.

"Even less than that, if you take into account the fact that the watchman has to fix it before the boy can use it," Mr. Jollysnaps said.

"Right you are," the fox replied, "I am sure the watchman and his Patron friends will be giving the young lad a crash course on *how* to use it, *where* to use it—and just as important, *when* to use it."

"I understand the 'how', but please explain to me further the 'where' and 'when' you speak of," Flamario spat out.

"Of course. The importance of each Object of Magic lies within its ability to guide its user to one of the sacred Kingdom Crystals. There are five in all. Not only that—and this is key, it gives the one who wields its power the ability to ACQUIRE the crystal."

"So, a big strong man like me could not walk up and take it?" Flamario asked, pounding his chest with his fist.

The fox rolled his eyes and lowered his head. "No my friend, there's a little more to it than that. Each crystal is hidden and protected by Patron magic. Only a chosen outsider who possesses an Object of Magic can find AND acquire a Kingdom Crystal. Even someone of your size and strength could not remove a crystal from where it rests."

"And why not?"

"Because, big fellow, like I told you, only a chosen outsider can harness the power of an Object of Magic. And you my friend, are not a chosen outsider."

"This boy who carries the watch, he is a chosen outsider?"

"Exactly."

"So why are we going to take the watch if only the chosen outsider can use it? The Dark Thorns did not tell us to bring the boy *and* the watch back?"

"Yes, why aren't we bringing the boy along?" Jolly asked.

"Good question," the fox replied, rubbing his chin in thought. "I don't really know. The Dark Thorns never miss a thing, so I'm sure they have a reason."

"I bet you're right, mate," Mr. Jollysnaps added.

"Oh, and there is one more detail I forgot to mention."

"Well, spit it out my little genius," Flamario said with a big devilish smile.

Not only are the Kingdom Crystals hidden, the locations in which they are hidden magically change from time to time as well."

"Ahhhh, and now I see the importance of the where and when," Flamario said.

"Precisely my friend. Precisely indeed," the fox said with a sly smile.

The golden coach continued on across the sky.

Daylight had all but disappeared. The animated ban of Patrons were exhausted from their long journey through the woods and over the snow-capped mountains. Far below, and now well behind them, sat the tiny little village where Raphael had once lived. As they passed over the mountain top, the sun glowed softly in hues of orange and purple on the horizon of an unfamiliar, grass-filled valley below. No sign of where Raphael may live, could be seen. Everyone took a minute to catch their breaths, as Midnight's curiosity got the best of him.

"Do you see anything?" the cat asked Ben, who was bent over catching his breath.

"See . . . what . . . you . . . silly cat?" Ben replied—his words broken by several deep breaths.

"Anything that looks remotely like Raphael's workshop."

Ben stared intently towards the valley below, as he tried to discover what his friend could not. "No sir, I don't see a bloomin' thing."

Frustrated by Ben's words, Midnight turned to a set of younger eyes, hoping his luck may change. "Michael, scan the valley below and tell me if you see anything, would you please."

Michael stared towards the valley, scratching his head. "Uhhh, nnnnope, I, I don't see anything either."

"Ha! You see, you furry feline. Our young lad here can't see any better than me," Ben proudly proclaimed.

"Well of course he can't," Featherwink said, standing on Charlie's shoulder.

"Oh really," Midnight snipped at Ben. "Do you really think you can see as well as our young friend, Michael?"

"Ho-ho, hold on fellas. Just because *you* can't see anything, doesn't mean there's nothing to be seen," Featherwink said.

"I beg your pardon little frog, but I'm quite sure you can't hide something out in plain site," Midnight said, pointing his furry paw towards the empty valley below.

"I am afraid I have to agree with the cat on this one," Provo squeaked out.

"As do I," Sassyfran added.

"If you just give me a second, I'll introduce you to somebody who can clear things up," the frog replied. He flew off Charlie's shoulder and onto a large rock—the perfect stage for a tiny frog. Standing on his hind legs, Featherwink began to sing out in frog language, creating a beautiful sound like no other. His body shimmered, emitting a soft, purple glow. The music echoed through the mountains, carrying upwards towards the snow-capped peaks.

"Look, what is that over there?" Charlie said, pointing towards the highest peak of the surrounding mountains.

"I see it too," Ben added.

A steady stream of sparkling snow swirled through the air, growing in size, as it moved closer towards Charlie and the others. Spiraling faster and faster, it formed a funnel-like mass, which emitted bright, radiant light from it's core. And then . . . the funnel dissipated, the light receded, and a beautiful winged fairy was revealed. Her translucent figure hovered effortlessly in the air as her white gown and long, curly, snow-frosted hair danced and flowed gently around her pristine figure. Her skin was a radiant crystal blue, and her eyes, a deeper shade of indigo blue—which sparkled as she looked upon those who stood before her. In her right hand, she held a wand made of clear crystal, tipped by a brilliant white light. From underneath her gown, flakes of snow gently fell, cascading through the air and evaporating before reaching the ground.

"When I was a wee lad, a wise, old Patron once told me a story about a snow fairy who dwelled among the mountains of the Watchmaker. But I thought he was making it up. I never knew she actually existed," Ben quietly whispered to Midnight.

"So, little man with the curly orange hair, you've heard of me before?" the fairy asked with a kind smile.

"Ye, yeah, yes," Ben stuttered—embarrassed that she had overheard what he had said.

"So, kind fairy, would you do the honor of telling us your name?" Midnight requested.

"I am Neve, snow fairy and silent protector of the watchmaker."

"See, I told you she was the snow fairy," Ben mumbled to Midnight.

"Yes. Well, I guess you were right, now weren't you?" Neve said with a tiny giggle.

The little red headed man blushed even more—being it was the second time he had been caught.

"Hello, Neve, it's me again. Featherwink. I hope I, I didn't bother you?"

"Of course not, Featherwink. It is always a pleasure to see you, my little friend." The frog and the snow fairy were close friends who had been introduced to each other many years ago by Frank—a good friend to both.

"We are trying to find our way to Raphael's workshop. Is there any chance you could point us in the right direction?" the frog asked.

"Well of course." Neve rose high into the sky, waved her magic wand, then recited:

Hidden in the land below, where trees, grass, and flowers grow.

Reveal to us so we shall see, a place where the watchmaker, is sure to be.

The tip of Neve's wand burst into a radiant ball of snowflakes. She cast her arm forward, sending an enormous cloud of snowflakes over the empty valley below. When the flakes reached a center point in the sky they exploded and shot in all directions, sparkling and tingling, like a giant firework. They quickly spread, covering the entire sky above the valley. Like a giant snow globe, the flakes peacefully floated downward.

To the amazement of Charlie and the others, the blanket of flakes did not reach the ground, but instead, began to reveal hidden shapes of buildings, roads, signs, wagons and other things. At first, everything was snow covered and no details were visible. But as the last flake came to rest, they quickly began to melt, revealing a quaint little village that did not exist seconds before. The cobble stone streets were populated by dozens of cute little houses, shops and things that were elaborately decorated with ornate patterns. Children frolicked and played as they ran about the village, with mothers following closely behind, making sure the little ones stayed out of harms way. A baker was standing out in front of his store, manning a table full of delicious goods he had worked hard to make, and was now trying to sell off before sundown. The blacksmith was pounding away on a new set of horse shoes for a lucky steed, which stood outside his barn. And a small group of jolly men stumbled out of the local tavern, joking and laughing as they made their way home for dinner. Behind it all, the low setting sun highlighted every nook and cranny—giving the village a warm, soft sense of peacefulness.

"Well I'll be," the mouse said, rubbing his eyes.

"I don't believe it," Ben added.

"That's quite a spell you cast," the cat said.

Charlie stood staring in silent amazement.

"So where? What? Huh? How, how is that even possible?" Michael stuttered.

"Yes, how *did* you do that? I've never seen anything quite like it before," Sassyfran said.

Neve giggled modestly. "It's really quite simple dear," she said to Michael. "That is, if you believe in the magic of fairies."

"Oh, there you go," Michael said in a sarcastic tone. I suppose next you're going to tell us that all you need is a little faith and trust?"

The fairy tilted her head in curiosity, as she looked at Michael.

"You know, 'faith, trust and pixie dust,' from the Peter Pan movie?" Michael said.

Neve giggled again. "Have you already forgotten where you are, Michael?" the snow fairy asked as she continued to hover in the air.

"In WONDER?" the young boy answered hesitantly.

"Exactly. And while you are in WONDER, don't you find it easy to believe that anything is possible? Including the ability to fly like Peter Pan?"

"I, uh, guess so?" Michael replied, as the others followed along with the conversation.

"Well then, let's see if we can make that happen, shall we?" The snow fairy waved her wand through the air—magic snow flakes shot out in every direction, gently falling upon the heads and shoulders of Charlie, Michael, and their friends. Instantly, they all began to rise up off the mountainous terrain. Their faces beamed with excitement, except for Midnight—who was having a most difficult time getting oriented in the air.

"Hold on tight, Provo," Sassyfran said to the furry little mouse nestled in her grassy head of hair."

"I'm not going anywhere," the mouse replied with a big grin.

"You too little fella," Charlie said to the frog, who he thought was on his shoulder. But to his surprise, Featherwink had already taken flight.

"How quickly you forget, young man," the frog replied, as he circled the boy repeatedly. "I too, have wings."

Charlie giggled with delight. "Oh, how did I ever forget. Sorry my friend."

The entire group was now aimlessly floating high above the mountainside—where they had been standing, mere seconds ago. The ban of merry friends had no idea what to do next.

"Is everyone ready?" Neve asked.

"Absolutely," Charlie said, with youthful excitement in his voice.

"Yeah, let's go," Michael added.

"Can we please get this over with," Midnight said, as he continued to roll like a barrel in the air—while Ben laughed hysterically at the expense of his friends misfortune.

"All right then," the snow fairy said. She flicked her wand—pulling everyone into formation. "Follow me!" Neve slowly took off towards the village below.

Michael, eager to fly, extended his arms out and focused on the snow fairy. Much to his surprise, he began to move forward. "Charlie, catch me if you can."

Charlie, seeing what his brother had done, followed suite and took off like a shot towards Michael. "Here I come," he hollered.

Ben, sensing it was time to go, grabbed hold of Midnight's large, striped tail. "Ready, my friend?"

"Are you kidding me?" the cat replied. "I can't see a thing with you pulling me by my tail."

Ben took off, with Midnight in tow, trying to keep up with those ahead. "Quit your wining, fluffy, and enjoy the ride," he said with a smile from ear to ear.

Sassyfran and Provo gladly joined Ben and Midnight to keep the frustrated cat calm.

As they soared through the sky, towards the village far-far below, incredible thoughts of pure joy raced through the minds of Charlie and Michael. This was a moment they would remember forever.

Chapter Eleven

As Neve and the others approached the watchmaker's workshop from the sky above, it became obvious that this was much more than a humble little workshop for an ordinary craftsman. In fact, it was more like the village focal point. Standing over two stories tall, with a giant clock tower sitting atop its steeply peaked, wood-shingled roof, the watchmaker's shop was covered from top to bottom with elaborately detailed, stone and wood carvings of timepiece gears and mechanisms, marionettes, toys, nutcrackers, animals, trees, flowers and other elements of nature. It was quite a site to behold. The clock atop the tower was nothing short of magnificent, it was ginormous, masterfully carved, and painted to resemble a traditional cuckoo clock. As the group flew in closer, the clock struck six and began to move—convincing Charlie and the others that it actually WAS a real, fully functional, giant cuckoo clock. There were three life size men enjoying food and beverages at a picnic table, as four dancing maidens twirled and circled around—entering through the right door of the clock, and exiting out the left door. To the left side were several animals, including a deer, several rabbits and a skunk—all moving their heads to the rhythm of the clock chime. And on the right side were two large, brown bears. One was sitting atop a tree stump tapping its foot to the chime, while the other was laying on its back with all four legs extended upward, as it tried to balance a large barrel of honey by rolling side to side. It was the most incredible cuckoo clock Charlie or his brother had ever seen.

As everyone landed in the cobble stone street in front of the watchmaker's dwelling, they walked up and gathered by the front door. Excited from their Peter Pan-like flight, everyone in the group was full of chatter, while continuing to gaze upwards and side to side, admiring the incredible craftsmanship of the watchmaker's home.

The snow fairy kindly called for attention. "Alright. Alright everyone. We mustn't be so loud. You never know who may be listening. Which reminds me." She flew high above the village, waved her wand, and once again, snow flakes spread all around, forming a transparent dome which covered the village. Immediately, the surrounding area outside the dome turned to clouds of white—similar to what Charlie and Michael had seen when they looked out of Geppetto's bedroom window the year before. It was like nothing existed outside the village.

"What was that you just did?" Charlie asked the fairy.

"She hid us from intruders," the frog replied.

"You mean, the village is invisible again?" Provo asked.

"Yes, Provo," the fairy replied.

"But, but—then, where are we?" Michael asked.

"The watchmaker will explain later. Now go and enjoy your visit," the fairy replied, as she rose into the air and disappeared—leaving behind traces of sparkling snow flakes, which gently floated to the ground.

Catching everyone by surprise, the front door opened. "Well-well, would you look at this. We have visitors," the old man said to his two cats, who circled and rubbed up against the watchmaker's legs to show their excitement.

"Hello Raphael, I brought some friends along that wanted to meet you," the frog said from atop Charlie's left shoulder.

"Oh, yes-yes-yes. Come in, come in—so we can get acquainted," the watchmaker replied. He opened the door wider to allow everyone in. "Please make yourselves at home."

Charlie, Michael, Ben and the others entered, taking in their surroundings.

Raphael's secret workshop was much different than what the boys had expected. Unlike the quaint workshop they had imagined, this shop was on a much grander scale. The dimly lit, sunken living room had an enormous fireplace, which was flanked by two fifteen foot tall, intricately carved totem poles that were built into the wall. Each, with faces of every expression imaginable, masterfully carved into their surface. The light from the fireplace added an even deeper sense of mystery and character to the faces. Sitting on the fireplace mantle were various posable figures made of wood. All with legs dangling over the edge. There was a toy soldier, a brown teddybear, and a princess dressed in blue on the left, and an elephant, a frog with a straw hat, and a woodsman with a beard, on the right. Hanging on the wall above the marionettes was a very large painting, with an ornately carved, wooden frame. It was a painting of a small boy sitting on his father's lap.

As Charlie looked closer, it appeared the boy was made of wood, though he did not resemble Pinocchio in any way. Instead, this wooden boy had brown eyes, sandy brown hair, and he was tall and lean. He was dressed in shorts, a button down shirt, and an ornately-stitched vest, with long white socks. His vest and shorts were brown, his shirt white, and his tie, red. Atop his head was a traditional brown hat with a blue band and a white feather. The father figure in the painting resembled the man who had just welcomed them in.

"So, who exactly is Raphael?" Charlie quietly asked the frog on his shoulder.

"He is the watchmaker, young man. Have you any doubt?" the frog replied.

"No, not really," Charlie said.

"I sense indecision in your voice. What is it you are thinking?"

"Well, the painting on the wall."

"Yes, what about it?"

"It is an old man with a wooden boy. You know. Like in Pinocchio. So I was thinking..."

"Ah, now I understand," the frog replied. "The painting reminds you of Geppetto and Pinocchio? Don't forget, everything you see in WONDER is conceptual or an unrealized dream. None of the finalized Disney characters exist here. They are well preserved within animation cels, or hard drives, to protect them from the evil clutches of the Dark Thorns and the FOTO army."

Charlie nodded to acknowledge the frog's words.

The man who let them in had a generous, well-rounded waistline. His face was plump and jolly with welcoming eyes, full, rosy cheeks, and a large round nose, on which his circular glasses rested. His gray hairline had receded somewhat, though it was still very full along the sides and back. And he was clothed as one would expect a master craftsman to be clothed, with a light blue shirt and socks, black pants, brown shoes, and a brown leather apron.

"Follow me," Raphael said, as he led Charlie and the others into the dimly lit living room, up two shallow steps, and through another doorway with a hand carved wooden sign overhead that read: MAKING HAPPINESS.

As Charlie and the others passed through the doorway, everything suddenly became brighter—changing the mood from comfy and cozy to colorful and lively. Dozens of candles were scattered throughout the room, and hanging above, were two large circular chandeliers—providing an abundant supply of light, covering every square inch of the enormous room with twenty foot high ceilings. The wall facing them as they walked into the room was filled with shelving from top to bottom, and was paired with a ladder that had fanciful scrolling on its side rails. It could slide back and forth like a library ladder. The towering shelves were occupied with countless numbers of colorful, and very playful, timepieces, music boxes, nutcrackers, wagons, animals, and other interesting things. The far wall to the left had a large bay window, with two sets of shelves flanking it, and one long shelf above. All were filled with wooden, posable figures, including young girls and boys, old men and women, dancers, kings, queens, soldiers, and jesters—not to mention, a slew of circus animals and fairytale characters. And the wall to their right was occupied by Raphael's work bench. The bench was centered with shelves on each side that were fully stocked with paints, paint brushes, pencils, piles of sketch sheets used to plan out his masterpieces, and so much more. On the sides below the bench were half opened drawers overflowing with every type of tool you could imagine. And on the messy bench itself, sat several vices, a large magnifying glass with multiple lenses, and a variety of brushes, tools, wood shavings and things that had been used on his most recent projects.

But now it was time for more important matters.

"So, which one of you boys did my dear friend Ruth give the watch to?" the watchmaker asked.

"That would be me, sir," Charlie replied.

"Ahhhhh, of course. You have the watch with you, yes?"

Charlie pulled the damaged watch out of his short's pocket and handed it to Raphael.

Handling it gently, like a small, delicate bird, the watchmaker pulled the magic timepiece in closely, so that it almost was touching his red nose. He carefully assessed the damage through his thick glasses. "Why someone would want to harm such a nice timepiece, I do not understand. They must have been VERY unhappy." He continued to examine the watch from every possible angle. "This is going to take me all night to repair. Don't you agree Ticky and Tocky?" he asked his cats.

"Bell's father, Maurice, from *Beauty and the Beast* could help you fix it. He can fix anything," Michael said jokingly. He did not expect an answer in return.

"Oh, no-no-no, my young friend. Finalized characters are NEVER released in WONDER. The Patrons keep them tightly concealed, far away from this place," the watchmaker said with a stern look on his face.

"Sorry, I forgot," Michael said, with an embarrassed expression. "What about your two cats? Aren't you afraid they could get hurt?"

"No. You see, uh, Michael, is it? Ticky and Tocky are here to protect me."

"Really? They look like regular cats to me," Michael replied.

Ticky was a grey, short hair male cat with a lean build, while Tocky was a white, long haired female. And while they first appeared quite different in looks, the shape and crystal blue color of their eyes were exactly the same.

"Be kind, Michael," his brother warned. "I am sure he has a perfectly good explanation, right Mr. Watchmaker?"

"Yes...I for one would most certainly like to hear more," Provo kindly added.

"I wish I had time to explain, little mouse friend, but there is so much more we need to do," the watchmaker replied. "Like getting to know all my wonderful new friends."

"Why of course, what was I thinking," Featherwink replied. "I guess formal introductions are in order."

"I say we start with the cute little log over here who is carrying the tiny mouse on her head," Raphael motioned with his hands towards Sassyfran.

"Thank you, Mr. Watchmaker," she replied, fluffing up her grassy hair, and nearly knocking Provo out of his nest.

"Young lady, would you mind. I count too you know," the mouse hollered from above with his little voice.

"Ha-ha-ha-ha-ha!" Raphael broke into laughter, which caused the others to laugh as well. "Be careful. You don't want to make the little fellow angry."

"Don't worry Mr. Watchmaker, he'll be over it in a minute," Sassyfran replied.

The old man stared at the log with great curiosity. "You look... familiar, Raphael said. Have we met before?" I mean, you appear to have quite a bit of magic in you. Just like the piece of wood old Raspberry once showed me, which from what I understand, Pinocchio was carved from."

"Funny you should say that," she replied. It just so happens I once sat on the same log pile as Pinocchio at Mr. Raspberry's cottage."

"You don't say?" Raphael replied. "Why, old Raspberry is a good friend of mine. He has been supplying me with wood for many years, which I use for all my projects."

"And, did you know," Sassyfras added, "Pinocchio and I came from the same enchanted forest in a far away land?"

"That is very interesting." The old man placed a hand on his head, which quickly filled with endless possibilities for all the wood from the enchanted forest.

"Boy, just imagine what Raphael could do with an entire stack of magic wood," Ben said. "Why, it makes me tingle all over just thinking about it."

"Me too," Charlie added.

"Oh dear, too many things to think about." The watchmaker shook his head clear of thought and refocused. "Now, where were we? Oh yes, we were making introductions. I forgot, did you give me your name?" he said to the little wooden log.

"I must have gotten caught up in the moment as well," she said with a giggle. So sorry. My name is Sassyfran. It is an honor to meet you, Mr. Raphael."

The old man let out a laugh. "Just Raphael is fine, my dear. I am nothing more than a humble craftsman."

"Very well then. Raphael, it is very nice to meet you," Sassyfran replied.

"And who is the little fellow on top of your head with the big blue eyes?"

"I'm Provo, the local field mouse. Well, almost local. I live on the other side of the mountains."

"How do you do, Provo. It is good to meet you."

"It is my pleasure, watchmaker," the mouse kindly replied.

"Hello, Mr. Watchmaker, I mean Raphael. I'm Ben, assistant to—"

"Frank Wellington, yes, he has told me all about you."

"All good I hope?" Ben replied with a nervous chuckle.

"Yes, yes, yes. Ohhhh, he has nothing but praise for you my friend."

"Whew, glad to hear it. For a minute there, you had me nervous," Ben said, wiping the sweat from his brow.

Midnight rolled his eyes at Ben's choice of words, then introduced himself. "Good evening Raphael. My name is Midnight, Frank's living companion. I'm sure he must has spoken about me as well?"

"The big black WONDER cat with a grey striped tail and sparkling green eyes. Yes, he has told me all about you as well. I believe you already met my two cats, Ticky and Tocky? From what Frank has told me, I think the three of you will get along tremendously," Raphael said. "Ticky, Tocky," he called on his cats, who were curled up by the fireplace in the living room. "Why don't the two of you come in here and introduce yourselves."

Ticky and Tocky walked into the room, stretched as cats do, then addressed their new, and very large, friend with a couple of, "meows".

"Nice to meet the two of you as well," Midnight replied. His fluency in the feline language was as good as his English, though he never really spoke it, since most of the cats in WONDER could understand the human language perfectly.

The watchmaker smiled then turned to Charlie's brother. "And what about you young fellow. Do you have a name?"

"I'm Michael."

"Very nice to meet you Michael. So you are helping your brother, yes?"

"I guess you could say that. It's not like I had a choice," Michael replied sarcastically.

"Yes, I can see that. It is hard to refuse a siblings request for help. Especially when you love them as much as you love your brother."

Michael's frown was melted away by the watchmaker's words. He turned to Charlie, then slowly back to Raphael. "Yeah, I guess you're right," he answered in a humbled tone.

"And you. You must be Charlie," Raphael said with a twinkle of admiration in his eyes.

"Yes sir. I mean, yes Raphael," the boy replied nervously.

"Frank has told me all about the great adventures you shared together last year."

"He did?"

"Why of course. You are *the* chosen outsider. A very big role for such a young boy."

"So why do they call you the watchmaker?" Michael interrupted.

"Uh, hmm?" The old man was initially caught off guard by the question, as he scratched his head in thought. "Oh, uh, yes. How did I get the title of watchmaker. Let me think a moment...oh yes, now I have it. One day, many-many years ago—when I was still living in the peaceful village on the other side of the mountain, Frank's Great Uncle, Waldo Wellington, and several other Patrons came to ask me a favor. They were looking for someone who could build a magical device to track down one of five Kingdom Crystals if it were hidden away from the evil Dark Thorns, or any other members of FOTO. You are all familiar with the crystals, Dark Thorns and the Forest of Thorns Order, yes?"

The boys and everyone else in the room nodded yes to confirm they did.

"Very good," Raphael continued. "I told the Patrons I would be honored to do so, but that I would need a great deal of time to think up such a device. They granted me all the time I needed, and said they would be back in three months to check on my progress. As soon as the Patrons left, I rolled up my sleeves and went to my bench to start thinking up whatever came to mind. I sketched pages upon pages of ideas. I started with simple things, like a flute and a whistle. But neither was complex enough for such a task. Then I thought, maybe a music box or a cuckoo clock would work. But they were too large to carry around. I continued to think, day and night, night and day. My mind and body were exhausted. I could barely keep my eyes open. That is when I left the workbench to go sit by the fireplace in my big comfy chair. I started to fall asleep, when the pocket watch in my vest began to chime. I pulled the watch out to look at the time, and THAT is when it came to me! It was small, it was complex, and it was portable. I decided a watch would make the perfect object to pair with a Kingdom Crystal."

"I think I understand now," Charlie said. "You made a watch for the Patrons to use as an Object of Magic, so naturally they named you the watchmaker?"

"Ha-ha! Yes, Charlie, that is right. You are a very smart boy."

"But how do you turn a Mickey watch into something like an Object of Magic?" Provo asked.

"Yes, can you explain to us how something like that even works?" Ben added. "Besides telling time, what else can a watch—like the one you hold in your hands, possibly do?"

"Ohhh, huh-huh-huh," the watchmaker chuckled. "You see, this watch—"

"Is a magical watch. Ruth, the Keeper of the Watch from the jewelry store, already told us how it works," Michael interrupted.

"Shhh," the frog said. "If you give the watchmaker a chance, you might just learn a thing or two."

"Thank you, Featherwink." I'm sure my younger brother would love to hear what you have to say, Raphael," Charlie said, while bumping his brother in the shoulder. "Isn't that right, Michael?"

"I guess so," Michael replied—even though he still believed there was nothing more to learn about the watch ."

The watchman looked at Michael, shook his head, sighed, then continued on. "This watch is much more than a timepiece. And yes, while I am sure, young man, Ruth explained, very thoroughly, that the watch can be used to get you and your brother from one place to another within WONDER, I am *also* sure, she did not explain *HOW* to use it, in order to do so."

"How would you know that?" Michael asked.

"Because, there is only one person who knows such details."

"And who would that be?" Charlie asked out of curiosity.

"You are looking at him," Raphael said, with a proud smile.

"Now I see why the Patrons chose to hide you away in such a secret place," Midnight said. "If something were to happen to you, then no one would be left to explain how the watch works. Nor would there be anyone to fix it."

"You are a very smart kitty. Remind me to get you a nice bowl of milk later for being so smart."

"If it is not too much to ask, I would much rather prefer a nice bowl of spaghetti and meatballs, if you have it," Midnight replied.

Raphael gave the cat a look of bewilderment.

To break the awkward moment of silence, Ben jumped into the conversation. "He has what you might consider, a rather *unusual* appetite for a cat."

"Ahhh, now I see why he is so BIG," Raphael replied, spreading his arms apart in a humorous manner to exaggerate the size of the cat.

Everyone in the room burst into laughter, except for Midnight of course. He turned away and began to study some of the beautiful work on the shelves that the master craftsman had created.

"Oh come now Midnight, we were only kidding," Ben said, to lure his friend back to the conversation.

The large cat turned back towards everyone and said, "You know, I have never been one to turn down a good plate of food," followed by a small chuckle.

"I knew you couldn't stay mad for long. Get back here you silly cat," Ben replied.

"Yes, please come back and join us," Raphael added. "I want to explain a few things about the watch you have brought me to fix."

Midnight quickly scurried back to the work bench and eagerly waited for the crafty watchmaker to begin.

"I am sorry, Midnight. I did not mean to upset you," Raphael said. I do hope you will forgive me." The big cat nodded to acknowledged his apology then the watchmaker continued. "So the watch you see before you can do many things. But, in order for you, Charlie, to use it correctly, there are details I must first explain. Which, you will need to remember."

"I would be taking notes if I were you right about now," the frog whispered softly to the boy.

Without missing a beat, Raphael reached across his bench and picked up a pad of paper and a pencil, then handed it to Charlie.

"See, what did I tell ya," Featherwink said to the young boy.

"Now, to begin with, I understand that Frank Wellington and Ruth have already explained to Charlie and Michael the meaning of the phrase: forwards, backwards, sideways and magic."

"Yes, that's right," Charlie replied.

"Good. While you are busy writing down what it means, I will explain it to the others," Raphael replied. "Now then, the Watch of WONDER does not tell time, but rather, allows one to travel to *conceptual realities* that Disney has dreamt up, or will dream up. These include park, resort, ship, movie, and other concepts—combined with all other dreams that never reached the concept stage. More importantly, the watch will lead the chosen outsider, that being you Charlie, to the second Kingdom Crystal by utilizing these magical places—which are all connected AND preserved in WONDER, thanks to the Magic Dream Expander.

"So how exactly does the watch take you to all of these wonderful places?" Midnight asked.

"Ahhh, that is the best part. You simply push the button on the side, then ask, or tell, Mickey where you want to go."

"So if Charlie wanted to go to a simulated version of the Haunted Mansion the day it opened in Walt Disney World, all he would have to do is ask the watch to take him there?"

"Precisely, Midnight."

"Fascinating," Provo replied.

"What if he wanted to go somewhere in WONDER that was movie-related, like a conceptual scene from Fantasia?"

"Yes, the watch would take him there too," Raphael said with confidence. "In fact, the Watch of WONDER, when it is fixed, will take Charlie, and whoever is with him, *anywhere* they want to go within the magical boundaries of WONDER."

"Anywhere?" Sassyfran asked.

"Well, almost anywhere. There are two limitations when using an Objects of Magic. They *cannot* access any of the finalized scenes or characters used in a Disney movie. These are all carefully locked away in WONDER, and are strictly off limits to everyone, except a select group of Patrons. Nor can an Object of Magic access the actual parks, resorts, ships, or anything else created by Disney, which exist in reality. Simply because, they can only exist in the real world, and not in WONDER."

"So basically," Charlie said, "any Disney-related dreams, or concepts that have not been finalized, can be accessed using an Object of Magic—as long as they are preserved within WONDER?"

"Precisely," Raphael replied.

"Still, seems pretty amazing to me," Featherwink added.

"Oh, and I almost forgot," Raphael said. "The Mickey watch can also be used to locate dream dots. Making it easier to navigate around WONDER."

"Sounds like that would come in handy if the boys needed to make a quick getaway," Ben said.

"Exactly, the watchmaker replied. "Now, everyone gather in closely, so I can show you how it works."

Everyone huddled around Raphael and the watch.

"First, everyone must understand the meaning of *forwards, backwards, sideways and magic,* and how it relates to the watch. Forwards represents the future realities of WONDER. So if the watch is asked to travel into the future, Mickey's hands will both point to the three on the watch face, representing forwards. If it is asked to travel backwards, the hands will both point to nine. To travel sideways, one hand will point to three, and one to nine. And finally, if the watch is asked to travel to a place of magic, both hands will point to twelve. Everyone understand, so far?"

Charlie and the others nodded their heads, yes.

"Good. Now let's say Charlie wants to visit Frank at his apartment in WONDER, which would be considered sideways, or present time. First, he would press the button on the right side, to activate the watch. Then he would ask the watch to take him to Frank's apartment. Immediately, Mickey's hands would begin to spin rapidly, in ether direction—and the watch would start to flash in a brilliant pattern of purple, orange, blue and red light. Each color represents a layer of WONDER. The magic rim is purple, WONDER is orange, Deep WONDER is blue, and the Dream Core is red. When the watch finds its location, which in this case is Frank's apartment in WONDER, Mickey's hands would snap into place—one hand would be on three and the other on nine. Then the watch would illuminate orange, and POOF, Charlie would immediately be sent to Frank's apartment.

"Very impressive," Midnight said.

"So what are the small, green circles surrounding the face for?" Michael asked.

"Ahh yes. Good question, Michael. The small, green circles around the perimeter of the watch face are activated when you get close to a dream dot. The closer you get to a dream dot, the faster the green circles blink in a clockwise succession. Once you are at your location, they turn solid green, and the watch would illuminate green. Which is precisely when Charlie, and whoever is with him, will want to touch or walk through the dream dot."

"So if we were using the snow man in Hollywood Studios, like last year, everyone would have to touch him when the green lights on the watch turn solid?"

"Exactly, Charlie. See, the watch is actually quite easy to understand, once you understand its basic functions," the old man replied with a chuckle.

"I don't understand, how do the green circles light up, if they are made of wood?" Michael asked.

"Disney Magic, Michael," the watchmaker replied.

"That is quite the watch," Ben said. "It would make a great gift for a friend of mine. He loves his Mickey watches."

"Yeah, if only he could use it," Featherwink replied, jokingly.

"Oh, that's right. I plumb forgot. Only the chosen outsider can do that," Ben said, blushing. Everyone in the room burst into laughter.

"That was a good one," Raphael said, "but now it's time we all go and relax, yes? Everyone, please, go into the living room and sit around the fireplace. Make yourselves comfortable. We can chat for a while over a nice cup of hot cocoa before I fix the watch, eh? Except for you Midnight, I will get you a nice big bowl of spaghetti and meatballs."

Midnight's eye's lit up.

Everyone burst into laughter once more, as they headed towards the living room.

The watchmaker went to prepare food and several warm mugs of cocoa. He even had miniature wooden mugs for Mr. Featherwink and Provo the mouse.

They all sat by the fireplace, as the watchmaker shared tall tales about the many adventures he had had through the years in his realm of WONDER. Several included the likes of Featherwink, the snow fairy, and even Ticky and Tocky.

It was then that Midnight asked a question that everyone in the group had wanted to ask. "Those are all such marvelous stories, Raphael, but there is still something that has had me baffled ever since the snow fairy unveiled the hidden village we are in right now."

"Oh, and what is that, my friend?"

"How in the name of WONDER is it possible to hide an entire village? And even if it is invisible, how does the snow fairy keep those who travel through this valley from bumping into it? I mean, even if they cannot see it, it is *still* physically sitting here, correct? Or, isn't it?"

Raphael gazed deep into the burning embers of the fireplace. A look of seriousness blanketed his face. "You met the snow fairy, yes?" he asked.

"Why sure we did," Ben replied.

"Without the assistance of Mr. Featherwink, we never would have met her," Sassyfran added.

"And if we had not met the snow fairy, we never would have found the hidden village," Provo said.

"Right. That is a very good point, my little mouse friend," the watchmaker said. So, let me try and explain to you how the snow fairy makes it allllll possible." He turned his attention away from the fire and towards his newfound friends. "A long time ago, shortly after I designed the Watch of WONDER as a favor to the Patrons, it was decided by their council that my well being was too valuable to leave unprotected. In turn, they dreamt up the snow fairy and released her into WONDER to guard me from the evil forces of the Forest of Thorns Order."

"I think we all understand that the snow fairy is responsible for keeping the village hidden," Midnight said, "but what I think we are all having a hard time comprehending is exactly how she can keep it hidden, both visually AND physically."

"Yeah, how can anyone have the power to make something disappear, yet still exist?" Michael questioned.

"That is where the real magic of WONDER shines, my friends," the watchmaker said, with a grin from ear-to-ear. "In the real world, people only see what their eyes reveal—which is one reality. But in WONDER, there are many conceptual realities which coexist within each layer. Which is why this world is called the World of Natural Dream Enhanced *Realities,* and not, the World of Dream Enhanced *Reality.*" The old man paused for a moment and turned quickly towards the front door.

"Did you hear something?" Charlie asked.

"Naaaah. I don't think so. It may just be the wind, a squirrel or something," Raphael replied. "Now, where was I?"

"You were explaining the conceptual realities of WONDER," Provo said.

"Ahhhhh yes. Thank you my little mouse friend. As I was saying, there are a multitude of realities which coexist within each level of WONDER. Like for instance, the snow fairy, being the clever guardian she is, placed a dimensional charm over this entire village, which when used, transports the village from where it is now, to a magic dimension in the exact same location."

"And because it is transported into a 'magic dimension', it is both invisible and untouchable?" Midnight asked.

"Precisely, Mr. Kitty," the watchmaker said. "Which keeps the village hidden from the dark forces of FOTO. But there is even more. Don't forget, we have FOUR dimensions in each level of WONDER that can be utilized, as I mentioned earlier when showing you the watch."

"Right," Charlie proclaimed. "Forwards, backwards, sideways and magic."

"Ha-haaaaa! I am so proud of you, Charlie," Raphael said. "You are a very smart boy. That is exactly right. Not only can the village be transported to the magic dimension of Deep WONDER—"

"It can also be sent forwards, backwards or sideways?" Charlie asked.

Raphael looked upon Charlie with his chin down, proudly observing the boy over the rims of his glasses—his hand, resting gently on the boys shoulder. "Now I can see why Frank Wellington chose you to help our team. You are wise beyond your years, Charlie."

"What? Him?" Michael intervened, as he jumped out of his chair. "I'm the one who gets straight A's, not him."

"You know, Michael," the frog hinted, "there are all types of 'wisdom' in this world. Not just the type that comes from books."

"My little purple friend is right, Michael," Raphael added. "Wisdom can come from almost any type of experience one goes through in life. And some, like your brother, are naturally gifted with what I like to refer to as, *simple wisdom.*"

"Oh, you mean like common sense?" Michael asked.

"Yes, something like that," Raphael said with a chuckle. "For example, it is getting late, and a young boy like you needs a good nights sleep in order to be productive the next day."

"I'm not tired," Michael replied with a yawn.

"And I'm not made of wood," Sassyfran said.

"Besides, I need to get the watch fixed before sunrise, and the night isn't getting any younger," Raphael added.

Everyone in the room received the watchmaker's message well and collectively decided to call it a night.

The watchmaker showed everyone upstairs to their rooms, said his goodnights, then headed back down to his workbench, where the watch of WONDER awaited his magical touch.

All fell silent. The fire burned brightly in the adjoining room, casting long shadows throughout a dwelling where only the tick-tock sounds of the watchmaker's clocks remained. He began to work diligently, yet carefully, on the magical timepiece with his skillful hands.

Tomorrow was going to be a busy day for all.

Chapter Twelve

"Charlie, wake up!" Charlie, wake up now," Michael said, as he pushed on his brother's shoulder.

Day three of their vacation had begun. But not from where they had thought.

Charlie slowly pulled the covers from his eyes and was greeted by the sunlight breaking through the balcony blinds. He rubbed the sleep from his eyes, scratched his head, and sat up, heavily disoriented. As his eyes and mind cleared, the young boy took in his surroundings. It was a moment difficult to comprehend. They were no longer in Deep WONDER, but rather, back at the Beach Club Resort.

"What happened, Charlie? How did we get back here? I, I don't get it."

"Shhhhh. Keep it down, Michael, I think mom is in the bathroom."

The door latch clicked, and Mr. Z came walking in—startling the boys. "Goooooood morning fellas. Looks like we're going to have another perfect day."

"Oh. Yeah. Sure, Dad. Looks pretty nice out," Charlie replied.

"Hey Susie, you gonna be a while?" her husband asked. "Cause if you are, I'm going to run down and grab a coffee at the Marketplace."

"Sure Ed, go ahead, the boys still have to get ready anyway. Could you get me one of those special coffees as well?"

"Sure. You boys need anything?"

"Too early for me, Dad," Charlie answered. "My stomach isn't awake yet."

"Can you get me a chocolate milk, Dad?"

"You got it. Be back in a minute." As quickly as he had showed up, their dad was out the door—clearing the room for Charlie and Michael to speak freely about the unusual string of events they had experienced over the past twenty four hours.

"Do you see the watch anywhere, Michael?" Charlie asked quietly—not wanting his mother to hear.

The younger brother scanned the room. "I don't see anything Charlie. You mean, Raphael never gave you the watch back last night?"

"How would I know? I was sleeping, just like you."

"Well, I don't know. I thought maybe the watchmaker might have given you the watch when I was sleeping?"

"I wish that were true, but unfortunately, it's not."

The bathroom door opened. "OK, Michael. Why don't you grab your things and get ready," their mother said, as she walked out of the bathroom in search of her shoes.

The boys conversation would have to continue later on.

With no watch, no watchmaker, and no clue as to what happened, Charlie and Michael could do nothing but guess about what lied ahead that day.

What happened to their friends? Were they all OK? Was the watchmaker able to fix the watch? A looping cycle of questions continued to run through Charlie's mind as he walked along with his family. They were headed from the boat dock to the Hollywood Studios entryway.

The lines were long and moving slowly to get into the park. A typical day for the summer vacation rush. Charlie continued to think, playing back everything in his mind from the night before in Deep WONDER. It was hard for him to see the magic band kiosks past the crowd. *Will we ever get into the park?* He impatiently thought to himself. Which for Charlie, was unusual. His eagerness was getting the best of him.

The family ahead of theirs finally reached the magic band kiosk and checked in quickly.

As they cleared out, and the Zastawits family stepped up, a pleasant surprise was revealed.

Charlie held his MagicBand up to the kiosk—instead of lighting up green, the Mickey icon lit up in a rainbow of colors. The female cast member looked at the young boy with a smile and said, "Welcome back. Make sure you give Toy Story Mania a try this morning, I heard it's *full* of surprises today."

Caught off guard by the cast member's recommendation, Charlie only managed to stutter out a few words. "Uh, yeah. Sure. Thank you." He walked over to join his family, where his father was picking up park maps.

"So where would you like to start, Susie?" Mr. Z asked, while reviewing a park map. Knowing every square inch of the property, their father did it simply because he thought it necessary to get the *full* Disney experience. And they made great collectibles as well.

"I don't know, Ed. Maybe we should just let the boys decide."

"Yeah, I vote for that idea," Michael blurted out.

"What about you, Charlie. Any ideas where we should start?" their mother asked.

"I think Toy Story Mania would be a fun place to begin," he said.

"I like it," Mrs. Z replied. "Ed, what you think? Sound good?"

Charlie's father was scrolling through the My Disney Experience app on his phone. "One second dear, I juuuust want to check something."

"Check what, Ed? We're here. Now. Don't you think we need to—"

"Well I'll be. Would you look at that."

"What dear?"

"I don't know how to explain it, but it looks like we have FastPasses for Toy Story Mania at 9:45 this morning? Not sure how that happened?" Did you—"

"No, Ed, I didn't book any FastPasses," she replied with a confused look on her face.

"But, how then did...well...how did...who...what?"

"I don't think it really matters, does it, Dad?" Charlie asked.

"I guess you're right?" his father replied, scratching his head.

The Zastawits family took off down Hollywood Boulevard towards Pixar Studios with great anticipation.

"Since we have time, what do say we stop by One Man's Dream and look around? This may be the last time we get to see it in its current format," Mr. Z said.

"Oh, that's right, I read about that somewhere. Or maybe I heard them talking about it on one of the Disney podcasts?" Not sure which one, but yeah, great idea," Mrs. Z replied.

"What do ya say, boys?"

"Sure, Michael and I are always up for checking out the details of the miniature park models," Charlie said.

"Yeah, like Charlie said, we love checking out the models. Especially the ones that draw us *into* their world." Charlie gave his brother a wide-eyed look.

"What? Draw you into their world?" their mother questioned.

Charlie elbowed his brother in the side as a warning not to tell their parents what had happened by the Tree of Life model the previous year.

"Ouch! Watch it, Charlie," Michael said.

"Charlie, be nice to your brother," their mom said.

"I'll do my best," Charlie replied with a grin—happy to have succeeded in making his mother forget the question she had asked. A question that would have revealed the magical experience Charlie and his brother encountered the year before in the One Man's Dream exhibit.

"What do we do with the little fella? And what about the watch?" Duke asked his captain.

"I tell ya what we're going to do. We take him straight away to hiding until we can figure out exactly how we're going to explain what happened to the Dark Thorns," Captain Fibs replied.

"We? Who's we?" Flamario blurted out. "I say we take the little red headed man, tie him to a stick, then slowly turn him as I roast him like a marshmallow with fire from my belly. Then he will tell us where the watch is, yes?"

Everyone went silent, then looked at the fire breather like he had lost his mind.

"I'm not quite sure that will work," replied the silver fox. "But you are on to something my overgrown friend. We do need to find the watch before meeting up with the Dark Thorns. Otherwise, as everyone here knows, there will be dire consequences to pay."

"Ha-ha-ha! Oh, sure. So who left you in charge?" Captain Fibs snapped at the fox. "Do ya really think me and my men are gonna listen to you, ya furry critter?"

"Better you listen to me and get the watch, then the alternative."

"Alternative?" Fibs replied. His face growing redder by the second, as beads of sweat rolled down his forehead and over his puffy cheeks.

"Yes, that's precisely what I said," the fox replied. "The alternative. Do you care to hear what it is?"

"No, not really," Fibs said with a scowl—knowing his reply would hold no weight.

"Well, I'll tell you anyway," the fox said with an inflated ego. "You and your two pathetic spies would crawl back to the Dark Thorns and beg for forgiveness, after telling them you were unable to obtain the watch. At which point, they will most likely turn you into cowardly toads or possibly even freeze you for an eternity. Who knows, the dreadful possibilities are endless when it comes to the power of the Dark Thorns. Then after they are done taking out their frustrations on the three of you, they will turn to the *real* help—that being the three of us, in order to get the job done."

"I'm no coward, and don't you go saying I am," Fibs spat back at the fox. "You might have a way with words ya silver-tongued fox, but me, I'm a man of action. Get 'em boys!"

On the captain's command, Duke and Grim hit their belt buckles and instantly transformed into two very large troll-like toad creatures. Their skin was spotted with brown and green. Their dirty yellow eyes bulged out of their oversized, and oddly-shaped, heads. Warts and imperfections populated their tough, well worn skin, which was protected by heavily spiked, tarnished metal armor. Their feet were webbed and the legs on which they stood were short and muscular, which easily supported their obese figures, and could be used to leap great distances. Their ginormous toad-like hands could grab the largest of objects with ease, including things such as giant boulders, tree limbs and what not. And when they weren't using their enormous hands for such unruly tasks, they hung so low, that their knuckles almost scraped the ground. Amongst the dwellers of WONDER, these ghastly creatures were commonly referred to as toady trolls, and were usually avoided if at all possible by the Patrons and their friends.

"Alright, then. Let us see how well the two of you match up against someone as mighty as me," Flamario shouted. He took an aggressive stance and prepared for battle.

Duke and Grim countered with the same.

Just as the battle between two colossal evils was about to begin, Mr. Jollysnaps came running out from within his secret mine of gold on Mischief Island—where Ben was being held against his will. It was a strange and mysterious place, and its only inhabitants were the coachman, his goons, and the innocent victims of mischief.

"Stop it, would you, please," Mr. Jollysnaps shouted.

Conversations between Flamario, the silver fox, Captain Fibs, and the toady trolls came to an abrupt halt. Everyone turned and directed their attention to Mr. Jollysnaps.

"Our little friend has something to tell us. Now, instead of sitting here arguing amongst yourselves, why don't you all follow me down into me lair and listen to what he has to say."

"What makes you think he's going to tell us anything worth listening to," Fibs blurted out.

"Yes, why would the little man have any reason to tell us the truth," Flamario added, as small puffs of fire shot out of his mouth and nostrils.

"Now-now, fellas, no need to start getting all worked up about it. What's done is done. I know we missed our opportunity to get the watch last night, but if we can persuade little Benny to tell us what he knows, then we'll get another shot."

"Lets say we do convince him to tell us what the Patrons and their little outsider are up to. And, we get another shot at the Watch of WONDER. Who's to say you fellas won't go and mess it up again, like you did last night," Duke said, pointing his large, ugly, toad-like finger at the shadow villains.

"What? Are you blaming us for not getting the watch last night?" Flamario shouted. Again, he took a stance and prepared himself for battle.

"Gentlemen, gentlemen," the silver fox said, stepping in between the giant man and the toady trolls to make peace. " I believe Mr. Jollysnap's idea has merit. If we can persuade the red headed fellow to tell us what the Patron's plans are, and I'm sure I will have *no* problem doing so, then our chances of getting ahold of the watch will improve dramatically."

"What makes you so sure you can persuade Ben to tell us what he knows, foxy?" Fibs asked.

"My good fellow, the silver fox is the best persuader in the land," Mr. Jollysnaps said.

"Though I don't like to brag, I must say, Mr. Jollysnaps does have a point," the silver-tongued fox added, striking a noble pose.

Captain Fibs paused...he rubbed his chin and stared at the fox and coachman over the rim of his steamed up glasses—contemplating whether he should believe the shadow villains or not. Then he looked at Duke and Grim and gave them a nod.

They pushed their belt buckles and returned to their human animation forms.

"Alright then fellas," the captain said to the fox and coachman. "If you can persuade old Benny to tell us what the Patrons and their little outsider friend are up to, then we'll back you up. After all, getting our hands on that watch is the most important thing. No matter how we do it."

"Precisely," the fox replied with a grin, as the two shook on it.

It was 9:40. Charlie and his family were closing in on Toy Story Mania, weaving in and out of the crowd. Their father was leading the way, while Charlie, Michael, and their mother followed close behind. As they entered the attraction FastPass queue, it was clear to see it was going to take a few minutes before they reached the loading area.

Then, something odd happened. Charlie, who was passing time by taking photos of the queue area, noticed through his phone screen that everything began to move in fast-forward. People moved ten times faster, and their speech was ten times quicker and very high pitched. It gave the term FastPass a whole new meaning. He turned to his family and even they were moving and speaking in rapid motion. Everyone, that is, except for Charlie. At ten times the pace, the queue line moved quickly—turning a ten minute wait into just one minute. Just as they approached the vehicle boarding area, everything magically snapped back to normal.

"Michael, you feel OK?" Charlie asked.

"Yeah, why?"

"Never mind."

As the vehicles approached, Charlie mumbled to Michael, "We need to ride together."

His brother nodded to confirm.

"Mom, we're riding together, OK?"

"Sure honey, go ahead. We'll be riding on the other side of the same vehicle."

The two boys jumped into their vehicle and donned 3D glasses, as they readied for action.

"So what are we looking for, Charlie?"

"I have no idea, but according to the cast member at the gate entrance, 'something special' is going to happen on this attraction. So keep your eyes peeled."

"You talked to the cast member?"

"It was more like she talked to me."

"Why would she do that?"

"I don't know. Does it really matter? No. Just help me out here, would ya."

The boys warmed up with the Pie Throw Practice round, while Charlie's mind eagerly waited for something special to happen.

The attraction did not disappoint. On their first spin around, the boys landed at the Ham and Eggs booth. Immediately they started launching plastic eggs at Barnyard characters—knocking them down one after another. But is was a yellow duck that caught Charlie's attention. The duck broke free from the row it was fixated to and began to fly around sporadically—doing loop-de-loops, and what not, around the entire booth. Then, breaking out of the booth completely, the duck shot off like a yellow blur—quacking uncontrollably, as it took off over their vehicle, spun around, then zoomed back, landing on top of the young man's head. Charlie turned left, right, up, down, and any other way he could possibly position his head to try and get a glimpse of the crazy duck. Just as he was about to give up,"QUACK-QUACK-QUACK," the inverted face of the duck came face-to-face with his own.

"See the sweeper! See the sweeper! For he's the keeper! QUACK-QUACK-QUACK!"

Then just like that, BOING! The duck snapped back into line with the other targets in the booth, as if nothing had happened. Their ride vehicle moved on to the next booth.

"What was that?" Charlie blurted out—his hair all a mess, and his 3D glasses sitting cockeyed upon his nose. "Did you see that, Michael?"

"See what, Charlie?"

"Ugh! Never mind."

Over the next few minutes the two brothers enjoyed the rest of the attraction—slinging, shooting and tossing stuff at the moving targets in each booth. During the entire time, Charlie's mind was preoccupied, playing back what the duck had said, over and over again.

Visiting the Star Wars Launch Bay, checking out several shops, and watching the Voyage of The Little Mermaid show rounded out the morning of magical activities for the Zastawits family. Which also meant it was close to noon and time for lunch. Charlie had well over two hours to think about the crazy duck's message and saw lunch as the perfect time to run his thoughts past Michael. After everyone had sat down to eat at the ABC Commissary, Charlie pulled out his phone to begin a text conversation with Michael:

> Put your phone on vibrate so Mom and Dad don't get suspicious.
>
> OK.
>
> Looking for a sweeper.
>
> A sweeper?
>
> Yes.
>
> Like someone with a broom?
>
> Maybe.

Could it be someone who works here?

Possibly. But I think it might be someone famous.

Like someone on an attraction?

Yes.

Star Wars?

No.

Indiana Jones?

No.

Muppets?

I don't think so.

What about The Great Movie Ride? Any sweepers there?

Let me do a visual search online. Just a sec.

OK.

BINGO.

You found something?

Mary Poppins. On roof with Bert.

Bert?

He's a chimney sweep.

Gotcha.

After lunch we go there.

10-4.

"You guys need to put those phones down and finish your meals," Mrs. Z said.

The boys respected their mother's wish, put away their phones, and, quickly finished eating. Shortly after, Charlie and his family headed out the door for more Hollywood Studios fun and adventure.

"Well what next, Ed?" Mrs. Z asked.

"It's beginning to heat up. What do you say we go check out the Great Movie Ride. Should be nice and cool in there."

"What do you boys think?"

"Sounds good to me," Charlie said. He gave his brother a secret thumbs up.

Based on the video he had watched earlier, Charlie positioned himself on the far right side of the Great Movie ride vehicle so he would be nice and close to the Mary Poppins scene. Bert's secret message was not to be missed. As the ride vehicle rounded the corner and slowly made its way towards Mary Poppins the young outsider focused intently on Bert, the chimney sweep. Charlie continued to stare, waiting for something magical to happen. Yet, nothing did. Feeling let down, he began to lose hope, as the ride vehicle continued onward.

Then, everything went blurry and started to move in slow motion. Everything that is, except for the area surrounding Bert.

But it wasn't Bert that delivered the message. Instead, it was the silhouette of a chimney sweep, just to his right, that spoke.

"This evening you'll gather where all are around.

A place full of magic and water abound.

Good things and bad things will be shown in the spray.

Where you'll learn from a friend what's happened and what may."

As quickly as the silhouetted sweep came to life, he snapped back into a static pose. It all happened in the briefest of moments. Fortunately, Charlie had been prepared, and was able to record the message clearly with his phone. His work was done for now. With a relaxed smile on his face, the young adventurer sat back and enjoyed the remainder of the attraction with his family and other guests, who as usual, were totally unaware of the magic that had just taken place.

Through the rest of the afternoon and early evening the Zastawits family enjoyed a multitude of laughs and adventures, with attractions such as Muppet Vision 3D, Star Tours and the Indiana Jones Epic Stunt Spectacular show. And in between, they had managed to get in an ice cream snack, several popcorns, a few bottles of water and a tasty dinner at Mama Melrose, which included passes to the Fantasmic nighttime show—here, the Zastawits family planned to end their day. During their busy afternoon, Charlie had managed to review the chimney sweeps message and thoroughly dissected it with the help of his younger brother. Just before dinner, the boys had reached a decisive conclusion. The message was to be delivered during the Fantasmic show.

Dusk had settled in. The soft hues of orange, purple, yellow and blue painted the skyline. People were filtering into the stadium and grabbing quick snacks of popcorn, cotton candy and other tasty treats from the concession stand at the top of the stadium, as they eagerly awaited the big finale show of the evening, Fantasmic. The stadium continued to fill, cast members entertained the seated guests with sing alongs and other fun activities. Soon, the sun retired below the horizon and the evening sky set the mood for the show, which was about to begin. All was dark, as the narration of a female voice flooded the stadium, and then... "IIIIMAAAGINAAAATION," echoed through the silence. An arrangement of random flashing lights and smoke filled the area. Concentrated streams of water shot skyward and were highlighted with colored lights—followed by giant, misty water walls, which captured a series of beautifully animated scenes. One of which, was a series of characters encapsulated in giant floating bubbles.

At that moment, as Charlie and the rest of his family were fully entranced by the show, the young outsider was pulled back to his purpose by an incredible occurrence. About half way through the series, one of the bubbles jumped out to capture Charlie's full attention. It was a large animated head of Frank—all distorted in and arrangement of psychedelic colors. The bubble took a steady position, holding up the rest that were still to follow. And just like all of Charlie's previous magical encounters in the parks, the entire audience and crew of cast members began to move and talk in slow motion. It was time for something special.

"Hello my friend," Frank said.

"Hey Frank."

"I have some very interesting news for you, my boy. The Patron council just received word today, from a source we wish to keep secret at this time, that Bella Bark, witch of the enchanted forest, was the shadow villain who tried to destroy the Watch of WONDER by casting down a lightning bolt from Big Thunder Mountain Railroad."

"Bella Bark? I don't believe I've ever heard of her," Charlie replied.

"Most have not. In fact, I'm almost certain nobody, except those familiar with WONDER, have ever heard of her."

"And why is that?"

"Well, for one thing, I've been told by other members of the Patron council that she was once a young princess."

"A princess?"

"Yes, a princess of a magical forest. Which, by the way, is the same forest where the magical wood of Pinocchio and Sassyfran came from."

"So the two are related?" Charlie asked.

"In a strange and magical way, yes, you could say that," Frank replied.

"So why did the princess become a witch?" the young boy asked. "I mean, after all, she was a princess and probably had more than any normal person could ever wish for."

"Under normal circumstances, one would think this to be true," Frank replied. "But from what the Patron council has told me, Bella Bark, formerly known as Princess of the Enchanted Woods, did not listen to the warnings handed down by her royal family. And in a moment of misguided temptation, she picked a magical pear from the golden tree of hope and took a bite in her moment of weakness. Little did she know, a tree with such beauty as this carried with it a terrible curse. Instantly, the young, beautiful princess grasped her throat, as her mouth became dry and hoarse. Her hair turned white and frazzled, her skin shriveled up and turned a grey-like brown, with deep lines and wrinkles, resembling the old bark of a tree. The whites of her eyes grew dim, yellow and lifeless—no longer carrying within them a glimmer of joy. And her shriveled body became cloaked by a gown made of old, weathered leaves. The young princess had been transformed into a hideous and hateful witch, who swore there would never be another peaceful day in the enchanted woods as long as she lived."

"Sounds like she made the wrong decision," Charlie said.

"Yes, a very keen observation for a young man of your age," Frank replied. "Just remember, Charlie, the choices we make in life are a direct reflection upon who we become. Anyway, she's out there... somewhere. And we are quite positive she will be looking for the watch. So be on your guard."

"So the Patrons still have the watch?"

"Indeed we do. Ticky, Tocky and Midnight escaped with the watch last night, while the rest of your party held off a sneak attack from a few Thorns and shadow villains. Fortunately for us, they were unable to get their hands on what they came for. Including you and your brother."

"We were attacked last night? But how...why...what?" Charlie said with a look of confusion.

"Raphael will explain tomorrow. For now, all you need to know is that the watchmaker is safe—hidden away in the snow fairy's secret cottage."

"How are we supposed to find them?"

"That's the easy part. Tomorrow morning you and Michael will meet Midnight on the west side of the World of Disney Store, near the plush section. And from there, he will help you find your way back to the watchmaker."

"Sure, but—"

"Don't worry, Charlie, we've taken every precaution to make sure you and your brother remain safe on your journey tomorrow. "And our parents?"

"They'll be taken care of in your absence as well. Now, it's time for me to go. I have other things to attend to. Besides, we need to let the guests get back to their show."

"Oh, right. I guess that would be good."

"Indeed it would, Charlie. And remember, tomorrow you will need to follow the frost trail to find the snow fairies cottage. There you will find the watchmaker."

"Frost trail?" But how—"

"You'll know when you see it. Plus, Midnight will be there to assist you. Good luck, and enjoy the rest of the show." POP! Frank's bubble burst, and he was gone.

The Fantasmic show continued—guests and cast members carried on as if nothing had happened.

Charlie pretended to enjoy the rest of the evening with his family, though deep inside his head, all he could think about was the upcoming day and the challenges he and his brother would soon face.

Chapter Thirteen

Day four of their vacation began just like the first three. The boys awoke, their mother was already in the restroom doing her hair, the early sun was shining through the cracks of the blinds, and their father was out taking his early morning stroll. An ordinary beginning to what Charlie anticipated would become a very unordinary day. On their way back to the resort the night before, it had been decided today would be a "break from the parks day," which meant the family was headed to Disney Springs for a slow day of shopping, eating and possibly a movie or bowling.

As the bus hummed and bumped along, and the narration continued to play over the speaker system—highlighting all the wonderful things to do in Disney Springs, Charlie and Michael sat far back in the rear, going over a vague game plan for their day of uncertainty. Neither one knew what the day ahead would bring.

"OK, I brought you to the back of the bus so we could talk without Mom and Dad hearing us," Charlie said.

"Obviously," Michael replied, in typical, younger brother fashion.

Charlie shook off his brother's remark, while rolling his eyes and clenching his right fist—wanting to punch his brother in the arm for the way he was behaving. But knowing it would only turn out bad for him in the end, he kept his composure and calmly continued. "So, as I was about to say, last night during the Fantasmic show, I spoke with Frank, and he informed me that we're to meet Midnight on the west side of the World of Disney Store, near the plush section."

"You spoke to Frank?" Michael said with a scrunched up face.

"Yeah, I did."

"And when are we supposed to do this?"

"This morning."

"But I was sitting right next to you. I didn't see or hear Frank say anything."

"That's because the secret message he passed on was only meant for me. Besides, when have you *ever* been able to see or hear any of the secret messages I've received outside of WONDER?" Charlie said in an angry, yet lower tone.

"Mmm? I guess your'e right," Michael replied with a smirk— knowing well he had gotten the best of his brother during their conversation.

Charlie exhaled, then continued on. "Anyway, when we get to Disney Springs I need you to help me persuade Mom and Dad to take us to the World of Disney Store before the morning is over and mom gets into one of her go-go-go shopping modes. Got it?"

Michael looked at his brother out of the right corners of his eyes and said, "piece of cake."

The bus rolled on.

There it was. Bigger than life. The largest Disney character store in the world. And looming over the east corner entrance was a larger than life Stitch, who shot streams of water from his mouth—catching many unsuspecting passerby's by surprise in hilarious fashion.

As they entered the store, passed through the section of cups and kitchen accessories in the east wing, and into the heart of the store, their mouths fell agape. Their eyes looked forwards, backwards, upwards and down. The boys could not believe the overwhelming presence of characters, color and merchandise that surrounded them from floor to ceiling. It was the most amazing display of Disney character merchandise they had ever seen in their lives. There were hats, shirts, plushes and balls. Ears, glasses and toys on the walls.

From one room to the next, the Zastawits family slowly made their way from the east wing towards the west, as their mother collected items from one section after another—handing them to her husband to hold onto until they had reached the other end of the store, at which point she claimed, they could sort through and pick one item each to be purchased as a souvenir. It wasn't really the buying she enjoyed, but rather the hunt for that *perfect something* to make someone happy, that brought joy to her heart.

As they neared the west wing, Charlie and his brother noticed a huge selection of character plushes. "This has to be it, don't you think?" Charlie whispered to his brother.

"Has to be what, dear?" his mother asked.

Caught off guard, Charlie thought up a quick lie. "Oh, I've been, uhhhh, looking for a particular plush Mickey," he replied.

"Oh?"

"Yeah, I thought if there was one place I could find it, it would be here." He nervously awaited his mother's response.

"Well, if you want to look around, go ahead. It's not like we live next door to Disney World or anything like that," his mother said jokingly.

"Is it alright if Michael helps me look?"

"Of course. Just make sure you stay where we can see you. Your father and I will be right over there by the picture frames and such."

Charlie felt a surge of relief shoot through his body, as he exhaled then replied, "thank you, Mom."

"Of course dear, that's why we're here, isn't it? You go ahead and search for your special Mickey."

Charlie returned the smile then called to his younger brother, who was preoccupied with something cool on a shelf near by, "Michael, come on, I need you to help me out," he said with urgency.

Michael picked up on the vibe his brother was sending, and immediately walked over to help.

"Alright, it's time to comb through all these characters until we find Midnight."

"That should be pretty easy, since he's not a Disney character. Don't you think, Charlie?"

"Usually I would say yes, but since we're dealing with a magical cat from WONDER...who knows," he replied. "You start over their on the right, and I'll start on the other side."

"Got it."

As they scanned the area—searching shelf by shelf, wall by wall, stack by stack of colorful plushes, it became obvious that finding Frank's large, black cat was going to be more challenging than antic-ipated. "Here kitty-kitty," Michael said softly to a cluster of plush Plutos. No response. Then he moved to a group of Nemo plushes and repeated his words. Again, no response.

On the other side of the room, Charlie was busy searching as well. "Midnight. Are you there? Midnight, where are you?" he quietly said to a wall full of Minnie and Goofy plushes. Still, no response.

After a long and tedious effort of looking, Michael reached the final section of the wall he was scanning. There were plushes of Stitch, Pooh, Tigger, Simba, Sorcerer Mickey, Dumbo and more. In a last ditch effort to find the magical cat, he whispered with a hint of aggravation, "Kitty, where are you, I think you've been hiding long enough." One of the pink Cheshire Cats just above to his right winked! "What? Did you just wink at me cat?" Michael said a little louder, staring intently at one of the pink cats with the large grin. Quickly, he walked over and pulled his brother by the shirt sleeve.

"What? Why'd you do that? What's wrong?"

"Follow me. C'mon. Over this way. Now," Michael said as he turned and anxiously walked back towards the group of Cheshire Cat plushes on the wall.

As his brother walked up beside him, Michael said softly, "OK, cat, do it again."

"Who are you talking to? There's nothing here but a bunch of plush characters."

"Really? Is that what you think?"

"Looks that way to me," Charlie replied. "I mean, I don't see any-thing on the shelf that even comes close to resembling Midnight."

"Oh, so you think I'm making this all up?"

"Yes, you could say that. Either that, or you didn't get enough sleep last night."

"The two of you really need to stop with all the bickering. It's beginning to give me a headache."

"What? Who said that?" Charlie asked, whipping his head around in the general direction of the voice.

"See, I told you, Charlie."

"Told me what, Michael. I still don't see anything that looks like Midnight."

"You need to try a little harder, young man," the voice whispered.

Charlie turned his head once again, facing the plush-lined shelves.

"Pssst, up here." The patient young boy, who had anything but patients at the moment, glanced upwards and to his right—focusing all his attention on the cluster of pink Cheshire Cats. To his surprise, the second cat from the left turned from pink, to purple, then blue. Its eyes glowed yellow, and the grin on his face grew even larger, exposing a big set of pearly whites. And then...he spoke. "Glad you could make it boys," the blue cat said.

"Midnight?" Charlie said with a perplexed look on his face.

"The one and only," the cat replied.

"But—"

"I know. I look nothing at all like myself. It's a gift. A little extra something-something Frank threw in when he thought me up."

"So you can change into other things?"

"And then some," Midnight replied.

"That's amazing," Michael said. "So can you like, change into an orange elephant, or a clock?"

"Anything," the cat replied. "But now we need to move the conversation onto more important matters. Like getting you boys to the watchmaker."

"Right," Charlie added."The watchmaker. So how do we get started?"

"Simple. Pick me up and hold me in your arms. As you do, have your brother touch my tail."

"And then what?" Michael asked.

"You'll see," the blue cat replied with a grin. "So Charlie, if you would please."

"Sure," the boy replied. He picked the blue cat off the shelf and held him in his arms.

"And now it's your turn, Michael." The young boy gently grabbed hold of the feline's tail, which was sticking out through Charlie's arms.

The room began to spin—all became a blur of colors, distorted voices and unrecognizable music. Faster and faster the room continued to spin—to the point that everything turned to bright white and silver-like dust. Round and round and round the funnel of sparkling dazzlement continued to spin. And standing dead center in the eye of the magic were the two boys and Midnight, who was still comfortably nestled in the arms of Charlie.

THHHHHHWOOOSH!

The funnel broke apart, disappearing into thin air and exposing a place vaguely familiar to the boys—who were now fully animated.

"Where are we?" Charlie asked, looking around from high atop a mountainside.

"You don't recognize the forest below?" Midnight asked.

"The realm of the watchmaker?" Michael replied.

The blue cat jumped out of Charlie's arms, and in mid air, transformed back into the overly large black cat the boys had come to know. "Very good, Michael."

"It was pretty obvious, I mean, since we're searching for the watchmaker, I assumed it would have to be in the realm where he lived," Michael replied confidently.

"Yes. While that *is* true in this particular instance, sometimes it is not."

"And why is that?"

"Well, Michael, there *are* times when certain characters, creatures or whatever may jump to another realm within WONDER. There are no limitations here," Midnight replied.

"So this is where we met Provo, Sassyfran, and Fethearwink?" Charlie asked.

"Indeed it is."

"The forest below looks different than it did the last time we were here."

"Which it not unusual in a realm of WONDER," Midnight replied.

"How so?" Charlie asked.

"Remember, the realms of WONDER are based on concepts and dreams of the Imagineers and animators, so they are in a state of flux. What you see today, may be different tomorrow, because Disney is constantly thinking and dreaming up new things. Which is the way Walt intended it to be. At least that's what Frank has told me."

"So Frank was actually working for Disney when Walt was alive?"

"Absolutely."

"Wow! That must have been pretty neat," Charlie said. "How old is Frank? He must be quite old. He doesn't seem that old?"

"Yes, Frank is quite spry for someone his age, I must say," the cat answered with a chuckle. "Anyway boys, we need to keep moving. This way gentlemen," the cat said. He headed up the narrow mountainside path, but was suddenly stopped by Charlie's words.

"I almost forgot. Last night Frank told me we needed to follow the frost trail? So, what exactly is that?"

"It's a hidden trail left by Neve the snow fairy, which can only be seen for the briefest of moments in temperatures above freezing.

Once it melts, no trace of it can be found. Which reduces the risk of any unlikely threats—such as Thorns and shadow villains."

"That's all good and such, but what about us? What if we don't spot a part of the trail before it melts? Then what?" Michael asked.

"Not to worry, young man. The frost trail is charmed. So it will not melt until after those intended to see it, such as us, lay their eyes upon it."

"But what if, say a Thorn sees it before we do?" Charlie asked.

"Again, it is a charmed trail, which is only visible the moment a friendly ally comes near it," Midnight replied.

"It sounds as if there are only a few seconds from the time we see the trail, to the time that it melts?"

"Exactly, Charlie."

"You said that the frost trail can only be seen for the briefest of moments in temperatures above freezing. So what happens if we go somewhere below freezing?" Michael asked.

"Yeah, that's a good question," Charlie added. "I would imagine the snow fairy's ice cottage is definitely located where temperatures stay below freezing. And if that is actually the case, how would the frost trail ever melt?"

"Freezing temperatures to one, may be balmy temperatures to another," the cat replied. As I've said before, and I'm sure I'll say again, here in WONDER, anything is possible." On his word, Midnight transformed again. But this time he became a large polar bear—making him well equipped for the chilly temperatures that lied ahead.

"Huh?" Michael reacted.

"It's going to be a little cooler where we are headed, boys. I highly suggest you follow suite."

"But...but that's not possible. I mean, how are we...I mean, we just can't turn ourselves into polar bears," Charlie replied.

"Why not?" Midnight answered back. "The only limitation you have here is your own imagination."

Charlie and his brother looked at the bear like he was crazy.

"Go ahead, what are you waiting for? Think it, then be it."

"Think what?" Charlie said. He continued to deny the fact that he could change himself into anything he wanted.

"Anything. Anything you can imagine. Just look at me, it's really not that difficult. Just think it, then be it. Go ahead, give it a try, Michael. I can see the wheels turning in your head. Just let it out and see what happens."

Michael squeezed his eyes shut with excitement and thought up something wonderful. Instantly, he transformed into a half-grown reindeer. "How do I look?"

"Ha-ha! Rather cute. I mean, magnificent," Midnight replied. "You'll do well where we are headed. OK, now it's your turn, Charlie. Give it a go, young fella."

Charlie closed his eyes and thought really hard—possibly too hard. POOF, he was a snow owl—POOF, then a seal—POOF, next a penguin—POOF, and finally...a funny looking elf?

"What?" Michael spat out." An elf? How in the world is that going to help where we are headed?"

"I saw you change into a reindeer, then I began thinking snow, which made me think of the watchmaker—who is sort of a toy-maker, like Santa. Then, you know, I put it all together and started thinking Christmas. So, now I'm a little guy who likes to help others, drinks hot cocoa and builds toys."

"You forgot to add, someone who does *very well* in bitterly cold weather," the bear said. "Not to mention, is the type of fellow who can conjure up a nice bit of magic if the need arises."

"Hmm," was all that Michael could manage to say in response to the polar bear's brilliant assessment of Charlie's choice.

"Speaking of magic," Charlie said, "it looks like a frost trail is forming over on that cluster of mountain shrubs."

Just a little ways from where they were standing, a miraculous trail of sparkling frost began to grow and spiral around the plant life on the side of the mountain. However, instead of leading up the mountain-side, the magic frost trail led downward towards the woods, where Charlie and Michael had met Featherwink the frog just the other day.

"Huh? What on earth is going on?" Michael said in a bewildered state. "Shouldn't the frost trail be traveling up the mountain? I mean, you would think the snow fairy's ice cottage would have to be somewhere up that way," he said, pointing up the mountainside. "At least that would be the *normal* choice. Right?"

"Well, this isn't exactly a normal place, now is it," Midnight answered. "And a polar bear will be far too warm where we are headed." The large white bear instantly turned back into a cat.

"Now I get it," Charlie replied. The boy switched from an elf back into his animated self.

"Well I'm not changing back, I still believe we're headed some-where cold," Michael added, reluctantly.

"Suit yourself, but it may get a little warm for a reindeer," the cat replied.

Large, chubby hands pulled away a pair binoculars from the staring eyes of Captain Fibs, as his sunglasses slid back down—stopping at the bridge of his large, red nose. He pushed his portly body away from the large rock he was leaning on, then handed the binoculars to the silver fox, continuing to look towards the mountainside. "Looks like your plan is working, foxy. Those two little brats and the chubby cat are headed this way."

"And to think you ever doubted me, Captain," the fox replied, as he held the binoculars to his eyes. He located the threesome as they descended down the mountainside—his sly smile growing larger by the second.

"Alright, alright, so we agree, it looks like your plan is working—"

"Now hold on there Duke," Fibs interjected. "I may have agreed with the old fox here, but that don't mean I believe this plan of his is gonna work. In fact, until I see the watch in my hands, as I hand it over to the Dark Thorns, I really don't believe much at all."

"Oh, it's going to work, Fibs," the fox snarled back, as he continued to follow the three watch seekers down the mountainside. "Yes, there's no doubt about it. The outsider and his two little helpers are going to lead us right to the watch, just as Ben promised."

"What makes you so certain the red headed fella told us the truth?" Grim asked.

"Consequences, my good man. Consequences."

Grim's looked confused, as he stared blankly at the fox. "I'm not following ya."

"Yes, I can see that," the fox answered back in a sarcastic tone. "Let's just say, if Ben chose not to tell me the truth, then he would have to deal with my little friend."

"And by little friend he means me," Flamario blurted out—cracking his knuckles.

"Oh, I get it now," Duke replied. "The fox used mister hot belly here as an intimidation factor to get what he wanted outta Benny."

"It's a wonder the two of them have survived this long under the command of the Dark Thorns," the fox replied under his breath, allowing only Flamario and Mr. Jollysnaps to hear what he said.

"Come again, fur brain," Fibs snipped back. He was sure the fox had made a crude comment directed at him and his men.

"It was nothing," the fox replied in a condescending manner. "Just mumbling to myself."

"Well, I think that's enough chit chatting gents," Mr. Jollysnaps jumped into the conversation to break things up. "What do ya say we get a move on? Our three little friends should be reaching the woods shortly, and we need to get into position to follow 'em to the watchmaker, eh?"

"Right you are mate," Fibs replied. "Duke, Grim, get off your duffs. We got work to do," the captain spat out, as he hoisted up his shorts.

"Yes, we've got work to do," Flamario added.

"Very well then," the fox said.

"I'll fetch me coach and head to the skies for a better view, while the five of you cover the ground," Mr. Jollysnaps said, as he pulled back and cracked his whip—turning a random branch in a nearby tree to gold.

Everyone let out an evil fit of laughter, while marching off into the woods to find the perfect hiding spot. There, they would wait for the arrival of their unsuspecting victims.

Michael had given in to the cat's suggestion and changed back to his human, cartoon form, finally admitting the course they were on would be far too warm for a reindeer.

"The frost trail leads deep into the woods," Midnight proclaimed. He pointed towards the ice-coated trail, which continued to magically wind its way over, under and around a multitude of shrubs, flowers, logs, rocks, tree branches, and even a slow moving stream. As sections of the trail were passed by the three adventurers, it quickly melted away, leaving no trace behind.

Further and deeper into the woods the two boys and cat carried on until the sunny, blue sky above had been completely shut out by the densely covered branches from the overhanging trees.

Midnight marched confidently onward, while Charlie and his brother's eyes began to wander, wondering if they were indeed headed in the right direction. It was hard for them to believe that a place so dark and eerie as this was fit for the cottage of a snow fairy.

"Are you sure we're heading in the right direction?" Charlie asked.

"It sure doesn't feel right," Michael added.

"The frost trail is still very much alive and moving," young men. "Why, just look at how she sparkles and glows. We need to keep up."

The two brothers looked at each other and shrugged their shoulders. "I guess you're right?" Charlie said, with doubt blanketing his mind.

"Right as a rainy day, Charlie," Midnight replied.

On the feline's last word, the three adventurers came upon a small clearing in the woods. In it's center was a very young tree— only eighteen inches tall at most. Under it was a small, moss-covered rock, no larger than an egg. And from above, filtered rays of sunlight shined through the overhanging leaves—highlighting the very spot upon which the small tree and stone sat. As Midnight, Charlie and Michael watched in wonderment from just outside the clearing, the magic frost trail began to spin in a tight, funnel-like manner until the frost became nothing more than radiant waves of silvery flakes, which gently floated downward upon the tiny tree and mossy stone. Each was sufficiently covered as if they were part of a miniature winter scene.

The three seekers slowly approached the incredibly small, yet quite astonishing, setting.

Rays of sunshine magically fused with the silvery flakes, setting off a dazzling display of blue and white sparks—and underneath its surface, the tiny little tree and stone began to grow at an enormously rapid rate!

Midnight and the boys quickly retreated back to their original viewpoint, as they witnessed a most amazing thing.

The tiny tree shot up and sprouted out into a full grown willow tree. And right beside it, before their very eyes, a cottage made of snowy, white stones, frozen sticks, leaves and straw grew from the size of a small stone, into a full-scale cottage with warm lights beaming from within.

The front door opened and a majestic, female voice called from within, "Please, come join us."

Hesitant to accept the invitation, Midnight spoke out, "And who is it that requests our company?"

"It is I, the snow fairy, Neve. Your friend and silent protector of the watchmaker. Please come in and join us, won't you?"

The boys, trusting what they had heard, immediately began to walk towards the open door, but were called back by the hesitant cat.

"Uh-uh-uh-uh-uhhhh, just a moment gentlemen. We need to make sure she is who she says she is before we go trouncing through that door."

"But you heard her, Midnight, it's the snow fairy," Charlie said. "You know, the one who led us to the watchmaker's hidden village? Why would she ever want to cause us harm?"

"Good point, young man," an older male voice called out from within the cottage.

"Is, is that you Raphael?" Midnight questioned.

A mature, well rounded man, short in stature, with rosy cheeks emerged from within the frost-covered cottage with open arms. "Welcome, welcome my friends. It is so good to see that you made it here safely."

"Raphael, it is you," Charlie said with excitement. He marched towards the watchmaker to give him a hug.

"Excuse me gentleman, I don't mean to break up your special moment, but I think it's best we all gather inside," a small voice beyond the entryway said.

"Yes, he is right. We should probably get inside before someone sees us," Raphael replied, stopping in his tracks. "Come-come, follow me inside where we can safely discuss our plans."

Charlie, Michael and Midnight followed the watchmaker into the cottage—the door gently closed behind them.

SHWOOOOOP! On the click of the door latch, the frosty cottage and willow tree immediately shrunk back down to their original miniature sizes, assuring no unwanted attention would come their way.

"Did you happen to see which way they turned?" A gravely voice asked from behind a small cluster of oak trees.

"Now why would the captain be looking for someone he expects us to keep track of?" Duke asked.

"Oh, I don't know," Grim replied. "Perhaps I thought three pairs of eyes for look'n would be better than two? Wouldn't you agree, Captain?"

"Depends how smart the ones doing the look'n are," Fibs replied, rolling his eyes.

"Really?" The fox said in a sarcastic tone to Fibs' response. "You mean to tell us your two best spies aren't even capable of following two little boys and a cat?"

"More capable than you, fluffy," Grim spat back to the fox.

"Ha-ha-ha-ha! My little friend here is a fox, in case you didn't realize," Flamario said. "Why, he could do a better job of tracking than you, or your pathetic friend, with both eyes closed."

"Is that so, you big overgrown hot head?" Duke said in defense of his friend, positioning a hand over his belt buckle—ready to transform into a toady troll for battle.

Flamario picked up on Duke's action and prepared to fight as well.

"Now, now gentleman," the silver fox interjected. "It's time to rise above these feeble grudges you share amongst one another and focus on the task at hand. Where was the last trace of the boys and cat?" he asked.

"Over there near the creek," Grim replied.

The silver fox walked over and sniffed the ground near the water's edge where Grim had pointed. "Their scent grows stronger in this direction," he said, pointing with his paw towards a pathway that led deeper into the woods.

"Alright, alright," Fibs replied, shaking his head and flailing his arms in the air. "C'mon-c'mon, let's get a move on before old fluffy here looses the scent."

The fox and fire breather smirked at the captain's frustrated remark and gestures.

Meanwhile, Mr. Jollysnaps continued to circle the woods from the sky above in his golden coach pulled by flying mules, to assure the seekers of the watch did not escape the forest.

As Midnight and the boys walked into the snow fairy's cottage, they were pleasantly surprised to also see sitting before them, Featherwink, Provo, and Ticky and Tocky. Unbeknownst to the boys, everyone was now the size of a tiny bug in a cottage no larger than an egg. And though everything was extremely small, the details of the snow fairy's humble abode were quite breathtaking. The walls were made of packed snow and tiny fragments of ice, which sparkled just so. Above was an extraordinarily high ceiling from which snow gently fell and bonded with the crystal-like floor to create an intricate snow flake pattern. The furniture was sculpted from ice and snow, yet when touched, was not cold. Upon the dining room table sat a bouquet of crystalized flowers which captured fragments of reflected light from the small, icicle chandelier above.

"Please, sit down," Neve said. "We have much to tell you, and very little time to do so."

"Yes-yes-yes, the snow fairy is correct," Raphael added. "Charlie, I have something special for you." The watchmaker reached into his vest pocket and pulled out the watch and showed it to the outsider.

"It's magnificent. Does it work?" Charlie asked.

"Oh yes, it works quite well. Do you remember everything I explained to you last night?"

"Like how to use the green dream dot sensors, and that kind of stuff?"

"Heh, heh, heh. Yes, all that, what do you call it? Stuff."

"I sure do. It was all I could think about last night."

"OK then, lets see how you do." Raphael carefully handed the watch to the boy. "Now, put it on, to see how it fits."

Charlie slowly moved the watch over his hand and onto his left wrist, which seemed way too small for the size of the watchband. "I, uh...I think it's a little big," the boy said, giving the watchmaker a baffled look.

"Are you sure?" Raphael replied. He nodded towards the watch.

"Even I can see it's too big," Michael said.

"Hey! Whats going on," Charlie blurted out. The watch magically adjusted to fit perfectly around his wrist. Not too tight. Not too loose.

"Looks like a good fit to me," Featherwink added.

"Yes, I must say, the watch does fit the boy rather well," Provo said.

"What kind of watch is that?" Michael said, staring intently at the timepiece.

Raphael smiled at the young boy. "Go ahead, Charlie, try it out, I'm anxious to see what you can do with it.

Neve interjected. "Just a little test for now. You must stay in the cottage. We don't know who may be out there looking for it."

"Yes, that would be smart," Raphael added. "Charlie, why don't you try something simple at first. Like say..."

"How about moving from here to that chair over there," Michael said, pointing towards a corner of the room, some twenty feet away.

Neve approved. "Yes, try moving to the chair using the watch, Charlie."

The young boy nodded. He pushed the button on the side, then spoke into the watch. "Take me to the chair in the corner of the snow fairy's cottage." Instantly, Mickey's hands began to spin, faster and faster, while at the same time, a brilliant pattern of purple, orange, blue and red light lit up the face. Suddenly, the hands snapped in place, a blue light expanded outward, from the watch, encompassing Charlie completely. SHWOOOP! Charlie disappeared from the dining area, then reappeared, sitting in the chair by the corner.

"It worked," Michael proclaimed.

Everyone joined in and celebrated Charlie's success. Featherwink and Provo danced on the dining room table, Raphael spun arm and arm in circles with the snow fairy, and Ticky, Tocky and Midnight all skipped around the legs of the dining room table.

"It works, it works," Raphael said in joyous celebration. After taking a few deep breaths to calm himself, the watchmaker continued. "Now remember, you can also use the watch to locate, and use, the nearest dream dot."

"Yes sir, I remember what you told us last night about the green dots."

"Good. Then you are *all* set. I wish you, your brother, and your kitty friend, good luck."

"Thank you, sir," Charlie said, as he started walking over to hug the watchmaker.

But just as he did, out of the corner of his eye, he saw a figure come walking into view from another room. The shape of the silhouetted figure appeared to be that of a young girl. Moving closer, the soft lit room revealed a beautifully crafted, wooden girl.

"Hello, Charlie. It's good to see you again," she said.

Charlie pulled back from the watchmaker, startled by the girl's words. "How...how do you know my name?" The young boy didn't know how to respond. All he could do was stand and stare—his mouth agape, as he took in the lovely features of the intricately carved, wooden girl.

Her hair was dark brown and wavy—pulled back and tied with a red bow. Her sparkling blue eyes were surrounded by long, lush lashes. Her cheeks were perfectly pronounced, and her lips, tight and pouty. She had on a sleeveless white shirt with a lace-patterned collar and cute blue shorts that fit just so. Her short laced socks were also white, and her shoes brown, with a subtle flower pattern on the tops.

"You don't remember me, do you?"

"Uhhhh, nope."

"It's me, Sassyfran."

"Ohhhh. It's, you? But...but, you look so..."

"Different. Yeah, I know. When Raphael finished fixing the watch, he was nice enough to change me into something a little more presentable. So, what do you think?"

Charlie sat in silence, continuing to stare.

"What? Am I really that hideous to look at?"

"No-no-no, just the opposite. I mean, you look very nice." Trying to get out of an embarrassing situation, Charlie turned to Raphael to offer his compliments. "You did an incredible job. I mean, uh, you are more talented than I ever thought. Um, what I'm trying to say is—"

The watchmaker giggled, as did the others. "It's OK, Charlie. I understand. And thank you. Creating this little girl is some of the best work I have done in a long, long time," he said with a humble smile.

"I'll say," Charlie added.

Everyone broke into laughter. They could clearly tell the young boy thought *quite highly* of Raphael's latest achievement in woodworking.

The snow fairy stepped forward and spoke, sensing it was time for the boys and Midnight to depart. "I have something for you, Charlie." She handed a small, clear object to the boy.

"What is it?" Michael asked. "It looks like an icicle."

"Yes. But it is much more than that, Michael, the snow fairy said as she looked at Charlie. "Keep it with you at all times. If you ever need my help, just hold it in your hand and call my name—I'll hear you."

"But it's made of ice. Won't it melt if he carries it around?" Michael asked.

"It will only melt if taken by someone not deserving of its power."

"Like a Thorn or a shadow villain?" Charlie asked.

"Yes, Charlie. Now put it into your pocket and make sure to carry it with you at all times."

The outsider carefully placed the magic icicle into his pocket.

"Very well then, it's time you head back to your parents."

"Neve is right. It would be best if you go back before it gets too late. Besides, you don't want to miss out on all the fun your parents are having in Disney Springs," Raphael added.

"Yes, it would be nice to spend time with our parents," Charlie replied. "OK, lets go" he said, while motioning to his brother and Midnight to come closer.

Michael responded, but the cat did not move.

"What about you, Midnight?"

"I uh, have to stay a little while longer. You two go on ahead, and I'll see you in the morning," the cat said, in a suspiciously strange manner.

"Yes, go enjoy a little Disney magic with your parents," Featherwink added.

"Well. OK. We'll see you tomorrow morning then. Right Midnight?"

"Without question," the cat replied.

"Good," he answered back. "Ready Michael?"

"Ready."

Charlie pushed the watch button, then said,: "Take us to our parents." Mickey's hands spun faster and faster, the watch face glowed brilliantly in multiple colors. SNAP! The hands locked into place, a bright, purple mass of light engulfed the boys. SHWOOP! They were gone.

"They should be safe now," the snow fairy said in relief.

"And not a minute too soon," Raphael added.

"Darkness is upon us. Tomorrow you will tell the boys about Ben and what needs to be done?" Neve asked.

"Indeed, I will," Midnight replied.

Chapter Fourteen

Heavy storm clouds had snuck in overnight. Not only into the morning sky, but into the outsider's *mind* as well. Who, at the moment, was staring out a rain-drizzled window from within the Beach Club Resort. His parents, contemplating whether to hike through the thunderstorm to Epcot or to wait it out in the lobby. Either way, it made no difference to Charlie. His thoughts were consumed with one single thing. *Why was Ben not at Neve's cottage yesterday?*

The doorman in the resort lobby approached the family. "I see we're having a little bit of weather out there," he said, peering out towards the unpleasant sky.

"Is it supposed to be like this all day?" Mrs. Z asked.

"Ohhhh, it should only last for another twenty or thirty minutes. After that, you should be good until around three this afternoon." It's Florida, and it's summertime. Which means, a chance of rain and thunderstorms are likely almost every day. Good news is, the rain usually doesn't last long. And with the Florida sun, things dry off in a hurry. Speaking of a hurry, your boys look like they're anxious to get somewhere."

"Awww. Yes, it's only their second visit to Walt Disney World and there are a lot of things they want to see and do," Mrs. Z replied.

"Say, that's a nice Mickey watch you got there, young man, where did you get it?"

Put on the spot by the doorman's question, Charlie was speechless. He struggled to come up with an answer.

"Yes, that is a good question. Where *did* you get the watch?" his dad asked.

"I uh...uh...I got it in the Magic Kingdom on our first day here, remember?" Charlie was sure his parents would never go for the lame answer he just dished out.

"From Uptown Jewelers on Main Street?" his father replied. "I don't remember you buying a watch that day. Are you sure you got it from there?"

"Oh yeah-yeah-yeah," the doorman said. "That's right. I've seen the watches in that jewelry store. They have some pretty cool stuff for younger folks."

"They do?" Charlie's dad was still was not convinced. "But I don't remember you wearing a watch that day."

Charlie's eyes grew large, his mind searching for an answer. "Uhhh, that's because I had it in the bag the store gave me," the boy nervously replied, hoping his answer would work.

"You know, now that I think about it, we probably did get it there, Ed," Mrs. Z said with a chuckle. We've been to so many stores, it's hard to keep track."

"Charlie joined his mother and the doorman in a good laugh to relieve the tension. "Yeah, Dad, don't you remember?"

"Not really. "

"You don't pay much attention when we're shopping anyway, Ed," his wife added. "And chances are you were probably distracted by something else when we were in the store."

"Yeah, you're probably right. Forget I even mentioned it," Charlie's father replied, which made everyone, including the doorman, laugh even more.

"Well, you folks have a wonderful day. Looks like the sun is beginning to peek through the clouds," the doorman said, pointing out the window towards the sky.

"What do ya know. This truly is a magical place," Mrs. Z declared.

Charlie was off the hook. He put on a big smile for the doorman, yet still, he could not stop thinking about the whereabouts of their good friend, Ben Glimmer.

The cast member pushed open the door and the Zastawits family headed out towards Epcot. Charlie was the last to exit, and as he did, the doorman stopped him. "That was a close one, don't you think? Make sure you ride Spaceship Earth today," he said with a wink and the tip of his hat.

Caught off guard by the remark, Charlie's eyes opened wide, then returned to normal. Excited by the doorman's comment, the young boy picked up his stride and led the way to the International Gateway—the rear entrance into Epcot.

The Zastawits family were well into their morning. They had made their way from the back entrance of Epcot, through the west side of World Showcase, and all the way to the Land Pavilion, which included a thrilling experience on Soarin'. Lunchtime was nearing and most guests had set their sites on a place to eat.

Eager to ride Spaceship Earth, Charlie came up with a brilliant suggestion. "Hey Dad, we should ride while others eat. I bet the line on Spaceship Earth would be short right now?"

"You know Charlie, that's not a bad idea. What do you think, Susie?"

"Works for me. What about you, Michael. Can you wait a little while longer for lunch?"

Charlie had told Michael earlier what the doorman had said. So, he was quick to oblige. "Yes, mom. I can wait."

"Done. Spaceship Earth, here we come," their dad said.

"The Dark Thorns have informed me that the outsider and his side-kicks will be returning to the realm of the watchmaker today, and that they will be doing so using a dream dot in Spaceship Earth."

"I can send Duke and Grim back to follow 'em, foxy," Fibs replied. "Should be pretty easy."

"Yes, I would think so, but lately it seems like the easiest of things have been rather *difficult* to carry out," the silver fox replied.

"Not this time. When they transport, my boys will be right behind 'em. And when they touch down in WONDER, they'll have a big surprise wait'n for 'em. This time, we, get, the watch," Fibs said with a snarl, as he held up a clenched fist.

"You just make sure they get here," Mr. Jollysnaps said. "We'll handle the rest."

"Why you over-shined golden boy," what makes you think you can handle the outsider and his gang any better than we can?"

"Do you have a plan once they arrive in WONDER?" the fox calmly asked.

"No."

"Well, there you have it. Let's just stick to what we're good at for now, shall we. You send your men to track 'em, and we'll work on the watch once they get here."

"Ohhhhp!" Fibs' face turned bright red and sweat began to poor over his forehead and cheeks—trying to control his temper. "All right then," he said while exhaling. Duke, Grim."

"Yes, Captain?" they replied.

"Transport to Epcot and go hang out by the ball. When the outsider and his brother show up, follow 'em onto the attraction and hitch a ride back here to Deep WONDER. Got it?"

"No worries, Captain. We'll stick with 'em like bees on honey," Duke said, as both spies set their brushed steel wristband devices for Epcot's Future World. "See ya soon Captain." SHWOOP! They were gone.

The line was minimal, only a short ten minute wait. Charlie and Michael held a quiet conversation, discussing their plan of attack once on the attraction.

"I'm not sure exactly what's going to happen once we're on the ride, but judging by the experiences we've had here so far, I'd say anything is possible."

"You're not kidding," Michael replied.

"Since nobody really gave us specific directions, I guess we just keep our eyes open and be ready for whatever happens?"

"I guess so, Charlie."

A younger, married couple with no children were right behind the boys and overheard their conversation.

"Oh dear, so is this a scary ride?" the wife asked in a heavy English accent. "This is our first time here."

"Yeah, and from what you were saying, it sounds like it might be a tad bit scary," the husband added. "Is it a rollercoaster with loops that turn you upside-down?"

The boys looked at each other and giggled. "No, not at all, Charlie replied. "It's a slow moving dark ride. Kind of like the Haunted Mansion."

"Ohhhh. Right-right-right. Like the Mansion you say," the husband replied. "We were just in the Magic Kingdom yesterday. What a jolly good time that was. Well darling, looks like we have nothing to worry about then. Thank you, gents."

"No problem," Charlie said, as they approached the loading area.

"Looks like it's your turn to board," the young, English lady said with a smile.

"Yes, good luck, mates. We'll see you on the other side," her husband added, giving the boys a thumbs up.

The boys looked back and returned the gesture, then spun around to face forward—each looking at one another with raised brows.

"What kind of conversation was that?" Michael asked.

"Uh, I don't know," his brother replied. "But it's time to get ready."

"Ready for what?"

"Whatever," Charlie said, as they began their journey through Spaceship Earth.

Their ride vehicle had just passed the halfway point and was approaching the newspaper boy, who was standing on the street corner shouting out for sales. To the boys, it was a memorable part of the attraction, simply because the paper boy was similar in age. To the paper boy's left was a box on which newspapers were stacked, and just ahead of him, a black light post. As the boys continued to study the scene, a bit of unexpected magic popped into view.

Appearing out of thin air, and wrapped around the light post, was a black fury creature who's eyes glowed green in the darkness. as it stared at the boys. Next came a big grin of white teeth. It spun quickly around the post several times, then looked at the boys again. It became much clearer who it was.

"Look at your watch, Charlie," the creature, cloaked by shadow, said.

Everything around them slowed to a snails pace and became blurry, just as it had the year before on the Jungle Cruise attraction.

The watch began to vibrate, Charlie glanced down. To his surprise, the small, green dots surrounding the watch face were fully lit. "C'mon Michael, it's time to go! He grabbed his brother's arm and somehow managed to leap out of the ride vehicle towards the center of the light post. Instantly, they were surrounded by a sphere-like mass of swirling green lights. The boys made contact with the post. SHOOP! They were gone.

Right behind them, the young English couple did the same—morphing into their true identities.

"There they go Grimsly, now's our chance!" Duke shouted, as the Thorn spies activated their wristbands and leaped towards the dream dot, following the outsider and his brother. SHOOP!

And right behind the Thorn spies, from high atop the street light, the furry black creature spun round and round the pole, before shooting like a meteor into the swirling lights."Lookout boys, they're coming!"

THOOP! The dream dot closed and everything returned to normal.

Mr. and Mrs. Zastawits, who had been sharing the same ride vehicle with their boys, were oblivious to what had happened. Their children were headed into another dimension, with trouble following close behind.

SHOOP! The boys were back in the fully animated world of Deep WONDER. But where? And why had they turned into toys?

"Michael, you look like an overgrown, wooden soldier."

"Well, at least I'm not a giant, overstuffed blue bear, like you, Michael fired back with his clickity jaw.

"Huh? A blue what?" Charlie said. He looked down at his fluffy paws.

"Ha-ha-ha! See, I told ya. What? Why does my jaw keep clicking?"

"Looks to me like you're all cracked up, Michael," Charlie roared and snorted in laughter. Indeed he was right. Michael was a life-sized nutcracker, with the largest set of teeth he had ever seen.

"Oh, real funny, Mr. Cuddly Bear."

"Now-now, boys. No need to argue. Midnight made sure you were both transformed into toys on your journey here."

The boys, so caught up in themselves, had not in the least bit bothered to stop and take in the environment around them.

An elderly lady in a wheel chair rolled in closer to greet them. Her hair was white as snow, her eyes—which sat behind a lowered set of glasses, a sparkling hazel. And her kind smile, warm as the sun.

"Transformed?" Michael asked.

"Yes, so that you fit in," the kind, old lady replied. She spread out her arms, inviting the boys to look around.

"Toys," Michael said with his giant, wooden jaw agape.

"Lots of toys," Charlie added, while slowly turning to take in the room.

There were dolls, spinning tops, building blocks, horses, trains, trucks and cars. Jack in the box's, stuffed animals, balls, planes, yo-yo's, pogo sticks and more. Shelves upon shelves of any toy imaginable surrounded the boys on every wall of the room.

"So who are all these toys for?" Charlie asked.

"It's just a little collection of mine. Something I do to keep myself busy."

"By the looks of it, I'd say you've been collecting for a long-long time," Michael said.

"Yes, heh-heh-heh, you could say that," she replied.

THUMP!-THUMP!-THUMP!

Someone was at the door.

Startled by the unexpected knocking, the kind old lady quickly rolled around in her chair—instructing the boys where to hide.

"You, blue bear, jump into that pile of plushes over in the corner. And you, soldier boy, go stand in line with the other nutcrackers over by the window.

The boys were quick to respond, as the elderly lady rolled her way to the door in her beautifully carved wooden wheel chair. Slowly, she opened the door, blocking the view of who stood before her.

"Ohhhhhh, why it's you. Are you OK? You look like you need some rest. Please, come in and join us."

I wonder who it is?, Charlie thought to himself. He laid motionless amongst the other plush animals.

"It's alright, boys. You can come out now," the kind lady said.

As she rolled back towards the center of the room, the mysterious guest following her in was revealed. It was their good friend, Midnight. It looked as though he had been through a frantic experience. His hair was ruffled and gnarly, with tiny twigs, shrubbery peddles and dirt mixed in. His breath was short and his large green eyes, tired.

"Midnight, are you alright? What happened?" Charlie asked.

"Thorn spies...two of em...followed you through the...the... dream dot."

"Thorn spies?" Charlie said with a quizzical look. "We didn't see any Thorns on Spaceship Earth before we transported here?"

"They...were right...behind...you."

Charlie and Michael turned and looked at each other. Neither one knew how to react.

"Remember? The couple behind you?"

"Behind us?" Michael said.

"The only one behind us were the people from England," Charlie added.

"It was...a...disguise," Midnight said, gathering his breath.

"You have to always be watching for those pesky Thorn spies," the kind old lady added. "They can pop up any place, any time, looking like anybody or anything." She sat a bowl of water in front of the cat.

Midnight took a hearty drink, exhaled, then addressed the boys. "I guess I should introduce you to our friend here. Charlie. Michael. This is Angelina, keeper of lost toys. Angelina, this is Charlie—the chosen outsider Raphael told you about earlier. And this is Michael, his brother, and a valuable contributor to our cause.

"It's nice to meet you Charlie and Michael."

"Nice to meet you as well," the boys replied.

"So how did you know there were two Thorns behind us?" Charlie asked the cat.

"I was there keeping an eye on the two of you, to make sure everything went according to plan. That's when I saw them. But by then, it was too late for me to do anything. So I followed them into the dream dot and managed to cause quite a distraction. Enough so, that we ended up in an entirely different realm of Deep WONDER."

"Wow, really?" Michael said.

"And where was that?" Charlie added.

"You know, I'm not quite sure...but wherever it was, it's a long ways from here, which should give us plenty of time to complete our tasks for today."

"Which is?" Michael asked.

"To find and rescue Ben."

"Ben! You know where he is?" Charlie asked.

"Hold on there, lad. I said we have to find him first.

"Oh. Yeah. Right. Sorry. Go on.

"So, what I need the two of you to do, is to sit tight and visit with Angelina, while I venture out and pinpoint Ben's location."

"You just want us to sit here and pretend to be toys?" Michael replied sarcastically.

"Well...yes. That *was* the reason we had you brought into Deep WONDER as toys."

"But I thought we could change into whatever we wanted in Deep WONDER?" Charlie asked.

"Yeah, so if we wanted, we could change back to ourselves right now," Michael added.

"Yes...I guess that's true, Midnight said. But if you do, it will increase the risk of the Dark Thorns tracking you down. They have the ability to look into all realms of WONDER, and Deep WONDER using dark magic. How, I'm not exactly sure. But there have been instances in the past where it was the only way they could have possibly found out what we were doing, or where we were going."

"Like when they sent the Yeti after us last year in the simulated world of the Animal Kingdom?" Charlie asked.

"Precisely," Midnight replied.

"Ohhhh, right," Michael said.

"So now you see why it is important you remain toys and stay with me for now," Angelina said. "We need to keep you hidden away from the dark forces for as long as we can.

"We understand now," Charlie said.

"Besides, I have a good idea where they're keeping Ben, thanks to the watchmaker's advice," the cat said. "So I should be back shortly."

"And then what?" Michael asked.

"And then, you and your brother get to come with me to rescue him," Midnight said, as he jumped onto the ledge of an open window, smiling.

"I can't wait," Michael said.

"Yeah, see ya soon, Midnight," Charlie added.

"Indeed you shall." The cat winked, then leaped off the window ledge—out of sight.

Hours passed. Charlie, Michael and Angelina had enjoyed a thorough conversation, learning many interesting things about one another, while waiting for Midnight's return.

There was a knock at the door.

Just as before, the old lady sent the boys to their respective hiding positions. When Angelina opened the front door, before her stood the sliver fox and Mr. Jollysnaps, posing as sellers of potions.

"Hello there, young lady. Is your mother home?" the fox said with a flirtatious grin.

The elderly lady's blue eyes grew large, then receded quickly behind her glasses. *I know what they're up to and they're not going to get away with it,* she thought to herself. Angelina giggled and said out loud, "Why no, I don't think you will find anyone here who is older than the one who stands before you."

The fox let out a thunderous laugh. "But of course, you must be the lady of the house. My friend and I are here to make your life easier."

"Easier?" she replied

"Yes, easier. The briefcase I carry in my hands contains a remedy for allllll your aches and pains. Guaranteed to make you feel at least thirty years younger."

"Is that so? Sounds amazing," Angelina replied, thinking to herself, *what a liar this silly fox is.*

"One sip will have you up and out of that wheelchair, dancing around like a young school girl. Ask my assistant here, he has seen it happen right before his very own eyes."

"He's right me lady. My own mother was bedridden, barely able to feed herself. But after she took a spoonful of our magic potion, she practically jumped out of bed and started doing cartwheels around the bedroom," Mr Jollysnaps replied.

"Why, that's the most incredible story I have ever heard," Angelina said, not believing a single word they had told her.

"If you let us in ma'am, we'd be more than happy to give you a free taste," the silver fox insisted.

The elderly lady played along to humor the fox, and to buy herself time—hoping that Midnight would soon return so they could end the silly game of lies the fox and coachman were playing.

"Well...alright, come in. You can set up over there on the table," she said, pointing towards the kitchen. As she followed the two shady guests into the kitchen, Angelina glanced at the pile of plushes and the row of nutcracker soldiers by the window, to check on the boys. Both were still holding steady.

As the fox and coachman set up their display of fake potions and continued to spin their web of lies, they scoured the room with quick glances. Both were positive the outsider, who carried the Watch of WONDER, was hiding nearby.

"What a lovely place you have here, uhhhh...I don't believe we've been formally introduced yet," the fox said, while at the same time thinking, *I know you're here little boy, but where are you hiding?* "I'm fox, Mr. Fox. And my assistant here is Mr. Jollysnaps."

"But you can call me Jolly, me lady."

"And what...may I ask," *there you are, we've got you now, boy,* "is your name, young lady?" The fox spotted the blue bear wearing the watch. He nodded to the coachman—pointing out the bear in the corner.

"My name is Angelina, keeper of—"

"Keeper of lost toys—which you will *never* get your hands on, you filthy scoundrels!" Midnight shouted from the windowsill.

"Grab that blue bear!" the fox shouted, as he swept his arm across the table, knocking all the potion-filled bottles to the floor—which shattered into hundreds of pieces and created a hindrance to the cat.

The coachman pulled the golden whip handle from his long jacket, holding it in his right hand. He made a casting motion towards the bear in the corner. A magic whip sprouted outward from the golden handle and quickly wrapped itself around Charlie before he could move. Jollysnaps gave it a firm tug, immobilizing the outsider, giving the fox an opportunity to remove the watch from the blue bear's wrist.

Angelina somehow managed to build up enough momentum in her wheelchair, running straight into the coachman—knocking the whip handle loose from his grip.

"I've lost the whip," Jollysnaps called out to the fox.

The silver fox charged towards Charlie, who was battling to regain his freedom from the whip.

Leaping into the air, the fox's eyes grew large—his silvery hair, standing on end. *The watch is finally ours*, he thought to himself.

SMACK!

Blindsided by the giant wooden nutcracker head of Michael, the fox fell fast to the floor, almost unconscious.

What was that? What just hit me?

Jollysnaps grabbed hold of the whip and lashed out at Michael, wrapping up his legs and tugging hard. The nutcracker fell to the floor with a loud THUNK!

The coachman reached down and pulled his partner off the floor. "You alright mate?"

The fox nodded, as he rubbed the side of his head then asked,"Where's the bear? We need to get that watch."

Meanwhile, Charlie had changed into an animated version of himself, making him a much more formidable opponent for the fox and coachman. "Over here, you lug heads," he shouted. "Looking for this?" He held up his arm, showcasing the watch.

"The watch! That belongs to us now," the fox growled, "and we're not leaving without it."

The shadow villains charged the outsider. One from the left, the other from the right.

Fearing the worst was about to happen, Charlie froze.

The fox and coachman leaped into the air towards the boy—both ready to seize the watch.

There was a sudden burst of light and magic flares from a corner of the room.

Featherwink shot out of its center, and while suspended in mid air, turned and threw a ball of radiant light in the direction of Charlie, striking him in the mid section. SHOOOP! Charlie shrunk to the size of a pin.

The shadow villains collided in midair, both falling hard to the wooden floor.

Feathwink clapped his hands together. ZWINK! Charlie grew back to regular size.

"Over here lad," Midnight called out to Charlie.

The outsider jumped to his feet and ran across the room where the cat and Michael were standing by the fireplace.

"Not so fast fellas," the fox growled, as he regained his footing. "We still have unfinished business."

"Not today my friend," the cat replied. He jumped in the air and flicked his large striped tail at the foul creature. A large stream of magical light shot from Midnight's tail, wrapped itself multiple times around the fox, grew wings, then flew out through the window—carrying the fox deep into the woods. He would not be returning anytime soon.

"Lookout, Charlie!" Michael yelled.

Mr. Jollynsaps had regained his composure, and cast his golden whip towards the outsider's watch arm.

In a split second, Featherwink thrust his hands towards the coachman. A meteor-like burst of magic dust shot out from his palms, striking the shadow villain squarely in the chest—instantly, shrinking him, and his whip, down to the size of a harmless field mouse.

"Aghh! What in the devil have you done to me you silly purple frog," Jollysnaps squeaked out in a fitful rage. "You...you turn me back this instant."

Midnight charged the mouse, hissing and meowing with his claws out.

Mr. Jollysnaps shrieked from fear, then took off like a dart towards the gap underneath the front door—quickly disappearing from sight.

Everyone let out a big roar of laughter, including Angelina.

"Oh, I haven't laughed like that in ages. You should come around more often," she said to the cat and frog.

"It's been a pleasure, dear," Midnight replied with a nod.

"Yes, a true delight," Featherwink added.

"What now, Midnight? Did you find Ben?" Charlie asked.

"Yes, I was able to locate our friend."

"So where is he? Can we go save him?" Michael impatiently asked, as he morphed back into his animated human form.

Featherwink looked at the cat and said with a nod, "Tell him."

"Well, the good news is, we know where Ben is, and he is safe. The bad news is, I received word from Frank that the second Kingdom Crystal location has been discovered."

"And? Why is that bad news?" Charlie asked.

"Well...the Patrons believe the crystal's location is going to change before sundown tomorrow, the purple frog said."

"I see where you're going with this, and I don't think I like it," Charlie replied.

"So you understand what needs to be done?" Midnight asked.

"Yes...I do."

"What? Did I miss something?" Michael blurted out.

"You and I have to help these two find the second Kingdom Crystal before we save Ben," Charlie said to his brother in a somber tone.

"No. No-no-NO!" Michael shouted back. "Ben is our friend. We need to save him before we go looking for some stupid crystal."

The cat and frog bowed and shook their heads. Both looked up, ready to council the young boy. But they were called off by the keeper of lost toys.

Rolling her chair close to Michael, she said, "Young man, if you think for one moment that we, or any of the other Patrons, do not value Ben's life more than the crystal, then you are sadly mistaken. *Any one of us* would put Ben's life ahead of the crystal if we had a choice.

Michael looked to Angelina with teary eyes and said, "We...don't have a choice? Why don't we have a choice?"

"Ben is but a single individual. But if we fail to gain control of the second crystal before the evil forces of FOTO...why then, all of us will face extinction. WONDER and all that surrounds it, will face extinction...including Ben, the parks, the movies and everything else we've come to know and love about Disney."

Michael stood and stared, with a blank expression, into the kind, old woman's eyes.

"Have faith in the Parton's decision, Michael. Trust...trust in your friends. You must believe, that THIS decision, is the right decision," said Angelina. "As for Ben, we know where he is," Midnight added. And I promise you this, Michael, once we get the crystal, rescuing him will be our highest priority."

There was a moment of silence. The young boy lowered his head to weigh the options in his mind. Then he looked up—his eyes void of all emotion. "Very well."

Chapter Fifteen

The sun rose, painting the sky with warm hues of yellow and orange, day six of their vacation had begun. Repeated thoughts of Ben's whereabouts had looped through Charlie's mind over and over the entire night before—leaving him sleep deprived. His concerns to find the second Kingdom Crystal, with only the guidance of a large black cat and a purple frog with wings, had only added to his night of sleeplessness. And though Midnight and Featherwink were quite capable in helping the outsider, without Frank Wellington's assistance, Charlie was most certain finding the crystal would be nearly, if not totally, impossible.

Where are you Frank? Charlie thought, staring into the steam-coated bathroom mirror. *I know he said there were other things he needed to attend to, but how long does that take? Really? If he doesn't get back here soon—*

THUMP-THUMP-THUMP.

"Charlie, what's taking so long? I need to take a shower too," Michael shouted through the bathroom door.

"I'll be out in a minute. Just chill out." *Geeez, that kid has no patience,* Charlie thought. *Now what was I thinking? Oh yeah. If Frank doesn't come back soon, I don't know how we're EVER going to find the second crystal. Not a chance.*

THUMP-THUMP-THUMP.

"Done yet?" Michael barked again.

"Charlie, you've been in there long enough," his mother said. "Come on out so your brother can get cleaned up, please."

"Just give me one, more, second, pleeeease," Charlie said—almost falling, as he pulled his shorts up. "Doesn't anybody have any patience around here?" he mumbled to himself.

"But, Dark Leader, if we—"

"There is no more time for fiddle-faddle, Captain Fibs," Senkrad said, raising a hand to silence the captain.

"But, but we know where the second crystal is, and—"

"Yes, for the most part, you and your spies *have* done well to track down the young boy and the Object of Magic he holds in his possession. However, you have FAILED miserably to capture this so-called, outsider, or at the very least, to bring us the watch upon his wrist. And now you want us to believe that you can *not only* get the watch, *but also,* the second Kingdom Crystal?" Senkrad questioned.

Fibs shrunk into his chair like a frightened little child.

The Dark Leader went silent and turned to Fibs. "The other Dark Thorns and I presented you with several opportunities to retrieve the watch. You failed. We *even* sent shadow villains to assist you in capturing *this illusive* Object of Magic. Yet still...nothing.

Fibs swallowed deeply. "And?"

"And," Senkrad said in a cold, gravelly voice—his dark, lifeless eyes staring right through the Captain's, "We. Will. NOT. Fail. Again."

Charlie had heard people using the phrase "Animal Kingdom hot" on the bus ride over from their resort to the park. Though he really didn't think much about it until now—as he and his family waited in line for the It's Tough to be a Bug! attraction.

The line curled endlessly towards, around and under the spectacular Tree of Life, and all the lush foliage that surrounded it—which offered only temporary relief from the hot, mid-morning sun, as everyone slowly crept along.

"Mommy, can we go inside now.? It's hot," a little girl, no more than five, said to her mother—who was doing all she could to keep her daughter cool.

"Michael, here, you need to drink some of this, honey." His mother handed him a partially frozen bottle of water. "Here's one for you too, Charlie."

Relieved by the ice-cold touch of the plastic, Charlie rubbed the bottle across his forehead, then twisted off the cap—chugging nearly a third in a matter of seconds. As he tilted his head back to take another swig, the giant monkey head near the attraction entrance came to life—directing its attention towards Charlie.

"Ooh-ooh-ooh, young boy wait here with brother, Ooh-ooh. Let parents go ahead."

Charlie looked down at his watch, confused by what he saw. The green dots were fully lit and small. A swirling mass of colorful, green light began to rise up from the watch face. It was time to go.

"Michael, wait here," Charlie said, holding his brother back—allowing their parents to walk inside while they remained outside.

"Ooh-Ooh, watch take you to Epcot, Ooh," the giant monkey said.

"Epcot?" Charlie questioned.

"Ooh, cat and frog in Epcot, Ooh-Ooh."

"What's going on, Charlie? Who are you talking to? And why is your watch lighting up like that?"

"The big monkey."

"You mean that big head?" Michael said, pointing to the monkey head.

"Where in Epcot?" Charlie asked.

"Ooh-Ooh, dolphin head."

"Dolphin head?"

"Charlie, what in the world are you talking about? Dolphin head?"

"I'm still talking with the monkey, be quiet, Michael."

"Dolphin head go through before, Ooh."

"Oh, you mean the dolphin at the Neptune fountain? In the Italy Pavilion?"

"Charlie, those people over there are giving us funny looks. I bet they think you're nuts. Something better happen soon, or they're going to point us out to a cast member," Michael said.

"Yes, ooh. Italy, ooh-ooh."

"Got it," Charlie replied.

The monkey's eyes lit green and a large mass of bright light pushed its way outward from the edges—outlining the giant head.

The swirling mass of lights on the watch spun faster and faster—growing brighter and larger, eventually encapsulating the boys.

The giant monkey head opened up as if it were hinged from the top. The light unleashed from behind blinded their vision, forcing the boys to look away and shield their eyes.

Instantly, Charlie and Michael were pulled into the light. SHOOOOOOP!

The giant head slammed shut with a giant THUD!

They were gone.

And their parents, unaware.

Charlie and Michael sat on the bench nearest the Neptune fountain, waiting for the arrival of their two magical friends.

"Well, we're here," Michael remarked.

"I'm sure...", his brother stopped mid-speech, caught off guard by something rather unusual.

"What is it, Charlie?"

Pointing towards the fountain statues, he said: "Dolphin head."

Michael turned, his eyes went wide as saucers.

The left dolphin had Midnight's face, and the right, Featherwink's. So flanking Neptune were two smiling dolphins, one with a cat's head, the other a frog's head.

"Morning chaps," Featherwink said. "Are we all set to go?"

"Can anyone else see you besides us?" Charlie asked.

The boys nervously looked around. Worried someone would see what they were seeing.

"Not at all lad," Midnight said with a chuckle.

"Whew, that's a relief. Yeah, we're ready," the outsider said. "Wait. What...what's that?"

The Neptune statue had taken on life and was rotating the trident above its head in a large circular motion. A gust of tornado-like wind grew out from the statue and picked up the boys. Round and round they spun—screaming and kicking in the air. A whirlpool opened up at the foot of the statue. Neptune cast the trident downward towards the spiraling water. The boys, controlled by the motion of Neptune's trident, followed suite and shot down into the whirlpool. Shrinking along the way on every rotation.

Then suddenly. SHOOP! Everything went silent.

They uncovered their eyes, and were amazed by what they saw.

Charlie and Michael were in the club car of a passenger train... traveling through a small village, scaled to the size of a model train. They were still in Epcot's World Showcase, only now they were in WONDER's Germany pavilion. And they were...MUCH smaller.

The tiny train rolled on along the tracks. Sitting across from Charlie and his brother were Midnight and Featherwink.

"So, what do you think, boys?" Midnight asked, as he looked towards the window, queueing the boys to do the same.

Giant guests beyond the enormous iron fence were pointing, smiling and admiring the miniature train system the boys and their two friends were traveling around, over and over again.

Charlie gave it a good look over, and was astonished by what he saw.

Michael did the same.

"It's amazing," Charlie said. His mouth agape, as he and his brother continued to stare out the club car window.

"You're probably wondering why we're here?" Midnight asked.

"What?...oh, yes," Charlie replied. His eyes still occupied by the view. "So what *are* we doing here, and why..."

"Why are we SOOOOOO small?" Michael blurted out.

"Yes. Exactly." Charlie added.

"We needed to find a place to talk. A place, where there was *absolutely* no chance someone would overhear. Especially Thorns," the cat replied.

"Oh, that makes sense," Charlie said, continuing to look out the window. "And I definitely think you managed to do that."

"Now then, if you would please," Midnight said, to call the boy's attention away from the window. "We need to discuss the location of the second Kingdom Crystal."

Charlie's ears perked up.

"It has been brought to our attention by some of our best Patron spies that the second crystal is currently hidden somewhere on the Western River Expedition attraction."

"Western River what?" Charlie replied.

"The Western River Expedition attraction," the cat answered back.

"I've never heard of it. Which park is it in?" Charlie asked.

"I've never heard of it, either," Michael added.

Featherwink chuckled. "Well, that's probably because it was never really created."

"Huh?" the boys replied.

"You see, Western River Expedition was a boat ride dreamt up by legendary imagineer, Marc Davis, that never came to be. It would have taken guests on an extraordinary, and very entertaining, journey through the old west."

"Similar to Pirates of the Caribbean, only with cowboys, if you can imagine that," Midnight added.

"WHOOOA, cool. If they would have built it, where was it going to be?" Charlie asked.

"It would have been an integral part of a western themed area in Fronteirland, called Thunder Mesa. Which, would have contained multiple attractions in one incredibly themed area. And it would have been laid out right where Splash Mountain and Big Thunder Mountain Railroad now reside," Midnight explained.

"But anyway...back to the crystal," Featherwink blurted out.

"Yes. Right. Heh-heh. The Kingdom Crystal," Midnight said; embarrassed he had gotten off topic.

"Yes, please tell us about the crystal, Midnight," Charlie politely insisted.

"So we know that the second crystal is currently hidden somewhere on the Western River Expedition attraction, as I already mentioned. But there are still *two* obstacles standing in our way."

"And what are those?" Michael asked.

"One: we don't know exactly *where* on the attraction to look. Two...and this is a big one: neither Featherwink nor myself knows exactly how to...well, find the attraction."

"What? You mean the Patron spies, Frank, or whoever, didn't tell you how to find the place where the crystal is hidden?" Michael shouted.

"Yes-yes-yes, we know. It's going to be a bit of a challenge," Featherwink said. "But me and the cat here are pretty sure we can figure it out."

Charlie stood up from his seat and began to pace the floor. " 'A *bit* of a challenge', I'd say it's a lot more than that."

"More like impossible," Michael added.

"Now-now, boys, we just need to think things through," Midnight said, attempting to calm Charlie and his brother down.

"Think? Think using what? We have NOTHING to go by," Charlie said in a panic.

"We're doooooomed," Michael moaned, while sliding down in his seat.

"Come now, chaps. We gotta look at this on the bright side," Featherwink said. He rose off his seat and into the air—his wings flapping fast as a humming bird's wings. "We do have *one thing* that may help us."

"And what is that?" Charlie asked in a defeated tone.

"A rhyme," the frog proclaimed.

"A what?"

"A rhyme."

"That's right," Midnight stated. "I almost forgot. Frank did tell us a rhyme, didn't he...but, I can't quite remember how it goes?"

"No need to worry about that, my friend. I've got it right up here in the old noggin," the frog said, pointing to his head. Then he descended back to his seat.

"Oh, thank heavens for that," the cat replied, sighing in relief.

"So? Let's hear it," Michael demanded.—his eyes bulging with impatient curiosity.

Without hesitation, the purple frog struck a pose and recited the rhyme:

> "Off in the distance, the sun drenched hills.
> A magic place, with lots of thrills.
> Marked in orange, red and gold.
> The thing you seek, not to be told.
>
> To find it well, an object from a friend.
> Will take you to it's glorious end.
> Begin where it drops, a prickly theme.
> Where once could have been, a brilliant dream."

Charlie's fingers moved quickly, typing the eloquently spoken words of Featherwink into his phone.

"So it sounds like we're headed to the Magic Kingdom?" Charlie asked.

"My assumption, precisely," Midnight answered.

All four exchanged glances. The outsider pushed the button on the watch and said, "Take us to the Magic Kingdom."

The watch hands began to spin faster and faster, as a pattern of bright colors looped quickly behind them. POP! Mickey's hands snapped into place—one pointing left, the other right. A brilliant orange light exploded outward from the watch face and engulfed all four seekers. SHHHWOOP! They were gone.

SHHHHHHUP! Charlie, and the others popped into WONDER's Magic Kingdom, tucked away in a hidden nook near the Country Bear Jamboree attraction.

The sky was perfectly blue. The temperature, spot on. And every detail from the walkway to the shrubbery was flawless. Even the bird in a nearby tree was chirping in perfect harmony to the music cascading through the air from the Country Bear's show.

"Hmmmmm? So where do we go now?" Michael asked.

"Thunder Mesa, if built, would have been somewhere over in that direction," Midnight replied, pointing left with his paw. "I say we head that way."

As the four adventurers made their way out of the shadows and past the Country Bear Jamboree, it was difficult to tell where they should begin their search for the second Kingdom Crystal.

Even though everything appeared to be normal at first glance, it was clearly obvious they were in WONDER.

Tom Sawyer Island was much larger, at least twice as big as the real island. There were multiple riverboats circling the island—all, filled to maximum capacity with happy guests. And all, three decks high, instead of two.

Whistling in the distance, Big Thunder Mountain Railroad's full scale ride vehicles chugged along—pulling screaming guests in their passenger cars, all detailed to perfection. Instead of just two rail systems, there were six. And the mountainous terrain, which the large steam-powered beasts traveled upon, was far beyond the size and believability of the real attraction back in the Magic Kingdom most were familiar with. Traveling through ginormous caves, over towering railed bridges, and up, over and around enormous western-themed terrain, the giant steam locomotives chugged, huffed and hissed along at break-neck speeds, giving their happy passengers the thrill of a lifetime.

But the most dominant of all attractions to capture their attention, was Splash Mountain. As the foursome set their eyes upon it, the sheer immensity of the mountain left them speechless. In the real Fronteirland, Big Thunder Mountain Railroad was the larger of the two mountains. But in WONDER, Splash Mountain was far superior. In fact, the peak of the mountain rose so high, that it nearly touched a small, single cluster of perfectly shaped clouds which sat above it—defining the mountain's enormity.

"So, which do we choose first?" Midnight asked Charlie.

"I'm not quite sure," the boy replied.

"Maybe I could help?" a young, and quite beautiful, cast member asked.

"Uh...uh...I, uh..." Charlie could not find his words.

"Hi, I'm Valerie, a Patron friend of Franks. He told me you'd be in the area. And you are?" she said, extending her hand out for Charlie to shake.

"Uh..." The boy was petrified by her beauty. Valerie's long black hair was pulled into a ponytail, and her stunning green eyes were simply too much for the young man.

"We're trying to decide which attraction to ride first, Miss," Featherwink replied. "They both look so appealing."

The girl covered her mouth and giggled.

"What is it you find so funny, dear?" Featherwink asked.

"Is that really the best story you can come up with?" She said.

"Story?" It's...it's not a story, young lady," the frog replied. Rattled by her answer.

"Well, if you say so, I guess I have no choice but to believe you."

"Yes, I guess you—"

"It's *not* the truth," Charlie confessed—his will, broken by the girls good looks.

Featherwink's eyes opened wide, his face turned red with frustration, as he gave the outsider an angry stare.

"Ohhh? Really?" Valerie said.

"No. Actually, it's not even close to the truth," Charlie replied.

"CHARLIE. We don't really know her," Featherwink mumbled under his breath, as he hovered near the young boys ear.

"But she said she's a Patron friend of Franks. That's a pretty trustworthy statement, don't you agree?"

Midnight looked at the boy, then the frog. He turned to the young cast member and said, "The boy is right, we need to trust her."

"So what is it you're *really* trying to do?" she asked.

"We're...well, trying to find one of the crystals," Charlie said.

"Crystals?" the young lady replied. "As in one of the Kingdom Crystals?"

"You got it."

The girl giggled again. "Frank told me that you would be looking for the crystal."

"He did? Well...why...why didn't you say that in the first place?" Featherwink barked out."

The cast member giggled even more. "I wanted to earn your trust, and I thought, maybe it would be best if I let you and your friends explain what you were trying to do, instead of me trying to push my way into the group."

"She has a good point," Midnight said. "Go ahead, Charlie. Let her read the rhyme."

The boy pulled out his phone and showed Valerie the rhyme.

> Off in the distance, the sun drenched hills.
> A magic place, with lots of thrills.
> Marked in orange, red and gold.
> The thing you seek, not to be told.
>
> To find it well, an object from a friend.
> Will take you to it's glorious end.
> Begin where it drops, a prickly theme.
> Where once could have been, a brilliant dream.

After a minute of analyzing the rhyme, Valerie advised, "I think I can help you."

"Really? That would be *such* a big help," Charlie said, exhaling.

"Yes, any information you can pass along from Frank would prove most helpful," Midnight proclaimed.

Valerie looked at the others, then back at the rhyme on Charlie's phone. She smiled, then explained while pointing, "You see, the sun drenched hills are clearly the two mountains that stand before you. All highlighted in orange and red. As for the magic place where this 'thing' resides, I have a hunch we will find it on one of *these* two attractions."

"But an 'object' is also mentioned in the rhyme?" Charlie questioned.

"Yes, this is the Object of Magic given to you by the watchmaker."

"Oh, you mean this watch," Charlie said, holding up his arm to show the cast member.

The Patron's eyes opened wide with excitement.

"Why yes. There...it...is," Valerie said in admiration. "It's so... beautiful. And yet, so powerful at the same time."

"So what else can you tell us?" Midnight asked.

She broke away from admiring the watch. "Oh. Sorry. It's just... I've never actually *seen* an Object of Magic before."

"Understood, my dear," Featherwink said.

The young lady continued. "The only thing we can really do now is to ride both attractions. It's clear to me that the watch will 'find it well', with 'it' being the crystal, once we are in the right place on the attraction. Which, by the way, will be marked in gold."

"How do you know it will be marked in gold?" Michael asked.

"Easy. Gold was the third color listed in the rhyme. And there is *obviously* no gold shown on the outside of either attraction," she stated, while guiding her hand along the mountainous landscaped area—showcasing her point.

"Well, one thing is *clearly* evident," Midnight said.

"And what is that?" Valerie asked politely with a smile.

"Without Frank sending you to help us, we would be *totally* lost."

Everyone burst into laughter, then headed for the Splash Mountain queue.

The WONDER version of Splash Mountain was proving to be nothing short of spectacular. The animatronic characters throughout the ride were so life-like, one would swear they were real. The flume logs themselves appeared to be quite real as well, and even smelled of real wood. Yet still, they were very clean, with no hints of wood dust or shavings. The waterway, along which they traveled, was on a much grander scale, and bared with it a full flowing river which cut through a country landscape that was so real, it was just like being outdoors on a sunny afternoon. Birds chirped, bees hummed, the summer breeze brushed against the cheeks of passerby, and the smells of nature bombarded their senses.

But just as Charlie and the others began to relax, Valerie turned and said to the young outsider, "This is where the fun begins. Are you ready to go to your laughing place, Charlie?"

Michael and the others looked at the young lady with quizzical expressions.

Two large vultures perched above the river came into view and said, "So, you're looking for a Laughing Place, eh? We'll show *you* a Laughing Place! Time to be turnin' around. If only *you* could!"

The young boy pulled the rhyme up on his phone and read the last two lines as their ride vehicle slowly ascended up the waterway:

> Begin where it drops, a prickly theme.
> Where once could have been, a brilliant dream.

Drops? He thought to himself. *Prickly theme?* "Michael, hold on! Things are about to get CRAZZYYYYYYYYYYYYYYY!"

Their log vessel hit the tipping point and rushed down the giant waterfall—forty, eighty, at least one hundred and twenty feet down!

Charlie's watch began to spin uncontrollably half way through their descent, fully illuminated in a multiple-colored pattern of brilliant, swirling lights and miniature star bursts.

SNAP—the watch hands locked into place. Both pointing to twelve. The face released a brilliant burst of orange light, sending them to a "magical place" in WONDER.

Their ride vehicle continued to plummet downward.

Another giant burst of orange light shot out in all directions from the watch, blinding its passengers, who were holding on for dear life.

There was a supersonic BOOM.

The log vessel launched into an even higher plunge speed.

Everyone's cheeks began to flap like jello in a hurricane.

Charlie's grip on the ride handle was beginning to loosen, as were the others.

All eyes were closed, as streaks of light flashed past the plummeting vessel—SPLOOSH!

The nose of the log bottomed out, popped upwards and slammed into the water—leveling off in a peaceful river flanked by a twisted arrangement of thorny briar bushes.

And just beyond the bushes to the left, a clearing, where guests were unloading from an unfamiliar site.

"This...this isn't Splash Mountain", Charlie mumbled, as he looked around.

"Isn't it breathtaking?" Valerie said, stepping out of their log vehicle to admire what stood behind them—her arms opened wide.

Everyone turned around, as they unloaded from the flume vessel, to take in one of Disney's greatest ideas that was never realized. Thunder Mesa. More than just an attraction, the majestic, table-top mountain range, painted in breathtaking shades of orange and red, acted as a scenic backdrop for all of Fronteirland, and included within it's parameters, such attractions as the flume ride they had just ridden, a runaway mine train, and most importantly, the Western River Expedition.

"There it is," Michael said, pointing to the sign.

"The Western River Expedition," Charlie said in belief.

"Yes indeed," Valerie added. "What do you say we go check it out?"

"That's precisely what I was thinking," Featherwink added, landing on Charlie's shoulder to ring out the water from his yellow scarf.

"Right you are," Midnight proclaimed. "Very well, young lady, show us the way."

Boarding the boat-like ride vehicle for the Western River Expedition, Charlie and Michael sat in the front row. Midnight and Featherwink occupied the second row. Valerie kindly volunteered to ride in the back—telling the others she wanted to give them the best chance possible to spot the location of the 2nd Kingdom Crystal.

As they entered the cave-like attraction, they were instantly surrounded by stalactites, some of which were in the subtle shapes of both animals and people. Everything around them was either flickering like a loosely connected light bulb or fuzzy like a television station with bad reception. Either way, it made it hard for Charlie and the others to make out any specific details.

"What's going on with all the flickering lights and stuff," Michael asked. "It's driving me crazy."

"Sometimes when an attraction only reaches the concept stage and is never actually developed, this is what happens," Midnight explained.

"So it's like an incomplete thought?" Charlie asked.

"Exactly, Charlie," the cat replied.

"But we rode the Rhine River Cruise last year in Germany and everything looked good," Michael said.

"I said *sometimes*, Michael. Not *always*," the cat replied.

The ride vehicle turned and entered the next setting of the attraction. It was a prairie scene, which included, several wild buffalo, howling coyotes, a cowboy sitting on his horse while serenading a group of steers, and three cowboys around a campfire playing a song, while the surrounding cactuses sang in harmony.

As their boat slowly past the singing cactuses, one broke off from the others and began to sing in riddle:

> "Oh give me a tune, from Big Jack's Salooooooon.
> Where the piano man and cowboys go plaaaaay.
> There's a man on the roof.
> And his horse is a goof.
> Cause the gold in the safe sure did paaaaay.

Gold? That's it, Featherwink thought to himself.

The frog flew up to Charlie's ear and whispered what he had just discovered.

"The gold, Charlie. Remember the magic place is marked by orange, red and gold."

"Yeah, I know. The entire Thunder Mesa area is made up of orange and red rock formations," Charlie replied, appearing half interested.

"I know, boy, but the gold," Featherwink fired back.

"What about it?"

"The gold is in the safe, Charlie. The gold is the marker for the 2nd Kingdom Crystal."

Immediately, the outsider's eyes lit up.

He stood up and shouted out to everyone on the boat, "That's it! The crystal is *in* the safe!"

"What are you talking about, Charlie?" his brother asked.

Midnight was also bewildered by the young man's proclamation. "Exactly what safe are you talking about, lad? And please, sit down before you fall off the boat."

"I...I'm not exactly sure? But Featherwink is right. I mean, it all makes sense. Doesn't it?"

"What makes sense, lad?"

"The two rhymes, silly," Valerie said. "Can't you see? They're both tied to one another. And the common link...is the gold."

Everyone turned back towards Valerie.

"She's right," Michael said.

Midnight turned back around to face Michael.

"Yep, she's definitely right," Michael said again.

Finally grasping the concept, the cat sat up tall, cleared his throat, and announced, "Very well then, let's keep our eyes open for this *magic safe*. And Charlie, I'd keep a special eye on that watch of yours, if I were you."

As they approached the magic elixir wagon, where a city slicker was working hard to sell his bottled up lies, Charlie's watch began to glow softly and Mickey's hands started to slowly spin.

To everyone else, these actions went unnoticed. But to Charlie, the slow movement of the hands and the subtle glow of the face were obviously different than what he was used to.

Next came a cowboy firing off his twin six shooters to the dismay of a Native American. As their boat passed under the wooden bridge, where the two animatronic figures stood, and around the bend towards the gunfight scene, something terribly unexpected found them.

The river suddenly split and a mysterious storm front with strong winds began to build.

Instead of banking right to continue through the attraction, their boat turned left and was blown towards a massive whirlpool.

"I...I don't know what's happening!" Valerie yelled out from the back seat.

The boat plunged violently downward towards the whirlpool and began to follow the current round and round, getting closer to the center with each passing rotation. The front end of the ride vehicle tipped forward, throwing Valerie out of the boat and onto a nearby rocky bank.

Charlie, was holding on tight to the boat rail with one hand, while his other arm protected Midnight, who's claws were fully dug into the seat.

Michael was now next to Midnight, his hands wrapped around the railing. Featherwink was clinging tightly to Michael's shirt sleeve.

Everyone in the boat screamed out in fear, as they continued spiraling downward towards the unknown abyss of the whirlpool—all the while, holding on for dear life.

"I'm sorry, Charlie, I don't know what to do! I'll see if I can get help!" Valerie shouted, as she stood braced against the rocky wall on the left side of the waterway, trying to avoid the violent storm winds and the possibility of being blown into the whirlpool.

Charlie could not see nor hear her.

The boat carrying the four helpless passengers reached the core of the whirlpool and disappeared.

Hidden within the conceptual realities of WONDER—in shadow, high up in the tallest tower of the full-to-scale Beast castle of Fantasyland, the first step towards capturing the watch had just been successfully executed.

"There, that should make it *easy* for our villainous friends," Dark Thorn Elontra said with an evil laugh. She turned and walked away from her magic fire pit, a tool of dark magic that allowed her to see, and control, anything within WONDER's Magic Kingdom—the realm she ruled. "We should have *no* trouble getting the watch, now."

"I agree," Captain Plank replied. "So what do we do next?"

"What do we do? I'll tell you what we do, Mr. Plank. You go tell your captain friend, Mr. Fibs, and his blithering sidekicks, they are cleared to enter our realm of WONDER and guard the safe until we get the watch from that pesky little boy and his friends."

"Where...uh, and where is that again, master of darkness?"

Elontra turned and stared through the captain's soul with her lifeless eyes.

"Oh. Oh yeah. I plum forgot. It's in the Western River Expedition over there in Fronteirland," Plank replied—nervously rubbing his sweaty forehead.

Elontra remained perfectly still and quiet, making the captain even more unsettled.

"And what...what about me and my crew?"

"Ohhh...I guess it wouldn't hurt for you and a few of your men to help guard the safe as well," Elontra said, rolling her eyes. "You never know who else the Patrons may send after the crystal. But one thing is *certain*. It WON'T be anyone who was on that boat."

Dark Thorn Elontra exploded into a bone-chilling fit of laughter, which echoed down the winding staircase of WONDER's abandoned Beast castle tower.

Chapter Sixteen

Their boat continued spiraling downward through darkness, deep into a place Charlie, Michael, Midnight and Featherwink were likely to never return from. Though now, instead of water, it felt like they were falling through air.

Click...click-click-click-SMASH-CRUNCH-BUMP-BUMP, THUD!

Darkness surrounded them. Above sat a pale moon, skirted by unruly clouds. A gust of wind danced through the trees—rustling the partially dead leaves. The sounds of owls, crickets, howling wolves, and other creatures of the night, surrounded their senses. Below them sat a leaf-covered terrain. They had not yet reached the ground.

"Oh my, I can honestly say, I have never been here before," Midnight proclaimed.

"Nor...nor have I," the frog added—snuggling close to the cat for protection.

"If neither of you know where we're at, how are we supposed to get back?" Charlie questioned. He looked at his watch, which had stopped moving.

Michael leaned over to peak at the watch. "It doesn't look like Mickey is going to do us any good."

"Never mind the watch," Charlie replied, looking down over the side of the boat. "The first thing we need to do is get out of this tree."

No longer had Charlie spoken, when a pack of wolves approached the base of the trunk—their red eyes staring intently at the boat passengers. First one, then three, then six of the wolves stood up on their hind legs—jumping upwards, clawing, growling, snarling and drooling for a taste of Patron meat.

SNAP! The crack of a whip scattered the wolves below, and turned the tree to gold.

Mr. Jollysnaps emerged from the shadows of the woods and into the clearing—his lean figure highlighted by the pale moon beams.

"I don't suppose you want to come down from there and give us the watch, like a good boy, now do you?" the coachman said, glaring up at the stranded passengers in the boat.

There was a pause of silence...nobody knew how to respond to the coachman's request. Tthey did know, however, not to give up the Watch of WONDER to such evil filth.

Jollysnaps let out a creepy chuckle, as he turned his attention away from the boat. "I guess *not*." he said, signaling towards the edge of the woods.

From the dark shadows of the forest, the sound of thunderous footsteps erupted, growing louder with each step—shaking the tree their boat was nested in. Branches cracked, snapped and popped. A ginormous man stepped into the moonlit clearing, revealing his identity. Large, burly and staring right at them, their worst fears became reality. It was Flamario.

Charlie felt his heart drop into his stomach as a barrage of panic-like thoughts rushed through his mind—*we'll never make it back to find the crystal, which means we'll never find Ben, and what about our parents, Frank, or even, our new friend, Valerie? Is she still alive? How will we get out of here alive? Why won't this stupid watch work? What are we supposed to do?*

"Now I bring you down from tree," Flamario said in a thunderous tone. "Mr. Fox, bring me the fire."

"Coming right up," a voice called from the woods.

Featherwink and Michael spun their heads around, searching for the unidentified voice.

Click, click, click—the sound of two rocks being struck together echoed from the woods.

"I tried to tell him, really, I did. I said, look big guy, this kid is smart. And the last thing he wants to do is see his friends, or his brother, get hurt."

Click-click-click.

"Then I said, why don't you let me talk to him. I'm sure he would gladly hand over the watch once he weighs his options."

Click-click-click.

"I mean, who wants to get cooked like a roasted marshmallow? I know I don't."

Click-click-POOF! The torch caught flame.

"But then, old fire breath made a good point," the silver fox said, as he came walking out of the woods carrying a lit torch in his right paw. "Patrons DO NOT bargain."

The light of the torch cast a shadow across the fox's face, as he stared upwards at the boat, giving the passengers a toothy grin.

"Quick, think of something," Featherwink frantically whispered to Midnight.

"I am, I am. Don't rush me."

The fox continued to stare at Charlie and the others, giving them one last chance to surrender the watch.

"Hurry up, we're about to be roasted like ducks," Michael barked.

"Almost there," Midnight said.

"Almost? Almost isn't gonna get us anywhere but cooked," Featherwink insisted.

"Hmm? As you wish. I thought you were smarter than that, young fellow," the silver fox said.

"Aha! I got it!" the cat proclaimed. Jumping to the front of the boat, he spun around, faced the boys and frog, then curled his tail over his back so that is was aimed towards Featherwink.

"Enough chit chat," Flamario shouted. "Give me the torch."

"Farewell Patrons of WONDER," the fox announced, as he spread his arms apart, gracefully bowed, then handed the torch to his enormous friend.

"And now it is my turn," Flamario shouted. The giant of a man inhaled a flame from the torch, his chest puffed out like a rooster about to crow. With one mighty exhale, he unleashed a furious stream of fire towards the trunk of the tree.

Charlie and the others frantically scrambled, the tree of gold began to melt like butter.

As the tree continued melting, the boat shifted amongst the branches, causing Midnight to temporarily lose his footing.

With cat-like reflexes, the Patron feline gathered his balance, dug his claws into the boat, and with the flick of his tail, said,"Little winged frog of purple delight, grow much bigger and take to flight!" A sparkling stream of magical light shot out from Midnight's tail and struck the frog, who instantly grew to the size of an elephant.

Without hesitation, the giant, winged frog, grabbed hold of the boat and took to the air—carrying his friends away from their attackers.

"Huh? What? Get back here you big purple frog!" Flamario shouted. He took another deep breath, then shot multiple bursts of flames from his mouth, attempting to knock the flying frog, and the boat he was carrying, out of the sky.

"Jolly, get your coach. We've got a flying frog to catch!" the crafty fox hollered.

The coachman put two fingers to his mouth and whistled loudly.

From out of the woods came a golden coach, glistening in the moonlight. The eight, winged mules, all white in coat, nervously pranced in place, for they knew it was time to get crack'n—as in Mr. Jollysnaps crack'n their hind quarters with his magic whip. Not a good thing, as far as they were concerned.

"Alright then, climb aboard gents. We got a frog to fetch," the coachman said to his villainous friends. He climbed atop the coach, pulled the whip from his jacket, grabbed the reigns, then cast out— giving his whip a mighty CRACK! Magic sparks, followed by glittery, gold and silver sparks exploded off the tip of the whip in all directions. "Hee-yah!" the coachman shouted.

The mules shot off into the air, throwing the skinny man back into his seat, as he held onto the reigns.

"Make haste, you hairy herd of critters." CRACK! "It's time to earn your keep," the coachman yelled, as he pulled hard on the right reign—putting them directly on line to intercept Featherwink and the others. CRACK! Mr. Jollysnaps struck the lead mule on the left, a female named Hinny. Short tempered and ill mannered, she did not deal well with taking orders from others. As the whip struck her, she let out a loud, whinny-like "hee-haw," then flew even harder out of frustration. Frustrated that she had gotten herself into such a predicament as this. And frustrated she could not chew up and spit out the coachman's golden whip, which she hated.

The fox stuck his head out the side window of the flying coach and hollered, "We're really moving, Jolly."

Flamario followed suite from the other side window, though it was a tight fit for such a large head. His long black beard flapped in the wind, as he shouted, "Yes, we will catch the big frog and his friends in little time."

"Not a very friendly looking place is it?" Midnight said from the boat, as Featherwink continued on through the night sky, his arms and legs weakening each passing minute from the strain of carrying the boat.

"I need to land soon, I don't know how much longer I can keep this up," the frog replied.

Below lay nothing but dark forest, full of partially leafed, old twisted trees, thorny bushes and other unwelcoming terrain. Populating the forest were scores of unfriendly wildlife and unusual creatures, found only within the dark shadows of WONDER.

Suddenly, a noise rang out in the distant sky.

Charlie turned to his left. A small shiny dot was dancing through the sky, highlighted by moon rays. It was graceful and soothing. And more importantly, it kept the chosen outsider's mind off their current situation, as he continued to follow its path.

The tiny dot began to grow larger, when Charlie realized it was much more than a soothing spec in the sky. A bright ball of orange and yellow shot out from the growing spec, approaching their boat at a rapid rate. *Was it a ball of fire? It is.* The boy thought to himself. "Featherwink, head towards the ground. Quickly!"

What had been beautiful seconds ago, was now threatening their very existence. The small, sparkling dot was the coachman's wagon, and the yellow and orange ball was definitely no ball at all, but rather, bursts of flames shooting out from the mouth of Flamario.

The first burst of fire shot past the right side of the boat.

"They're moving too fast. I can't outfly them. We're going to have to land," the frog shouted.

"Watch out!" Michael yelled. Another meteor-like burst shot past the left side.

"OK, that's it, we're going down! I can't keep this up any longer." The frog hugged the boat tightly, sheltering his friends, as they went into a dive.

Charlie, Michael and Midnight braced themselves for impact. "Hang on EVERYBOOOOOODYYYYYY!"

"Now they will feel the *wrath* of the shadow villains," Flamario proclaimed, as they closed in on Charlie and the others.

"Looks like they're going to crash into the woods," Mr. Jollysnaps said.

"Perfect, they'll have nowhere to run once they're down," the fox added. "Jolly, drop the big guy off on the east side of our friends, me on the north side, and you take the west."

"What about the south side?" Flamario asked.

"The trees, vines and bushes will take care of that," the fox replied with a sneer.

"But how? I do not understand," Flamario asked.

"And that's why our old friend, Mr. Jollysnaps is going to take care of it, right Jolly?"

"Indeed, my furry friend." CRACK! "He-yah you furry critters. The mules continued to fly hard, as the coachman turned and cast his whip towards the rear of the coach, striking a hidden hatch, which opened and released a stream of magically cursed dust—coating the entire south side of the forest.

The fox let out a loud, bellowing laugh then said, "Wonderful my friend. Simply wonderful."

The secret hatch slammed closed as the coachman tugged hard on the reigns—the mules banked right, then straightened out.

"OK, we're nearing your drop point, be ready to jump," Mr. Jollynsaps said to Flamario.

Charlie opened his eyes, temporarily knocked out from the crash landing. Rubbing his head, he looked around. "Everybody here? Michael? You here?"

"Over here, in the bushes. "Ow! Could someone please, ouch, help me get out of here? I feel like a human, ouch!, pin cushion."

Charlie stood up and staggered over to the group of thorn bushes Michael had fallen into. "Give me your hand so I can pull you out. Ow!"

Michael chuckled. "See, I told you."

"OK, quit complaining and give me your, ouch!, hand," Charlie said, attempting, unsuccessfully, to reach into the bushes and pull Michael out.

"Maybe I can be of some assistance," Midnight said, slowly regaining his composure from the crash. "Please, Charlie if you would kindly step aside, I may be able to improve the situation."

The young boy stepped back and gave the cat room to work his magic. Aiming just above the bushes, Midnight shot from his tail, a miniature storm cloud which soaked the dry, thorny bushes.

Instantly they turned into green, plush shrubs with giant pink and white flowers.

Amazed by what he saw, Charlie dove right into the bushes, without fear, and pulled his brother out. "Well, that wasn't so bad."

"Sure, that's easy for you to say. You weren't the one getting poked every time you tried to move," Michael said in a cranky tone.

Switching the subject to avoid further bickering, Midnight asked,"Has anyone seen Featherwink?"

"No, but it shouldn't be hard to spot a giant purple frog with wings," Charlie said.

"I'm down here," a voice echoed nearby.

"Where?" Midnight asked.

"Over here, down in a hole."

Midnight and the boys walked over to investigate.

As they made their way around three large boulders, a giant, roughly-shaped hole in the ground came into view.

"Featherwink? You down there?" Midnight hesitantly asked.

"Yes, but it's so dark I can't see a thing."

"Now would be a good time to have a flashlight," Michael said.

"I don't think they have flashlights in WONDER," Charlie replied.

"Wait a tic. If I can just remember how to do this," the frog said.

The sound of snapping fingers echoed through the cavernous hole: snap...snap...snap...snap...buzzzzzzzzzz. Featherwink's middle fingertip began to glow, lighting up the area in which he had fallen. Allowing the others to see him from above.

Midnight slowly crawled down into the hole towards his large, purple friend, who at the moment, was in very tight quarters for such a giant frog.

Charlie and Michael followed the cat down into the hole. The rocky walls were covered with strange drawings of human and animal figures, symbols, odd creatures, and writing of some sort. The further down they climbed, the more obvious it became. This was no hole created by their friend who had just fallen, but rather, a hidden cave.

"Hey, fellas, I see a couple torches over there on the wall. If you would please go grab them and bring them over here, that would be most helpful," Featherwink asked politely.

Midnight flicked his tail, lighting the torches so they could see.

"Now, good friend, if you wouldn't mind? It's a little cramped in here for someone of my size, and I can't free my arms up enough to change back to my usual tiny self."

"Oh, right, right, right," the cat said. Midnight flicked his tail again, this time, returning Featherwink back to normal.

"That's more like it." The frog flew up out of the hole and onto Charlie's shoulder.

"So what is this place?" Charlie asked.

"Whatever it is, it doesn't look very inviting," Midnight said.

"Can we get out of here now?" Michael asked.

"I think that's a—"

There was a noise up above. A loud thunderous noise. Footsteps, growing louder with each step. Shaking the ground so hard, dirt and rocky debris fell from the ceiling of the cave.

"Quick, over here," Charlie said. He had found a niche in the cave wall. Everyone gathered tightly together—hiding from whoever, or whatever was approaching from above.

"The torches," Featherwink whispered. "Put out the torches."

Just as Midnight put out the torch lights with the flick of his tail, another light source lit up the cave entrance. A large hand, highlighted by the light, reached in, grabbing along the outer edge of the cave. A giant head peeked in with big round eyes and a long beard. It was Flamario. His giant face was hauntingly backlit by the torch, creating dark, long shadows, which made his appearance all the more menacing. His piercing eyes stared deeply into the cave, then quietly, he pulled his head back out.

There was a deep inhale, then the crackle-pop sound of fire. Flamario's head reappeared in the cave entrance, this time with puffy cheeks and bulging red eyes.

"Shield your eyes," Midnight whispered.

The fire breather unleashed a firestorm that roared through the cave, past Charlie, Michael, Midnight and Featherwink.

They pushed back towards the wall, turning their heads, to avoid the flames and tremendous surge of heat, which could easily claim the life of any living thing in its path.

When the flames retreated, Flamario's head emerged once again for another look inside the smoldering cave. Satisfied nobody could survive the flames, he moved on—his thunderous footsteps faded away into the distance.

"OK, go ahead and light the torches back up, the frog said.

"I think it would be wise if we head that way," the cat stated, gesturing towards the path leading deeper into the cave. "The last thing we need right now, is to have another run-in with *that* hot head."

"I agree," Charlie said."

"We stand just as good a chance down here as we do up there," Featherwink added.

Michael nodded.

"Very well then, keep your eyes peeled and your ears open," the cat said. "I think it is safe to say, we are in a Shadow of WONDER."

"A Shadow of WONDER?" I think Frank told us about those earlier this week," Charlie said.

"Yes, I believe you're right, Charlie. As you may recall, shadows are dark places. Undesirable places. Hidden within, or between, the realms of WONDER," Midnight said.

"Usually...they are places we try to avoid," the frog added.

"Yes. Well unfortunately, it looks like they have found a way to pull us into *one* of their shadows," Midnight said. He began walking further into the cave, leading the way for the others to follow.

"So there are more shadows?" Michael asked.

"Oh yes. Many more," Featherwink said.

"And growing larger in number all the time," Midnight added. "Which is why we can NOT afford to waste any time. Each day the dark forces continue to grow, decreases our chances of stopping them from taking over WONDER."

"Yes, Frank has explained to us why the Patrons can not allow this to happen. That's why Michael and I are here to help," Charlie said.

"You are both good boys," the cat replied.

They continued to walk deeper into the cave—their pathway lit only by the torches carried by the boys.

Charlie and the others had been walking through the cave for a lengthy period of time. Until now, there had only been one path to follow.

"What do we do now?" Charlie asked, as they stared at five alternate pathways. Featherwink flew off Charlie's shoulder, turned to face the others, then said in a decisive tone, "Simple, we pick one and move on.

"But what if the one we choose is more dangerous than the others?" Michael asked.

"No reason to worry about that now, young man," Midnight said. "The frog is right. We need to make a decision and deal with whatever comes our way, without fear or hesitation."

Feeling encouraged by the cat's words, Charlie spoke out, "Choose a path, Midnight, and we'll move forward."

The cat picked the pathway second from the right. "This way, gents."

The boys followed their feline friend, with Featherwink riding along on Charlie's left shoulder.

The cave bent left, then right, then rose upward, before bending right again. As they leveled off, a slight breeze met their faces. The sounds of crickets, owls and other creatures of the night could be heard. Then, an opening appeared, highlighted by the soft glow of the moon.

"We did it," Michael proclaimed, as they exited the cave into a small clearing in the forest.

"See, it wasn't really that bad after—"

"Well, well, well, what do we have here?"

Charlie and the others spun their heads around.

It was the silver fox, perched above the cave opening. And gathered around him, a pack of wild, gnarly-haired wolves, waiting on his word to attack.

"But...but-but, how did you find us?" Midnight stuttered.

"It was *only* a matter of time. Really, I'm surprised it took us this long to track you down," the silver fox said, staring up at the moon. "Lovely night, isn't it?"

"So what do you want?" Charlie asked with a stern look.

"Hmmm, heh-heh-heh. Oh, I think you know what we're after. And it isn't your fluffy cat friend, or the little purple guy with wings."

A large python snake slowly slithered down to a lower branch in the tree behind them.

"If it's the watch you're after, you can forget it," Featherwink shouted.

"Really?" the fox questioned. "And how do you plan to keep it from us? It appears to me that you are surrounded."

"There's always a way out," Midnight replied in an angry tone.

"Not likely," the fox said. "Get 'em!"

The pack of wolves leaped down off the rocks and charged Midnight.

The elusive cat spun around and took off in the opposite direction of his agressors.

"Run boys!" Featherwink shouted, as he leaped off Charlie's shoulder and took to flight. "Head into the woods, it's our only chance to escape."

Charlie and Michael turned and ran as fast as they could towards the woods.

Everything was happening fast. The forest was a blur of snapping sticks, crunchy, dead leaves, rattling shrubbery, long shadows and darkness, as the boys ran deeper and deeper into the woods. The torches each carried in their hand were the only source of light to help them through the dark, wooded terrain.

"Do you see Midnight anywhere, Michael?"

"I haven't had time to look. Ouch." Michael's shirt sleeve got snagged and torn by a low-hanging branch, which left a deep scratch on his upper left arm.

"You OK?"

"Yeah, I'm fine," Michael replied as they kept running.

Charlie came to a sudden stop. Michael followed suit.

"What is it, Charlie?"

"You hear that?"

"What? I don't hear anything."

"Exactly. We've lost our friends."

Midnight was in a full-out sprint, staying merely seconds away from his hungry pursuers. Ducking, leaping and cutting from side to side, the frantic feline gave it his all to increase the distance between him and the pack of hungry wolves. But it was no use, the panting and growling sounds only grew closer. He needed to find an alternative way to escape.

Where, where, where can I go? the cat thought, scanning the woods as he continued to run. *Up? Up is good.* Midnight leaped and dug his claws into the nearest tree—climbing, clawing and scratching his way out of site.

One, three, six, nine wolves went streaking by, their focus straight ahead on their intended prey.

The cat was safe for the moment.

Buzzing up, down, in and out, and around the forest trees, like a bug hopped up on Red Bull—Featherwink frantically searched for his friends with his enormous, lime-green eyes, which also acted as headlights.

There was a howl in the distance, *Midnight,* he thought. The frog landed on a rotted tree branch. *I should help him. But what about the boys? Midnight can survive without me, the boys cannot.*

There was a CLICK several hundred feet to the left from where he was perched. The purple, winged frog took off from the branch to investigate—his eyes, shining brightly through the dark woods, as he zipped along.

Where are you? he thought. Hopeful it was the boys.

Two more clicks came from nearby.

He was getting closer. *It has to be the boys. But I must remain quiet until I know for sure. Just in case. The sound is coming from just around that big tree up there,* Featherwink thought.

As the frog circled around, he found a large branch, hanging just so, it would serve his purpose well as a vantage point to scan the area. Silently landing on the branch, Feathwerink searched the area below. *Hmmm? I don't see them. Maybe they've already moved on? Let's take a look over by—*

Psssssssssssssssst—THWAK!

Just as the frog leaped from the branch to take flight, the tail end of a giant python snake blind-sided him—sending the unsuspecting frog into the trunk, which knocked him unconscious and sent his tiny, limp body plummeting to the leaf-covered ground below.

CRACK, "Helloooo fellas," Mr. Jollysnaps said, while striking a large rock—turning it to gold, as the boys came into a small clearing on the west side of the woods.

Charlie and Michael spun around and shot off in the opposite direction.

Jollysnaps leapt to his coach and took to the air. Within seconds, he cracked his whip, nearly striking the backsides of the terrified boys—both running in full stride with torches in hand.

Each strike of the whip turned whatever it touched to gold. The coachman laughed wildly, knowing well the surprise that lied ahead for the chosen outsider and his younger brother. "Run boys, run! Ha! Ha! Ha! Ha! Ha!"

They sprinted left, right, then straight on through a thick cluster of shrubs and trees, where Charlie almost tripped and fell over a fallen branch. No matter which way they turned, or how fast they ran, the coachman, with his golden whip snapping, stayed close behind—forcing the boys due east.

Having eluded the pack of wolves, Midnight slowly, and ever so quietly, climbed down out of the tree and worked his way towards the south end of the woods. His eyes were fully dilated, allowing him to see every detail of the dark forest which surrounded him. The magical feline kept low to the ground, moving carefully with each step as to not make a sound.

The wolves will return soon, he thought. *Keep calm Midnight, you can do this. On this course, I should have a very good chance of finding Charlie and Michael.*

The cat came upon a clearing in the woods. He was back where he had started, by the cave. But this time, no one was around.

There was a rustle of bushes, two snaps of a twig, and footsteps crunching leaves.

Midnight hugged the ground, then turned to look west. *With my black fur, they will not see me if I remain still.*

The rustling noises and footsteps crunching leaves combined—growing louder with each passing second.

Two figures emerged from the shadows of the woods and into the moonlit clearing. They stopped suddenly, putting their hands on their knees, trying to catch their breaths.

The black feline focused in on the two figures, trying to make out their faces. Identified!

"Charlie. Michael, psssst, over here," Midnight whispered.

The two boys looked up towards the hidden voice.

"Midnight? Is that you?" Charlie whispered back.

The cat rose to his feet and began to quietly walk towards them. "Indeed it is."

"Ohhhh, Midnight, you don't know how good it is to see a friendly—"

CRACK...CRACK-CRACK! Two small trees and a shrub near the boys and cat turned to gold.

"It's over mates," Mr. Jollysnaps shouted, as he swooped down from sky on the west side of the woods, landing in the clearing.

Before Midnight or the boys could get a word in, the silver fox emerged from the north side of the clearing. "Hello-hello boys, it appears you may have gotten yourselves into a little bit of a pickle." The fox stuck two fingers in his mouth and whistled loudly. Come on out, gents, and have a look at what *we've* found."

The pack of wolves leaped out of the woods, blocking off the north side of the clearing.

CRACK! CRUNCH! POP! SNAP! BOOM! BOOM! THUD!

Treetops shook back and forth as others snapped and fell, creating a giant pathway. In the center of it all was Flamario, who swung his arms outwards, snapping in half the remaining two trees between him and the clearing, where the others had gathered. The giant of a man stepped forward in intimidating fashion.

"Ohhhh, I see you've run out of places to hide my little sneaky Patrons," the fire breather said, followed by thunderous laughter. "This will be the end for you, *and* your friends too. Now hand over the watch little boy, or I snap you in two just like big tree." Flamario gestured towards the waste of trees that laid in his wake.

"Run!" Midnight shouted.

The boys turned and sprinted towards the south side of the woods.

"This should be interesting to watch," the fox said with a smirk.

As they sprinted along, the cat turned to glance back. To his surprise, *none* of the shadow villains had moved an inch. He turned back around and said to the boys, "Hold on fellows, something's not right."

The boys screeched to a halt.

"What was that?" Charlie asked, trying to catch his breath.

"The villains. They're not chasing after us," the cat replied. "It's as if they know something we don't."

"Well, whatever it is, we can figure it out later," Michael said.

"I think Michael is right," Charlie added. "I say we get through the woods and as far away from those guys as we can. We can worry about their plans later."

"Right. What was I thinking?" Midnight said.

Everyone agreed, then turned and headed into the south side of the woods.

Only ten steps in, Charlie felt something wrap tightly around his left leg, which lifted him high into the air—holding the boy in an upside down position. He screamed for help, but it did not matter.

At the same time, two large vines reached out and wrapped around Michael's body—pulling him back so snug against the trunk of a willow tree that he could barely breath.

Hearing the boys screams and calls for help, Midnight struggled to come up with a plan. The weight of the situation was almost unbearable. *A freedom spell? No, too slow.* His mind continued to spin. *Petrified wood? Yes, that should do it,* he thought. The cat turned and aimed his magic tail in Charlie's direction, but something grabbed it and tugged hard. Midnight let out a loud MEOW, jumping straight up into the air with all four legs extended out horizontally. Two roots shot up from the ground—wrapped around the feline's airborne body, then slammed him hard to the leafy ground, while a third root restrained his magical tail.

The fox and coachman's plan had worked. The magic dust they had scattered earlier over the south side of the woods had transformed the trees, vines and all other elements of the forest into a giant barrier of wicked woods. Charlie and the others were at the mercy of the shadow villains.

Chapter Seventeen

Against their will, Charlie, Michael and Midnight had been thrown into a wooden cage and were taken out of the forest on a wagon pulled by two small, thorny-scaled dragons to one of the deepest and darkest places known in WONDER, a shadow realm castle. Patron legend has it, few who have been taken into a shadow realm have ever made it out unscathed.

Overseeing the captured Patron's delivery from high above, in a golden coach pulled by flying mules, were Mr. Jollysnaps, the silver fox and Flamario—to assure Midnight and the boys did not try and escape.

The rickety old wagon's driver was a gruesome looking creature. With a body covered in dark brown hair, a curved spine, large snout for a nose, and two tusks protruding upwards from its mouth, the beast resembled some sort of mix between troll and wild bore.

Midnight tried speaking to the driver, attempting to cut a deal that would set them free, but all the beastly creature did was turn and grunt with an unfriendly snarl—making it very clear that Midnight and the boys would *not* be talking their way to freedom anytime soon.

As the wagon slowly clicked and clunked its way down the bumpy roadway, Charlie became cautiously aware of his unpromising surroundings. From high above, the full moon peeked through jagged clouds and twisted, monster-like trees—highlighting the unwelcoming landscape which flanked the road on which they were traveling. To their left were dozens of glowing eyes of all shapes, sizes and colors, which followed the wagon from a distance as it clanked along—eagerly waiting, hoping at some point, the cage would fall from the wagon and leave behind a late-night snack or two. But of course, they would first have to deal with the two Giggletorian guards trailing behind the wagon on foot. The Giggletorians were named so because of their interesting genetics. While their bodies resembled that of strong, muscular men, it was their hyena heads and persistent giggling that clearly set them apart from any other creatures of WONDER. In their overly large hands they carried long, axe-like weapons with spear tips, in case someone, or something, were to attack their precious cargo during its transport to the shadow realm castle.

To the right of the road were a hundred plus shadow nibblers, who's small green bodies, well rounded and covered with spikes, resembled what many in WONDER would describe as possessed chestnut shells, with big appetites for hair, that grew and fell from various trees of the forest. They too, were wishing for the cage to fall and break open, as they rolled and bounced alongside the wagon. But unlike the other creatures, the shadow nibblers only craved hair. To them it was like very fine spaghetti. It did not matter what type of hair—human, cat, horse, dog, goat, lion, tiger, bear or whatever, the shadow nibblers would eat up all the hair on a body until it was silky smooth. But since hair grows back, the nibblers were really nothing more than a common nuisance.

The driver of the wagon had no time for nibblers, nor was he concerned with the other creatures. His deep-seated commitment to his dark leader far outweighed any meager threats posed by the immediate surroundings.

But to Charlie and Michael, two young boys who had never before known or seen such things or shadows, it was a most frightening experience.

"When is morning going to get here?" Charlie asked, while nervously looking around.

"I'm afraid that in shadow realms, darkness is perpetual, Charlie," the cat replied.

Michael looked up towards the sky. "So that's why the moon hasn't moved since we got here."

"Right you are, Michael. And it won't."

"And my watch still isn't showing any signs of life," Charlie added, with doubt painted across his face.

Michael read his brother's expression, then rested his head on Charlie's shoulder, worried they would never get back to reality.

The cat lifted his tail, surprised by its limp posture. "My tail appears to be out of order as well. Only black magic of the worst kind could have such an effect as this."

Charlie patted his lap, inviting the cat to curl up and take a nap.

The old rickety wagon pulled by the two thorny-scaled dragons continued on down the dark, muddy road, while Charlie, Michael and Midnight all quietly, and hopelessly, cuddled together in a cage from which there was no escape.

THWAK! One of the Giggletorians smacked the cage, startling the boys, and causing Midnight to spring straight up in the air and back down into Charlie's lap. It was an uncomfortable landing from Charlie's perspective, to say the least.

"C'mon, wake up-wake up. We don't wants to upset the master now do we?" the guard said with snarl lips, triggering his partner to let out a bellowing, hyena laugh.

Charlie readjusted his sitting position, hugged Michael to ease his tension, then focused on what lied ahead, as he rested his head on one hand, while petting the cat with the other.

As they came over the hilltop and out of the woods, the serpentine roadway curled downwards into a deep valley, surrounded on three sides by jagged, volcanic mountains. In the center of the valley, surrounded by a lava-filled molt, was a ragged castle of sorts, built out of dark, slate-like stone, which looked as though it could tumble down at any second.

"Looks like we're here," Midnight said quietly to the boys. "If at all possible, we need to stick together."

SMACK! One of the guardsman hit the cage again, causing the boys and cat to flinch. "Hey, quiet down in there. No talking."

Charlie gave the Giggletorian a dirty look, showing he would not be intimidated that easily. Then he turned to Midnight and whispered back, "We'll do our best."

Michael nodded in agreement as all three locked eyes.

The rickety wagon had reached the valley and was approaching the castle entryway, flanked by two large, purple rhino's. Both stood upright on two legs, and were dressed in shiny black armor with an ornate "S" crest, painted in red, yellow and white, across the chest plate. This was the same crest which adorned the flapping black flags atop the castle walls. Between the unfriendly rhino's rose a large iron-bar gate, with rivets that loosely held it together.

One of the rhino's turned, looked upward towards the gate tower, then snarled and grunted out, "Visitors approaching."

There was a series of loud clanks and clicks. The gate slowly began to rise, clearing the way for the wagon, as it entered the castle property.

The rhino's nostrils flared, and their eyes beamed, as the two unfriendly creatures stared down the caged prisoners entering the heavily guarded property.

The giant iron gate came down with a THUNK. The wagon turned left down a cobble stone road, with the castle wall on one side and resident facilities on the other. The air was hot and heavy from the surrounding lava. Steam randomly popped through the cracks in the unstable roadway, as the wagon continued on around the castle's inner perimeter before turning right and heading through a smaller entryway with no gate. The entryway was guarded by two rock-like soldiers who's facial expressions reflected what they were made of, hard, emotionless matter. They were at least five feet in diameter with short, stocky legs, enormous feet and long arms with giant hands that hung slightly above the ground. One carried with them a rock sword, and the other, a large rock hammer. Both stepped aside to let the wagon pass.

Rising up before them stood a large, intimidating stairway flanked by fifteen foot high raven statues. Some forty to fifty feet above where their wagon came to rest sat a giant, arched doorway made of wood with dragon-head knockers and serpent handles.

The ghastly driver turned back to the hyena guardsmen and grunted out commands, "Take the prisoners to the Dark Thorn master."

The wooden cage was unlocked and opened. Charlie, Michael and Midnight were poked and prodded by the Giggletorians, who escorted them towards the stairway.

"Alright, lets get a move on ya filthy little buggers," the guardsman on the left said.

Midnight glared at the guard.

"Yeah, that means you too, fur ball, he-he-he-ha-ha-he-he-ha!"

As they begrudgingly worked their way up the giant stairway towards the enormous doors, the cat and his two friends glanced around at the frighteningly dark, and very detailed, entryway into Senkrad's unpleasant shadow dwelling. Skirting each side of the rising stairs were intricate patterns, carved in stone, of haunting faces, wicked foliage, prickly thorns and other frightful things. Strangely enough, the faces appeared to turn and follow them as they continued upward, making young Michael feel most uncomfortable. Perched in the center, above the arched doorways, was a winged demon of sorts, who's hollow eyes glowed green. The chiseled beast's shadow, cast down and to the left by the moonlight, made his presence even more gruesome than it would have been if it were daylight. Two enormous stone torches, covered with carved skeletons and demon-like creatures, sat on each side of the doorway. Tall flames of green and yellow rose up from within their structures, flooding the arched doorways with unwelcoming flickers of dancing light.

One of the Giggletorians reached for a dragon-head door knocker to signal their arrival, nearly loosing a hand to the feisty head with razor sharp teeth. Finally winning out, he slammed the knocker repeatedly against the wooden door—which echoed throughout the chambers within.

The left door creaked open. A small whiff of spirit cloud escaped from inside. Then ever so slowly, a ghostly female figure appeared in the doorway, welcoming the two Giggletorians. "So nice to... see you. Please...won't you come in," the graceful, blue figure with a porcelain-like face and white flowing hair said—gesturing for the prisoners to enter.

The spirit hostess effortlessly led the others through the castle—reciting details of each room they passed along the way. After an eerie stroll down a torch-lit corridor filled with unfamiliar works of famous Disney villain art, such as Ursula the Sea Witch, Maleficent, the evil Queen from Snow White and numerous others, they came upon a bat patterned, spiral staircase forged in black iron.

"So what's with all the villain art?" Michael asked.

"They are mainly here for inspiration," the spirit replied.

"Inspiration?" Who would want to be inspired by roll models like that?" Michael spat out.

"Someone you are about to meet," she said, turning and gesturing towards the staircase with an open hand. "Please, follow me...and, *watch* your step."

"Someone we're about to meet?" Michael asked with a quizzical expression.

Midnight and the boys cautiously followed the spirit down the winding staircase—the temperature rising with each step. As they reached the last few stairs it became very apparent why.

Opening up before them was an expansive underground passage with towering tree-like, stone pillars. The pillars were sculpted with ravens and thorny vines, and supported three stories of dark corridors on the right. On the left was an elevated walkway, where lava surrounding the castle, flowed along the jagged banks.

As they walked along the lava banks, Charlie, his brother and Midnight continued to look around. High above on the ceiling was a painted mural of creatures peering out from behind stones, bushes and trees—silhouetted by the crescent moonlight on the far right side of the enormous painting. Only their eyes were clearly visible. Unlike other paintings, the creatures in the shadows on the ceiling appeared to be quietly moving—following along, as Charlie and the others passed by.

The spirit hostess turned towards the sixth corridor on the first level and quietly continued on. The others followed, including two Giggletorians, making sure the Patron team did not try and escape.

The corridor was dust-covered and web-filled. Midnight sneezed, as did Michael, then Charlie. The narrow hall was dimly lit by low-flamed torches on the walls. One hundred feet down the hallway, the spirit stopped and turned to face a door on her left. She waved her left hand and the solid metal door slowly opened. Everyone entered, went up a tall flight of stairs, turned right, walked across and elevated walkway, turned left, went up another flight of stairs, then turned right again and walked thirty more feet. On their left was a wooden door, with the "S" emblem they had seen earlier, carved into the center of an ornate, rose bush pattern.

Charlie, Michael and Midnight had lost all sense of direction.

"Any idea where we are?" Charlie whispered to the cat.

Before he could answer, the door latch clicked, then creaked open. A large, thin figure, sitting in a stone-sculpted throne resembling a dragon, sat well beyond the doorway. The identity of the figure was masked by a hooded, black cloak. To the left and right of the throne sat two green flame torches.

It took all of Charlie's youthful eyesight to try and make out who, or possibly even what, sat in the dimly lit room before them.

The seated figure raised its skinny blue arm and flicked a bony hand.

The spirit hostess vanished into thin air.

The black cloaked figure raised its other arm, and clinched its bony fist.

Suddenly, Midnight and the boys were pulled through the doorway and into the center of the circular room by an unexplainable force of dark magic.

The mysterious figure dropped its arms quickly—the door behind them slammed closed, leaving the Giggletorians outside to stand guard. The others stood trapped inside the room against their will.

The cloaked figure snapped its boney fingers and the green torches grew taller and brighter, exposing the three shadow villains, Flamario, Mr. Jollysnaps and the silver fox, who were sitting along the right side wall. Eagerly, they awaited the fate of their victims, who were about to be dealt with by the dark figure seated before them.

Midnight stepped ahead of the boys to offer protection. Not knowing what to expect.

Slowly, the tall rail-like figure stood up from the throne, lowering the hood concealing their identity.

"Oh...oh no," Midnight said softly.

"What? What is it?" Charlie asked.

"Go ahead, Mr. Kitty, tell them...tell them what you know," the pale, blue-skinned figure with large black eyes said with a stone cold stare.

"It...it's D...Dar...Dark....Dark Thorn S...Sen...Senkrad. One of FOTO's dark leaders."

"Oh, come now kitty, you make it sound so negative?" Senkrad replied.

Reading the expression on Midnight's face, Charlie's stomach began to turn. Inside, he could sense great danger. He tried his hardest to be strong, if not for himself, then for his younger brother, Michael. It was their first time coming face-to-face with a Dark Thorn. "What do you want? Why are we here?" the outsider demanded.

"I think you already *know* the answer to that question, boy," Senkrad said in an gravelly tone.

"Maybe I do. But, I don't know?, maybe what I'm thinking, and what you are thinking, are two different things," Charlie snapped back.

"Come off it boy, we both know that watch around your wrist is much more than an ordinary watch."

"What, this old thing?" Charlie said as he held up his arm. "Why, it's nothing but a beat up timepiece my grandfather gave me."

"Please boy, don't try and play me for a fool. I can see and hear all that goes on within the realms of WONDER. And one thing *I know* for certain is that the watch around your wrist is *indeed* an Object of Magic. And that, boy, is about to become quite unfortunate for you AND your little friends."

Senkrad stepped back then lifted his arms quickly towards the ceiling, palms up. The green flame torches shot upwards—then out and around, Charlie, Michael and Midnight. The Dark Thorn threw his arms to the right, and the flames pulled tight, restraining the three figures. He threw his arms upwards and the flames lifted them high above the ground, as they kicked their legs and swung their arms—helpless against Senkrad's powers.

The flames continued to swirl around its victims, still holding them tightly, humming, popping and cracking, as they lowered Charlie and the others back towards the ground. Senkrad approached Charlie. "So boy, would you like to...change your story and hand over the watch? Or, would you and your helpless friends like to endure more pain?"

"D...Don't...do it," Midnight said—barely able to get his words out.

Charlie looked at the cat, then his brother, who nodded in approval. "Not a chance."

Senkrad looked at the boy with no emotion, then turned and took several steps. "Very well, if that is your wish." Spinning around quickly, the Dark Thorn thrust his open palms towards the threesome. The green flames grew brighter and tightened their grip—causing Charlie and the other two to grunt, moan and scream out in pain.

"Urrraaaaah! I'm...n...not...giv...giving you th...the...watch. No matter what you do to me," Charlie shouted.

"YOU will, boy. Indeed, you will," Senkrad snapped back."

"Or what? You're not even real. Why...why you couldn't do anything to me in the real world."

The Dark Thorn flew across the room, mere inches from Charlie's face. He stared into his youthful eyes, wanting to intimidate the boy. "No matter, I can do plenty to you HERE."

The shadow villain's dark eyes lit up with excitement.

Senkrad clenched his right fist, the flames tightened around their bodies even more. The Dark Thorn reared back then made a throwing motion with his right arm, sending the flames, along with Charlie, Michael and Midnight, over the balcony behind his throne and down into a holding cell below—they smashed against the back wall and were knocked unconscious. The iron door slammed closed behind them, as the green flames released their grip and returned to the torches.

"Hey, young fella, wake up," a familiar voice said.

"Huh?" Charlie replied, blurry-eyed and fuzzy-brained from their encounter with Senkrad.

"It's me, Featherwink. You know, the little purple guy with wings."

"Whah? Purple frog...wings...oh...right," Charlie said.

Tink-tinkety-tink-tink-tink!

Something fell from Charlie's pocket, waking his brother and Midnight.

"Hey, who...who's making all that racket," Midnight asked. He shook his head to clear his thoughts.

Michael looked down, as did the others, and said while pointing, "It's the icicle. The one the snow fairy gave you."

"Where?" Charlie asked.

"Behind you, over there by the wall," Featherwink said.

Charlie turned around and spotted the magic icicle laying on the ground.

"Hey, Feathewink, when did you get here?" Michael asked.

The outsider picked up the magic icicle—admiring its flawless details.

"Ohhh, I arrived quite some time before the three of you," the frog replied. "That sneaky snake gave me a good *smack* with his tail end when I wasn't looking, and when I woke up, I was here."

"What did Neve say about the icicle?" Midnight asked Charlie.

"She said that if we ever needed her help, to hold it in my hand and call her name."

"Who? What...what are you talking about?" Michael said. His mind still focused on Featherwink's story.

"The magic icicle the snow fairy gave me, you nitwit. She said that if we ever needed her help, all I had to do was hold it in my hand and call her name."

"Ohhh, heh-heh, now I remember," Michael replied. "Do you think it will really work?"

"I don't know. Maybe?" Charlie answered with a shrug.

Everyone in the cell looked at each other, then mutually agreed they should try.

"Well then, what are you waiting for, young lad," the cat said, "go ahead and see if it works."

Charlie nodded, then held up the icicle. He called out her name, "Neve".

The snow fairy's name echoed around the holding cell, over and over. A burst of bright light expanded outward from the magic icicle, speckled with sparkling silver dust. It continued to grow larger and larger, until the entire room was filled by the light— now so bright, that everyone in the cell had to shield their eyes.

As the lights retreated, there—hovering before them, with flakes of snow gently cascading down from her gown, was the snow fairy.

"I am still trying to figure out *what* could have happened to Charlie and the others," Frank said to his Patron friend, as he nervously paced the floor of his apartment—his hands clinching and pulling his long, frazzled grey hair. "If everything had gone to plan, they should have reached the current hiding place of the Kingdom Crystal by now, and we...we should have heard back from them." He paused, then turned around. "You, you *know* what needs to be done, right?"

"Without question, Frank," the Patron replied.

"Very well then, be swift and true. Fear is not an option," the eccentric Imagineer said with a noble expression, pointing upwards, then towards his friend. He touched the light charm around his neck with his free hand. A bright stream of light out shot from his index finger, and into the chest of his brave friend—sending him to another realm of WONDER."

"Duke, Grim, quit cowering behind those horses, and get over here to keep an eye on this safe," Captain Fibs yelled. "These cowboys ain't gonna shoot ya, ya yellow livered ninnies."

"But Captain, those two burly cowboys guarding the safe don't look like they wants to give it up."

"Come off it lads, those western fellas is just a couple-a ride prop cowboys. In other words, no way they're packing real heat."

"No disrespect, Captain, but they are shoot'n every and anyone who tries to get near that safe," Duke replied, as he and Grim continued to hide behind two horses nearby. "I mean, just take a look at the bodies they've piled up near the river bank."

The captain rolled his eyes. "They're props lads, props," he said, as his face began to turn red with anger while standing out in the open— not phased by the gunfire the cowboys were dealing out.

"Well, if you two fellas can't handle it, I'm pretty certain me three mates here can," Captain Plank said, as he and three of his Thorns walked out from behind the Miner's Bank Building and up to where the safe sat on its side.

"What? Why...what are ya doing here, Plank?" Fibs questioned, caught off guard by the sudden appearance of Plank and his men. "Me and my boys here got everything under control."

"Really? Cause to me the only thing your boys seem to have under control is them two horses they're hiding behind. And even then, I'm not so sure that'd be the case," Plank replied.

His mates broke into a hysterical fit of laughter.

"Oh, really?" Fibs spat back in defense of Duke and Grim. "Boys, why don't you show these Magic Kingdom fellas how we do things over in Epcot," the sweaty, out-of-shape, captain squawked, motioning for his men to move towards the safe.

Still petrified by the gunfire, Duke and Grim refused to budge.

"Ha! Ha! Ha! Ha! Ha! Why, I can see you've got yourself a set of really brave lads there, ol' Fibsy," Plank said, bent over with laughter. "Alright, Martin, Robert, Joe; take control of that safe, would ya."

The three men paused and stared at their captain, unsure what to think.

"On the double, or ya be swimming with the sharks tonight."

"Yes, Cap'n, right away. We...we're on it, sir," Joe replied.

Plank's men scurried over, grabbed hold of the two armed cowboys, wrestled their pistols away from them, then tossed them into the river against their will—which carried the cowboys down stream and out of sight.

Captain Plank let out a hearty burst of laughter. "Ha! Ha! Ha! Ha! Ha! There, ya see. Now that's how ya get things done around here."

Captain Fibs shook his head in disgust, then gave his cowardly sidekicks an evil glare—embarrassed by their lack of courage.

"Neve? You, you heard me?" Charlie said with a gleam in his eye.

"Well of course I did. You seem surprised."

"I, I mean we...we weren't sure if the icicle would work or not."

The snow fairy chuckled. "Have you forgotten where you are?"

"Oh, heh-heh, I guess...I guess you're right. I should have given it a little more thought before speaking," the boy replied, embarrassed by his previous comments.

"I'll say," Featherwink said, smirking and rolling his eyes at the boy.

"Very well then, everyone gather close together, come-come, we haven't much time. They could return at any moment," Neve added, looking back towards the cell door.

Charlie, Michael, Midnight and Featherwink huddled together.

"OK, we're ready," the cat replied.

Neve raised her arms, holding the crystal wand with the left hand, she recited:

"Make them tiny so they shall be, hidden from those they wish not see."

The boys, cat and frog were instantly shrunk down to the size of fleas.

The snow fairy continued on, her raised arms now swirling about...

"Carry our friends where they shall go, winter winds stir and blow!"

Neve cast her wand hand towards the microscopic Patrons, sending a blast of never-ending snow flakes, which engulfed Charlie and the others, lifting them up into the air, and swirling them about. There was a burst of light, followed by twinkling silver dust. They were gone.

The fairy swung her arms upwards, creating a funnel-like snow storm that surrounded her. Neve became one with the storm of glittering light and snow, which shrunk smaller and smaller, continuing to spin rapidly. FFFFIP! It vanished—taking the snow fairy with it.

Chapter Eighteen

Tiny as fleas, Charlie, Michael, Midnight and Featherwink easily snuck by Plank, Fibs and their crew, then managed to transport into the safe where the 2nd Kingdom Crystal was rumored to be—thanks to Midnight's magical powers.

The inside looked nothing like a safe at all, but rather, an endless expanse of rolling, golden terrain in the form of coins, on which golden cacti and shrubs grew. Centered amongst the hills, and quite some distance away, was a massive rock structure, similar to what can be seen in an American desert, except that is was made entirely of gold. Partially carved into the mass of rock was a herd of wild galloping horses, that rose up, and out of, the enormous, rocky formation.

"This is no safe, this is no safe at all," Featherwink claimed.

"I think you're right about that one froggy," Midnight said. "I've heard of this place before. Something Frank mentioned to me quite some time ago. But I never believed it actually existed. Not even in WONDER."

"So? What exactly is this place?" Charlie asked, as he and the others continued to turn in all directions—their mouths agape.

"They call it the Desert of the Golden Safe," Midnight replied. "And I think it's pretty obvious to see why."

"I'll say," Michael said.

"Legend has it, that anybody who has heard of it, and tries to find it, can't, because they are always looking for a golden safe. Including myself. But, as you saw before we transported inside, the exterior looks like an ordinary, run-of-the-mill safe. And as far as I know, from what Frank has told me, nobody had ever set eyes upon this place, except for those who dreamt it up back when Walt Disney World was in its infancy."

Charlie looked at his feline friend, scanned the area one more time, then pulled out his phone to review the rhyme Frank had recited to Midnight and Featherwink. "Well, one thing is certain, this is definitely the golden marker referred to in the rhyme, so it looks like we're on the right track."

Catching everyone off guard, just over the horizon past the giant rock formation, a burst of light, and a sudden BOOM, took them by surprise. Everyone snapped to attention.

Something small, moving quickly through the air, emerged from the light burst and rapidly approached, leaving behind a glittery trail. The mysterious flying object, banked hard left, then circled around them multiple times—so quickly, that no one in the group could make out who or what it was.

On the third pass around, the supersonic anomaly shot upwards, before looping and heading back down at a ridiculous speed, straight towards Charlie and the others, who were now covering their heads and ducking for protection.

Then...silence.

"Ahhhh, I've always enjoyed making an entrance like that," a familiar voice said. "It brings back so many good memories."

Charlie, recognizing the voice instantly, pulled his hands away from his eyes. "Alexios!"

Hovering just above where Charlie and the others stood was their wise, old owl friend— defender of the Kingdom Crystals, Alexios.

"Hello there young squire, I told you I would be back," the owl said.

"I guess you were right," said Michael. "It's good to see you again."

"And you as well, Michael," the owl said with a wink, as he gracefully landed on a nearby rock.

"Frank? Did Frank send you?" Midnight asked.

"Yes he did."

"So how is he? It's been, what day is it?" Charlie asked.

"It is now day seven of your vacation," Midnight said.

"Day seven?" Michael blurted out. "So we missed all of day six?"

"Yes, I'm afraid so, young man."

"So we've been here at Walt Disney World, going on our seventh day, and have barely seen Frank at all. Plus we've missed all of day six?" Charlie said, with his hands on his forehead, pulling back his hair.

"Time moves quickly when you're dealing with Dark Thorns, shadow villains, and trying to rescue friends," Featherwink replied.

"Yeah, I guess you're right," Charlie replied. "So our parents are doing well? And, and what about Frank? When will we see him again?"

"Patients, my boy, patients. Frank has been very busy over the past several days. He has been trying to prepare for whatever dangers FOTO and their evil army may throw at us, as our quest for the second crystal continues," the owl said.

"Precisely," Midnight added. "You see boys, now that FOTO has brought shadow villains into the mix, the tasks at hand have become much more difficult, and dangerous, to carry out."

"Which means more preparation time for us. This...you see, young man, is why Frank has been so busy since you arrived," Alexios added.

"I see," Charle said. "And what about our parents?"

"Your parents are doing splendidly. They were placed under a memory knot spell immediately after you last saw them, and have no idea you've been gone."

"So they're still enjoying themselves in the parks?" Michael asked.

"The parks, and anywhere else they have been on property, since yesterday when you last saw them."

"That's good to hear," Charlie said, relieved by the owl's words.

"Um...hey there, young fellow, I think it might be time to start paying attention to your watch. What do you think?" Featherwink said, landing on Charlie's shoulder and pointing to the Object of Magic—which had lit up like a Christmas tree and was spinning out of control.

"I'll say," Michael said.

"It looks like we're in the right place," Midnight added, "so where do we start?"

A sudden burst of laughter rang out from above. Not a threatening laugh, but rather, one of friendship.

Everyone turned to see who it was. They were surprised by what happened next.

A large mound of the rolling desert surface, made of glistening, gold coins, began to rise upwards towards the clear blue sky—the only thing not gold in the desert. It rose higher and higher, growing in scale some eighty to one hundred feet higher than the miniature Patron crew. The enormous mound of golden coins began to morph, changing into a giant, silhouetted figure—unfamiliar at first, but then, as the figure was refined, it became clear to Charlie and the others who it was. Frank Wellington.

"Well, hello there everyone, so glad to see you finally made it to this *special* place," Frank said, his avatar of golden coins spread its arms and looked around. "So you're probably wondering why I'm popping in at a time like this?"

"Yes, I was just about to ask, Frank, what are you doing here?" Charlie asked.

"As you know, from last year's experience, finding a Kingdom Crystal can be *quite* challenging. Which is why I sent Alexios to help you again."

"Yes, we were happy to see him again," Charlie replied.

"Just as I was to see you," the owl replied.

Frank continued. "Yes-yes-yes. Now, as I was saying, finding a crystal can be quite challenging, which is why, not only did I send my trusted friend to help you, but I too needed to speak to you, so I could pass along a little bit of Patron wisdom, you could say."

"So Frank, how is it you are able to make appearances such as this inside WONDER?" Charlie asked.

"For now, let's just say it's connected to my dreams."

"Your dreams? Interesting."

"Yes, I'll explain later, Charlie, when we have more time. But for now, we need to set you on course to find the crystal, before it moves."

"Right, Frank. Just tell us what we need to do, and we can take it from there," Charlie said with a look of determination.

"Very well then, where was I? Oh yes, yes of course,"Frank said, scratching his head. He turned to the large rock formation with the carved horses and pointed. "So by now I'm sure you and the others have taken notice of the large rock formation over there?"

"Oh, yes. Absolutely, it's amazing."

"Well I'm glad you like it, Charlie, cause *that* is where you and the others need to go."

"Is the Kingdom Crystal inside there?"

"Yes, you could say that. But to get in, you will need to find the hidden entrance."

"How do we do that?"

"You ask Alexios to show you, of course."

"Now I see why you sent him to help us," Michael said.

"Yes, Michael, since Alexios is the guardian of the crystals, he is always aware of where they are hidden, and, for the most part, *how* to get to them."

The young boy looked at the owl, who winked to confirm Frank's statement.

"Now then, as I said, our friend Alexios, for the most part, knows how to get the crystals. But there are a few additional details that he is not aware of, which, you will also need to know. Details, that only a Patron Council member, such as myself, can tell you."

"We're ready to listen, right everyone?" Charlie said, spreading out his arms to include the others standing around him.

Michael, Midnight, Featherwink and Alexios all agreed.

"Splendid," Frank replied. "Now then, once you pass through the secret entrance, you will be required to climb an intricate, maze-like stairway. Make sure you stay on course."

"How do we do that?"

"Simple, Charlie. Just keep a close eye on the watch and *listen* to what it tells you."

"And how will I know when it is trying to tell me something?"

"Oh, heh-heh-heh, you'll know. Believe me, you'll know.

Charlie nodded to confirm he understood.

"Once, or I should say, *if*, you reach the top of the stairway, there will be two magical horse-like creatures waiting for you. You and your brother will have to choose between the horses. And once you do, mount them and pull on the reigns. The horses will do the rest."

"So let me get this straight, there are horses inside that *giant* rock thing, and we have to climb some *crazy* staircase to find them—then we jump on the horses, and they'll take us to the crystal?" Yeah, that makes perfect sense," Michael said sarcastically.

"Hush, Michael," his brother said with a stern look. "Frank, so the horses will guide us to the crystal?"

"That's quite alright, my boy. I can see why your brother has his doubts. If I were in his shoes, I probably would too."

Michael looked at his brother and smirked.

"Yes, Charlie, you could say the horses will lead you to the crystal, but, it won't be as simple as you may think."

The chosen outsider gave his giant friend a look of bafflement. "Terrific, I guess...we'll...be...on our way? Come on everyone," he motioned for the others to follow him towards the giant rock formation.

"Aren't you forgetting something?" Frank asked.

"Um, not that I can think of," the boy replied.

"Ahh-hmmm-hmmm-hmmmmmm," Alexios cleared his throat to gain everyone's attention, then he took flight, hovering above Charlie and the others. "It seems you have already forgotten who the leader is?"

"Oh. Oh, that's right, I'm so sorry," Charlie said. "Please, lead the way Alexios."

"I'm right behind you," Featherwink said, as he leaped off Charlie's shoulder and took off into the air.

"Very well then, gentlemen, good luck. I will see you real soon," Frank's avatar, made of golden coins, disbanded and fell to the ground.

"Follow me lads, there's work to do," the owl said, while taking off towards the magnificent rock formation.

"Well this is gett'n pretty bloom'n boring if you ask me," Captain Fibs said to Plank. Questioning Elontra's decision to have them stay and guard the safe.

She has never been wrong, and if I were you, Fibsy, I wouldn't be doubting her word," Plank replied. "Besides, she might be listening in on us right this very minute," he whispered, while cautiously looking around.

"Come off it chap. You really think she's watching us?"

"You know how the Dark Thorns are, Fibs. I'm sure you've experienced it once or twice before. They seem to have an uncanny ability to see and know all that goes on around here."

"Such a *keen* observation, Captain Plank. I'm quite impressed, really," a female voice echoed down from above.

"Where?...who?...what?" Fibs said, as he and the others looked up, down, and all around, trying to pinpoint the voice.

"Oh. Oh, dear, now we're in for it," Plank said. He knew exactly who the voice belonged to.

"No need to worry your tiny little mind, Captain Plank. I just wanted to check in and see how things are going."

The voice stopped. A giant pair of dark, feminine eyes opened up on the large canyon wall—just across the river from where Fibs, Plank and the others stood guard over the safe. As they continued to watch, facial features, such as a nose, cheeks and mouth, grew out of the canyon surface—completing the face Plank had already identified in his mind.

It was Dark Thorn Elontra, and her giant, stone face, which protruded out of the canyon wall, was larger than two school buses on top of one another.

"Aye, it's good to see ya, your Dark Excellency," Plank said with a bow.

Fibs, Duke, Grim and Plank's crewmen followed suite, out of fear for their lives, while the characters of the simulated attraction continued to carry on as if nothing had happened. They were oblivious to anything that occurred outside of the ride's storyline.

"So, *Captain Fibs,* what do you have to tell me? Something *good* I hope, for your sake," Elontra stated, looking a hundred times more intimidating with her ginormous face.

"I...I uh...I, or I should say we...we uh, haven't seen the boy with the watch or his...his uh, friends, since we...we uh...since we got here." A bead of sweat rolled down the side of his forehead.

"That's right your Excellency," Grim spat out in the captains defense, "there's nothing going on here, nothing at all, as far as we can tell, heh-heh."

There was silence...Elontra closed her eyes for a moment of thought. She opened them again. This time, they burned with anger and disappointment. "Captain Fibs, your dark leader, Senkrad, and I spoke just a short while ago and he passed on some rather *curious* information, which I am *most certain,* you would be interested to hear."

"I...I would?" Fibs said nervously.

"Yes. Especially since, how did your little sidekick put it? Oh yes, especially since there appears to be, 'nothing going on here'."

Fibs swallowed deeply. "Ohhhh, he did say that didn't he, heh-heh. Well uh...well I think he's uh, he's...I think he's right.

"YOU, you trust his judgement over mine?" Elontra asked, followed by a booming fit of evil laughter, which echoed throughout the attraction. "My dear captain, it appears you have...*much to learn.* You see, Captain, what you and your insignificant little *fool* of a friend here DOES NOT know, is that just a short while ago, the chosen outsider escaped from Senkrad's shadow kingdom by way of magic. And *more* than likely, he is headed here to retrieve the second Kingdom Crystal from the very safe, upon which, your arm rests. As. We. SPEAK!"

The unnerved captain began sweating profusely.

"Has it occurred to you, to ANY of you—including you Captain Plank, that the chosen outsider and his jolly little band of friends might be in the safe at this very minute? Retrieving the second crystal? Hmmmmmm?"

"Well uh...I guess we uh....we never even gave it a thought," Plank replied.

"Yeah, we figured the little bloke and his mates would be showing up in a boat along the river, here," said Fibs.

Elontra's giant face let out another booming fit of laughter. She shook it from side to side. "Ohhh, you fools. You silly, insignificant fools. All of you! Never, and I mean NEVER, assume the obvious when it comes to dealing with Patron scum and their chosen outsider.

"But, your Excellency—"

"But? But nothing! As far as we know, they may have already found the crystal and be well on their way to doing whatever it is they plan to do next. Is that what you want? Do you want them to succeed? I suppose you'd be perfectly happy singing the Small World theme song, and wearing those ridiculous Mickey ears, as you merrily skip around the parks eating one of those tooty-fruity Dole whips for the rest of your *pathetic* lives?"

"Oh no, not in the least bit. Why...I, I'd rather dye me hair pink and wear a polka dotted dress than having to hear that dreadful song again," Plank replied.

"Yeah, and you wouldn't catch me on me worst of days wearing a pair of those stink'n ears or skipping around the parks," Fibs added.

"And those Dole whips? You can have 'em," Duke said, "why they—"

"All right, ENOUGH!" Elontra shouted. Her eyes opened wide, shooting a steady stream of blue lightning into the bodies of the captains and their crew—sending them to a place they had never been.

Elontra's eyes calmed, her giant stone face receded back into the cavernous wall of the simulated Western River Expedition attraction without a trace.

As they approached the giant rock formation, Charlie and the others tilted their heads way back—taking in the enormity of what stood before them.

Alexios swooped down and landed on a rocky ledge some ten feet above where the others stood. He held a wingtip to his beak, quieting the others, then turned left to face what looked like nothing but a large flat area of the giant rock formation. With confidence in his voice, he spoke out. "Ever magnificent, ever kind, allow us the way, beyond common mind!"

Some thirty feet apart, at the base of the giant rock, two cracks rose up from the coin-covered ground, zigging and zagging along the way, until they met at the pinnacle of what looked like a colossal, arched doorway. As the two cracks collided, a pair of illuminated, flowing lines quickly, and symmetrically, moved down and about, leaving behind tracks of organically etched shapes, which decorated the giant golden door, with no handles. As each flow line reached its end, both sides of the arched doorway opened inwards, revealing to Charlie and the others, an incredible entryway.

"Would you look at that," Midnight said in awe.

Before them, rising up into an endless expanse of darkness, was a massive stairway made of large, flat-surfaced rocks. Each of which, floated in the air. The rocks were random in size, ranging from four to ten feet in diameter, and were highlighted by mysterious light sources. As the intricate stairway rose higher, it split into multiple paths, then again, and again, and again...until it disappeared into the vast darkness high above where they stood.

Everyone stepped through the giant doorway and approached the stairway, their footsteps echoing on the polished stone floor.

"I guess Frank wasn't joking when he said it was a maze-like staircase, eh Charlie?" Midnight said.

"No, I guess not," he said while gazing upwards, carefully studying the multitude of paths they would have to choose from."

Alexios landed on the fourth stone up, just in front of the group. "Well, at least there is only one path to start on. So I say we get a move on gentlemen. I will fly ahead to scout out any potential danger, while the four of you start climbing. Understood?"

"Yeah-yeah, we got it, Michael said, rushing up the first six steps, which tipped downward, then back up, as he landed on them. "Hey, check it out. This is cool."

"Michael, you mustn't run ahead like that. It is VERY important that your brother leads the way. *He* is the one wearing the watch," Midnight said.

"But these stairs, they really *do* float, and—"

"Yes, we can see that, young man, but we don't know what might happen if you step on the *wrong one*, understand?" Alexios replied with a stern look. "Now come back down here and let Charlie lead the way."

Feeling dejected, Michael lowered his head and slowly walked back down, not saying a word.

"It's for your own safety, Michael, as well as the others," Charlie said, placing his hand on Michael's shoulder. "Don't worry about it, I know you mean well. I just don't want to see you get hurt. I mean, could you imagine how terrible Mom and Dad would feel?"

"That would be horrible, your'e right. I'm sorry." Michael gave Charlie a humble smile.

"What da ya say we get a move on boys," Featherwink insisted, as he flew up to join Alexios. "Yes, your little friend is right," the wise owl added. "We must keep moving."

The first five stories of the stairway were easy to navigate, with only one path to choose from. As the sixth story began the path split into two.

"Hold on," Charlie said, suddenly stopping in his tracks. The watch had unexpectedly begun to move in an uncontrollable fashion. "The watch, it's, it's acting all crazy and stuff."

Mickey's hands spun faster and faster as the watch face glowed brightly in multiple colors. It spun so fast, everything blurred together. Then, the watch face changed.

"That's...what in the...well, that's interesting," Charlie stuttered—unable to get out a full sentence.

Amazed by what he saw, the young boy stood and stared, as the blurry watch face began to morph into a subtle, yet familiar, holographic face. It was the watchmaker, Raphael.

The 3D face opened its eyes and spoke. "Hello, my young friend, I see you have made it safely to the stairway, yes?"

Charlie and the others stood speechless, staring at the watch.

"It's alright, Charlie, I'm here to help. Unlike some characters of WONDER, I cannot leave the realm in which I live, so *this* was the only way I could join you. Cat got your tongue?"

"N...no. I mean, no, sorry, you kind of caught me by surprise."

"Ohhh, Heh-heh, I see. Now, where was I? Oh, right-right-right. You are at the first split in the stairway, yes?"

Charlie looked up to confirm their current position. "Yes, sir."

"I want you to listen carefully. It is *very* important, as the path you take must be picked by you, the chosen outsider. Understand?"

"I do...I, I mean, yes, I will," the boy replied. The others all gave Charlie a look of concern. Great responsibility had just been placed upon his shoulders, and they all knew it.

"OK," Raphael said, clearing his throat. "Ready?"

"Ready," Charlie replied. A shot of nervous energy ran through his mind and across his face.

"Look but once, and not again, the path you trust will be your friend."

There was a moment of silence as everyone stood around the watch wondering what Raphael's words meant.

"So what does it mean?" Featherwink asked, breaking the silence.

"It's a riddle," Midnight replied.

"I know that, you overgrown fur ball, but about what?"

"It's something that only the chosen outsider can answer," Alexios said. "Charlie, you must decide."

The young boy closed his eyes tightly, focusing on the riddle... searching for an answer. A cloud of thoughts and possible solutions blanketed his mind. *What should I do?* He thought to himself. *There is only one right answer. Or is there?*

The boy opened his eyes, then looked upwards towards the rising stairway. "It's a question of faith," Charlie said.

"Faith?" Featherwink replied.

"Yes, the choice I make must be the one I believe in. I have to have faith in my decision."

"Well then, pick one," Alexios said, attempting to instill confidence in the boy.

Charlie closed his eyes tightly one more time, then opened them again. "Right. We go right." Without hesitation, he turned to the right stairway and confidently took his first step up. Nothing happened.

Everyone, including Charlie, let out a sigh or relief.

"OK, lets keep moving. No time for drama," Alexios said from above. "It looks like you'll need to climb another three to four stories before it's time to make another decision."

Charlie and the others continued on. Steps turned to stories, which turned to more stairway splits and more choices. Sometimes the stairway split into two paths, sometimes three. All of which, intertwined with the stairways that had come before them, making it virtually impossible to trace a path to the top. And yet, the chosen outsider continued to pick the right stairway, each and every time, until eventually, they reached the forty-second story.

On level forty-two Charlie closed his eyes, just like before, and searched his feelings for the right choice. And just like before, he confidently opened his eyes. "Left," the young boy said as he pointed.

But unlike all times prior, this time, Michael jumped ahead and took off in a full sprint up the stairway, confident his older brother's choice was the absolute, right choice.

POOF!

On the fifth step Michael disappeared, then reappeared on a floating stone, completely isolated from the stairways, four hundred feet above the ground.

"Michael!" Charlie shouted in a panic.

"What have you done, boy?" Midnight said.

"Help. Help me, Charlie," Michael said, looking in all directions for a way off the isolated stone. "I, I didn't mean to do it, it just kind of happened."

"Well, it's a little late for excuses now," Charlie replied. He put his palms to his forehead, grabbing and pulling his hair.

"Oh dear," Alexios mumbled, while circling from above. "Hold on young squire, I'm on my way." The owl dove towards the boy.

Restless from the sudden turn of events, the frantic boy began pacing around the stone, looking for a way off. As he stepped towards the edge, a chunk of rock broke off—Michael slipped, tumbling forward, then off the rock—he grabbed onto the edge with both hands, as he helplessly dangled high above the ground. "Help!" he shouted, "I ca...can't hang on much longer!"

"Almost there, hang on," the owl said. He shot off like a supersonic missile, leaving behind a glittering trail of silvery dust.

"I...I can't hang on!" The young boy cried out. His fingers straightened, weak from the unexpected effort put upon them. Michael lost his grip and plummeted towards the ground. "Aghhhhhhhhhhhh! Charlieeeeeeeeeeee!"

"Michael, no!" Charlie shouted—his face stricken with fear. His stomach, twisted in knots. There was nothing he could do. Helplessly, he watched, as his brother continued to fall towards the end of his mortality—tumbling end over end.

SWOOOSH!

"Ugh!" Something had broken the young boys fall. Something large and feathery.

Michael grabbed on tight with both hands and regained his bearings. "Wha...what's going on?" He looked around, taking in what, or who, had saved him. The breeze blew through his hair as the large, winged creature ascended upwards towards the others.

"I trust that you learned your lesson?"

"Alexjos?"

"Yes?"

"But...you...how'd you get so big. How did..."

"Oh, I still have a few tricks up my wing, young squire."

"Well that was the best one I've seen yet," Michael said, as he squinted from the force of the wind hitting his face.

Seconds later, the giant owl came to rest on the floating stairway, next to where the others resided.

Everyone was speechless from what they had just seen.

Michael climbed down off the great white owl, who returned to his original size.

Charlie rushed up and smothered Michael with a giant hug, then pushed him back, still holding on to his brother's shoulders. "Don't you EVER do that again, you hear me?"

"Ye...yeah, I do," Michael replied in a grateful manner.

"Today you learned a valuable lesson, young squire, one which almost cost you your life," the owl said, giving Michael a stern look. He peered over the top of his glasses. "I trust, young man, that from now on you will *listen* to what you are told?"

"Oh, absolutely, I mean, yes...yes sir. I, I'll definitely start doing a better job of listening...sir."

Alexios tilted his head back and continued to give the young boy a look, expecting more.

"And, and I...I promise to never pull a stunt like that again...cross my heart."

The owl remained silent for a moment, then took off into the air. Turning his head back while flying away, he said, "Well, come on the then, we are waisting precious time."

"You heard him, time to get crackin'," Featherwink said. He leaped off Charlie's shoulder, and took off to catch Alexios.

"Alright gentlemen," Midnight said, "lets be on our way."

Charlie cleared his thoughts, then refocused on the task at hand. He and his faithful group headed up the next story of floating stairs.

This time, Michael made sure to let his brother lead the way.

The climb had been quite the workout. Even for two young fellows such as Charlie and Michael. Midnight on the other hand, had chosen the easy way out by turning his tail into a helicopter-like propeller, which carried him up the stairway with no leg effort at all.

"There it is," Michael said, pointing upwards. "Only three stories to go."

"Yeah, I see it too, "Charlie replied, relieved they had almost reached the top.

"Are those horses at the top?" Michael questioned.

"It would appear so," Midnight answered back.

"They're beautiful," Charlie remarked.

"And their eyes," Michael added, "they have blue eyes that glow."

When they reached the top, all that existed was a large, floating slab of rock, twenty by thirty feet wide, with nothing else around it. Next to the two horses, one black and one light grey, stood a thin, older gentleman, some seventy to eighty years old. He was wearing a pair of worn jeans, a plain white shirt with an unbuttoned collar, some old leather boots and a brown cowboy hat. His face was weathered like fine leather, his eyes steely blue. And just under his nose, around his chapped lips, was a large white mustache that curled up on the ends. He was feeding the horses hay. But not just ordinary hay. As the horses chewed, enjoying their meals, magic glitter cascaded downward from the corners of their mouths, which they gladly bent down to nibble off the ground. With every bite they took, their radiant, blue eyes and diamond-like coats shined brighter. These were no ordinary horses.

"H...Hello sir, my name is Charlie, this is my brother, Michael, and our friend Midnight."

The old cowboy turned around to address Charlie. His steel blue eyes sparkled with honesty. Taking off his hat, he scratched his head, which was full of long, silvery-white hair. "Yep, been expecting ya. Glad to see you finally made it up to see us. Ol' Ellie and Maybelle here are juuuust about ready."

"Ready? Ready for what?" Charlie asked.

"Ready for you to take 'em on a ride."

"A ride? To where?" Charlie said, looking around, searching for a place they might go. "I'm sorry sir—"

"No sirs around here, young fella, you can call me Lipkin," the old man interrupted.

"Oh, OK, Lipkin, so...I'm a little confused."

"Confused about what, young fella?"

"Well...uh, I...I don't see anywhere around here to take your horses for a ride."

The crusty old cowboy stood still and gave the boy a blank stare.

"I think what the young fellow here is trying to say, is that we're standing on a large, floating rock, with nowhere to go but in circles," Midnight said.

The cowboy smirked, then chuckled. "Yeaaah, well I guess that is what a stranger would see. But these here horses ain't your regular kind of horses, they're more of what you might like to call—"

Alexios and Featherwink zoomed down, landing next to Charlie and the others.

"All clear," the owl reported to Lipkin.

The cowboy turned to acknowledge the owl and frog by tipping his hat. Then he went back to where he started with Charlie. "As I was say'n, these two horses here is what I like to call Reinhorses."

"Reinhorses? Never heard of 'em," Charlie replied.

"Well, you've heard of reindeer, right?"

"Yes."

"So these here horses have what you might call, the same kind of abilities. You know, like Santa with his flying reindeer and all."

"You mean they can fly?" Michael asked.

"You betcha. And they're pretty darn good at it too."

"But reinhorses? That sounds made up," Charlie stated.

"Well, we're not exactly dealing with reality here in WONDER, now are we, young fella?"

"Oh, right. I guess not,"

"How are we doing?" Alexios asked the cowboy.

"Looks like they're just about ready to go. Now, you young fellas need to get on the left side of Ellie and Maybelle here so they know you are ready to climb aboard."

Charlie and Michael, with little hesitation, did as they were told.

Lipkin prepared the reigns on the horses.

The horses gracefully kneeled down, making it easy for the boys to climb up onto their bear backs.

"No saddles?" Charlie asked.

"Not necessary with these two beauties," Lipkin replied. "Go ahead, climb on and grab hold of the reigns."

Charlie mounted the black horse, while Michael climbed onto the grey one.

"And, what about me?" Midnight asked.

"Oh, right. Heh-heh, almost forgot about you kitty," the cowboy chuckled. "Why don't you ride with Michael, he's a little younger, so he could probably use a little help."

"Yes, brilliant idea," Midnight replied. "Very well then, make way, Michael, I'm coming aboard." The large, black cat leaped up behind the boy, then magically extended his tail, wrapping it twice around the boy's torso to secure his position on the reinhorse.

"All set?" Lipkin asked, signaling the beautiful creatures to rise to their feet. Ready, girls?"

The two reinhorses whinnied and raised their magnificent heads. Their eyes shined bright blue, as they pranced in place—their sparkling coats, glistening from the mysterious lighting.

"So what do you do while we're gone?" Charlie asked, trying to stay balanced on the reinhorse.

"Don't worry about me none. I'll be over there in my shack," Lipkin said, pointing towards an old outhouse with a half moon rudely cut into the door for a window.

"Where'd that come from?" the boy asked, positive it wasn't there just a minute ago.

"It's there when I need it," the cowboy replied.

"Seems kind of small."

"There's actually quite a bit of room once you get inside."

Charlie gave the old man a quizzical look.

"Any hoot, time to fly. Everybody hang on now. Yah!" Lipkin hollered, as he smacked the reinhorses simultaneously on the hind end, triggering their takeoff.

Twenty, fifteen, ten, five feet, they were off! The reinhorses leaped of the end of the large, floating rock and soared high into the darkness above. Side by side, the two magnificent reinhorses galloped along effortlessly through the air, with Alexios and Featherwink following along just overhead. They continued to climb higher and higher through the endless night sky, all of which, was strangely enough, still inside the giant rock formation.

Similar to what happened when they first began their climb up the stairway, Mickey's watch hands began to spin out of control, the face became blurry, and a holographic face of Raphael emerged. "Looks like you are headed in the right direction."

"We are?" Charlie asked.

"Of course you are. I'll see you when you get there."

"Get where? I don't have any idea where we're going."

"You'll know when you see it," the watchmaker replied.

"See what?"

"Ha-ha, something *unusual*," Raphael answered back.

"Can you at least give me a hint?" Charlie asked, as the reinhorses continued to climb.

"I would if I knew. But I know very little, just like you. So keep your eyes and mind open."

"OK, I'll do my best," Charlie replied. He turned and focused on the dark sky ahead.

Seconds later, Alexios spotted something breaking through the darkness. As did Featherwink. Something, rather peculiar. "There appears to be a light up ahead, young squire," the owl shouted down to Charlie.

As the owl spoke, the magic watch began to work hard. The hands spun rapidly in every direction, just as they had done before. But this time, instead of the face getting blurry, hundreds, if not thousands, of tiny little sparks of multicolored light began to shoot out in random directions, like a miniature fireworks show. The colorful streams of light created by the sparks grew larger and more pronounced as they left the watch face, traveling up, over and around the bodies of Charlie and his faithful steed, like electrons around an atom.

Alexios and the others flew in close, riding alongside the chosen outsider and his reinhorse, who were giving off and almost god-like aura of multiple colors.

"Charlie, can you hear me?" the owl shouted.

The boy calmly turned his head and nodded to confirm he could hear the owl. He moved as if his entire being were a hypnotic spell.

"Just ahead is a miniature sun-like mass of purple flames. Within that mass lies the 2nd Kingdom Crystal. To free the crystal from the flames, you will need to repeat what Midnight tells you. Do you understand?"

Charlie turned and nodded again to confirm his understanding.

"Very well. Good luck, young man," Alexios said. He broke off his flight pattern and rejoined Featherwink to watch from a distance.

As Charlie and Ellie rapidly approached the small, purple mass of flames, the young boy confidently smirked. It appeared their task at hand would be rather simple. The mass was no larger than a basketball, and there was little to no heat, as far as he could tell.

The reinhorse carrying Michael and Midnight swooped in to join Charlie and Ellie. They circled the mass, side by side.

"Charlie," Midnight said, "Repeat what I say, then hold on tight."

The chosen outsider nodded a third time, as they continued to circle the purple ball of fire.

"Ever more, ever lasting, a gift, not to be told. Sworn by those who shall protect, its past, its present, its future to behold," the cat recited.

Charlie repeated the words, which echoed through the vast darkness surrounding them.

The grey reinhorse carrying Michael and Midnight broke off to join Alexios and Feathwerwink, who were watching from a safe distance above.

Charlie snapped the reigns of his flying steed, they took off like a shooting star, leaving behind a blurred trail of spectacular light and multi-colored, glittery dust, as they sped round and round the small sun.

The purple mass began to spin, slow at first, then faster and faster, as the chosen outsider and his reinhorse circled round, over and over again. The ball of fire spun so fast its flames were extinguished, leaving a solid, crystal-like orb, which continued to spin round and round. From within its core, shining through the transparent shell in all directions, was an intense green light—almost too bright for Alexios and the others to look at. And though the clear sphere-like shell continued to spin rapidly, the green object within remained still.

Charlie brought his steed to a sudden halt in the air, pausing to observe the magic before him. The outer shell began to hum in a low pitch, which then turned to a high pitch, as its rotational speed increased even more. The green light inside continued to grow, larger and brighter, as if it were trying to push its way out. The crystal-like shell began to crack in multiple places, which traveled the surface, as piercing rays of bright green light shot through the imperfections in all directions.

Michael and the others shielded their eyes.

Without warning, the sphere exploded into thousands of tiny pieces, which vanished into darkness. All that remained, suspended in air and shining brilliant green, was a teardrop-shaped crystal, no larger than a child's hand. It was the second Kingdom Crystal.

"Hurry boy, grab the crystal before it vanishes!" Alexios called out from a distance.

Charlie swooped in with his black reinhorse, then leaned hard to his left, snagging the crystal with his left hand, while holding onto the reigns with his right. He pulled himself upright as Ellie galloped through the air towards the others. The magic aura surrounding the boy and his steed slowly disappeared. Charlie proudly held the crystal, which had now dimmed, high above his head, signaling to the others that he had it.

CRACK...CRACK-CRACK, THUNDER-CRACK-BOOM! An unexpected display of blue lighting lit up the sky, dancing across the darkness. From it emerged seven ghost-like figures—all electrically charged with bright red eyes. It was Captain Plank, Captain Fibs, and their five crew members—all of whom, had been sent by way of Elontra's evil, lightning-charged eyes, to steal the crystal away from Charlie.

"Charlie, above you!" Michael shouted, pointing towards the rapidly approaching ghosts.

SWOOSH, SWOOSH-SHOOSH-SHOOSH!

It was too late, the ghosts were on him. Charlie brought the crystal down to his lap, as he pulled on the reigns, banking hard left.

"Coming, Charlie," Alexios said. The mighty owl shot off towards three of the swarming ghosts trying to fend them off.

"Good thinking," the winged frog said. Fetherwink transformed to a larger size and headed towards two more of the ghosts.

SWOOSH, SHOOSH, HISS! The ghosts moved quickly, making them nearly impossible to catch. The one resembling Captain Plank zoomed high, paused, then turned and shot bolts of lightning through his fingers toward Featherwink—stunning the giant purple frog, and sending him into a free-fall.

"Featherwink!" Charlie shouted.

"We've got 'em," Midnight said, as he patted Michael on the shoulder with his paw, "Ok young man, it's time to take action. Dive boy, dive."

Michael pulled on the reigns, directing Maybelle to dive after their unconscious friend. The reinhorse turned and banked hard, diving at a ridiculous speed—her head and wings tucked, her front legs pulled in towards her body.

"Hang on young man, this could get rather interesting," Midnight said, gripping the boy tightly with his tail.

"Interesting? I think it's going to be far more than interesting," Michael said. He and Midnight screamed as they hung on for dear life.

"Behind you, Charlie," Alexios said. He looped around to make another pass at the pestering ghosts.

"Wha...where?" The boy replied, struggling to look back.

Just as he turned back around, the ghost of Captain Fibs popped up from below, right in front of Ellie's face—startling the reinhorse and causing her to buck wildly.

"Calm down girl," Charlie said, attempting to get Ellie back under control. But it was too late—the reinhorse's right shoulder struck Charlie's leg hard, which bumped his hand and caused him to lose control of his prized possession. The green crystal bounced off his lap and out into the dark expanse. "Noooooooo!" Charlie shouted, as he tried to reach down and grab it, but the crystal was already well out of reach, falling rapidly.

"I've got it, don't worry," Alexios called out. He dove towards the crystal, his large yellow eyes focused intently on the target.

SWIIIISHHHH! "Not today old fellow," Duke snagged the crystal before the owl could get to it. "I've got it Captain, I've got it!"

"Good job Duke," Fibs replied. "Alright boys, it looks like our job is done here, eh Plank?"

"Aye, that it is," Captain Plank, replied.

Before another word was said, a series of lightning bolts danced across the darkness, each striking one of the ghosts and taking them away.

Michael and Midnight had managed to save Featherwink by way of the cat's magic tail, which had shrunk the stunned frog back down to regular size so Michael could catch him in his hand.

Charlie and Alexios flew down to join them, as they all returned to Lipkin's rock.

"Well, that was rather unfortunate," the cowboy said.

"What do we do now?" Charlie asked Midnight in a defeated tone.

"I need to meet with Frank as quickly as possible. Not only will the Patron Council need to decide what to do about the crystal, but we still have Ben to worry about as well," the cat replied.

"Right," Alexios added. "Featherwink and I will head back to the watchmaker's realm and see what we can do. We're going to need all the help we can get."

"But first, we need to get the boys back to their parents until we figure this out," Midnight said.

"Absolutely. Charlie, you still have the watch I see?" Alexios said. "Just have Mickey take you back to your parents."

"Right," Charlie half-heartedly said, looking down at the watch.

"We'll be in touch soon," the cat said.

"Yes, we'll see you soon," Alexios added. "And don't worry young man, I am HIGHLY confident the Patron Council will come up with a brilliant solution for our troubles."

Charlie gave the owl a somber smile, though deep down inside, he felt there was little chance they would succeed.

"Very well then, off you go," Midnight said.

Charlie nodded, pushed the button, then spoke to the watch with his brother next to him: "Take us to our parents." The watch lit up, engulfing the boys in a spectrum of magical light, taking them away.

"I hope for the boys sake, Alexios, what you told them is true," Midnight said.

"So do I...so do I," the owl replied.

The cat, owl and frog said their goodbyes to Lipkin.

Then Midnight flicked his tail and vanished. Only a cloud of sparkling dust remained. The magic cat was headed back to Frank's secret apartment to wait for his return. There, they would have to decide what to do about the crystal and their good friend Ben.

Alexios and Featherwink were next. The frog snapped his fingers, sending them to the watchmaker's realm, where they would gather up all the help they could find, while waiting for word from Midnight on what to do next.

Buried deep below the Haunted Mansion, in the simulated Magic Kingdom of WONDER, a series of lightning bolts erupted. The two captains and their men returned with the Kingdom Crystal in hand.

Dark Thorns Elontra and Senkrad were sitting patiently, waiting to greet them. Each, flanking a large, green-flamed fireplace.

"We have it," Fibs proudly proclaimed. He held up the Kingdom Crystal for the Dark Thorns to see.

"Yes, I can see that," Senkrad replied with little, to no emotion. "You've done...quite well."

"Tha...thank you sir," Fibs replied with a bow.

"But this is only the first step," Elontra said, turning towards Senkrad.

"First step?" Fibs replied.

"Yessss," Senkrad said. "You see, now that we have the crystal, *and* Ben as well, you can rest assured the Patrons will make an attempt, however feeble it is, to play the hero and save the day."

Fibs and Plank gave each other a look, then shook their heads. "I...I'm not quite sure we're following ya," Plank replied.

"We are going to CRUSH them," Elontra said, pounding her pale, boney fist on the arm of her chair.

"Take what is ours," Senkrad added.

"Leave no hope."

"And above all, wipe the Patron scum completely from existence," Senkard added.

"Then the ENTIRE Disney empire, and it's precious WONDER will be ours to rule forever!" Elontra shouted, as she and Senkrad enjoyed a frightfully evil laugh together.

POOF! Charlie and Michael reentered reality, midway down the big drop of Splash Mountain. "Aghhhhhhhhh!" the boys screamed out.

KERSPLOOSH!

They were soaked to the bone.

It was well into the seventh day of their vacation. At the attraction's exit point, their parents stood waiting, as if the boys had been with them all along.

"Well boys, what did you think?" their mother asked.

Charlie and Michael glanced at each other, then Charlie replied in an exhausted voice, "It was...unbelievable?"

"Wow, the big drop tired you out that much, did it?" their father asked.

"You have no idea," Charlie answered back.

The remainder of the day, the boys and their parents toured the lands of the Magic Kingdom, riding attractions, snacking on snacks, and combing the shops.

Though neither boy was paying much attention to what they were doing. Their minds were occupied with only two thoughts. Where was the crystal? And, where was Ben?.

As evening settled in, Charlie and his family enjoyed the fireworks show. Shortly afterwards, they returned to their resort, where he and his brother quickly fell asleep—physically tired from the past day's experiences, and mentally tired from thinking about the next day, and what it may bring.

Chapter Nineteen

Morning had come. The final day of Charlie and Michael's Walt Disney World vacation began like any ordinary day. Not that any day was ever ordinary when spent at the most magical place on earth, but compared to the Zastawits brother's experiences, a day spent at Walt Disney World was just the tip of the iceberg compared to a day spent in WONDER.

Their morning had been filled with a quick grab and go breakfast from the Beach Club Marketplace, a handful of attractions at the Magic Kingdom, and a sad farewell, as they walked down Main Street and out under the railroad station for the final time during their visit.

But there was still plenty of time before they had to leave. And better still, it was time to eat lunch.

After a short boat ride, the Zastawits family arrived at the Wilderness Lodge for a root'n toot'n good time, not to mention a mighty fine meal, at the Whispering Canyon Cafe.

Despite all the tasty fare, ketchup bottles, and generous hospitality from their entertaining waitress, Boxcar Barbara, Charlie could not escape his thoughts about the crystal and Ben. The more time passed, the more consuming his thoughts became. If Midnight did not contact them soon, Charlie was almost certain he would lose his mind.

The afternoon began at the Tri-Circle-D Ranch, where each member of the family saddled up and prepared for a relaxing horseback ride. Mrs. Z was first behind their guide, with Michael, Charlie, and their father bringing up the rear. The natural rhythm of the ride, combined with the peacefulness of their surroundings, helped to ease the tension in Charlie's mind. There were deer, rabbits, ducks on a pond, and the soothing sound of trees swaying in the breeze, as they made their way through the trails of the Fort Wilderness Resort.

All was peaceful and quiet, when the most unexpected of things happened.

Charlie's horse spoke.

"I'm sorry, did you not hear me the first time?"

Charlie looked around, trying to pinpoint the voice, as their group continued down the trail. The young boy leaned over, placing his head close to the horse's face.

"Yes?" the horse said.

"Whoa! That was you?" Charlie whispered.

"Well of course it was. You didn't think the ducks were talking, did you?"

"I wasn't sure. Out here on the trails there are all sorts of animals. And after what I've seen, I wouldn't be surprised if *all* the animals here could talk.

"Really, Charlie? *All* the animals? Even the most magical place on earth has its limits."

"I'm not so sure. I mean, you're talking to me right now."

"Oh, heh-heh, quite right you are," the horse replied.

"Say, your voice sounds familiar."

"I sure hope so. I mean, after all we've been through."

Charlie leaned over again and looked into the horses eyes, which sparkled electric green. "Midnight?"

"In person."

"But...we're not in WONDER. How...how did you manage to transport into reality?"

The horse neighed at the boy. "The same way I met you in the World of Disney Store as a plush Cheshire Cat. I guess Frank didn't tell you *everything* about me? You see, Charlie, since I was dreamt up for Frank's own personal companionship, he wanted to make sure I could travel anywhere he could. So unlike most animated characters from WONDER, he made sure I had the ability to transport into reality. Not only that, I have the ability to appear in any shape or form I choose."

"Like a horse?"

"Ye...yeees, like a horse. Exactly."

"So how does—"

"Charlie, who on earth are you talking to? The horse?" his fathered interrupted, startling the boy.

"Wha...what? Who, me?"

"No, I'm talking to your horse. Of course you, Charlie."

"Oh, heh-heh, that's a good one, Dad." Quickly thinking, the boy replied, "Actually, I was talking to the horse to keep him company. You know, like we talk to the cats at home."

"Well, as long as you don't expect him to talk back."

"Of course not Dad, that would be crazy," Charlie replied.

Mr. Z chuckled at the boy's answer, "I guess your'e right," he said, brushing it off while continuing to take in nature's beauty.

"Whew, that was a close one," Midnight said. "Way to be on your toes, Charlie. So where were we?"

"You were telling me about your abilities for transporting into reality?"

"Oh, yes. So, I can pretty much pop into reality as any type of creature I choose, and at any time I choose, as long as I am only interacting with Frank or chosen guests of his. I think it has something to do with the micro-dream particles he told you about last year? Anyway, back to why I am here."

"Is it about Ben and the crystal?"

"Yes...and no."

"Huh?"

"All I can tell you now, is that you and your brother are to join us at Raphael's shop."

"And then we will talk about Ben and the crystal?"

"Yes."

"Now I get it, but—"

"What is it, Charlie? I sense you still have more to say."

"So when are we going to meet up?"

"Precisely one hour from now."

The boy thought for a second. "OK, I'll figure it out."

"Very good. Now, enjoy the rest of your ride."

For the short remainder of the trail ride, Charlie and Midnight did not talk.

As the boy unmounted the horse and started walking away with his family, he looked back. The horse winked.

Charlie returned the wink with a subtle nod.

The doors slid open, Charlie and his family boarded the monorail, the doors closed, and the narration began, as the monorail started off for Epcot. Seated across from them was a young lady cast member, who smiled and looked as though she wanted to start a conversation.

Mrs. Z was happy to oblige. "So what do you do here?" she asked.

The young cast member gave Charlie's parents a hypnotic smile, her eyes sparkled and gleamed, as she snapped her fingers with both hands, then replied, "Why it seems like yesterday I just started here, but really..." the cast member flicked her fingers towards the boy's parents. Instantly, they were thrown into a memory knot.

Charlie, suspecting what had just happened, looked at each of his parents then turned to the cast member, who's name tag read, Lucy. "So I take it you are here to help us?"

"At your service, young man. Frank has told us so much about you *and* your brother. You know, he really does think a great deal of both of you."

"Really? Michael questioned, "cause—"

Charlie held up a finger to silence his brother. "Will we see him soon?"

"That I don't know, but rest assured, he is fully aware of where you are at all times, and is doing what he can to help you succeed."

"So you've seen him recently?"

"Why yes, just yesterday we talked."

"Well, if you see him soon, could you please pass the word along that we would like to talk to him again before we leave tonight."

"Oh, I don't think you'll have to worry about that," Lucy replied.

"Really?" the chosen outsider said with a quizzical look.

"You and your brother better get moving, you don't want to be late."

"Oh, right." Charlie pushed the watch button, then said, "Take us to Raphael's workshop." An orb of light engulfed the boys, sparks flew round.

"Good luck, Charlie," the cast member said, waving goodbye.

The orb around the boys grew brighter, there was a sudden burst, and then they were gone.

Charlie's parents remained seated across from Lucy, happily smiling and totally unaware of what had happened. They would remain safely in transit on the monorail until the boys returned.

"The chosen outsider and his brother have just transported into the watchmaker's realm. I am most certain they will be teaming up with their little ban of friends and will soon be headed your way," Elontra said, her face superimposed on the painting above the giant fireplace in Mr. Jollysnap's, grand dining hall on Mischief Island.

The fox and Flamario were also present, as all three were enjoying a feast-like meal.

"We will be ready, Elontra. I have a little surprise all set and ready to go, when they arrive," Jollysnaps replied.

"Very good. And just to make sure you do not fail, Dark Thorn Senkrad and I will be joining you."

The silver fox nearly choked on a chicken bone, after hearing Elontra's words. He gave the coachman a look of concern.

"The more the merrier, ma'am," the coachman replied, confident they would succeed.

"Excellent, prepare yourselves. We will arrive shortly."

Before Mr. Jollysnaps could get another word in, Elonta's face vanished from the painting.

Upon their arrival at Raphael's workshop, Charlie and Michael were surprised to see Midnight and Alexios already there, discussing a plan of attack to rescue Ben and regain control of the crystal.

"Ahhhhh, the boys have arrived. So good to see you again," Raphael said. "Come in and join us. We were just talking about you."

Charlie smiled humbly.

"Please, sit down, sit down, we have much talking to do," Raphael said, encouraging the boys to take a seat around the dining table.

Charlie turned to Alexios, who was perched up on the back of his chair. "A most dangerous, evil-ridden, and challenging task, lies ahead young squires."

"More so than any you have ever faced before, my young friends," Raphael added.

"If we are to succeed in rescuing Ben and regaining control of the crystal, much will be asked, and even more will be expected, from the two of you," Midnight said.

"And especially you, Charlie," Raphael said.

The owl, cat and watchmaker continued on, explaining every detail, as the animated brothers remained silent and still—staring straight ahead, their eyes glassed over, fearful of what lied ahead.

Somewhere deep in the woods, at the fork in the path where Charlie and Michael had originally met Featherwink, the three wooden signs stood quietly. There was a sudden flash of blue light, which left behind Charlie, Michael, Alexios and Midnight.

"Well, here we are," Midnight said.

"Our path lies this way," the owl said, landing on the lake sign.

"The lake?" Charlie asked.

"There's an island, on the far side of the lake," Midnight said.

"An island?"

"Yes, Charlie," the owl said. "An island known to those in WONDER as Mischief Island.

"There, inside a mountain, we'll find the coachman's mine of golden statues," Midnight added. "Legend has it, the statues were once playful children that had been instantly turned to gold by a single crack of Mr. Jollysnaps's magical whip, if they were deemed not worthy of being changed into working mules."

"And in this mine of gold, lies the coachman's holding cells," Alexios added.

"Where they're holding Ben?" Charlie asked.

"We hope so," Midnight answered.

"Why don't I just use the watch to transport us there?" Charlie asked. "Wouldn't that be easier?"

"Ah-ah-ah-ah-ah, they're expecting that," Alexios replied.

"Right," the cat added. "So we're going to travel by foot."

"And by air," Alexios said.

"So we best be on our way," Midnight said, as he turned and headed down the wooded trail towards the lake.

Michael and Charlie followed close behind, while the owl kept a sharp eye out from the sky above.

Back at Raphael's workshop there was a knock at the door. "Frank, so glad to see you could make it. Please, come in."

"Thank you, my old friend," Frank replied. He curiously stared at the grinning watchmaker. "Is it ready?"

"Yes, yes, yes. Please, come this way," Raphael quickly marched towards his shop room. Frank eagerly followed close behind.

There, sitting on his work bench, highlighted by the soft glow of the candlelight, was a special gift Frank had requested. The old Imagineer picked it up and admired the watchmaker's craftsmanship with wide open eyes. "It's perfect."

Rays of sunshine cut through the canopy of overhanging trees, as Charlie and the small ban of Patrons continued to make their way through the thick forest, towards the lake.

"So, does this lake have a name?" Michael asked.

"Actually, it does not," Midnight replied, leading the way.

"A lake with no name? I've never heard of such a thing," Charlie said.

"Of course you haven't. You had never heard of WONDER before last year either."

"There's a clearing ahead," Alexeios shouted down from the sky above, though the others could not see him through the treetops. "Only about a twenty minute walk from here."

"Good, cause my feet are killing me," Michael wined and moaned.

"If your feet are tired, you could always *change* into something else, you know," the cat replied.

"Change into something else?"

Midnight rolled his eyes. Fortunately the young boy could not see the feline's expression.

"What he means is, we're in Deep WONDER, so you could change into anything you're imagination can think up, Michael," Charlie said. "A squirrel, a rabbit, a unicorn...anything."

"If your feet need a rest young man, may I suggest a creature with wings?" the cat said.

Michael closed his eyes tight and concentrated hard. POOF! Instantly, he changed into a robin. "Hey, it worked. I feel lighter than air." The boy flew in sporadic circles and loops around Midnight and his brother, who continued to march on.

"Yes, yes, I can see that," Midnight said, ignoring the boy's jubilation. "Now that you can fly, why don't you go up and give Alexios a little help in the sky."

"That's a great idea." Filled with excitement, Michael shot through the overhanging trees, high above the forest, where he located the owl—and within seconds, was flying circles around him.

"Great scats! What on earth is wrong with you, bird?" Alexios screeched, irritated by the strange bird's actions.

The robin pulled up next to the great white owl, and matched his flight speed. "It's me," the bird said, while glancing over at Alexios.

"Michael?"

"Yeah," the robin replied.

Alexios did a double-take, adjusted his glasses, then sighed. "Well, stay close to me young squire. Flying may seem like fun at the moment, but it can become QUITE challenging during times of distress if you don't have a lot of practice."

"Okaaaaaaaaaay," Michael said, tailing off into a dive, before rising back up to join the owl.

"Oh brother," Alexios sighed again.

"How's everything going up there?" Charlie called out from below.

"Splendidly, young squire. Just splendidly," the owl replied, looking over at the robin.

Michael responded with a big grin.

Alexios shook his head, as they flew on towards the clearing.

The band of crystal seekers had reached the lake with no name. It was much larger than they had expected. In fact, it was so large they could not even see the Island.

"Where do we go from here?" Charlie asked.

"Yeah, it looks too far to swim," Michael added.

"You're thinking too much like a *human*, young fellow," Midnight replied. "It may be too far for a person, but for a fish, it would be rather easy to swim across."

"And to fly across would be just as easy," Alexios added.

"Hey...yeah," Michael replied, suddenly realizing that he was a bird.

"See," Midnight said, as he dove towards the water—transforming into a lake trout in midair. SPLASH! Then he surfaced and asked the boy, "So how are you going to get across, Charlie? By water or by air?"

I think I'll swim," the boy replied.

"Before you do, make sure you put the watch in your pocket for safe keeping," the cat said.

"Oh, right." Charlie removed the watch from his wrist and tucked it into his left pocket before diving into the water with his eyes closed tight. SPLOOSH! For almost a full minute there was nothing...and then, he broke the water's surface. "I never dreamt this could be so much fun," he shouted out, splashing and swimming around in a playful manner.

"Now, now, boy, just because you're an otter doesn't mean you get to swim about without worry," Midnight said.

Charlie swam up next to Midnight. "Just wanted to try out the new me, but you're right. I'm sorry. So where do we go from here?"

"We head east," Alexios called out from the shoreline, pointing with his right wing across the lake.

The trout and otter watched from the lake as the majestic owl took off into the sky with Michael following close behind.

"C'mon lad, it's time we get moving," Midnight said.

The trout and otter swam off through the sun-drenched water, leaving behind a glistening wake, as they caught up to Alexios and Michael.

"So, no sign of them yet?"

"No, Senkrad, neither the boy, nor any of his friends, have been spotted on the island yet," Mr.Jollysnaps replied.

The Dark Thorn paused. He closed his eyes, then tilted his head back, transcending the realms of Deep WONDER using his mind.

The coachman, fox and fire breather observed the Dark Thorn's actions by way of a magic water fall in the coachman's hidden mine.

"I sense their presence," Senkrad said. His eyes still closed. "A short distance off shore, rapidly approaching from the west side of the island. Two by water...and two by air."

"I'll send out a team, to comb the area," Jollysnaps replied.

"No," the Dark Thorn said in a slow, raspy tone. He opened his cold, black eyes and stared through the coachman. "Actually, let them come to shore. I have a better idea."

As they approached Mischief Island, it immediately became clear that this was not an ordinary place. The sandy shoreline was populated with enormous, spiraled trees that doubled as water slides, which emptied into the lake with no name, and as flume rides that ran wildly, end to end, along the island's coastline. The trees were swarming with children, all playing and carrying on without worry, as they swung from vines, swooshed down the water slides, rode the flume rides, and climbed amongst the spiral tree's branches.

Alexios flew down from above, hovering close to the water's surface. He brought everyone to an abrupt stop. "We need to be very careful when we get to the island. The last thing we want to do is give ourselves away to the enemy, so try to blend in and keep your eyes open for anything suspicious."

Charlie and his brother were half paying attention to the owl's words, distracted by the noisy children along the tree-covered shoreline.

"Pssst, Charlie. Did you hear what I said?" Alexios whispered.

Charlie snapped to attention. "Oh. Yes. Yes, I heard you, Alexios. Blend in and keep our eyes open. Got it. Right. Heh-heh."

The owl gave Charlie a raised brow, then turned to Michael, who was hovering beside him. "And what about you?"

Michael was still entranced by all the playful children.

Alexios snipped at the young boy, "MICHAEL."

"Wha, what?" The robin replied, spinning around to face the owl.

"Did you even hear a word I said?"

"Ye, yes. Yes I did. I, I'll make sure to be careful when we get to the island."

Alexios looked at the little bird and shook his head, then turned to Midnight and Charlie. "I think we'll need to keep a close eye on this one," he said while nodding towards Michael.

"I believe your'e right," Midnight replied.

"OK then. I see a nice spot, just a few hundred yards away, for us to go ashore without drawing too much attention. Over near the boat dock. Follow me." Alexios headed towards the island. Michael, Charlie and Midnight quietly followed close behind.

Midnight and the boys had successfully snuck onto the island, all transforming back to their normal, animated selves. Immediately, they began searching for Ben, with Alexios surveying the area from above—carefully guiding them through the forested shoreline, deeper towards the island core. As far as they knew, nobody suspected they were there.

The twisted woods gave way to even more unusual things. Things that could never be found in the real world. There was a root beer river, which foamed up at the base of a waterfall. Charlie and the others crossed over the river on a bridge made of a colorful assortment of hard candy. Some of which, the boys could not resist trying a piece or two. The foliage was made of cotton candy bushes, licorice sticks with bubble gum flowers, and leaves made of taffy. The rocks were made of chocolate, and the dirt, brown sugar. Everything was sugar-filled and yummy, exactly the kinds of things kids loved to enjoy. Exactly the kinds of things Charlie and Michael enjoyed.

"I know it all looks tasty boys," Midnight said, "but something doesn't seem right about all this."

"What could be wrong with candy?" Michael said to the cat.

"Yeah, acres and acres of it," Charlie added, as he snapped off a bubble gum flower.

"Midnight is right," Alexios said. He flew down and landed on a giant jawbreaker. "The only thing the two of you are going to get out of eating all this candy is a giant belly ache. So please, let's not get carried away."

"Yes, focus on what we're here for," the cat added.

Charlie stopped chewing the wad of gum in his mouth, then spit it out. "You're right. Michael, put it down."

Michael looked at his brother with a dejected expression.

"You heard me, put, it, down."

Michael sighed, then dropped the licorice candy shrubs he held in his arms. "Geez, you guys really know how to spoil all the fun."

"You'll thank us for it later," the owl replied.

As they continued on, the forest changed yet again. This time from candy to currency. The leaves in the trees and bushes were now made of money, ranging from one to one hundred dollar bills. And clusters of bright, shiny coins were scattered throughout. But again, the boys were warned not to give in to temptation.

A short distance later, the owl called out from above, "There's a clearing ahead. You really need to see this."

As the cat and boys emerged from the woods, they could not believe their eyes.

"How did we not see this from the lake?" Midnight asked.

"The tree-covered shoreline," Alexios replied. "The trees keep the mountain hidden from plain sight.

A short distance away stood a giant, low lying, mountain with multiple peaks. Centered at its base, above the enormous entryway, were incredibly large letters carved into the rocky surface which read: JOLLY MOUNTAIN.

"So what exactly do you think is in there?" Charlie asked.

"Nobody really knows," the owl replied, while circling from above. "Some say it contains all the fun a child could ever imagine."

"While others say it holds the end to all childhoods," Midnight added.

"Yeah, right. Neither of you have ever even seen it before, so how would you know?" Michael said.

"That may be true, young squire, but whatever is in that mountain, I assure you, cannot be good," the owl replied with a serious tone.

"Well I say we go find out, don't you?" Charlie began walking towards the mountain. "C'mon everyone, let's go see for ourselves what's in there. Something tells me we'll find Ben inside."

On Charlie's word, they started off towards the mountain entryway.

But as they were walking, there was a sudden change in the surroundings. The sky darkened, as a large mass of unwelcoming clouds rapidly formed and expanded over the mountaintop, completely blocking out the sun and beautiful blue sky.

Charlie and the others, unsure what to make of the situation, stopped in their tracks. Alexios swooped down and landed on a shrub branch next to Charlie.

"I don't like the looks of this," Midnight said.

Bolts of blue lightning shot out in every direction, as the mass of dark clouds rolled over the mountain and down across the landscape. The Patrons stood frozen, not knowing whether to turn and run, or stand and face whatever unpleasantness was headed their way.

A large flash of light burst out from the core of the clouds, as smoky figures grew out of the fog-like formations. Slowly, they descended towards the ground, developing one by one, into definable figures.

The first to be recognized by Charlie and the others was the short and portly Captain Fibs. Flanking him were the two large toady trolls, Duke and Grim. Next to appear was an unfamiliar figure. It was an older woman with white, frazzled hair and grey, tree bark-like skin. All cloaked in a gown of weathered leaves. Her eyes were dim, yellow and almost lifeless in appearance. In her right hand she held a tall crooked stick-like staff, which she slammed to the ground, summoning a force even greater than her own. A jagged bolt of light shot out from the top of her wooden staff and into the sky, forming a large ball of lightning. From it emerged Dark Thorns Senkrad and Elontra. Slowly, they descended to the ground as a gust of wind stirred up behind them.

"Looks like we have our work cut out for us," Alexios calmly stated.

"Oh, there will be no heroic victories here today," Elontra responded. "I assume this is one of the things you came for?" she said, holding up the brilliant green Kingdom Crystal in her bony right hand, as she let out a wicked bit of laughter.

"THAT is where you are mistaken," Midnight snipped back. "Patrons never give up. And we're not going anywhere until we get what we came for. Which includes that pretty green crystal you are holding in your hand, PLUS, our good friend, Ben."

"Well, one thing is for certain, you ARE going to get what you... came for." Senkrad looked towards the mountain, signaling with his bony finger for someone to join them.

Emerging from the darkness of the mountain entryway was a small army of shady, no-good characters. They were mean, ugly, covered in filth, and definitely up to something terrible. The ground shook as a large central figure led the way. Quickly, the evil band surrounded the Patrons. And worse yet, included in the group were the silver fox, Mr. Jollysnaps, and Flamario.

"It looks like we will crush you for good this time," Flamario shouted, as fire and smoke shot out from his nostrils.

"We need to protect Charlie and the watch as best we can," Alexios whispered to the others. "No matter what happens."

"My colleague here, Mr. Jollysnaps, would be *more* than happy to hand over your little friend," Senkrad said. "But of course, we'd expect something in return."

"Such as?" Alexios asked.

"Give us the boy," Elontra demanded, pointing towards Charlie.

Jollysnap's band of island goons tightened their parameter, slowly moving closer towards the Patrons.

Midnight let out a sarcastic laugh. "You must be kidding."

"If you will not hand over the chosen outsider, we will TAKE him by force!" Elontra shouted, as she magically created a necklace to safely hold the Kingdom Crystal during the battle that was about to begin.

"Allllright here we go mates," Midnight said. He took a deep breath then said the magic words, "Izza bazoo!" Sparks flew out of the black cat's giant, fluffy tail—swirling around him, as he morphed into a fierce black jaguar. "Prepare yourselves," he said, followed by a growl.

"Right," Alexios replied. Shooting straight up off the ground, high into the sky, the majestic white owl clapped his wings together. There was a burst of silvery light. Instantly, the owl's feathers transformed into titanium armor, his eyes turned to blazing yellow, and his razor-like talons grew long and sharp.

"Get the boy!" Fibs shouted to his two giant, toady trolls, Duke and Grim.

They took off in a full sprint towards Charlie.

Quick to respond, Charlie shouted out, "small and furry," instantly changing himself into a tiny mouse—just as Duke and Grim were leaping to grab him.

The toady trolls over pursued their target—now much smaller, grabbing only air with their giant, clawed hands, as they tumbled end over end across the ground.

Charlie scampered away towards a cluster of nearby bushes. But before he could reach them, Flamario burnt the shrubs to a crisp, leaving nothing but a pile of ash.

"Get him, you fools," Elontra shouted.

The coachman snapped his fingers. Ten of his island goons took off towards the mouse, who scampered into the nearby woods.

"What about you, young lad?" the fox asked Michael. "Wouldn't you like to get paid like a hero? My friend here, Mr. Jollysnaps could pay you handsomely with more gold than you could *ever* imagine." The fox locked eyes with the boy, luring him into a hypnotic trap.

"Look away, Michael," Midnight yelled. The jaguar leaped towards the silver fox—forcing him to break eye contact and flee.

"Now-now kitty, play nice," Senkrad said as he rose into the air and cast a bolt of lightning, striking the mighty jaguar, and taking his life.

"Midnight!" Charlie squeaked. He came running out of the woods towards the jaguar, changing from a mouse back into a cartoon version of himself. But this time, the Watch of WONDER was back on his wrist.

"Use the watch, lad," Alexios yelled from the sky, as he began his descent upon the giant fire breather and two toady trolls.

"Got it!" Charlie shouted back.

SWOOOOOSH, the mighty owl swooped down, and around, Flamario, the toady trolls and Captain Fibs—causing them all to get twisted up in knots and fall to the ground.

CRACK! "What the devil!" Alexios shouted, suddenly halted in his ascent. He began to tumble uncontrollably towards the ground.

The coachman had managed to strike the flying Patron, reaching Alexios all the way from the ground, with his magically extended, golden whip—temporarily rendering the mighty owl's wings useless.

"Hang on Alexios!" Charlie hollered. He activated the watch, then said, "Freedom to fly." The watch hands spun out of control, faster and faster, as the face began to shine brightly. The hands snapped into place. A burst of golden light shot out of the watch and struck the owl squarely in the chest. His wings broke free from the coach-man's spell and spread into gliding positions.

WHOOOSH, mighty Alexios skirted the ground and exploded into supersonic mode, heading straight for a cluster of goons led by the three shadow villains. BOOM! The owl struck the large group perfectly, knocking them all off their feet like a set of bowling pins. He rose back up into the sky at a blistering speed.

"Why you little ball of feathers!" Flamario shouted in anger. The giant man jumped back onto his feet. "Now, I will turn you into roasted chicken. The fire breather inhaled flames from his torch as he calculated the owl's flight path. In one big burst, he exhaled—shooting a hundred foot stream of fire towards Alexios.

The owl was too fast, and too wise, for the overgrown hothead's attack. He easily avoided the flames.

"Mr. Jollysnaps, go inside and bring out the little red headed man," Elontra commanded.

The coachman nodded and dashed into the mountain.

"I think it's time we tug on the young man's heart strings a little harder, wouldn't you agree, Sendkrad?"

"Yes, it's time we put an end to all this nonsense."

"Precisely," Elontra said. She shot into the air, transforming into a trail of blue smoke, disappearing from plane sight.

Senkrad turned his attention towards Charlie, then stomped on the ground with his right foot—sending a wave of earth towards the unsuspecting boy, whose back was facing the approaching doom.

"Charlie, behind you!" Michael shouted.

"Quiet boy," Senkrad said. He threw a spell towards Michael, sealing his mouth shut and freezing the boy in place.

"Aghhhh! What the—" Charlie hollered. A dozen vine-like appendages made of roots and soil rose up from the ground below and wrapped themselves around his body. The vines started at the legs and worked their way up around his head. Lifting Charlie up and suspending him above the ground. The boy was helpless and afraid—only his face and left arm were exposed.

With both boys detained and Midnight laying lifeless on the ground, it was up to the mighty owl to reset the balance of things. From high up in the sky, the owl adjusted his glasses and set his sights on Dark Thorn Senkrad. "This is for you my friend," Alexios said, picturing Ben in his mind. The mighty owl dove hard towards his target.

There was a sudden flash of light. ZAPOW! Alexios was stunned, speechless, and temporally blinded. He felt an electrical force wrap around him.

"You're mine now, owl," a gravelly voice said from behind.

The owl was spun around against his will to face upward, as he helplessly fell towards the ground. Slowly, his vision returned. *You,* Alexios thought to himself. *But how did you...*

"Yes, little owl, even your speed and cunningness is no match for *my* powers, "Elontra said. She returned to the ground and restrained the owl with her forcefield. "Now, I will end you." Elontra thrust her open palms towards the owl. Jagged streams of lighting shot into the owl from every direction. Alexios screamed in agony. His body went limp, as he fell hard to the ground.

Not more than five feet away from the owl laid his friend, Midnight.

Charlie and Michael, still restrained by Senkrad, watched in fear as their two courageous friends lay defeated before them.

Mr. Jollysnaps emerged from within the shadows of the mountain. Walking feebly beside him, with the coachman's whip wrapped tightly around his body, was Ben.

"Bring him here," Elontra commanded, as she stood with Senkrad and Bella Bark next to the watch-bearing outsider—still restrained from unfriendly vines.

"Gladly," the coachman replied.

Held tight by the coachman's whip, Ben stood helplessly next to Dark Thorn Elontra. She placed her left hand on his head, then touched the watch on Charlie's wrist with her other hand. Her body glowed blue, as she raised her head towards the dark sky and called out in an amplified voice, "Patron leaders come forth now...huh? What, what is that?"

A swirling mass of radiant snow flakes quickly grew from a tiny spec into a large blizzard-like mass near the edge of the clearing. A burst of light shot out in all directions from its core. Emerging before Elontra and the others were Featherwink, Sassyfran, Provo and Neve. Even though Charlie was wrapped in vines, somehow, some way, underneath it all, he had managed to find the magic icicle in his right pocket and quietly call on the snow fairy for help.

Caught off guard, Senkrad and the shadow villains assumed attack positions, breaking Elontra's concentration. Her hand pulled away from Ben and the Watch of WONDER around Charlie's wrist. "How dare you interrupt my calling," she said in anger.

"How dare us? How dare you try and harm our friends," Sassyfran replied, staring down the evil Dark Thorn.

"You have a lot of fight in you, little wooden girl," the silver fox said.

"I'm not falling for it, fox," Sassyfran replied. She continued to stare down Elontra. "I know your story, and you'll get no eye contact from me, nor do I care to listen to the hypnotic words which come from that deceiving tongue of yours."

"So it looks like the four of you didn't come here to talk?" Senkrad asked.

"That's right," Feathwink replied, transforming into a giant winged frog—well equipped with armored battle gear.

"Nice try. Really," Elontra calmly said, "but we have your precious boy and his Object of Magic, not to mention, the second Kingdom Crystal. Which, as you can see, works quite nicely as a necklace."

"Yeah, well, you've forgotten one thing," Provo shouted back.

"Oh really, and what is that you fury little, nuisance?"

"We've got a snow fairy."

"Elontra, turned to Flamario and grinned. "Melt her heart."

The giant fire breather let out a thunderous laugh, then turned towards the snow fairy. Inhaling fire from the torch, he unleashed a steady stream of flames upon her.

Featherwink, Sassyfran and Provo dove sideways to avoid the oncoming flames.

The snow fairy raised her crystal wand and spun it in a circular motion, creating an impenetrable ice shield, deflecting the fire breather's flames right back at him.

The giant man dove and rolled to his left, avoiding the flames.

Neve giggled. "One shouldn't play with fire."

"One should choose their words wisely, fairy," Bella Bark said. She cast a bolt of lighting, shattering the ice shield into tiny little pieces.

Provo leaped onto Sassyfran's shoulder, then said to the witch, "You might be good at destroying things that can't fight back, like watches and ice shields, but lets see how you deal with us."

"Aghhhh, little cheese eater, you dare challenge my powers?"

"Little cheese eater?" Provo replied.

"Don't let her name calling get to you," Sassyfran whispered to the mouse. "Instead, use it as motivation."

"Huh?" Provo replied.

"Just follow my lead," the wooden girl said.

"What?" Provo answered back, still confused.

"Well, crusty old tree witch, cheese isn't the only thing my friend is capable of chewing through," Sassyfran said. Then she whispered to the mouse, "The vines, Provo. Chew through the vines."

"What do you mean, little wooden girl?" the witch asked.

"She means, I'm a chewer," the mouse replied. He leaped off Sassyfran's shoulder and into her right hand. The wood maiden reared back and threw Provo towards the vine-wrapped outsider, his mouth ready to chew. The angry mouse chewed through the vines like a beaver on steroids. Dust flew everywhere, and within seconds, Charlie broke free from the grasp of the dreadful vines.

Simultaneously, Featherwink flew over and released a cloud of magic dust upon Michael, freeing him from Senkrad's spell.

You're free to do whatever you can imagine, Charlie, Neve called out.

Inspired by the snow fairy's words, Charlie leaped out of the chewed up vine debris and aimed the watch towards his two unconscious friends, then shouted, "Awaken!" A beam of golden light shot out of the watch face, split into two separate streams, circling around the jaguar and owl, faster and faster, until they collided, producing a burst of energy which shot through the lifeless bodies below—restoring them to their lively selves.

Midnight jumped to his feet and let out a mighty roar at the shadow villains, with Ben restrained by the coachman's golden whip.

Inspired by the cat's roar, Alexios soared into the dark grey sky, then took off like a shooting star, making him invisible to the naked eye. Only a trail of sparkling dust was left to be seen in his wake. The majestic owl, Defender of the Kingdom Crystals, was determined to repay the Dark Thorns for what they had done to him and his faithful friends.

"Aghhhh!" Senkrad screamed in anger. "You pesky little child, now I will deal with you once and for all." The Dark Thorn shaped a ball of lightning, then reared back to cast it upon Charlie.

As Senkrad's arm came forward, Michael, having changed into a billygoat, rammed the Dark Thorn's legs—making him overshoot his intended target. The sizzling ball flew high and far into the woods, behind where Charlie stood.

Senkrad screamed out in frustration.

SWOOOOSH! Alexios swept down, virtually out of nowhere, and struck the coachman firmly in his right arm, causing the shadow villain to spin rapidly in place and involuntarily free Ben from the whip's grasp.

Ben's eyes instantly lit up. The jolly little man stomped on the coachman's foot, pulled his hat down over his eyes, then darted off in a fit of happiness, crying out, "It's time to set things right!"

"Hey, get back here. Why, just wait 'til I get my hands on you, you little trouble maker," the coachman shouted, as he struggled to pull the tall, gold top hat off his head.

Charlie jumped onto the back of the large, black jaguar, teaming up with the snow fairy against Flamario and the silver fox.

The giant fire breather spat out multiple fireballs towards Charlie and the cat, which immediately were deflected by counter attacks of ice by Neve—who suddenly was stripped of her wand by the silver fox.

The fox ran off with the wand in his mouth towards the woods, where he was redirected back into the fray by the growling jaguar.

"Well, what are you waiting for?" Fibs called out to Duke and Grim "Get that wooden girl and her little mouse."

The two enormous trolls sprang into action, flanking the wood maiden and her faithful little friend from both sides.

Sassyfran called to the mouse, who jumped into her hands, as she did a reverse summersault, back into a standing position, avoiding Duke and Grim's attack.

The large trolls collided and fell to the ground.

"Get up you fools! They're behind you," Fibs shouted.

The ugly trolls jumped to their feet, spun around, and snarled at the wooden girl and the mouse.

"I think it's best, we get a move on," Provo said.

"Right," Sassyfran replied.

The wood maiden whirled around with Provo on her shoulder. SHAPOW!

Sassyfran felt a sudden jolt of energy rush through her, now splintered, body.

The mouse lay still in her hand. His whiskers, frazzled, his eyes, hypnotically glazed over—he looked like a toasted fur ball.

The wood maiden gingerly turned around—a tear was dangling from the corner of her right eye, as she looked upon her attacker. "The witch," she mumbled.

"That's right dear," Bella Bark let out an evil cackle, then struck them with another bolt. SHAPOW!

Sassyfran and Provo were instantly turned into a pile of ash.

"NO!" Michael shouted from behind a tree where he was hiding. Giving away his position, the young boy was now a vulnerable target.

Bella spun around, set her evil gaze upon Michael, then shot another bolt, splitting the tree in two and leaving the boy with nowhere to run. She prepared for another strike.

Michael raised his arms in defense. He fully expected to be turned to ash, just like the wood maiden and mouse.

"Don't you dare touch my brother!" Charlie shouted. He and the mighty black cat charged the witch from the left side. Charlie raised his left arm to ninety degrees, as a metallic silver shield grew out of the magical watch. Then he cupped his right hand, a magic lance appeared, as he and Midnight continued to charge.

Caught off guard, the wood witch turned toward the charging duo.

BLAM! Charlie was knocked off Midnight's back and thrown hard into the thick trunk of an old, scraggly tree, rendering him unconscious.

Midnight effortlessly changed directions and leaped into the air, his giant claws fully exposed, as he prepared to pounce upon the assailant.

CRACKLEY-CRACK-POW! A series of blue bolts sizzled from the fingertips of Dark Thorn Senkrad, forming a forcefield around the body of the airborne jaguar—pinning him against the base of the mountain. "Good, kitty," Senkrad said with a sneer.

Neve rose into the sky and opened up her right hand. The crystal wand was pulled loose from the running fox's mouth, and into the snow fairy's hand. She raised her arms high into the air and called out, "Wind and snow blow with fury, show this fox that he should scurry." She cast down a flurry of ice and snow towards the silver fox.

A sudden blaze of fire intercepted the snow fairy's wintery mix, instantly changing it to water—thoroughly soaking the fox.

The fire breather turned his fiery gaze upon Neve. He crouched down, then leaped high into the air, grabbing the snow fairy before she could move, with his enormous, and very powerful, right hand.

Neve struggled to free herself, but it was too late.

As Flamario's feet hit the ground, he inhaled flames from his torch, then unleashed a powerful stream of fire, while letting go of Neve at the same time. Nothing but a crystal wand sitting in a puddle of water remained upon the ground.

Ben, closely pursued by several island goons, zipped around Mr. Jollysnaps at an amazing speed, causing him to temporarily lose his footing.

In an effort to help his red headed friend, Michael imagined himself in a pair of super sneakers, giving him the ability to run at an amazing speed. He took off like a shot, barreling into the coachman's goons, which allowed Ben to help the others.

"Thanks—" SLAM!

Ben was blind sided in mid-stride by Grim, who picked up the jolly little man and tossed him to Duke.

"Tie 'em to that tree," Captain Fibs ordered, as he spat onto the ground. "We don't need him running about and causing anymore distractions."

"Yes sir, Captain," Duke replied. "Come on little fella, it's time we get you tied up nice and tight," the troll said, sharing a laugh with his unsightly partner, Grim.

Michael froze in his tracks. A sudden sense of helplessness took over his thoughts. Sassyfran, Provo, Charlie, Midnight, Neve, and now Ben, had all been bested by the evil Thorn army. *What are we going to do,* he thought to himself. *Without the others we are outnumbered and overpowered.*

"SNAP!"

The young boy felt something wrap around his torso. It was the golden whip of Mr. Jollysnaps. "Well-well, looks like we caught ourselves a good one this time," the coachman said, as the others joined in with a laugh.

"Hardly," Michael snipped back.

"Oh, we'll see about that, mate. Yes, we will see about that," Jollysnaps replied with a sinister grin, staring into the boys frightened eyes.

"We're coming lad, no need to fret," Alexios called out from the sky. The owl and Featherwink bared down on the coachman and his goons.

"NOT this time," Elontra proclaimed, suddenly appearing before Mr. Jollysnaps. Removing the crystal necklace from her neck, she spun it round, faster and faster. The crystal lit up, creating a piercing, green light. "Winds of peril, blow and swirl!" Her voice echoed through the air as she continued to spin the necklace around—creating a giant whirlwind of evil. Elontra released the whirlwind, hurling the chaotic mass directly towards the approaching owl and frog.

"Noooooooooo!" Michael screamed out.

The evil winds quickly consumed mighty Alexios and Featherwink, until all that remained was a whiff of green cloud.

"What have you done," Michael screamed at Elontra. "You...you... you don't scare me, Elontra. You don't scare me one bit."

"Oh really," Senkrad said, joining Elontra by her side. Then you must be a *very* foolish child."

"Coachman," Elontra said. "I think we've heard enough from this child. Maybe you should...add him to your collection?"

The coachman looked at Elontra, then turned towards the boy— his eyes wide open like saucers. His smile, wicked and intimidating. "Yeeeesss, what a wonderful addition he will make.

"And what a perfect way to lure in Frankie and the rest of those pathetic Patrons," the silver fox added.

"Yeah, the old coot and his friends wont be able to resist," Duke said.

Everyone from the Thorn army was now gathered around the helpless boy, laughing uncontrollably, which frightened and angered Michael, all at the same time.

"Well c'mon boy," Mr. Jollysnaps said, tugging on his whip, which tightened ever so slightly around Michael's body—forcing him to cooperate. Slowly they made their way towards the mountain entrance.

Captain Fibs and the others laughed even louder, as they watched the coachman lead the reluctant boy towards his perilous fate.

Just as they reached the mountain entrance, a voice called out from above. "Why wait. I have always been told there's no time like the present." A silvery burst of light broke through the grey skies above. A sudden gust of wind barreled down upon the evil Dark Thorns and their villainous friends. From the center of the light burst a white haired man, donning colorful clothing, white sneakers, and a confident smirk, appeared.

Frank Wellington had arrived, and following closely by his side were Ticky and Tocky, Raphael's magical cats.

"I agree, foolish old man," Elontra snarled. "There *is* no time like the PRESENT!" Lighting shot out from her fingertips towards Frank and the cats, attempting to knock them out of the sky.

The mighty Patron raised his arms above his head, exposing the light charm, which hung around his neck. The bolts cast by the wicked Dark Thorn were absorbed by the charm, then immediately shot back towards the gathering of villainous fiends and rabble rousers below.

SHAPOW!

Instantly they scattered like rats.

The sudden noise woke Charlie. Quietly he rose to his feet and gathered himself near the tree Bella Bark had blasted him into. As he looked up, his eyes were overwhelmingly surprised to see his good friends, Frank, Ticky and Tocky doing battle with the evil forces surrounding them.

Frank turned to the boy, winked, then turned towards the woods. With a mighty clap of his hands, he said, "Bring forth the wooden army." He raised his arms high—the light charm floated upwards, away from his body, shining brightly. The bushes and trees shook, and the leaves rustled, as the click-clack sound of a thousand wooden parts rose up from the forest. Then he turned towards his enemies and said, "Behold, Raphael's mighty wooden army."

Hundreds of carved, toy soldier figures—no larger than a small child, came rushing out of the woods, straight towards Flamario, the silver fox, and a group of island goons. Some of the soldiers were rough starts with bark-covered skin and hardly any recognizable features at all, while others were finely carved and intricately painted, right down to the smallest of details. All carried with them shields and small wooden swords or spears to help in the battle. And those leading the charge were riding atop a variety of wooden animals such as horses, elephants, giraffes and rhinos.

"Oh no you don't." CRACK-CRACK-SIZZLE-POW! Bella cast a strike towards Frank, who again, cast it back via the light charm—only this time, it was directed at the forcefield holding Midnight against the base of the mountain.

Instantly, the mighty black jaguar was freed, exploding into a full-out dash to join the battle.

Angered by the wise Patron's tactics, Senkrad shot up into the sky and cast the next bolt towards Frank, who yet again, redirected it towards the tree where Ben had been tied up. SIZZLE—CRACK—SHAPOW! The vines were broken and Ben was free.

"Mind if I help, old pal," Ben said with a smile. He jumped into a rolling juggernaut-like ball, and began bowling over dozens of Jollysnap's goons, one after another.

"This is not possible!" Senkrad shouted out in frustration—a rare thing for a Dark Thorn to do.

"Now it's my turn," Elontra calmly said. She disappeared into the ground. A moment later she reappeared, standing behind Frank and the cats. "Let's see how you deal with my pets." She raised her arms towards the sky, palms up. More than two dozen swirling balls of dirt rose up from the ground, which morphed into a pack of wolves.

"Wolves! Behind you! It's a pack of dirt wolves!" Charlie shouted to warn his friends.

Frank spun around and smirked, "You're up, kitties." He sprung into the air, did a triple summersault, then stuck the landing atop a large, nearby bolder from the mountain.

Ticky, the grey, short hair cat, took off in a full sprint away from the wolves.

Elontra laughed at the cat's cowardly actions. "Sic 'em, my pets," she called out, before turning her attention towards the other cat.

Half of the wolves looked at their creator, then turned and snarled with bright red eyes. They took off after their prey.

The pack quickly gained on the small, grey cat. Just as they were about to claim their prize, Ticky sprung straight up into the air, twisting, flipping and morphing into something much larger. As he landed on all fours, the wolves came to a startling halt, taken aback by the large snow leopard with crystal blue eyes which now stood before them.

Ticky let out a fierce growl.

The wolves growled back, surrounded the leopard and began their attack. One by one, they charged the fierce cat, who, with each strike of his mighty paws, turned the attackers back into what they really were. Nothing but dirt.

Sensing defeat, the few remaining wolves quickly retreated towards the woods, only to be hunted by the giant snow leopard, who was determined to return his foes back to where they came from.

Simultaneously, the other half of the wolf pack had turned their evil intentions upon Tocky, the white, long haired female, and were also eager to please their Dark Thorn master. Slowly they closed in on the small cat, their heads lowered, baring sharp, jagged teeth between their snarled snouts. The moment had come to attack.

Tocky frantically looked around for an escape. She darted towards a large cluster of nearby shrubs.

The hunt was on as the wolves pursued their prey, leaping into the shrubs after her.

"Charlie, my boy!" Frank shouted. "Use the icicle!"

The young boy was confused by all that was going on. He gave his Patron friend a look of bafflement.

"The icicle. Use it to bring her back," Frank said, pointing to his right pocket.

"Watch out, Frank!" Charlie shouted back.

SWOOSH-SWOOSH-SHOOSH!

Frank elevated high into the sky, easily dodging multiple flame burst delivered by Flamario.

Frank's words suddenly struck a chord with Charlie. "Ohhh, right. Now I get it." He pulled the magic icicle from his pocket. The young boy held the icicle high. "Return to us now."

A tiny mass of spiraling snowflakes began to form above the crystal wand, which laid upon the ground where Flamario had turned the snow fairy to water. The spiraling mass grew larger and more pronounced. There was a burst of sparkling flakes, the snow cleared. Neve had returned with crystal wand in hand. "Thank you, Charlie," she said to the young boy. Then she turned to Frank. "So good to see you again my old friend."

Frank acknowledged the snow fairy's words, then pointed behind her. "We have a few issues to take care of."

Neve turned, overcome by what she saw. "Understood."

Part of Raphael's wooden soldiers were swarming Flamario and the silver fox, trying their best to overcome the giant fire breather and his sly friend. But the two shadow villains were too powerful.

Flamario turned many of the soldiers to ash with streams of fire, including those riding animals, every time he exhaled.

The sliver fox, mostly known for his mind and hypnotic stare, could be quite physical in such battles. His lame paw was really just a ploy, as he moved quite well, tearing away limbs with his powerful jaws, and sweeping out legs from beneath the wooden soldiers, and the animals they rode, using his large, fluffy tale.

The soldier's weapons were rendered useless against their mighty foes. Every time a sword was drawn or a spear thrown, they were either disintegrated by the fire breather or snapped in half by the silver fox.

With the assistance of Midnight and Ben, the other half of the wooden army was having just as difficult a time battling Captain Fibs, his toady trolls, and a small army of island goons. And though they weren't as powerful as the shadow villains, they were able to hold their own. Overcoming anything Midnight, Ben and the wooden soldiers could throw at them.

The ground beneath them began to shake and rumble as cracks shot out in every direction. Not far away, Charlie and Neve stood and watched, unsure what to do. Frank leaped off the boulder and quickly ran over to join them.

The ground swelled and crumbled. There was a giant explosion. Rock and dirt flew everywhere, creating a giant dust cloud. When the air cleared, a giant crater remained.

An enormous claw emerged from the crater. Then another, and another. Large horn-tipped wings arose from both sides of the gigantic hole. Then two pale blue dragon heads with black eyes. The heads simultaneously looked towards the sky, then at Charlie, Frank and Neve, while letting out horrible shrieking growls. "EEERAHHHH!"

"Charlie, go back and get Alexios and Featherwink," Frank said.

The dragons climbed out of the crater, then exploded into the sky, letting out a multitude of shrieking growls.

Following the dragons with his eyes, the young boy replied to Frank, "I don't understand?"

"Look around you my boy, we are loosing this battle. We need all the help we can get, or our cause will be lost forever."

"Yes, that part I understand, but how do I go back and get Alexios and Featherwink?"

"The watch on your wrist, Charlie," Frank answered back. "Use the Object of Magic to travel back and get them."

"But...how exactly does that work?"

"You need to travel back in time, just before their end," Neve kindly explained. "At that very moment, you can save them. Then, bring them back to the present time."

"Now I get it," the boy replied—excited by the idea.

"And make sure they both are touching you before telling the watch to bring you back," Frank added.

"Got it." Charlie activated the watch. "Take me back to Alexios and Featherwink's end." The hands spun round and round, as the face lit up in a colorful pattern. Mickey's hands snapped to the backwards setting. There was a giant burst of light. The boy was gone.

Chapter Twenty

BOOM...BOOM! The giant dragons landed side by side, facing back to back. They surveyed the battles with their black, pearly eyes. Their large talons were dug well into the ground's surface, as their thorn-tipped tails, at least thirty feet long, swayed from side to side along the ground. The dragon's muscular, pail blue physiques were quite intimidating, even by the standards of Flamario and the fox. As they exhaled, small blue flames crept out of their fiercely-toothed mouthes.

"The one on the right bears what we need," Frank quietly said to Neve.

"I see it," the snow fairy replied—spotting the the Kingdom Crystal necklace around the dragon's long neck.

"Where is the boy?" the dragon wearing the necklace asked in a thunderous tone.

"Boy? What boy?" Frank said. Playing stupid to buy time.

"RAAARRRRRR!" the dragon responded in anger. She shot a stream of blue flames directly towards Frank and Neve.

The snow fairy flicked her wand—instantly freezing the blue flames before they struck them.

The male dragon responded with another fire stream.

Frank swirled his open hands around, then thrust them towards the approaching stream of fire. The charm around his neck released a magical burst of light, which traveled through his arms, then out through his hands, striking the oncoming flames dead center—pushing them all the way back towards the dragon until they had been extinguished.

"ROOOAAAAAAR! You'll pay for that," the male dragon proclaimed.

"I think not," Frank replied, sensing Charlie would return soon.

"Bring us the boy now, or I will end you," Elontra demanded from Frank, snapping her enormous dragon jaws.

SHOOOP!

Charlie had returned. With him were Alexios and Featherwink—alive and ready for battle.

"I hear you're looking for me?" the chosen outsider said in a confident tone.

The dragons quickly turned their attention towards the boy, as the owl and the giant, winged frog took to the air, traveling in opposite directions.

"Give us the watch, boy," Senkrad said in his deep dragon voice.

"Charlie, I brought you a gift from the watchmaker," Frank shouted from across the way—distracting the dragons.

"Gift? What gift?" Elontra growled with curios concern.

Frank smacked his hands together, magic sparks flew outward in every direction. He pulled his hands apart, a glittering trail followed each one, then dissipated, exposing a familiar walking stick in the wise Parton's hands.

"Oteza!" Charlie shouted. "You...you're alive? But how?"

"Magic. Purely magic," Frank replied. He reached back with the magic walking stick in his throwing hand, then launched her just out of reach of the dragons, towards Charlie.

Senkrad tried to reach out and snap the stick in half with his mighty jaws, but was too slow to react.

Charlie reached up and received Oteza perfectly in his left hand. He pulled the stick down to gaze upon her with teary eyes of happiness.

"I know you missed me, but *now* is not the time to get all emotional," Oteza said.

"Right," the boy said. He smiled and wiped the tears from his face.

"Oh, how sweet," Elontra growled with a sarcastic undertone, rolling her large dragon eyes.

"Charlie, you know what to do," Frank hollered.

"Just like old times, eh Charlie?" Oteza added. "Just tap me twice on the ground—that should do it."

"Do what?" The boy asked.

"JUST DO IT," Oteza demanded.

"Charlie took the magic ostrich stick in his right hand and tapped it two quick times on the ground. Instantly, he felt an invisible charge travel through his entire body and into the stick, which began to spark and hum. His body was magically shielded with carved, wooden armor that matched the engravings on the walking stick.

"It's time to go to work, my friend. Attack!" Oteza shouted.

"There's so much going on I...I don't know where to start," the boy replied, as he frantically looked around. "And where is Michael? I don't see him."

"Go to Frank, he should know," Oteza replied.

Charlie bolted towards his friend. The boy had forgotten what it was like to move with such power and energy—like the year before when they battled the Yeti. Once again, he was a warrior with mad skills and the ability to maneuver well beyond those of any normal human being. But this time was even more incredible than before, being they were in Deep WONDER.

"Stop that boy!" Elontra commanded. She and Senkrad took off into the air—trying to surround the chosen outsider and his magic stick with walls of fire.

But Charlie was too agile, too quick and had no fear or doubt in his abilities. Confidently, he maneuvered through and around all deadly obstacles the dragons could throw at him—reaching Frank and Neve without fatigue.

"So where is Michael?" Charlie asked.

"Watch out!" Frank shouted, as a stream of fire rained down from Senkrad in the sky above.

"Allow me," Neve replied. The snow fairy spun her crystal wand, creating and impenetrable dome, which easily deflected Senkrad's flames and all other fiery attempts the dragons sent towards her and her friends.

"My brother?" Charlie asked again.

"The coachman took him into his mountain," Frank replied.

"What is he going to do with Michael inside the mountain?"

Frank sighed. "More than likely, he will try to turn your brother into a worker mule that can be sold or used to mine his gold."

Charlie's eyes grew wide as saucers. "You mean like the ones that were pulling the coachman's coach?"

"Precisely."

"That's not going to happen."

"And worse yet, he may turn him to gold."

"What?" Like a statue?"

"Unfortunately, yes. The Patron council believes that Mr. Jollysnaps has a collection of golden statues hidden deep within the mines of the mountain."

The dragons swooped in for another attack, dousing the snow fairy's ice dome with even more fire.

The dome began to wear thin—hairline cracks started to form and grow all around its structure.

"We must hurry, the dome will not hold much longer," Neve said, as she surveyed the damage.

"Right," Frank replied. "Charlie, the sooner you find your brother, the better."

"Got it."

"And Charlie...be prepared for anything. Shadow villains are extremely powerful."

Charlie looked at his good friend and nodded.

"And watch out for those dragons!" Neve shouted, as the boy burst through the protective dome—rushing towards the mountain to save his brother.

"We'll take care of the dragons," Frank said to Neve, as he turned to face the flying fire breathers—ready for battle.

Inside the mountain, just beyond the entryway, was a long tunnel, lined with bright, lit arrows pointing towards a large, Illuminated sign at the end.

Charlie cautiously proceeded down the tunnel to take a closer look.

The sign read: THE JOLLY BIG ARCADE, COME IN AND HAVE A BALL!

The boy stepped into the arcade. It was massive—filled with colorful arcade machines and hundreds of lively gamers. The isles seemed endless, lined end to end with at least twenty of every arcade game one could imagine. At the center of the ginormous room was an expansive, rectangular soda bar, where gamers could enjoy a wide variety of bubbly, caffeinated sodas to keep their energy levels up. And if gamers didn't want to visit the soda bar, there were plenty of soda machines and candy-filled vending machines scattered throughout the arcade.

The chosen outsider made his way around the arcade, observing hundreds of children, all fixated on games they were playing, and all hopped up on candy and soda.

"Something's not right here," Oteza said to Charlie. "And where did these children get the money they're pumping into those arcade machines?"

The ostrich stick's words sparked a thought in Charlie's mind. "The woods," he said out loud.

"What? The woods?"

"Yes, the woods between here and the lake were made of candy, and then money."

"Are you thinking the coachman supplied candy and money to all the village kids visiting Mischief Island, so inevitably, they end up here, playing arcade games for hours on end?"

"Uh...Yeah...yes, that's exactly what I'm thinking," the boy replied.

"But why would the coachman do such a thing?"

"I say we go ask him ourselves," Charlie said.

"Good idea, but do you notice something strange about this room?"

The boy looked around. "No, not really."

"If we're going to go find Mr. Jollysnaps, wouldn't it be best if we could find a door to get out of here, first?"

Charlie carefully looked around again. "Hey, I don't see any exits."

"And the doorway we came in has vanished as well."

The boy snapped his head around, shocked by what he saw. "Wh... where did the entryway go?"

"Obviously we're supposed to stay here."

"Yeah, but for how long?"

HEEE-HAW! SHOOP!, HEEE-HAW! SHOOP!, HEEE-HAW! SHOOP! SHOOP! SHOOP!

One by one, the children in the arcade started changing into mules, and suddenly dropping through small trap doors in the floor beneath them.

"What's going on here?" Charlie said in a panic.

"The trap doors in front of the machines."

"I see them. What about 'em?"

"Don't you see, Charlie? That's our way out."

"Right, let's go."

"Behind you, Charlie. A girl just turned into a mule. The trap door beneath her should open any second now."

The trap door dropped down. Charlie leaped towards the opening—timing it perfectly. The boy and his handy stick screamed and hollered, as they slid down a shoot in total darkness—closely following the neighing mule ahead of them.

Flamario, the fox, Bella Bark, Captain Fibs and his two toady trolls stood triumphantly amongst the smokey air. Scattered around them, only ash, splintered wood and a few burning embers remained from Raphael's wooden army.

Broken down, ash covered, and defeated, Midnight and Ben stood quietly. They had fought bravely alongside the wooden army, but it had not been enough.

"I say, little red headed fellow. Why don't you bring your kitty friend over here," the silver fox said.

Ben kept his head down, refusing to acknowledge the shadow villain's request.

"Hey, little man. Did you hear what my friend asked of you?" Flamario spat out.

Both Ben and the black jaguar continued to ignore the shadow villain's words.

"Duke, Grim, go grab those two will ya," Fibs commanded.

The toady trolls marched over to fetch the Patrons.

Half way there, a giant white tiger with crystal blue eyes leaped out of the shrubs, cutting off the trolls. The tiger roared, suggesting the trolls should turn back.

Bella Bark reached back, then tossed a lightning bolt towards the tiger.

The bolt was deflected by a green counter bolt from the sky. Featherwink, the magic frog was helping Frank, Neve and Alexios battle the Dark Thorn dragons, and happened to fly by at just the perfect time.

The white tiger turned to the frog and thanked him, as Ticky, the large snow leopard, came to her side. The tiger and leopard's eyes were identical in every way. "Nice to see you brother," the tiger said quietly.

"Likewise," the snow leopard replied.

"Tocky, is that you?" Midnight asked. His curiosity peeked.

Ticky and Tocky both turned their attention towards the jaguar. "Well of course it is, silly."

"I did not realize you could talk," Midnight replied.

"You never asked," the tiger answered back.

"Behind you!" Ben shouted, pointing towards the shadow villains.

Flamario made the ground shake, as he charged towards Ticky and Tocky. And right behind him, was a small group of the coachman's goons, all bearing weapons.

Meanwhile, the fox had circled around and was mounting a charge towards Midnight and Ben from the opposite direction.

Elontra and Senkrad soared high into the sky, looped around each other, then dove aggressively towards Frank and the snow fairy, attempting to catch the Patrons in a crossfire of flames. They swept in low, one from each side, unleashing long streams of fire that left nothing behind but scorched trails.

Frank ran, then leaped upwards, changing into a giant hawk, as Neve took off into the sky, trailed by flakes of sparkling snow.

Elontra and Senkrad's flames collided, letting out a thunderous BOOM, as the low flying dragons crossed paths, heading in opposite directions.

As Senkrad circled back around, he was unexpectedly confronted by the snow fairy, who cast her wand in mid flight, sending a flurry of ice, which coated the dragon's wings and sent the giant beast spiraling towards the mountain.

KAPOW!

The giant creature crashed into the mountainside and tumbled downward. An avalanche of giant rocks followed—burying the unconscious dragon.

The snow fairy flew down and quickly concealed the pile of boulders in a giant glacier. "There, that should hold you for a while," Neve said.

On the opposite side of the mountain, high up in the sky, Frank attempted a surprise attack from the dragon's underside. The clever hawk rose up, eyeing the brilliant green Kingdom Crystal dangling from Elontra's neck.

Just as Frank was about to grab the crystal with his beak, she spotted the hawk and changed her course abruptly—swatting Frank away like a pesky fly, sending him into a tailspin, plummeting towards the ground.

Suddenly, Frank felt something grab hold of the light charm around his neck, pulling him out of his tailspin.

"Hello old friend. Looks like you could use some help."

Frank looked to his right as he regained control. "Alexios. So good to see you friend. And yes, I sure could use your help."

"If you can distract that overgrown lizard for just a second, I may be able to grab the crystal."

"That sounds like a wonderful plan," Frank replied.

"Very well, old chap, you get her to look up, and I'll take care of the rest.

"On my waaaaaay, the hawk said, as he tailed off—soaring at tremendous speeds, just beyond the reach of the dragon's deadly jaws.

SNAP. SNAP-SNAP. Elontra tried multiple time to snare the crafty hawk, as he swiftly flew by her again and again.

On the forth pass, Frank circled round and round, just above the dragon's head.

Elontra snarled, as she looked upward and said, "Come here you pesky bird, I need a snack." SNAP. SNAP-SNAP. The dragon tried again and again to snare the hawk.

A sparkling, silver blur rose up from below, shooting past the dragon's neck.

Elontra paused as if something was wrong. "What...what was that? Something seems amiss," she growled, continuing to fly along. Instinctively, the wicked dragon pulled up into a holding position in the sky. Looking downward with her black, pearly eyes, she reached for the crystal around her neck with her large front claws. Again and again, she felt for the crystal. But to her misfortune, the necklace holding the crystal was no longer there. Elontra's dark eyes turned fiery red, she screamed with rage—letting out a stream of fire so enormous, and for so long, that it filled the entire sky around the island.

"We have it," Alexios said, as he slowed down from supersonic speed, landing next to the hawk in an isolated tree on the mountainside. The owl raised his left wing, showing Frank the green crystal tucked away in his feathery pocket.

"Well, we're half way there," Frank replied.

"The boy?"

"Yes. I sent him after the coachman to rescue his brother," Frank replied with a concerned look.

"You go help the boy, I'll gather up Ben and the others."

Just before the hawk and owl parted ways, a large, horrifying series of screams rained down from the sky, catching their attention.

NO. NO. NOOOOOOOOOOOOO! Elontra had used so much energy to fill the sky with fire that she lost her power as a dragon. The evil Dark Thorn shedded her scales, transforming back into her hideous, human form, as she plummeted and slammed into the surrounding woods—leaving her unconscious.

Featherwink unleashed a large, gelatinous bubble, protecting Midnight and Ben from Flamario, the silver fox, and a few island goons, while he and Raphael's cats focused on Bella Bark and Captain Fibs' toady trolls.

"What happened to those big ugly trolls anyway?" Ticky, the snow leopard, asked.

"No idea," Featherwink replied.

"They probably ran into the woods to hide, once they saw what Frank and the snow fairy did to their precious Dark Thorn Dragons," the white tiger said.

"Nobody is running anywhere," Bella Bark declared. She took her staff and thrust it towards the white tiger, turning the fierce cat into a harmless plush animal.

The witch cackled.

Angered by her laughter, the snow leopard charged Bella head-on. The agile leopard leapt into the air, claws out.

Bella dodged the big cat's attack—she reached out with her staff, touching the pouncing leopard in the chest, which turned him into a harmless plush animal, just like his sister.

Midnight roared. "Enough." The mighty jaguar crouched down, green eyes glowing, as he flicked his magical tail at Bella. A stream of green light flew towards the witch.

Bella deflected the jaguars attack, sending it back towards Ben.

SHAPOW!

Ben dove out of the way.

The witch laughed even louder. "Really, is this all you can—"

ZZZING!

"Uhhhh...ahhhhh...what...what's happening to—"

SWOOOSH—KAPOW!

Bella was instantly crystalized by the snow fairy, then shattered into a thousand pieces from a blow by the supersonic owl, who flew right through her.

Charlie and Oteza found themselves in a giant stall filled with hay and a hundred noisy mules.

"Someone is coming. Quick, find a place to hide near the door, so we can slip out unnoticed," Oteza whispered.

The sound of footsteps grew louder. A soft glowing light pushed through the cracks of the doorway. There was jingling of keys, a click, then the door swung open.

A short, well-rounded man marched into the room. He was scruffy, dirty—dressed in tattered clothes, stained from years of neglect and lack of soap. He smelled. Even worse than the mules.

Charlie's nose crunched up, as he struggled to remain quiet.

The man marched towards the center of the room. "Alright, who will it be today," he announced, then snorted and spat onto the dirt floor.

"Now Charlie," the ostrich whispered.

The boy quietly slipped out the doorway, sprinting down the long and winding, torch-lit tunnel. Left, right, left, right and right again. For several minutes he continued on—at each bend wondering, would they be confronted by the enemy.

"I sense an ending soon," Oteza said, as the boy continued on down the tunnel. "Yes, two...maybe three more bends in the pathway and we'll be there."

The ostrich stick was right. After the third turn, the narrow tunnel opened up into a vast cavern filled with enormous stacks of gold coins, chalices, crowns, treasure chests and more. And planted throughout the stacks were hundreds of children that had been turned into gold statues—young, old and in between.

Charlie and Oteza had found the hidden mine of the coachman.

They both paused and stared, terrified by what they were seeing.

"Just a couple handfuls would probably be enough for our family to live off for the rest of our lives," Charlie said, his mind overtaken by what laid before him.

"We're here for your brother, not the gold," Oteza sternly reminded the boy.

Oteza's question refocused the boy. "Right. Sorry. Where...where do you think they took him?"

"They're here. We just have to find them." The ostrich stick scanned the area with her eyes.

They walked past and around mound after mound of gold coins and other riches—all the while, checking the statues to see if any resembled Michael. Fortunately, none had.

Flamario and the fox unexpectedly turned their attention away from the battle and retreated towards the mountain.

"Something strange is going on," Neve said. Observing the actions of the shadow villains.

"The glacier," Alexios said.

"It's melted," Neve added. "Come-come," she said, motioning to the owl and Midnight, "everyone huddle together. I will send you back to the watchmaker's workshop. The crystal should be safe there, while Feaherwink and I help Frank find the boys."

Midnight returned to his normal, cat form.

Ben grabbed the two plush animals in his arms. "All set," he said.

Midnight, Alexios, Ben and the others all gathered close together. Neve waved her wand and cast a magic spell upon the group. There was a flash of sparkling snowflakes. They were gone.

"Come, Featherwink. We need to go find Frank."

Neve and Featherwink flew off into the mountain.

"So, who are your lovely friends?" Michael asked in a sarcastic tone. Two smelly goons were tying him to a large, golden pole with aztec graphics populating its surface.

"Just a few of my helpers," the coachman replied.

"So like, they help you steal all the innocent children from the village to bring here and turn into gold statues?"

The coachman did not flinch. "Mules as well, my boy. You see, unlike you, some of the children from the village actually make good workers." He removed the golden rod from underneath his long coat. Gently flicking his wrist, the whip magically grew six to eight feet out from the rod's end.

The sight of the whip put Michael in a panic, but he tried his best to look calm on the outside. Attempting to distract the coachman, the clever boy kept the conversation going, as the two island goons stepped away from the pole and returned to their leader's side.

"How do you get all the kids here anyway?"

"Rides, candy, money, and games, boy. Rides, candy, money and games."

"It's quite the operation, if I do say so myself," the boy replied— feeding the shadow villain's ego to make him talk more.

"The rides attract the little boogers to the island, then I load 'em up on sugar, throw some money at 'em, then lead them into my arcade. And once they've had their fare share of mischief...they can't help but turn into worker mules. Mules I sell for money, HA! HA! HA! HA! HA!"

"But what if they *don't* turn?" The boy asked—terrified by Jollysnaps' greedy expression.

"Well, that's the best part, boy. If a kid don't turn into a mule, I take misses snaps here, and CRACK! Turn 'em into a nice shiny statue made of gold. HA! HA! HA! HA! HA!"

Michael's heart fell to his stomach, as he broke into a sweat.

"Free my brother. Now," Charlie said, stepping out of the shadows—his expression, calm and focused.

The coachman snapped his head around. "And what. If. I. Don't," he said with a sinister smile.

"That's your choice," Charlie replied. He crouched down into attack position—Oteza firmly held in his right hand. "But I promise you, you're not going to like it."

"Go get 'em," Oteza said.

The boy sprung high into the air, flipping and twirling, then pulling out into a karate-like kicking position, he descended upon the coachman's goons—knocking them thirty feet back into a wall. "Two down, one to go."

ZAPOW!

A bolt of lighting struck the ground, just a foot away from where Charlie stood.

The boy froze, then took a step back. He turned quickly towards the source of the attack.

High above, at the far end of the coachman's large whipping chamber, was a stairway. The only way in or out of the chamber. At the top of the stairway stood Elontra and Senkrad. And right behind them, Flamario, the silver fox, Captain Fibs and his two toady trolls.

There was clearly no easy way for Charlie and his brother to exit the room.

"Carry on, Jolly," Elontra said to the coachman.

Mr. Jollysnaps gave Charlie a look, then turned towards his brother, rearing back with his whip hand.

"Nooooooo!" Charlie screamed. He charged the coachman.

ZAAAAP!

The advancing boy was rudely thrown backwards into the wall. Held by a forcefield against his will.

The coachman cast the whip forward. CRACK! Striking Michael squarely in the chest.

A golden coat grew out from the striking point of the whip, covering the young boys body, it quickly moved upwards towards his face. The boy screamed out his brother's name, "Charlie, hel—"

Michael had been turned to solid gold.

"Ahhhhhh, NOOOOOOOOOOOO!!! Charlie shouted, overcome with emotion.

"Calm down, boy. There is nothing you can do now," Senkrad calmly said.

Senkrad's comment made Charlie grow even angrier inside, fueling the energy he received from Oteza. His body began to glow bright green, yellow, then white.

KAPOW!

Elontra's forcefield was obliterated. The boy was free and more powerful than ever, as he lifted Oteza high above his head.

"I am no longer a walking stick. Consider me your whomping stick," Oteza said to the boy. "Lets set things right."

Charlie gazed upon his enemies—his eyes, ablaze with fiery beams, burned bright yellow. Oteza was in his right hand, and a holographic light shield, projected from the magic watch, was in his left.

A sudden whirlwind of snow appeared then descended from the chamber ceiling—exploding into a brilliant display of flashing lights. As the lights receded, the friendly figures of Frank, Neve and Featherwink appeared.

"Frank, look what they've done to Michael," Charlie said.

"There may be time to reverse it," Frank replied, "but we have to act quickly."

"Not if we have anything to say about it," Elontra replied.

From the top of the stairway the fire breather leaped down and landed with a gigantic THUD on the main floor of the chamber.

The toady trolls, Duke and Grim followed suite.

"Time to heat this place up, Flamario said. He took in a deep breath, inhaling flames from his torch.

Anticipating the gigantic man's actions, Charlie took off running and exploded into the air towards the fire breather and trolls—his left leg fully extended in a kicking position.

The silver fox countered the boy's move—taking off in a full sprint, he leaped off the balcony, which surrounded the chamber floor, with intentions to blind side Charlie in mid-air.

Featherwink spotted the sly fox just as he leaped into the air. The tiny frog shot off like a bullet, heading straight for the shadow villain. Crossing the fox's path at its apex, Featherwink zapped the fox with a spell, sending him back to the woods where he belonged.

"So much for him," the frog declared.

Charlie's left foot caught Flamario squarely in the jaw, just as he unleashed the flames from his mouth intended for Frank and the snow fairy. The stream of fire swung wide of the Patrons, nearly scorching the coachman, who jumped out of the way.

"Get 'em boys," Captain Fibs hollered to his trolls.

Duke and Grim dove for the boy, one from each side. Grim managed to grab hold of Charlie's left arm, while Duke nabbed his right leg.

"What do ya say we tear 'em apart, Grimsly?"

"Sorry fellas, not going to happen," Oteza replied.

"What is that? A talk'n stick?" Grim said with a chuckle.

Charlie rapidly twirled Oteza like a baton with his free hand, smacking Grim in the side of the head—sending the troll flying into an empty holding cell, where he hit the wall so hard, the door slammed closed—locking the unconscious beast in.

"One troll down," Charlie proclaimed.

"Why you little twit," Duke said with an angry voice. He tightened his grip on the boy's leg, then spun him in circles above his head. Unfortunately, he forgot about Charlie's other leg.

As he brought the boy around for a fifth pass, the chosen outsider managed to swing his left leg around, making solid contact with Duke's backside. The sudden jolt forced the troll to let go of the boy. He flew towards another holding cell on the opposite side of the chamber from Grim. Duke skidded in to the cell face first. CRASH! The snow fairy waved her wand, slamming and locking the cell door behind him.

"That takes care of the trolls," Neve said, shooting Charlie a wink.

"*This* is where you end," Elontra stated. She hurled a series of fiery balls towards Frank.

Simultaneously, the coachman wrapped his golden whip around Neve, as Senkrad managed to pin Featherwink to the floor with a spell, allowing Flamario the opportunity to pounce upon the tiny frog and squash him like jelly.

But they had forgotten about Charlie. The young boy sprinted towards Frank, leaped into the air, landed with a summersault just in front of his friend, then held up his light shield—deflecting Elontra's fiery attack back in her direction.

The evil Dark Thorn dove out of the way.

POW, POW-POW, POW! The fireballs struck the corner of the entryway, collapsing the walls and sealing off the exit.

Frank seized the moment, swirling his arms around in waxing motions. The charm around his neck grew incredibly bright, sending a powerful beam of energy through his body and out of his open hands towards Elontra, who at the moment, was laying on the ground.

The radiant beams from Frank's hands quickly surrounded the Dark Thorn, wrapping themselves around her body.

The wise Patron pulled back with his hands. The beams tightened their grip on Elontra, as she let out screams of frustration, anger and pain.

"You. You'll pay for this, Patron," she said in a blood curdling tone.

Frank's body radiated even more, as did the beams—intensifying their strength. He thrust his hands towards a set of shackles on the wall—Elontra went flying through the air, then slammed against the wall. The illuminated shackles snapped around her wrists, ankles and neck.

"Ahhhhh! " The Dark Thorn screamed in anger, she knew she had been beaten.

"Free her or I'll turn your little ice princess into gold," Jollysnaps demanded. His golden whip, growing tighter around Neve's body.

"Meanwhile, Senkrad had managed to pin Charlie next to the frog on the chamber floor. Both helplessly awaited their fate, as Flamario prepared to dive off the balcony and crush them.

Not having time to save all his friends at once, Frank called to Charlie, "The watch can still hear you. Go back and save your brother."

"That is a brilliant idea, go young man," Featherwink whispered.

"I agree with the frog," Oteza added.

Charlie struggled, barely able to push the button—activating the watch of WONDER. "Take me back to Michael," he pleaded. The watch glowed, as the hands spun faster and faster. They snapped into place. SHOOP! The boy vanished.

Mr. Jollysnaps reared back with his whip hand.

SIZZLE-SIZZLE-CRACKETY-CRACK-POW! Charlie suddenly appeared next to his brother—about to be struck by the coachman's whip and turned to gold.

"Throw me," Oteza commanded.

Charlied turned towards Jollysnaps, and in one fluid motion, cast the magic ostrich stick towards the gold-loving shadow villain. Oteza flew straight and true, striking the evil coachman's whip hand.

"Noooooo!" Jollysnaps yelled.

The whip flew out of his hand and into a giant boiling kettle of gold, far away from where he stood.

The pot bubbled, popped, then spat out golden sparks. The whip was destroyed.

Quickly, Charlie used his light shield to cut the bands tied around his brother's wrists.

"Where did you come from?" Michael asked, happy to see his big brother.

"Never mind. Let's go." Charlie darted past the devastated coach-man, picked up Oteza, sprinted back to Michael, then returned them to present time.

Charlie had not given it any thought, but his actions had affected the present.

Because the coachman's whip had been destroyed in the past, it no longer existed in the present. Therefore, it was no longer restraining Neve.

"Thank you, Charlie," the snow fairy said.

"Wh...where did my whip go? What kind of magic is this?" Jollysnaps barked out in frustration, as he looked down upon his empty whip hand.

"The kind that's no good for you, my golden goose," Neve said. She flipped her wand hand, turning the coachman into a large golden goose. "There, now you know what it feels like to be turned to gold."

"Give me the crystal or your little friends die," Senkrad called out from atop the stairway. The Dark Thorn was confident he had the upper hand for two reasons: One, Flamario was ready to pounce on the restrained frog. And two, Michael had been quietly captured by Captain Fibs while Charlie was admiring the golden goose.

"That's right, give us the crystal and we'll let your friends go," Fibs demanded, holding a small dagger to Michael's throat.

Charlie, Oteza, Frank and Neve looked at each with silent confidence in their eyes.

Frank raised his head towards the chamber's arched ceiling. He noticed it was constructed of large golden blocks. Large enough in fact, to crush even the strongest of men. He turned and looked at Captain Fibs. "When will you ever learn, Patrons never give up."

On Frank's words, Charlie took action, diving towards Fibs into a summersault roll, which he leaped out of, then sprung into the air—flying over the heads of Fibs and his brother, he reached back and thunked the captain on the head with his walking stick. Fibs was out cold, and his brother was free once more.

"I told you I was a whomping stick, Charlie," Oteza said with a smirk.

Frank turned towards the fire breather, who was preparing to leap off the balcony. The mighty Patron reached out with his hands aglow, then pulled down. Three of the large, golden blocks from the ceiling came crashing down upon Flamario. He did not move.

Senkrad quickly began to conjure up a spell to make Frank pay for his actions, but the Dark Thorn was too slow.

Neve pulled back her arms, then thrust forward, sending an enormous wave of wintery magic, which engulfed Senkrad like a giant snow globe—rendering him powerless against the Patrons, and freeing their good friend Featherwink from the spell which had held him pinned to the floor.

Thank you, friend," the frog said to the snow fairy.

With the FOTO army defeated and the crystal in safe keeping, Frank gathered everyone together, and with the wave of his hand, the light charm flashed and the group vanished.

Back at the watchmaker's workshop, everyone had gathered to say their congratulations, thank you's and goodbyes for now. Alexios had given the second Kingdom Crystal to Frank for safe keeping, while Midnight, Ticky and Tocky agreed they would see each other again. Neve and Featherwink rejoiced with their good friend the watch-maker, as Charlie, Michael, Ben and Frank shared hugs, catching up on all they had done over the past week, and what what the boys had planned for the remainder of their Disney World vacation.

Charlie paused for a moment. Something was missing.

"What about Sassyfran and Provo?" Charlie asked. "They should be here to celebrate with us."

"Of course, Charlie. I could not agree more," Frank replied.

"You know what do," Oteza added.

"Right," Charlie said with a smile. He activated, then spoke to, the watch—vanishing with his magic stick in hand.

Mere seconds later, the boy returned with the cute, little wood maiden, and a mouse on her shoulder.

"Thank you, Charlie, Sassyfran said, kissing him on the cheek.

The boy's cheeks blushed. "You're welcome."

"Yes, thank you lad. Why, that's more than once you've saved my furry little hide this week. Let's not forget about that hawk you protected me from when we first met."

Charlie gave Provo a curious look.

"Ohhhh, the hawk. That's right," Charlie replied with a chuckle. "Well, now we can celebr...wait, there is one more thing," Charlie said. The boy looked over at Oteza, who was leaning against a chair. "What about her?"

"I will hold onto Oteza for safe keeping," Frank replied.

"Yes, the real world is no place for a walking stick like me," Oteza said jokingly.

Everyone joined in for a good laugh.

"Thank you Frank," Charlie said. "And you as well, Oteza," Charlie said , picking her up one last time before they parted. "I'll miss you." The boy sighed, then handed her to Frank.

"It's OK, Charlie. Somehow, I don't think this will be the last time we see each other," the ostrich stick said, trying to lift the boy's spirits up.

Charlie's eyes welled up. Goodbyes were never easy for him. "You...you are one of the best gifts anyone has ever given to me."

"Ohhh, please don't cry Charlie. It made me VERY happy to make this gift for a special person like you. As long as you hold her in your heart, you will never be apart. You are a good boy," Raphael said, placing a hand on Charlie's shoulder.

"And a good brother as well," Frank added, as he and Oteza glanced over at Michael—both smiling.

Michael returned the smile with much appreciation. Now, more than ever, he knew just how much his brother truly loved him. As did everyone else in the room.

Elontra, having freed herself from the shackles, was extremely frustrated. She helped Senkrad escape Neve's snow globe, then the two Dark Thorns looked around the chamber, assessing the results of their defeat.

"Should we help the others?" Senkrad asked, regarding Flamario, Mr. Jollysnaps, Captain Fibs, and his toady trolls.

"Leave them," Elontra said. "Consider it punishment for their failures. Besides, they are all plenty capable of finding a way out."

"This is only the beginning," Senkrad said.

"Yes, there will be more opportunities," Elontra replied. "We must inform the Shadow Queen immediately of our defeat."

"She will not be happy," Senkrad said.

The Dark Thorns blended into a dark, wicked funnel cloud, filled with lighting. CRACK, CRACK-CRACK, BOOM! They vanished from the coachman's chamber—leaving the others sealed in by the wall that had collapsed during the battle.

Charlie and Michael had returned to the real world, joining their parents back on the monorail. It was like they had never left. They were headed to Epcot for the final few hours of their vacation, before having to catch the Magical Express back to the airport.

Chapter Twenty-One

Charlie and his family were on their way to watch The American Adventure show. It would be the last thing they did before walking back to the Beach Club Resort to catch their bus to the airport. A rather ordinary ending to an unbelievable string of vacation experiences.

And that was exactly what Charlie was thinking. *How could it end like this? Besides, I'm still wearing the Object of Magic on my wrist. There has to be more.*

The door into the theatre opened and guests poured in, filling most of the seats.

"What is it, Charlie?" his brother asked.

"The watch," he replied quietly—as not to let their parents hear him."

"Yeah?"

"I'm still wearing it. Don't you think that's a little odd?"

"I never really thought about it."

Charlie rolled his eyes "Sit down, block head."

The show began. It was, magnificent. Possibly the best animatronic show Charlie had seen in Walt Disney World yet. Still, his thoughts kept reverting back to the watch.

The show was nearing its end, as Ben Franklin and Mark Twain had one final discussion atop the Statue of Liberty torch.

"Well, boys, it has truly been a great adventure. One I'm sure you will always remember," the Mark Twain animatronic said.

Charlie leaned towards his brother. "Did you catch that?"

"Catch what?"

Charlie rolled his eyes again, and continued to listen to Mark Twain's words carefully.

"But as you know, the time has come for us to part ways until your next visit."

"How about that? Did you hear that?"

"Here what, Charlie?"

"Are you even listening to what he's saying?" Charlie said in a frustrated tone.

Then Ben Franklin spoke. "However, we would like to show our gratitude for your brave and loyal efforts."

"So, it is with great honor, that we, members of the Patron Council, would like to give you a *second chance* on your vacation.

Most of which, was spent helping us protect WONDER and all that it represents," Mark Twain added.

"Now I know you heard that, right?"

Michael had frozen. His eyes and mouth, both wide open, as he stared at the figures on stage—amazed by what he was seeing and hearing.

Charlie nudged his brother in the arm, competing for his attention. "Michael. You alright?"

"Yeah," the younger brother replied. He continued to listen in utter disbelief.

"Just recite these magic words to the watch, and you'll be on your way," Ben Franklin said. "Forwards, backwards, sideways, magic."

Charlie looked at his brother with a big grin. "You ready?"

Michael, too excited to speak, nodded, then took hold of his brother's right hand.

"Alright, let's go have some fun." Charlie activated the watch, then said, "Forward, backwards, sideways, magic."

Mickey's hands spun madly round and round, faster and faster, as the face glowed in a repetitive, multicolored pattern. CLICK! The hands locked into place—both pointing towards twelve 'o clock. A burst of brilliant light exploded outward from the watch.

The boys shielded their eyes.

SHOOOOP!

The lights receded.

The boys found themselves sitting in the exact same place of The American Adventure attraction, their parents, still sitting next to them.

"Huh?" Michael said, as the boys looked around the room in bewildered fashion.

"Go on, young fellows, enjoy this special time together with your parents," Mark Twain said. The stage curtain lowered.

The audience clapped, unaware of what had just happened.

The theatre lights came up, then everyone stood to exit the theatre.

As Charlie and his family walked towards exit the doorway, the curious boy pulled out his phone to check the time. He was shocked by what he saw. Not only was it earlier in the day, it was also the first day of their vacation.

Charlie and Michael more than made up for everything they had originally missed on their eight day Disney World vacation. Endless attraction experiences, meals, snacks, shows, character greetings, fireworks, photo ops, and so much more. The weather had been perfect and the food delicious. The time spent with their parents at the most magical place on earth would be something to remember for the rest of their lives. Frank even made a couple surprise appearances throughout the week, just to check in and make sure the boys were enjoying themselves. And of course, Charlie, being the kind young man he was, repeatedly thanked his friend every time their paths crossed.

It was the last day, for the second time. Charlie and his family had magically caught up to the present day, thanks to the watch. The morning air was a perfect seventy two degrees, as the Zastaswits family passed through the gates of the Magic Kingdom. Their father had suggested they spend the morning there, and then take the monorail to Epcot for the final few hours of their trip. But Charlie and Michael had already experienced that ending of their vacation and wanted to try something different. Their parents, unknowingly, were more than happy to oblige.

The morning was filled with piratical adventure, jungle thrills, a thunderous rollercoaster ride, pleasant haunts, and the belief that one could fly.

After a brief lunch at Pinocchio's Village Haus, the family kicked off the afternoon with a FastPass ride on the Seven Dwarfs Mine Train. All had been normal up to that point, a few quick dips, turns and twists, as passengers screamed and shouted with delight. The ride vehicle banked one more time, then entered the mine, which was filled with colorful, illuminated jewels and the signing dwarves—the true highlight of the attraction. Charlie was cherishing every last detail, as the mine train slowly curved to the right. The clock bells rang, Doc called out, "Heigh-Ho", and the dwarf's shadows began their march home alongside the train, while it ascended out of the mine.

For most guests, the marching shadows of the dwarves were just a creative layer added to the experience of the attraction. However, for the Patrons of WONDER, it was the perfect opportunity to send Charlie and Michael one more secret message before their departure.

The train suddenly began to move in slow motion, as did all the sights and sounds around them. Grumpy's shadow turned towards the boys and spoke, "Frank will be want'n that watch back. So before you leave the park, make sure ya stop by Uptown Jewelers to drop it off. Ya get me?"

Charlie looked at Michael, his slack-jawed brother, then turned back towards the shadow to say, "We won't let you down."

"Hmm. Ya better not," the shadow replied, then turned and marched on, fading into the rocky formations.

The train exited the mine, breaking into daylight at normal speed. The ride, and all of its passengers, continued on as if nothing unusual had happened.

Late afternoon snuck up without warning. Charlie and his family were reluctantly making their way down Main Street towards the park exit.

It was time to return the watch.

"Hey Dad, I need to stop in the jewelry store before we leave, OK?"

"The jewelry store?" his dad replied. Curious to why his son would need to do such a thing, just before they were getting ready to leave the park.

Charlie was caught off guard. "Uhhh, I have to ask if they can fix my watch."

"Your watch? You mean the brand new watch you just got this week?" his mother asked.

"Yeah, the one I got on our first day here," Charlie replied. "Don't you remember? I told you and Dad a few days ago that it wasn't working right."

"Ed, did you know Charlie's watch was broken?"

"No, honey. Must have slipped my mine. You know, with all the fun going on around here, it's hard to keep track," Mr. Z said, shrugging his shoulders and laughing.

Charlie's mother gave the watch another serious look, trying to remember. She rolled her eyes. "Ugh, must have slipped my mind. I'm sorry, Charlie. Well, let's go see if we can get it fixed before we have to leave."

The two brothers both exhaled, as they looked at each other. Relieved that Charlie's strategy had worked.

Minutes later the entire family entered Uptown Jewelers. Mr. and Mrs Z approached the counter, and Charlie's mother asked for assistance—something he wished she had not done.

"Excuse me, miss, can someone help my son? He needs to have his watch looked at."

"Sure ma'am, it would be our pleasure," the cast member, Lisa, replied. "Can I see the watch sweetie?" she kindly asked Charlie.

Unsure how the watch would get back to Frank, the young boy hesitated.

"Oh, it's alright, I promise you'll get it back," Lisa said with a smile.

"Go ahead, sweetie," Mrs. Z added, encouraging her son.

Charlie nervously handed over the watch.

Lisa's eyes lit up. "Oh, you've got yourself quite the watch here. I...I'll be back right back."

Charlie carefully watched as Lisa took the watch over to an older gentleman working in the store.

"Don't worry, honey, I'm sure they'll be able to fix it."

Charlie looked up at his mother and smiled, his lips sealed tight, trying to hide his anxiety.

A voice called to him, "Well, hello, young fellow. Lucky for you, I think I can help."

Charlie spun his head around.

It was Frank, disguised using a face recognition spell so that Charlie's parents could not recognize him.

The anxiety in the young boy's mind was immediately washed away. "That would be terrific," he replied.

Frank reached down, and from underneath the display counter, pulled out a small watch box, decorated in silver and gold floral patterns. He sat it on the counter, slowly turned it towards the boys, then opened it— revealing an identical watch to the one Charlie had brought into the store. "What do you say we trade? Your watch for a brand new one," the old man said with a grin.

"Oh, thank you sir, I'm sure this will make my son, very happy, right, Charlie?" his mother replied.

Frank gestured for the boy to remove the new watch from the box.

Charlie smiled and gladly accepted. Removing the new watch, he fit it around his wrist. "Thank you, sir."

"My pleasure, young man," Frank said. He placed the watch of WONDER in the purple, velvet-lined box and gently closed the lid.

"See, all better now," Charlie's mom said. Then she slid a ways down the counter to engage her husband in meaningless conversation—leaving the boys to talk freely with their very special friend.

Frank leaned in towards the boys and tilted his head so their parents could not see what he was saying. "Thank you again, gentleman. What you did this week...that...that is something you should be very proud of. I'm not quite sure what we would do without your help." Frank gave the boys one more smile of gratitude.

"No. Thank you, Frank, for an unbelievable opportunity," Charlie replied.

"Yeah, thank you, Frank," Michael added.

The boys reached over the counter, each placing a hand atop their wise friend's left hand.

Frank smiled again, then placed his right hand atop theirs. "Well, boys, it's time for you and your parents to be moving along. Oh, I almost forgot. You still have the snow fairy's magic icicle, yes?"

Charlie felt around his left pocket. "Yeah, still there," he said—surprised he still had it.

"Good. Keep it in a safe place. You never know when it may come in handy."

"I will," Charlie replied.

"OK then, see ya around, boys." Frank picked up the watch box up off the counter and gave the boys a subtle, thumbs up.

"Right, c'mon, Michael," Charlie replied. "Mom, Dad, we're ready."

Charlie and his family headed for the door. As they exited, the chosen outsider turned to give his friend one last wave goodbye.

Frank returned the wave, as he stood near the back of the store.

Just as Charlie was about to let go of the door he had kindly held open for the others, a familiar face came walking in. The boy could not help but stare—certain he knew who it was.

The stunning young lady stopped and turned, locking eyes with the boy. "Hello, Charlie."

Her voice seemed familiar. "Valerie? You helped us locate the second Kingdom Crystal, right?"

"That's right," the young lady replied with a smile. She turned and continued to walk further into the store.

"Thanks again for your help," the boy replied, still standing in the doorway.

Valerie, stopped and turned once again. "My pleasure, she said with a smile," then turned and continued on.

"Maybe we'll see each other again."

The young lady gave the boy one last look, and grinned. "Oh, I'm *sure* we will," she said, then waved goodbye.

Excited to have made a new friend, Charlie let go of the door and sprinted to catch up with his family.

"What a silly little boy," the young lady mumbled to herself, as she searched the store for more important things.

Season of Shadows

A sneak peek at chapter one of the sequel to *The Watchmaker's Gift*...

In the not so distant past...

It was like any other ordinary day in the most magical place on earth. Beautiful sites, sounds, smells and memories to last a lifetime were everywhere to be found. A gentle, breeze danced through the autumn air as a little girl, no more than five, and her mother and father made their way down Main Street U.S.A. towards the hub. The buildings and store fronts were decorated in spectacular fall fashion with colorful foliage, bunting, and jolly jack-o-lanterns. And hanging on every lamppost was a Mickey pumpkin wreath.

"Mommy, when do we get to ride the horses?"

"Not too much longer, dear. The Prince Charming Regal Carrousel is just ahead, beyond the castle."

"Ooh, is that where Cinderella lives?"

"Yes, Samantha."

"I can't wait, Mommy. I can't wait to see..." The little girl stopped in her tracks. Her mouth agape. It was her first time seeing the castle.

"What is it Sam?" her father asked.

"I've never seen a real castle before."

Her father chuckled. "Would you like to walk through it? The carrousel is just on the other side."

"Yes, daddy, please, please, pretty please. Can we, pleeeeease?"

"Sure sweetie. Anything for my little girl."

While passing through the castle, Samantha's eyes sparkled in awe, taking in the dazzling mosaics on the left wall, which told the enchanted tale of Cinderella.

As they reached the end of the castle walkway and entered the courtyard, Samantha and her parents were welcomed into Fantasyland with warm rays of sunshine, which highlighted the young girl's heartfelt destination. Centered perfectly in the distance, between a series of buildings, was the colorful carrousel. The majestic white horses danced round and round to the carnival-like music—their golden posts glistening in the bright sun as the carrousel continued to move in spectacular fashion, spreading happiness to all who could see and hear the wonderful attraction.

"There it is, Mommy. The horses, I see them, I see them."

"Quick, let's get in line, then you can pick the horse you want to ride," her mother replied.

Samantha's eyes lit up with joy as they made their way into line.

"That one Daddy," she said while pointing. "The horse with the purple flowers on its neck. I want to ride that one."

The carrousel came to a stop, guests unmounted their horses and exited. The cast member gave the all clear, then opened the gate for those next in line to enter.

Samantha anxiously pulled her father along, making her way to the horse with purple flowers.

"Don't worry about me, I'm right behind you," the mother called out, scurrying to catch up.

Within seconds the little girl reached the magnificent horse and her father safely lifted Samantha up onto the saddle.

Now, hold onto the pole with both hands, sweetie. I'll be standing right next to you to make sure you don't fall."

Samantha did not reply to her father. Her mind was filled with too much excitement, as she anxiously bounced up and down on the saddle, waiting for the ride to begin.

All was clear, the horses slowly began to move, the carrousel started to rotate, and the music began to play.

Samantha's parents were cherishing the moment, taking in every precious second of happiness beaming from their daughter's face.

On their second pass by the castle, right as the young girl was at the hight of happiness, a wave of shadow passed through the carrousel.

Suddenly, everything on and around the rotating attraction was void of color, including her parents and other guests. Only the young girl and her purple flower horse remained unaffected and still in color. Everyone she could see became transparent and faded away into a blanket of darkness, which crept in over the castle, slowly filling the grounds of Fantasyland. Buildings, and everything in and around them, were transformed into frightfully unfamiliar places and things.

As the carrousel continued to move round and round, the music changed to a chilling tune. The brilliant white horses morphed into black and gray steeds with laser red eyes.

On the next turn around, Samantha glared to her right towards Rapunzel's Tower. Slowly appearing out of a thick rolling fog, between the Peter Pan and Small World attractions, and headed directly for the carrousel, were five dark, ghost-like figures on large black horses. Leading them was a sixth rider—a female wearing a gold, jeweled crown. Her transparent figure was cloaked in white, and her facial features masked by long, flowing white hair. She sat upon a golden saddle—strapped to the back of a small, white, horse-like creature with a dragon's head and claws. A gold harness decorated in jewels, hung down from the sides of the beast's snout, its radiant purple eyes staring straight ahead. Chartreuse flames shot out from between the dragon creatures jagged, tooth-lined jaws with each exhale, as it dug its rear claws into the ground—waiting with great anticipation to charge forward.

The lady in white called out to the others. The six riders began to advance, working their way from a slow trot into a steady gallop. Smoke shot out from the horse's nostrils, and flames from the dragon creature's, as they galloped madly towards the young girl. The cloaked riders rose off their saddles, picking up more momentum, as they continued to charge the carrousel. Left in their wake was a twisted, twirling trail of smokey grey, unfriendly-like creatures.

The carrousel continued to turn, Samantha was now at a disadvantage, scared, and unable to see the rapidly approaching riders. As she came back around, the horses and beast leapt high into the air towards the carrousel—their riders poised to attack.

Just as they began their aggressive descent upon the attraction, a shockwave of color exploded outward from the carrousel's hub, driving the riders backwards—erasing them from existence.

Everything returned to its normal state, as the carrousel slowly came to a stop.

Samantha's father helped her off the horse. He sensed something was wrong. "You're quiet. What's wrong princess?"

Samantha did not reply. Her mind was stuck on the ghostly riders.

"Honey, did you hear your father?"

"Yes...Mommy," the girl replied. She stared in bewilderment towards Rapunzel's Tower—unable to find the courage or words to describe what she, and she alone, had just experienced.

About the Author

Raised along the sandy shores of southwestern Michigan, Charles was always one sunset away from his dreams. A child of the 70s, his passion for Disney began in the summer of 1973 when he visited Disneyland for the first time with his mother, grandmother, and aunt.

Charles holds a B.A. in graphic design from Western Michigan University, and currently works as a brand Manager/art director for Round 2 Corporation in South Bend, Indiana.

ABOUT THEME PARK PRESS

Theme Park Press publishes books primarily about the Disney company, its history, culture, films, animation, and theme parks, as well as theme parks in general.

Our authors include noted historians, animators, Imagineers, and experts in the theme park industry.

We also publish many books by first-time authors, with topics ranging from fiction to theme park guides.

And we're always looking for new talent. If you'd like to write for us, or if you're interested in the many other titles in our catalog, please visit:

www.ThemeParkPress.com

• •

Theme Park Press Newsletter

Subscribe to our free email newsletter and enjoy:

- ◆ Free book downloads and giveaways
- ◆ Access to excerpts from our many books
- ◆ Announcements of forthcoming releases
- ◆ Exclusive additional content and chapters
- ◆ And more good stuff available nowhere else

To subscribe, visit www.ThemeParkPress.com, or send email to newsletter@themeparkpress.com.

Read more about these books
and our many other titles at:

www.ThemeParkPress.com

Made in the USA
Middletown, DE
27 May 2020